WINDS OF THE SOUTH

A novel by

Ben Walker

To Amanda
My best wishes,
Ben Walker

WINDS OF THE SOUTH

ISBN 978-0-9666145-0-3

Published in the United States by
Jamin Press
Jacksonville, FL
USA

Second Printing 2012

Acknowledgments

I owe much in the reading and preparation of this manuscript to friends of long-standing. They are: Ann Paine, Bernadette and Tom Polizzi, Barbara Pinkerton, and Preston Stevens, Jr.

For Julia V. and Pressley Walker

CHAPTER 1

Zimri shook the reins languorously with his wrists resting on his knees, clicking his tongue without conviction, as if the horses themselves would rebel against him for what he was about to do.

Clouds of red dust rose from the wheels, only to settle again on the four Negroes sitting shackled in iron on the wagon bed behind him. The dust adhered to the sweat of their bodies in the oppressive heat, giving them the appearance of rusted iron statues.

"Massa Zimri," the man said, "I been a good worker, you knows that."

"I know, Solomon," Zimri said. "I know that. It has nothing to do with your performance. It's just a thing that's got to be done, that's all."

The wife and the children said nothing, but all began to cough.

"Cain't hardly breathe in this dust, Massa," Solomon said.

"I know that, too, Solomon." Zimri snapped the reins a little more vigorously now. "We'll be there directly."

The horses picked up their gait as if the dust would somehow part like the Red Sea if only they moved smartly ahead.

Instead, as they approached the town square and other wagons came into the main road from various points of the compass, the dust increased considerably and Zimri himself began to cough.

"Best not to drive too fast, Massa," Solomon said.

"You're right, Solomon," Zimri said, stifling a second cough. "Looks like the whole county's turned out."

"Like they 'spect to see a lynching," Solomon said.

On hearing this, the boy began to cry. "Mama," he said, and clutched his mother's bosom.

"Hush, chile," his mother said, wrapping her arms around him. "This ain't no lynching…it's sumpin' worse."

Zimri heard this remark but made no comment. The boy dried his eyes with his little fists and peered through the settling dust at the covered platform in the middle of the square. There was grass all around it, with recently planted shrubs and bright flowers bordering the walkways that radiated from it—peonies, roses, geraniums, petunias, morning glories.

"Is the band gonna play?" the boy said.

"Ain't no band, chile," his mother said.

"Them roses we planted done bloomed out good, Massa," Solomon said.

Zimri pulled back on the reins at the edge of the square and the horses stopped. He tipped his hat to a neighboring driver, and got down from the seat. "That they did, Solomon, that they did." He tied the reins to the hitching rail, took off his broad-brimmed hat, and slapped the dust from his clothes as best he could. Then he went around to the back of the wagon to help Solomon and his wife, Betty, down from the wagon bed.

"Cain't hardly move with these chains, Massa," Solomon said. "I ain't gonna run away—not an' leave my wife and chillun."

Zimri took the length of chain between Betty's ankles and pulled them forward. "I know you won't, Solomon. But the others don't. Come on, Betty, put your hand on my shoulder."

"I thought you was a good man, Massa Zimri," Betty said. She slid her ample posterior towards the rear of the wagon, reluctantly, like a forlorn dog about to be given a bath. "But you ain't no better than the rest of 'em. Come on, Aaron, stay with your mama. You, too, Sally— ain't no place to hide in this wagon."

Zimri helped her down into the gravel, then lifted Aaron into his arms and set him down by his mother, where he immediately wrapped his arms around her legs and rolled his enormous eyes at him. He repeated the process with Sally, who grasped a piece of her mother's dress in her fist and put it in her mouth.

Betty slapped her hand away. "Whatcha doin,' girl? Cain't eat no cotton dress—you sho' to choke on it."

"You're next, Solomon," Zimri said.

"Don't need no help, Massa," Solomon said. He pushed the length of chain off the back of the wagon, where it fell in a heap, kicking up more dust.

"Suit yourself." Zimri didn't expect to actually lift Solomon completely off the wagon, anyway, though Solomon's admonition made him wonder if he could. He wasn't nearly as big a man as Solomon, barely 5'10" to Solomon's 6'4" or so, but he was broad-shouldered and liked to think he was stronger than most men.

Once down from the wagon, Solomon stood up with his bare feet on the gravel, where the red dust was beginning to settle. He seemed to tower over Zimri, and looked down at his master as if to confirm his physical, if not his social, superiority.

"Didn't know you owned no niggers, Zimri," called a gruff voice from the gathering crowd. "Thought you was just a newspaperman."

Zimri turned and saw that it was Charlie Whitbeck, a hardscrabble farmer who occasionally came into his office to place an ad, usually for slaves, though he never seemed to buy any.

"Dower slaves," Zimri said. "They came from my wife's people."

Charlie Whitbeck scratched the black stubble beneath his chin, eyeing Solomon in particular. "That's as strappin' a nigger as I've ever seen. Do he work hard?"

"Harder than most."

"How much do you want for him?"

"As much as the market will bear."

"Hmm," Charlie said, now eyeing Betty. "She go with him?"

"They all go together, Charlie. That's my only condition. Come on,

Zimri carried the length of chain in his hands as a sort of leash, leading Betty up the steps. He knew that, unlike her husband, she would not come along willingly. Solomon, by contrast, picked up his chain in his enormous hands, rolled the links back and forth between his thumb and fingers as if they were worry beads, and mounted the steps.

"I'll give you four hundred for the pair of 'em right now," Charlie said in a loud voice. "Not the little pickaninnies, though."

Zimri continued leading Betty up the steps to the platform. A considerable crowd was growing now. "I told you, they all stay together, Charlie."

Charlie scratched his stubble again. "It'll be a hard sell, then. You ain't a businessman like me, Zimri. You'll be wastin' your time."

Zimri shrugged his shoulders. "We'll see."

After running the chains through the eyebolts attached to the cement floor of the platform and padlocking the links together, Zimri spoke to several acquaintances, including a couple of his fellow city council members, and took his seat on one of the benches on either side of the auction block. There were about fifteen other slaves chained in similar fashion, some of whom Solomon knew, but he did not speak to them.

Aaron seemed fascinated by the chain links, and made a game of clinking them together as if they were parts of a puzzle that wouldn't quite fit together.

The crowd had grown to some fifty or sixty persons, all white, some already drunk, as there was little other source of entertainment in the town on a Saturday afternoon.

A rather stout middle-aged man, dressed in a black suit, white shirt, and Texas-style bow tie, stepped up on the raised block and addressed the crowd.

"La-a-a-dies and gentlemen," he said in an affected drawl, "welcome to the bi-monthly slave auction in Martinville, Georgia, in the year of our Lord, eighteen hundred and thirty."

Zimri was reminded of a referee for a prize fight he had once seen in New York City. The auctioneer cut a comical figure with his short stature, enormous belly, and string bow tie with the ends dangling nearly to his belt buckle.

"I must remind you that this is a business enterprise of the highest standard—it is not a sideshow or one of those burley-cues they have down in Savannah to entertain the sailors."

This statement was met with catcalls and whistles from several of the young men of Martinville who had only minutes before emerged from Murphy's Irish Saloon across the street.

"Hey, we ain't no sailors," one of them said. "We's gentlemen of the highest standard."

This comment was met with peals of laughter by his comrades, one of whom pushed the young man's hat down over his face and shoved him back into his seat.

"If you're a gentleman, I'm King George IV," his friend said to more peals of laughter.

The auctioneer seemed to take this distraction in stride and continued.

"Well, then," he said, "Now that we've established the dignified footing on which these proceedings are to be conducted, I will advise all interested buyers of the rules herewith.

Number One: The merchandise goes to the highest bidder—no if's, and's, but's or, 'you didn't hear me's.' Gentlemen, I have excellent hearing.

Number Two: All sales are final and cash-on-the-barrelhead. Installment contracts will not be considered, nor will barter-for-trade.

Number Three: Receipts will be provided for all buyers, signed and dated by both myself and the seller.

Number Four: 'Caveat Emptor.'"

The young man who had been shoved down into his seat stood up again. "What the hell does that mean?"

"Young man," the auctioneer said, "if you had spent more of your time in the school house and less in that saloon over yonder, you wouldn't have to ask that question."

This comment was met with more laughter. The young man, though his face reddened, nevertheless managed a smile. "Well, hell, I was in school long enough to know that you're spoutin' Latin—but what's that got to do with sellin' niggers?"

"It means 'buyer beware,' you dope," offered one of his comrades.

"Ah," the auctioneer said, "I see that one of your friends is a scholar—there is hope for your academic salvation yet."

Amid more laughter the young man was again pushed down into his seat and the proceedings were at last underway.

"I didn't know you were in the slave trade, Zimri."

Zimri didn't have to turn around to identify the owner of this voice. He knew it was Tom Pritchard, the mayor. "I'm not—my wife is. You might say she's cleaning house."

"Subscriptions falling off?"

Zimri didn't like the insinuation, but he knew it was true. "A bit. But mostly it's for general household expenses. We've got a baby on the way."

"Another one? Can't tell it. Elizabeth's still got her fine figure."

"Planning ahead, Tom. Planning for the future."

"The only prudent thing to do. And you're a prudent man, Zimri."

Zimri quietly fumed at the mayor's comments. Like Charlie Whitbeck, he knew Tom Pritchard didn't think much of his business ability. The newspaper had struggled over the past couple of years, partly due to Zimri's outspoken editorials, and partly due to the emergence of a competitor, the *Georgia Patriot*. Zimri's own *Mercury* was unabashedly pro-Union, while the Patriot appealed to the more provincial attitudes of the planters, who advocated states' rights over the interests of the nation. The mayor was a states' rights man and had been elected as such. Zimri often clashed with him in city council meetings.

The first slave to be auctioned was a mulatto girl of about fifteen or sixteen, with the 'high yaller' skin coloring that Zimri had heard Betty and other darker-skinned Negroes so often refer to with obvious disdain. Zimri recognized her as one of Jim Burkett's bastard children of whom he had many. It seemed that when they reached a certain age, particularly the females, he sold them off to placate his wife, who tolerated her husband's philandering among the slaves but drew the line at incest.

"An excellent breeder," the auctioneer said. "Lift your head up, my dear. Let'em see what a pretty wench you are." He put his fat forefinger under her chin and lifted it up.

She was, indeed, a pretty little thing, Zimri thought. But rather delicate-looking. One could see the Burkett family influence—high cheekbones; rather thin, upturned nose; alert, intelligent bluish-gray eyes. She could easily pass for white in some circles.

"Turn around—Elmira, is it?" The auctioneer glanced at his notes.

"Turn *all* the way around, Elmira. My, my, you must not have a bit of trouble attracting the young bucks, now do you?"

As Elmira turned slowly around as commanded, the auctioneer lifted the hem of her dress up with the hickory stick that he used as both a cane and a gavel, teasing the mostly male audience with a glimpse of first her buttocks, then, as she made a full revolution, her thighs up to, but just short of, the crotch.

"You see, gentlemen," he said, "The wench is stronger than she looks. Good, stout legs, a strong back, suitable for all manner of house work."

"Let's see her titties!" It was the young man who had earlier questioned the auctioneer's use of Latin.

"This is not a peep show, young man," the auctioneer said. "If you want to take such liberties with the wench, you'll have to put your money where your mouth is. Gentlemen! The bidding will start at $200. Do I hear $300?"

"Three hundred!" the young man said.

"Aw, Jack," a friend said. "You ain't got three hundred dollars."

"I can get it!" Jack said.

"Gentlemen," the auctioneer said. "I have a dubious bid of $300—do I hear $350?"

"Three-fifty!"

"Four hundred!"

The bidding quickly escalated until the bid reached $550, at which point the entire assembly grew eerily silent.

"Do I hear six hundred?" the auctioneer said.

There was no response. The auctioneer cast his gaze slowly around the premises as if admonishing everyone present. "Gentlemen—this is no ordinary nigger house slave. This is pedigreed horse flesh. Not a thoroughbred, but the highest order of the species just one notch below that. If she were a true thoroughbred, she wouldn't be for sale at all. Now, do I hear six hundred?"

"Six hundred!"

"Do I hear six-fifty?"

Silence. The auctioneer quickly scanned the audience one last time. He rapped his stick on the floor. "Sold! To the gentlemen in the yellow beaver hat. Be so kind as to settle with my assistant, Mr. Grimes. You've made a wise investment, sir. In Savannah, the wench would have gone for twice that amount!"

Zimri watched as the buyer, whom he recognized as Chauncey Taylor, a planter who had recently inherited a large estate from his father, approached Mr. Grimes, reaching inside his jacket for his billfold.

Chauncey was about Zimri's age, and had a reputation as a dissipated spendthrift. He was short and corpulent, gregarious to the point of being obnoxious, and known to have fathered a number of bastard children, both black and white. It was not hard to guess what Chauncey had in mind for young Elmira.

The next eight or ten sales went quickly, with little incident. Most of the slaves were sold individually, though one middle-aged couple, the husband completely blind, were sold to a candle-maker who only required two pairs of hands to pour tallow into moulds.

Zimri had allowed himself to slip into a sort of dream during this time, a dream of halcyon days as a young man in Connecticut. The candle-maker had reminded him of the chandler's shop in North Brantley, where he often accompanied his father to buy farming implements as well as candles. The chandler's daughter was a pretty, freckled girl of Scottish descent named Abigail. She would help him load goods onto the wagon while his father listened to the chandler's tales of his sailing days.

Zimri boasted to Abigail that he would someday become rich and then he would build the most stately mansion in New Haven, overlooking the harbor. There would be no farm work for him.

"Don't you like living on a farm?" Abigail would say as he lifted hoes, rakes and shovels onto the wagon.

"Like it?" Zimri would say. "I hate it—it's a mindless existence. Cows, horses, chickens, pigs—filthy animals and you become a slave to their needs. And there's no one to talk to—at least no one who's been anywhere or done anything but slop hogs and plant crops. I want to see the world."

Abigail smiled. "Then you should be a sailor."

"Not that way," Zimri said. "Sailors are a kind of slave themselves. I want to own my own ship and sail wherever I want to go—not where I'm ordered to go."

"You're a romantic."

"I suppose I am." Zimri would then gaze into that freckled face with the clear blue eyes. "Wouldn't you like to marry a romantic? As opposed to a drudge?"

"What's a drudge?"

"A kind of slave."

"Oh. Well, who would want to marry a slave? So I guess I would marry a romantic—but he wouldn't have to own a fleet of ships or live in a big house. He would only have to read poetry in the evenings by the fireside and tell me pretty lies."

Zimri took great pleasure in this answer and took her hand in his and recited the few lines that he knew from *Romeo and Juliet*:

> *O, she doth teach the torches to burn bright!*
> *It seems she hangs upon the cheek of night*
> *Like a rich jewel in an Ethiop's ear—*

"The man goes by the name of Solomon." The voice seemed to loom out of the mist. "The wench, by the name of Betty."

Zimri blinked a couple of times and saw Solomon, his huge figure towering over the auctioneer, looking towards him as if in supplication. Betty stood behind him, the children clinging to the hem of her dress. Zimri averted his eyes.

"Now this buck, here," the auctioneer said, "can do the work of two men—and maybe a mule, too. Look at those shoulders! Turn around there, Solomon, and show'em your back." He poked Solomon on the right shoulder with his cane and Solomon slowly turned to show his back. "I'm telling you, gentlemen, that's seven hands across from one shoulder to the other. There're horses that ain't that broad!"

"Bucks like that'll give you trouble," muttered one man in the front row.

"Trouble?" the auctioneer said. "Solomon's no trouble a'tall. His owner tells me he's as gentle as a lamb."

Zimri couldn't recall telling the auctioneer anything of the sort. But it was true that Solomon had a gentle disposition and had never raised a hand against him.

"Now what am I bid, gentlemen?" The auctioneer poked Solomon on the back of the opposite shoulder to indicate that he should face forward again. "Who'll say six hundred?"

"What about the wench and the pickaninnies?" another man said.

The auctioneer glanced at his notes. "They go together—that's the one condition of the sale."

"That's a lot of mouths to feed," the first man said.

"Ol' Betty looks like she eats right well," the young man from the saloon said. "Might need to hitch her up to the trough next to the hogs."

This comment created a wave of laughter that rippled through the crowd.

"Ol' Betty," the auctioneer said, "is nigh as strong as her husband. Can slaughter, skin, and dress a hog before breakfast and then serve him up in half the time it takes you, young man, to shave in the morning."

"And he ain't got nothin' but peach fuzz to clip off, no how!" one of his companions said.

This comment was met with even more laughter, and the auctioneer took advantage of the crowd's good humor. "Do I hear seven hundred?"

"Seven hundred."

"I have seven hundred," the auctioneer said. "Now gentleman, Solomon alone is worth more than that. Who'll say eight hundred?"

"Seven-fifty."

"Sir, you must be joking. Do I hear eight hundred?"

"Eight hundred."

"I have eight hundred. Do I hear eight-fifty?"

Silence fell over the crowd. Zimri was beginning to worry. He had hoped to get a thousand for the whole family.

"I'll give you nine hundred for the buck, but I got no use for the wench or the children," a voice in the rear of the crowd said.

"Sir," the auctioneer said, "you know the terms."

"Take it or leave it," the man said.

Zimri turned to see that the man was a tall, thin fellow with a gaunt, pockmarked face. He was dressed in black and carried a whip coiled up in his right hand.

The auctioneer glanced at Zimri for some sign, but Zimri gave none.

"You can get another three, four hundred for the others separately," the man with the whip said. "Take it or leave it."

Zimri supposed that the man was a trader, a professional who could possibly sell Solomon to a planter in Louisiana or Mississippi for twice that amount.

The auctioneer looked again to Zimri for a signal.

He stared at the trader for a moment, as if to study his character. His gaze returned to the platform where Betty caught his eye. She seemed to be pleading with him. He shook his head.

The auctioneer looked to the man in black.

"All right then. I'll take the pack of 'em for eleven hundred."

Zimri did not look at the trader this time, nor at Betty. He closed his eyes, exhaled slowly, and nodded.

The auctioneer rapped his cane on the floor. "Sold! To the man in black for eleven hundred."

Zimri heard a shrill cry like that of an injured bird and opened his eyes to see Betty collapse into the arms of Solomon.

CHAPTER 2

Elizabeth could not remember a time when she had been so angry with Zimri. Though they had been married only two years, she had known him since she was twelve, when he arrived from Connecticut and started the first newspaper in Martinville. Her father had brought her to town to place an ad for some property he wanted to sell. In spite of their age difference, she determined on the spot to marry him, and at the age of sixteen, she did. It never occurred to her that she would fail in her quest, notwithstanding the many beaus she had closer to her own age, and the desire of her father for her to marry not only a younger man, but preferably the son of a rich planter like himself.

"How could you do it, Zimri?" She ladled out a bisque soup that, ironically, Betty had prepared for them that morning before being trundled off to the slave auction. "Solomon was born on my father's plantation. Betty suckled me at her breast—"

"You're repeating yourself," Zimri said. He gazed down at the soup without interest. "Besides, it's done now. There's no going back."

Elizabeth served herself, returned the ladle to the tureen in the center of the table, and sat down. "I don't have any help now, and you're already planning a trip to Connecticut. The baby's due—"

"Patsy will be here."

"Patsy's a child. She can hardly dress herself."

"She'll learn quickly."

"She can't live with us indefinitely."

"I'll hire a nurse and a cook when I get back, I told you."

"With what? This trip of yours will be very expensive."

Zimri put his soup spoon down and wiped his lips with his napkin. "That's enough, Elizabeth. We've been over this."

Elizabeth knew just how far she could push Zimri, and she had now reached that point. It wasn't that she was afraid he would strike her, it was more a question of his cold resolve when he had made up his mind about something. She decided to change the subject.

"I saw Mrs. Laskey today."

"Oh? Did she say anything about the lending library?"

"Yes. She's convinced the Merchants' Association that it's in their best interest to contribute to the building committee."

"Excellent! That woman is a badger–all teeth and claws. How much?"

"Three hundred dollars."

Zimri turned the soup over with his spoon. "Well, it's a start. At least you've got them involved."

"Yes. That's important."

The rest of the meal went uneventfully, with the exception of the baby's crying and Elizabeth's getting up from the table to quiet her. The baby asleep again, Elizabeth returned to clear the table.

"I'll help," Zimri said, rising. "Now that Betty's gone—"

"No, no—I can do it myself," Elizabeth said. "Why don't you see about your roses? They're beautiful right now, but they could use some pruning."

"The roses? I hadn't noticed, really. I suppose you're right. There's still plenty of daylight left." He seemed about to say something more, thought better of it, and went out the front door to the garden.

Elizabeth knew how to get Zimri out of her sight when she was angry at him—all she had to do was mention his roses. Odd that a man of such assured masculinity should be so interested in flowers. But it was that combination of self-confidence and sensitivity to the finer things in life that had attracted her to him in the first place.

But he was so exasperating at times! Here she was four months pregnant with their second child, the newspaper struggling for survival—he refused to accept any financial help from her father—and he sells their most trusted slaves. Why, Betty was not only a wonderful cook, she practically anticipated her needs before she herself was even aware of them. And now he was going on a journey to Connecticut where he would be gone for two months! And for what? A death in the family? No...for a friend's wedding!

She finished washing the dishes—a novel experience for her—and went into the bedroom to check on the baby. Charlotte was sound asleep and looked as contented as could be. What an angel! People said she looked like her, with blond curls and blue eyes, but she saw much more of Zimri's features in her—the high forehead and square jaw, the small ears and sensuous mouth.

"Elizabeth!"

The sound of Zimri's voice startled her. She saw that the baby was still asleep and left the room quietly, closing the door behind her.

"Elizabeth!"

She saw Zimri standing in the doorway, half-in and half-out of the house. She put her forefinger to her lips. "Shh! Do you want to wake the baby?"

"I can't help that," Zimri said, nevertheless lowering his voice to a whisper. "Jim McDowell just came driving up while I was in the garden—the courthouse is on fire. I've got to get down there."

"Zimri—you're not a fireman. What can you do? Can't you wait until morning?"

"They'll need every available hand. Besides, I'll get an eyewitness account for the paper."

"Why can't—Oh, all right. Go!"

Zimri looked apologetic. It was the fifth night in a row he had had to go back to the office after supper. "It hasn't had a chance to get out of hand yet. I should be back within an hour."

Elizabeth sighed. "You'd better hurry."

Zimri disappeared from the doorway and Elizabeth stepped onto the front porch. She saw Zimri run down the garden path to the street and leap into Jim McDowell's gig. She waved to Jim, who acknowledged with his whip and immediately snapped it forward, striking the hindquarters of the horse. In a moment they were gone, leaving a cloud of red dust behind them.

She knew it would not be an hour, however quickly the fire was extinguished. Zimri would go back to the office afterwards and write the story. Then he would decide to set the type so that it would be ready to print first thing in the morning. He wouldn't be home until midnight, as usual.

She decided to while the time away in her usual fashion, by reading. She went in to check on Charlotte one more time, saw that she was sleeping soundly, and went back into what they called the hearth room. The house was a sort of double log cabin, with two bedrooms joined in the center by a large living area at one end and a makeshift library at the other. Zimri had built it with his own hands, albeit with the help of a few neighbors. It was rather rustic, to say the least, compared to the plantation house she grew up in, but it had a certain warmth to it that she found to be attractive and comfortable. There were numerous hooked rugs on the floor, some of which she had made herself, and a patchwork quilt over the back of the sofa that Betty had made while she was nursing her own children. The quilt was a pretty thing, a work of art, really, that would always remind her of Betty.

She found herself standing in front of one of the bookcases in Zimri's library, staring vacantly at the volumes. Swift, Pope, Fielding, Racine, Voltaire. What did they have to do with her? She smiled as she took down a volume of Voltaire's work and opened it to *Candide*. It was in French, of course, and she knew that Zimri could barely understand a word of it. She was fluent in French herself, since she had attended Mademoiselle Gaillard's Lycèe in Charleston for three years. They were allowed to speak only French morning, noon, and night. Two demerits if Mademoiselle, who was ubiquitous ('omniprésente!'), caught one speaking English, even in the dormitory. Ten demerits, and one was excluded from the Saturday evening soirées, which all the eligible young bachelors made a point to attend. Only at these soirées was English allowed, for the simple reason that few of the young men could speak French.

She replaced the volume of *Candide*, and continued to peruse the bookshelves. After passing over the male authors that Zimri largely preferred, her fingers stopped at a volume by Jane Austen—*Sense and Sensibility*. A curious name for a novel. It sounded more like a lecture. She took it down, however, and read the first paragraph or two. It seemed to be about a young woman much like herself. Finally, she pulled up Zimri's favorite chair, sat down, and continued reading.

The heroine, Marianne Dashwood, seemed so much like herself that she wondered how the author had been able to anticipate the very thoughts and feelings that she, Elizabeth, would have a generation or so later. She read eagerly and rapidly, and was completely oblivious of the time. She was reminded of a beau she had in Charleston by the character of Willoughby, Marianne's dashing and romantic young lover. She closed her eyes and let the open book fall to her lap as she drifted into reminiscence.

"Elizabeth?"

She seemed vaguely aware that someone was calling her name. She at first thought it was Randolph, her beau in Charleston, who was just on the verge of asking her to dance for the first time at one of Mademoiselle Gaillard's soirées.

"Elizabeth, you'll have a crick in your neck in the morning if you stay in that position. Come to bed."

She opened her eyes and saw that it was Zimri. He looked exhausted, with dark circles under his eyes and soot on his clothing.

"Oh—Zimri." She sat up suddenly in her chair and examined him more closely as if to determine whether it was indeed her husband. "The fire—you aren't hurt, are you?"

Zimri smiled. (He was always more handsome when he smiled.) "No, not at all. It was out in thirty minutes except for a few smoldering embers. But I'm afraid we'll need a new roof for the courthouse."

"New roof? Why, you're covered with soot. Did the ceiling fall on you?"

Zimri laughed heartily. "No, but a piece of it fell on Harry Ross. He wasn't hurt, but he came out of the courthouse looking like a darkie who had been standing under a privy at the wrong time."

She wrinkled her nose and frowned at him. "That's not a very romantic simile."

"Romantic? Of course it isn't." He picked up the book lying on her lap. "What have you been reading—*Sense and Sensibility*. Another English romance. Well, I'm glad you found something to divert you while I was away."

"Yes, it was diverting. Haven't you read it? It's your book."

"I can't remember. Perhaps I have. I have so many books. I don't suppose you'll allow me in the bed like this."

"Of course not. You're filthy. Get those clothes off and I'll give you a good scrubbing." She put the book aside, got up from the chair, and went to the kitchen to heat some water.

Zimri remained standing in the middle of the room, apparently at a loss as to what to do. He was too dirty to sit down anywhere, and too tired to remain standing. "How's the baby?"

"Asleep."

"That child could sleep through a cattle stampede."

"She inherited that trait from you. Come here, Zimri, and take your clothes off."

Ordinarily, these words would have greatly aroused him, but he was so tired that he simply obeyed her command like a small boy who had been playing where he shouldn't and marched passively to the sound of his wife's voice.

CHAPTER 3

Left Martinville just before daylight in the stage for Savannah in company with John Lewis, William Portman, and another man with whom I have no acquaintance. I think his name is Hurst, but not sure. Keeps to himself and avoids eye contact with the rest of us as we plunge ahead on the roads washed out from the recent rains.

Once through this rough, hilly section, we arrived in Dublin, situated on a plain near the Oconee River. The soil is generally fit for cultivating, but there are few inhabitants, with most of the buildings in a state of decay, and a general atmosphere of indolence and neglect. We dined at Yopp's Tavern , where the food was better than the accommodations, but not by much.

Left Dublin at daybreak, crossed the Oconee at a ferry. Weather improving, but a sameness of appearance in the countryside, the soil , the timber, the population, and every other object that meets the eye, continues for about a hundred miles, with nothing to relieve or amuse the mind. Even conversation with my companions, while amiable enough, suffered from a lack of stimulation from the passing display of poverty, ignorance and barrenness.

Zimri put down his pen as the stage approached the Ohoopie River. It was now about noon and the travelers were hungry and anxious to stop for dinner. An inn came into view as they turned towards the river, and it appeared to Zimri to be a well-kept establishment. There were horses and carriages parked outside, and people coming and going.

"Ah! An oasis in the desert!" John Lewis said. "I had thought we would all expire for lack of sustenance and libation."

Zimri knew that Lewis was primarily interested in the libations, as he seldom got through a day without imbibing at least a quart of whiskey. He had brought a flask with him, but unfortunately for him, Yopp's either would not or could not replenish it for him after the first leg of the journey. He was also prone to verbosity, especially when drunk, but the lack of his usual quota of spirits this fine morning had dampened his customary loquaciousness, a fact for which Zimri was grateful.

As the passengers got out of the stage to stretch their legs before going into the tavern to dine, Zimri noticed the man he thought was named Hurst staring at him with more than a passing interest. Their eyes met, 'Hurst' turned away, then, when he thought Zimri wasn't looking, their eyes met again. 'Hurst' again turned away.

Zimri wondered at this for a moment, trying to place the man. Where had he seen him?

"Wouldn't pay a plugged nickel for a hundred acres of this hardscrabble."

It was Bill Portman, a good-natured but highly opinionated planter who had done well with the small plot of land he had inherited from his father. Zimri liked Portman even though they often disagreed politically.

"Ain't no good for corn, or wheat, or even peanuts," Portman said. "You might could make it with livestock. But what're you gonna feed'em? Tumble weeds?"

Zimri laughed. "It's hardly that bad, Bill. Looks to me like the local planters just need some education about modern agriculture."

Portman gave Zimri a supercilious look. "There you go again, Zimri. All that Jeffersonian nonsense about 'scientific agriculture.' Just apply the right science and any idiot can grow buckwheat in the desert. It don't work like that. You ain't a planter like me, or you'd know that."

"Jefferson was a planter."

"Now don't get me started on Jefferson. Jefferson was a lah-tee-da dandy who never stepped in a cow patty 'cause his slaves picked 'em up before they could bespatter his shiny patent leather boots. No, what they got here is some poor soil that even God couldn't grow a turnip on."

Zimri laughed again at Portman's colorful way of expressing himself. He was amusing, even when, in Zimri's view, he was wrong. "The indigenous population lacks industry, that's all."

Portman shook his head. "That's a writer for you. Uses a big word when a little one will do. What the hell does 'indigenous' mean?"

"Native."

"Then why didn't you say so?" Portman looked around the premises. "I could eat a buffalo. Why don't we go inside and see what they got?"

"They must have some whiskey," Lewis said, licking his lips. "I saw a corn crib out back and what looks like a distilling mechanism."

"You're worse than he is. Why don't you two call things by their right names? 'Distilling mechanism.' It's a pot liquor still. Now let's go in before all them vittles get et up."

All seemed to be in favor of this suggestion, and the group began walking along the path to the front door of the inn.

Zimri noticed that 'Hurst' was hanging back somewhat, as if he felt excluded from the company. "Won't you join us, Mr. Hurst?"

"Herzen," the man said.

For the first time, Zimri noticed that he had a German accent. "Sorry, I misunderstood when we were introduced. Won't you join us, Mr. Herzen?"

Mr. Herzen looked hesitant, then nodded. "Yes. Thank you."

Once inside, the four men were escorted to a large table in the middle of the room, where several other diners were already seated. Their hostess was a rather energetic woman of middle age, slightly plump, and with a rather ugly scar that extended from one temple, disappeared briefly beneath the hair line, then emerged at the other temple and disappeared into the hairline again.

"Injuns," Portman said after the woman had taken their order for drinks. "Never seen a scar like that 'cept it was a scalping. Must have left her for dead and somehow she survived."

"Poor woman," Lewis said. "She must have been a beauty in her day."

Mr. Herzen seemed alarmed at this information. "Indians? I thought ze Indians were all on ze reservations. There is a treaty, no?"

"That's right, Herzen," Portman said. "But it ain't been twenty years since the treaty was signed. She was probably a young girl then."

"I hope her brain isn't so addled that she forgets to bring my whiskey," Lewis said.

"You'll be three sheets to the wind by sundown if she doesn't," Portman said. "Beats me how you make so much money with that millinery business of yours. I guess the ladies don't care whether you're sloshed or not so long as you sell 'em pretty hats."

Lewis was visibly offended but tried to slough it off. "It helps lubricate the transactions."

"'Lubricate,'" Portman said. "There's another good one. I know what that means—stewed to the gills."

"But zese Indians," Herzen said to Portman, "are they still 'scalping,' as you say?"

"Sure," Portman said gleefully. "Only they've moved out west. If you want a beaver cut, light out for Oklahoma. They're still open for business."

"We've had peace with the Creeks since 1821, Mr. Herzen," Zimri said. "There've been no significant outbreaks of violence since then."

Mr. Herzen looked dubious. "No *significant* outbreaks?"

"You were here before that, weren't you, Zimri?" Portman said. "Fightin' Indians out at Ft. Hawkins."

"I came to Ft. Hawkins in 1819," Zimri said. "But I didn't have to fight Indians. I ran the fort's newspaper."

Mr. Herzen seemed somewhat reassured by this new intelligence, and sat back in his chair as if he could now be permitted to relax.

Mrs. Connolly, the hostess, returned to their table with Lewis' whiskey and cider for the others. She seemed cheerful and attentive, calling many patrons—most of them men—by their first names, and carrying the hot food out from the kitchen with potholders. Her only assistants were her children, a boy about fifteen, and two girls around ten and twelve. She ordered them about as if they were raw recruits in a conscripted army.

At the end of the meal, Mr. Herzen, who ate voraciously, belying his small stature, turned to Zimri. "Do you remember the auction, Mr. Rhodes?"

Zimri finished his glass of cider and put the glass down on the table. "Auction?"

"Yes. The slave auction. I purchased your Betty."

Zimri wiped his lips with his napkin and examined Mr. Herzen's face more carefully. It was round, with a goatee that encircled his chin and joined a thin mustache over his lip. His eyes were set close together and he wore round-rimmed steel glasses. Zimri estimated his age to be about forty. "You must be mistaken, Mr. Herzen. I sold Betty and the children along with her husband to a trader."

"And I purchased the woman and the children from him."

Zimri was taken aback. "You bought them from—but you had no right! I specifically required that—"

"Pardon me, Mr. Rhodes. Regardless of your requirements before the sale, once the transaction was completed, the trader could sell them to whomever he pleased. No?"

Zimri struggled to control his temper. "That is true, Mr. Herzen. It's a free market place. But you must have been aware that—"

Herzen waved his hand as if to dismiss such sentimental nonsense. "I was only aware, Mr. Rhodes, that I was in need of servants and the trader wished to divest himself of the woman and her children. I paid nearly twice what they cost him."

Zimri glanced at Portman and Lewis, who seemed to take great interest in this conversation. "Well, Mr. Herzen, I assure you they are well worth whatever you paid for them. I only accepted the trader's offer because—"

"Zat Betty—she is a good worker, but she doesn't like field work."

"No, no," Zimri said. "She's a house slave. Trained as a cook and a seamstress."

"Vell," Mr. Herzen said with an air of resentment, "she cooks well enough—I am a bachelor, you see—but she is absolutely worthless in ze field. I had to beat her several times yust to get her to pick one basket of cotton."

"Beat her?"

Herzen smiled with a certain amount of satisfaction, it seemed. "Only with my riding crop. Zis got her attention, but she seemed to regard it only as a nuisance. As if she were swatting away flies."

Zimri, though still angry, could not help smiling at this comment. He knew Betty to be thick-skinned in every sense of the word. Still, it disturbed him that Herzen had so readily resorted to whipping. "Whippings are not the way to get her to cooperate, Mr. Herzen. Let her work in the kitchen as she was trained to do."

Herzen screwed his face into a kind of squashed pumpkin. "But I need field hands—that's why I am going to ze market in Savannah. In the meantime, the children will have to suffice."

"The children?"

"Zey are not old enough to be of much use, but zey are learning. Two, three baskets a day."

"Mr. Herzen—they are barely old enough to walk. Sally's about six, and Aaron's only four. Don't you think—"

"I am a small farmer, Mr. Rhodes. I cannot afford a division of labor like Mr. Portman here. I must make use of what I have."

"I ain't got but ten slaves," Portman said. "Ten slaves to work 300 acres. But I don't put children under seven out in the fields, Mr. Herzen. It ain't right."

Herzen dismissed Portman's comments with another wave of his hand. "You can say that with ze luxury of ten slaves at your disposal, Mr. Portman. I am buying two more in Savannah, but I will still be short of help. Ze children will have to do their part."

Zimri thought of Elizabeth and her reaction once she found out that the family had been split up. "I'll pay you whatever you paid for them, Mr. Herzen. It seems that by your own assessment that they will be of little use to you."

Herzen grinned. "By my own assessment, Mr. Rhodes, they will be quite useful to me. It will take time before I train them up, that's all."

Zimri studied Herzen for a moment. "You say you paid twice what the trader paid for them. What—four hundred?"

"I told you, Mr. Rhodes. They are not for sale. Betty will submit to my will soon enough. But if you are willing to pay, say, six hundred, I might be persuaded to—"

Zimri felt disgust at Herzen's attempt to drive up the price. Besides, he had just ordered a new printing press and now with the expense of the trip..."Four hundred, Mr. Herzen. That's all I can afford."

Herzen reached for his bill. "What a pity. Perhaps we can discuss it another time when you are, shall we say, feeling more prosperous."

"Perhaps."

The four men stood up to leave. Zimri picked up his bill and went to the front desk where Mrs. Connolly waited patiently. As he took out his billfold, he noticed an old man sitting in a chair next to the door. He must have been about eighty, with stooped shoulders, his right hand supported by a hickory cane, and a rather vacant look on his face.

"A fine meal, Mrs. Connolly," he said all the while looking at the old man.

"My pleasure," Mrs. Connolly said.

"Who's this gentleman? Your father?"

"My husband."

"Oh, I'm sorry—I didn't mean to—"

"That's all right. Dear Old Joseph is forty-two years my senior. But he saved my life and nursed me back to health, and now it's my turn to take care of him. Don't say much, but nothing gets by him."

"Yes," Zimri said, replacing his billfold in his coat pocket, "I can see that. But then you and your children run the place by yourselves, do you?"

Mrs. Connolly smiled. "Me, my children, and thirty slaves."

"Thirty?"

"Yep. Got over a thousand acres here. Mostly beef cattle. But we got pecans, peanuts, and cotton, too. Cotton's the thing, though. Next year, we'll have more cotton under cultivation than peanuts."

"You got that right," Portman said. "Cotton is king."

"Yes, it is. Have a good trip, gentlemen." She put the money in a drawer and slammed it shut. "I understand the weather's clear all the way to Savannah."

When they stepped outside into the sunlight, Zimri noticed for the first time that there was a large stable beneath a copse of oak trees that could accommodate perhaps a dozen horses with their carriages. Several black men were busy grooming the horses or repairing harnesses. One brought the stage out to the driveway to meet them.

"Thirty slaves," Portman said, letting out a low whistle. "That little lady is rich!"

"Industry," Herzen said, climbing back into the coach.

"Luck," Lewis said, following him. "Getting scalped and rescued by Old Joseph was the best thing that ever happened to her."

Zimri lingered a moment outside the coach, surveying the land around the inn. In the distance he could see what looked like dozens of black dots moving along a hillside. "Industry, luck…and thirty slaves."

Portman called to him from the stage. "Come on, Zimri—we ain't got all day."

Zimri barely heard him, focused as he was on the dots moving along the rows of cotton.

"Whatcha starin' at?" Portman said. "Let's go!"

Zimri adjusted his hat to shield his eyes from the sun and climbed into the stage.

CHAPTER 4

June 18, Friday

Arrived in Savannah at 7 a.m. and put up at the City Hotel.

Having nothing of importance to do while awaiting the arrival of the next packet for New York, I devoted most of my time to the observation of the country in the vicinity and the city. I had always had a favorable opinion of the beauty of Savannah and it was quite gratifying to see the improvements of ten years since I had first seen it.

There are many beautiful and costly dwellings in the city, most of which are enhanced in their elegance by various shade and fruit trees. Their yards are filled with orange, lemon, pomegranate, lagerstroemia, rosebay, frankliania, oleander, magnolia, and, in one garden, as great a variety of shrubs and plants as I have ever seen in one collection. A brick wall on one side of this garden is entirely covered with different kinds of European ivy, and intermingled with branches of Cape Jasmine, which have been trained against it.

Saturday

Attended the ship at 10 o'clock, with all the passengers, but the wind being unfavorable, did not sail, and returned to the hotel.

Sunday

Went on board the ship, got under way with a light breeze, went down the river about three miles, met a head wind—commenced to return, got aground twice, but soon got off. Passengers landed at the Rice Mill Wharf. I returned again to the hotel in bitter disappointment at the delay, and submitted with melancholy grace to the jokes of Portman and Lewis, who congratulated me on a safe arrival, and inquired of news from New York.

Monday

Said farewell to Portman and Lewis, who, having finished their business in Savannah, returned on the noon stage to Martinville. More ribbing, especially from Portman, who suggested that I might still be in residence at the hotel when they returned in the spring.

Tuesday, 2 p.m.

Again went on board the ship, and was towed out of the river by a steamboat. Passed Tybee lighthouse about two hours before sunset, a fine breeze sprang up, and at sunset the last glimpse of the low and level shores of Georgia sank beneath the blue waves.

Once out to sea, Zimri settled into his tiny cabin and unpacked his things. He shared this cabin with another passenger, a diminutive Frenchman, who introduced himself only as 'Alex.' Alex chose to sleep on the top bunk, joking that if they ran into stormy weather—as surely they would—he would rather fall on Zimri than have Zimri, with his greater bulk, fall on him.

Zimri found his companion quite agreeable, and noted that he had an aristocratic bearing and was possessed of considerable erudition. They were both invited to dine with the captain, which they did, and afterwards went out on deck for a cigar.

"Ah, Monsieur Zimri, is it not a lovely evening to be gazing out on the great expanse of this vast sea that separates our two countries?"

Zimri cupped his hands over a match, lit Alex's cigar, and then lit his own. "It is indeed a beautiful sight, Alex. It's almost worth it for the delay."

"Delay?"

"Yes. I've been waiting in Savannah for nearly a week for the ship to sail."

Alex puffed on his cigar. "Is that so? It's all a matter of timing, I suppose. I arrived from Charleston only the day before. A beautiful city, Charleston."

"I wouldn't know—I've never been there."

"What? But you live so close. Why, it's the Paris of your country!"

"So my wife tells me. She attended school there for several years. She's part French, actually."

Alex's eyes grew larger at this information. "Is that so? She was born in France?"

"No—her grandfather was."

"Ah—what part of France?"

"Bordeaux, I think. He and his brothers fled the Revolution."

"Aristocrats, then?"

"Yes, I believe so. Lost everything."

"Ah, yes, many did. It is a sad thing, no?"

"In some ways, yes. But they worked hard once they settled here and became quite prosperous."

"Yes, of course. That is the promise of America, is it not? I find your country fascinating in so many ways, Monsieur Zimri."

The two men fell into silence at this point, each gazing towards the west, enjoying the quiet serenity of the swelling sea, the last rays of the sun playing upon the crests with brilliant bursts of gold soon extinguished and replaced by red, purple and finally black. But this silence was soon broken by the boisterous sound of two men who had just emerged from the ship's mess, obviously having had too much to drink.

"I tell you, the black man is no more capable of living in civil society than the red," one of the men said in a booming baritone that could have been heard from bow to stern.

"Quiet, you drunken fool," the other said. "You'll have the ship's crew down on us in the blink of a whale's eye."

"Whales don't blink—they've got no eye lids."

"All right—a mule's eye, then. They'll be on us like flies on a dung heap."

"Why?"

The second man seemed to be teetering at the gunwale for a moment, having lost his train of thought. "Why? Why, because there's black men among 'em. Free blacks. They've sensitive about their color."

"Well, damn their sensitive souls, then! They ought to own up to their place in the scheme of things."

"What scheme is that?"

The baritone seemed to consider this for a moment. "Damned if I know…But I do know that blacks ain't got the same parts as the white man—or the red man."

"What makes you so partial to the red man—you got squaw blood in you?"

The baritone, whose physique fit the pitch of his voice, suddenly grabbed his companion by the lapel and threatened him with his fist. "You take that back, Jacob!"

The smaller man seemed not the least frightened, and brushed the larger man's hand away. "I'll not do it. Why should you be so offended when you say the red man is superior to the black?"

The baritone dropped his fist and turned to gaze at the sea. "I dunno.

I guess because neither red nor black adds up to white. But it just seems to me that the red man is smarter."

"Who says?"

"You're a cantankerous varmint for bein' such a runt, ain't you?" The baritone turned to Zimri and seemed to notice him for the first time. "Why don't we ask this gentleman to settle it. Got the look of an educated man. Sir!"

Zimri looked at Alex, who seemed amused, then at the baritone. "I believe you are addressing me, sir. How can I be of assistance?"

The baritone, well over six feet and outweighing Zimri by some fifty pounds, ambled rather unsteadily towards him, trying unsuccessfully to coordinate his movements with that of the rolling ship. "No doubt you've heard something of our conversation just now."

"Difficult not to," Zimri said.

The baritone seemed slightly embarrassed. "I hope we didn't disturb Your Honor. You have the look of a judge."

Zimri smiled. "No one ever accused me of being a judge before. I'm a newspaperman."

The baritone turned to his companion. "You see! I told you he was an educated man." He turned back to Zimri. "We'd like Your Honor to settle a little dispute we've been having."

"I'll do my best."

"All right, then. Who's smarter—the black man or the red man?"

Zimri removed the cigar from his mouth, placed his elbows on the railing, and gazed out to sea. "I've had considerable experience with both—but for the life of me, I can see no difference in native intelligence between the two, or between them and white men, for that matter."

The baritone seemed dumfounded, as did his companion. "You think niggers are as smart as white men?"

Zimri puffed on his cigar again. "I said that I could see no difference between them in the way of native intelligence. There are differences, of course, in the way of culture and circumstances."

The baritone seemed speechless for a moment, turned to look at his friend, then back to Zimri. "Let me ask you something if it ain't too personal."

"Feel free," Zimri said.

"Do you own slaves, sir?"

"I did at one time, but no longer."

"You're an abolitionist, then?"

Zimri had never been asked this question before and thought a moment before answering. "I suppose I am."

The baritone nodded his head briefly as if his suspicions were confirmed. "I'm much obliged, sir, for your opinion."

"I hope it was of some value to you."

The baritone did not answer but turned again to his companion. "Come on, Jacob. The air out here is gettin' a bit thick."

After the two men disappeared inside the ship's main cabin, which glowed with the light of oil lamps now, Zimri and Alex resumed their positions at the railing.

"Rather a rude fellow," Alex said.

"Oh, not a bad sort," Zimri said. "Just a bit limited in his horizons, you might say."

"Well put." Alex extinguished his cigar on the railing and tossed the stub into the sea. "Ironic, is it not, Monsieur Zimri, that so many Americans can be described as such when the 'horizons' of their country seem to be without limit."

Zimri chuckled. "I think you have a tendency to lump all Americans together, Alex. We're much like people everywhere—we simply don't have the barriers to advancement that you Europeans do."

"But do all Americans have this unobstructed path to wealth and happiness before them? It seems that some are excluded."

Zimri felt this thrust as a personal injury. "Yes. I cannot dispute that."

"It is a contradiction embedded in your beloved Constitution, is it not?"

"I wouldn't say it was 'embedded,' exactly. It is somewhat indirect. It can be changed."

"But that is a very difficult thing to do, is it not?"

"Yes. Very difficult."

Alex reached into his coat pocket and pulled out a fresh cigar. He clipped the end off and moistened it with his tongue. "You mentioned to the tipsy gentleman that you had once owned slaves."

"Yes."

"May I be so bold as to ask why you decided to sell them?"

Zimri felt more uncomfortable than ever, but was determined not to be ruffled by the Frenchman's trenchant inquiries. "It was more a matter of necessity than conscience. I simply needed the money."

"Ah, so giving them their freedom was out of the question?"

Zimri felt this last thrust as salt in the wound. "No, of course not. It was not out of the question. I simply did not consider it."

The two men remained silent for a minute or two, smoking. The wind began to pick up, and the ship heeled to the starboard side.

"Looks like a gale coming up," Zimri said. "Perhaps we'd better go inside."

"I hope I have not offended you, Monsieur Zimri."

Zimri turned to face the Frenchmen and saw that there was no malice in his eyes, only a fine, inquisitive intelligence. "No offense taken, Alex."

CHAPTER 5

Elizabeth stared dreamily out of the window, admiring Zimri's roses. They had come into full bloom since he had left for Connecticut and she marveled at his talent for coaxing even the most recalcitrant buds into dazzling displays of rapturous color. The deepest, most voluptuous reds, the softest, most sensuous shades of yellow, scarlet, and pink.

She missed him already and he had only been gone a week. How could she endure another two months!

"Lizzie!"

The sound of her younger sister calling her by her childhood nickname jolted her out of her melancholy reverie. She put down the copy of *Sense and Sensibility* that she had been reading since the night that Zimri had helped put out the fire.

"Lizzie!"

"I can hear you, Patsy—you needn't shout." She wondered at her own diction—'needn't shout.' It was this silly English novel that was making her talk that way.

"Lizzie! It's Jamie—and he's got someone with him!"

Elizabeth slowly rose from her chair. She was beginning to feel the weight of the baby within her. "Jamie? In the carriage?"

"No, no!" Patsy came running into the hearth room from the front porch where she had been sitting on the swing. "They're on horseback. Jamie on old Ginger, and the other man on a magnificent chestnut stallion. I don't think Papa even *has* such a horse! Come look!"

"Oh, Patsy," Elizabeth said, allowing her younger sister to pull her by the hand towards the front porch. "A horse is a horse. You get so excited over such trivial—" She interrupted herself when she recognized the figure on the chestnut stallion. He had an unmistakable profile, even seated on a galloping horse some one hundred yards off. It was Randolph Benson, her one-time beau in Charleston. "Randolph! I wonder what he's doing so far away from his beloved Lynwood?"

"What's Lynwood?" Patsy asked. They both watched as the two men came to an abrupt halt before the hitching rail in the road, throwing up a cloud of choking red dust.

"That's his father's plantation near Charleston. It's so large, it contains several towns and villages. Randolph is the eldest son."

"Then he must be very rich," Patsy said.

"He is…or soon will be."

"Elizabeth!" Jamie said, flinging the reins of his horse over the rail without bothering to secure them. "Look who I've brought with me!"

In contrast to Jamie, Randolph carefully wrapped his reins around the rail and secured them with a slip knot. Then he removed his riding cap, ran his fingers through his auburn hair, and began walking up the path to the house. Jamie walked ahead of him at a quick pace.

Patsy ran out to greet him. "Jamie, Jamie! We thought you'd never come—it's so boring here!"

Jamie wrapped his arms around Patsy in a big bear hug and lifted her feet off the ground. "Boring? Why—hasn't Elizabeth put you to work?"

"It's just baby-sitting," Patsy said. "Charlotte's so quiet and sleeps so much there's hardly anything to do."

"Well, you're also here to look after your older sister—don't you have games you can play?"

"Oh, we play checkers sometimes. But it's a stupid, boring game—besides, Lizzie just seems to want to read all the time."

"Read? Now that is boring." Jamie gave Elizabeth a look of mock admonishment and reached out to embrace her. "You should really try to think of some more entertaining things for Patsy to do, Elizabeth. A twelve year-old can't be expected to—"

"Patsy has the attention span of a butterfly," Elizabeth said. "She flits from one pretty thing to another. Actually, she's been enjoying Zimri's garden, haven't you, Patsy? Hello, Randolph."

Randolph stood as if at attention at a military parade. In fact, he looked much the military man, with his red riding jacket, white ruffled shirt, mouse-gray trousers and black riding boots. He even made a little bow. "It's been a long time, Elizabeth—too long."

"I suppose it has," she said. "What—two years? Two and a half? At the wedding."

"I'm afraid I missed the wedding."

"Missed it? I thought surely you were there—as a guest of Jamie's."

"If you'll recall," Randolph said coolly, "I was there shortly before the wedding to try to persuade you to put things off a bit."

"Oh," Elizabeth said. "Now I remember. You seemed to think I was too young for Zimri."

"Rather that he was too old for you," Jamie said, with a frown. "Too old and too much of a Yankee."

Elizabeth turned to Jamie. "Let's not go through that again, Jamie. Zimri's long since left his Yankee roots behind him."

"If that's so," Jamie said, slapping the dust off his trousers with his cap, "then why did he just go off to Connecticut? That's where he's from, isn't it? And you here with a baby, and another on the way."

This cut Elizabeth to the quick. "He *had* to go. His best friend is getting married. And, of course, I couldn't travel in my condition."

"No, certainly not," Jamie said. "So he should have stayed, too. Who knows? He might never come back—and good riddance!"

"Jamie," she said, "did you come all the way into town just to insult Zimri when he's not here to defend himself? If so—"

"All right, all right." Jamie gave her a hug. "I'm out of line, and I apologize. We came to cheer you up a little, not get your dander up. How about some lemonade? Randolph and I are as thirsty as a couple of billy goats."

"Zimri grows the biggest lemons you ever saw," Patsy said excitedly. "I picked some this morning."

"What a wonderful idea, Jamie," Elizabeth said. "Patsy, you go squeeze the lemons and I'll get some of that brown sugar that just came in from the West Indies. Randolph, it really is good to see you."

"It's good to see you, Elizabeth," Randolph said, making another little bow. "Charleston hasn't been the same without you."

"Nonsense. Charleston doesn't know or care whether I exist. I was just a school girl then, sillier even than Patsy. Gentlemen—won't you come inside?"

Randolph offered his arm. "If you will allow me, Miss Blake..."

She balked at Randolph's use of her maiden name, but then decided that it was merely a sentimental reminder of their earlier courtship. She placed her arm through his and allowed herself to be escorted up the path to the house. Jamie, who smiled with a perverse satisfaction, followed them at a discreet distance.

"How much property do you have here?" Randolph said. They sat on the veranda at the front of the house while Patsy served the lemonade.

"About four acres, I think. Does the lemonade need more sugar?"

"Not at all," Randolph said. "It's perfect."

"Delicious," Jamie said. "I'll have to give ol' Zim credit—he knows how to grow things."

"He's a man of many talents," Elizabeth said.

Randolph gazed out at the garden. "Roses seem to be his forte. I've never seen such a variety."

"It's both his recreation and his passion."

Randolph turned to her and their eyes met. "Passion? I would think that a man would not have much passion left for plants and flowers if he were married to you."

Elizabeth blushed and averted her eyes.

Jamie cleared his throat and stood up from his chair. "I think I'll explore the property a bit. Looks like you've got some new buildings out back."

"Oh—yes," she said, still a bit flustered at Randolph's comment. "Zimri's built a barn since you were here last—and a smoke house."

"A smoke house? Then you'll have some good meats this winter. Come on, Patsy, show me where the smoke house is."

Patsy leapt up from her chair and skipped down the front steps. "There's nothing in the smoke house but old smelly hams and turkeys. I'll show you the duck pond—we can feed the ducks!"

"Ducks," Jamie said. "Now there's an idea. I haven't shot one all year."

"No, no, no!" squealed Patsy. "I said feed them, not shoot them!"

"He's just teasing you, Patsy," Elizabeth said "Take some corn from the crib—they love corn."

"And it makes them nice and fat," Jamie said, descending the steps. "Corn-fed ducks are the best for eating."

"No, no, Jamie! These are tame ducks. I've given each a name. Promise me you won't hurt them."

Jamie winked at Elizabeth and Randolph. "All right, Sugar Plum, I promise."

Elizabeth and Randolph watched them as they took a path around the side of the house and through the garden until they disappeared from sight. Elizabeth was aware that Randolph was still staring at her and though this made her uncomfortable, it flattered her as well. It seemed so long ago that this handsome young man, the most eligible bachelor in Charleston, came courting her at Mademoiselle Gaillard's soirées.

"How do you stand it, Elizabeth?" Randolph said. "I mean this sort of life?"

Her eyes met his again, and again she looked away. "I don't know what you mean, Randolph. I'm quite happy here."

"Are you?" Randolph gestured towards the log walls of the house. "Look at this place! It's clean and neat enough, but it's a frontier cabin. We've got hunting lodges at Lynwood that are grander than this!"

Elizabeth sipped her lemonade. "I'm sorry you disapprove, Randolph. But it's quite enough for us."

Randolph gazed out at the garden again. "Is it? For you, I mean. It may be enough for a Yankee newspaperman who only needs a couple of acres to grow his roses and some fruits and vegetables for the dinner table, but it's…it's merely existing, Elizabeth. It's not living…especially for a woman of refinement like yourself. Where are the balls? Where are the smart shops? Where are the stables of thoroughbred horses and fine carriages with footmen and grooms? Where are the house servants?"

Elizabeth put her glass down on the table. "We had house servants until recently…and I'm sure we'll have them again."

Randolph looked at her dubiously. "When? Your husband no doubt sold them because he was short of cash. How many newspapers will he have to sell in this little backwater town before he has enough money to buy one or two more? A year? Two years? And then another financial crisis will come along and he'll have to sell those. You'll be living hand to mouth, Elizabeth, the rest of your life."

She stared out into the garden where a particular rose, a brilliant yellow one with flecks of red at the base of the petals, caught her eye. "What do you suggest, Randolph? Abandon Zimri and run off with you to Charleston?"

"No," he said.

"Well, that's a relief."

Randolph leaned across the table and placed his hand over hers. "I'm suggesting that you abandon your husband and come with me to Europe."

"Are you mad? I'm five months pregnant with his child. And Charlotte—"

"Bring them. I'll care for them as if they were my own. And they'll grow up in comfort and refinement and they'll go to the best schools, as you did."

Elizabeth looked away again, but she did not move her hand. "It seems that we've had this conversation before, Randolph. Only now I'm married and have two children. Whereas your proposition before was right and proper, it's now obscene and immoral. In fact, it's almost laughable."

Randolph looked down at their two hands. "Obscene and immoral? I notice that you have not removed your hand from mine."

She quickly withdrew her hand. "I didn't wish to be rude."

Randolph grinned. "You always were a well-mannered girl, Elizabeth."

"And you always were the most conceited rake I've ever known."

"You misunderstand me, Elizabeth—I am in love with you and always have been."

"Yes. Just as you love your horse, your dogs, your hunting lodges at

Lynwood, and a good cigar after dinner. You're a man of pleasure, Randolph, and that's all a woman is to you—another source of pleasure."

"You're wrong. Elizabeth. And I aim to prove it to you."

"You intend to reform yourself?"

"If that's what it takes."

"What's all this about reform? Are you talking politics now?" It was Jamie, mounting the steps that came up from the side yard, closest to the drive. Elizabeth and Randolph remained in their places, staring at each other.

"Uh, oh." Jamie executed an about face. "I think I came back too soon."

"No, no, Jamie," Elizabeth said. "Randolph was just leaving. He has to go back to Lynwood."

"Lynwood? What are you talking about? He's come here to go hunting with me for the next two weeks."

"Two weeks?" Elizabeth said. "Well, then, I guess Lynwood will have to get along without you, Randolph, until you've had your fill of hunting."

"Lynwood can wait," Randolph said. "I'll have to return in any case to clear things up before I sail."

"Sail?"

"Didn't he tell you, Elizabeth? He's leaving for Europe next month—taking the Grand Tour."

"The Grand Tour? No, he didn't tell me," she said, still looking into Randolph's eyes which had not left hers for a moment since Jamie arrived. "For how long?"

"Nine months," Randolph said. "The usual tenure."

"I've heard that travel abroad changes a person," she said.

"Yes," Randolph said. "I'm prepared for that."

"Are you? Well, I hope it will be for the better." She looked at Jamie. "What have you done with Patsy?"

"She's still feeding the ducks. I came back to get some more refreshment—it's hot down there."

"Help yourself," Elizabeth said. "There's plenty more. Oh—the baby's awake. Excuse me." She went into the house and passed through the hearth room to the bedroom where Charlotte had been sleeping. She picked her up from the crib, put her over her shoulder and patted her back. Then she took her out to the veranda and sat in a rocker.

"This is Charlotte," she said to Randolph. "Isn't she beautiful?"

"Yes," Randolph said without enthusiasm. "She's a beautiful child...I think we'd better be going, Jamie. The horses are exhausted from all that running and, like Charlotte, they're bound to be hungry."

"But I thought we'd stay and—" Jamie finally got the hint as his eyes met with disapproving glances. "Oh, right. I see your point, Randolph. Well, at least you got a chance to see Elizabeth and the baby. What if we return for dinner tomorrow?"

"We'll be hunting tomorrow," Randolph said.

"Oh, that's right. Well, perhaps Sunday, then. Would that be agreeable to you, Elizabeth?"

Elizabeth continued rocking and patting Charlotte on the back. "Suit yourself. Patsy and I aren't going anywhere."

"That's hardly a gracious invitation, Elizabeth," Jamie said.

"Oh—sorry. Please come again. Sunday will be fine."

Jamie looked at his companion apologetically, but Randolph seemed unperturbed. He made another little bow to Elizabeth.

"It would be my pleasure, Miss Blake " he said. "I hope Sunday will be a more opportune time for us to chat a little longer."

"Perhaps so," she said.

"So long, Elizabeth," her brother said. "The way Patsy's feeding the ducks, one of them may be fat enough to eat on Sunday."

"You're incorrigible, Jamie," she said. "But Patsy would defend her ducks with her life. Now go on, both of you."

"Yes, ma'am," Jamie said.

She watched as they walked down the path to the road, a distance of one hundred feet or so, and mounted their horses. She couldn't help but observe that Randolph was one of the handsomest men she had ever seen, and though merely twenty or so, carried himself with the dignity and bearing of a much older man. His horse suddenly reared as if on cue, he waved his cap in a grand gesture, and they galloped off.

CHAPTER 6

July 2, Friday

Wind generally light and sometimes a calm of a few hours...vessel laying her course, but the progress slow...passed Cape Hatteras, probably at a distance of fifty miles, so that it was not seen...

July 3, Sat.

Calm until 2 pm today, when the wind began to kick up...by 6 pm ran into a squall with thunder and heavy rain—swells to eighteen or twenty feet, which caused the ship to pitch and roll...poor Alex became suddenly sea-sick, as did many others, and retired to the cabin...to me, it seemed a great adventure and I remained on deck until it was over, getting soaked in the process.

July 6, Tues.

Passed Barnegat Point, with a favorable prospect of entering Sandy Hook by nightfall. Another thunder squall rising ahead threw the vessel out of its course, and afterwards it fell nearly calm. At sunset the lighthouses were but a few miles distant.

July 7, Wed.

Winds light and variable till 3 pm. Entered New York Harbor...all sea-sickness or indisposition seemed to be banished or forgotten in the joy that the haven was at last won. Alex and I stood on the forecastle deck along with the other passengers, and he remarked that the scenery was surpassed in beauty only by the port at Naples...arrived at sunset at the docks of the city. We put up at the American Hotel on Broadway.

July 8, Thurs.

Alex and I breakfasted together, and went our separate ways to renew old acquaintances. We vowed to meet again for afternoon tea.

The city, since I have seen it, has improved beyond any calculation I could have made, both in the widening of streets, and in public build-ings and stores. The stores, in particular, are chaste, substantial and elegant. The lower stories are composed of upright granite pillars; the rest of the building either granite or brick. Some neighborhoods that I had known only as a nuisance, or were in disrepair, were now occupied by the finest of edifices.

"It is the grandest theatre in New York, Monsieur Zimri." Alex stirred his tea as the two men sat in the dining room of the hotel with its floor-to-ceiling windows overlooking Broadway. It was a sunny, warm after-noon, but the windows were open and there was a light breeze that rustled the curtains. "It is surpassed, in my estimation, only by the Comédie Française."

Zimri stirred his tea as he gazed out the window at the carriages that passed by. "Well, I haven't been to the Comèdie Française, or even Paris for that matter, but I have been to the Park Theatre. I recall it being grand enough, but the play I saw was rather silly."

"And what play was that?"

"I believe it was *The Rivals*, by Sheridan. Yes, that was it. Complete with Mrs. Malaprop, who, of course, spewed out a constant stream of gibberish."

Alex smiled. "Yes, that was a bit tedious, wasn't it? But then it was amusing to the audiences, who fancied themselves infinitely more so-phisticated than Mrs. Malaprop."

Zimri sipped his tea. "I have no objection to the British theatre, really, but it is tired, worn out. There needs to be an indigenous theatre that reflects the energy and vitality of America."

"I quite agree. Perhaps the performance at the Park this evening is such a play."

Zimri set his cup down in its saucer. "I doubt it. But I suppose we should give it a try."

The Park Theatre was only a few steps from the hotel, but as it was considered to be a meeting place for high society, both men retired to their rooms to dress for the occasion. Zimri donned his best collar and waistcoat, along with a red cravat and blue silk jacket with velvet la-pels. A gold-headed cane (brass, actually) completed the ensemble, and after applying a bit of pomade to his hair, left his room and knocked on Alex's door down the hall. After a moment, the door opened.

"Voilá!" Alex had clearly exceeded Zimri in his elaborateness of dress. He was resplendent in a gold brocaded jacket, Venetian lace cuffs, red silk waistcoat, green pinstriped trousers, gold watch chain, and white spats. This ensemble was completed with an elaborately carved ivory cane crowned with the head of a wolf.

Zimri felt positively shabby by comparison. "I must say, Alex, you look prepared to be presented to a monarch!"

Alex waved his hand as if to dismiss such a notion. "Ah, Monsieur Zimri, I am so out of fashion it embarrasses me. This was the mode of dress for a gentleman in Paris ten years ago. Today, I believe, they dress quite differently."

"Believe me, no one here will know the difference."

"I'm not so sure," Alex said, closing the door to his room behind him. "But at least we shall not be denied admittance. Allons-y!"

The Park Theatre was indeed an elaborate and impressive edifice, particularly the interior, which contained a proscenium stage flanked by towering marble columns, a full orchestra pit with attendant musicians, and four tiers of balconies for the patrons. They were ushered to their seats in front of the orchestra by a young man in the livery of a great household.

"Not exactly reflective of a democratic society," Zimri said, as he perused his program.

"It is designed to impress." Alex began to examine his program as well, employing a monocle for the purpose. "And to rival the great theaters of Europe. I find it curious, Monsieur Zimri, that Americans, for all of their disdain for the European aristocracy, nevertheless seem determined to outdo one another in emulating its trappings."

Zimri smiled at this, knowing it to be true. "You should write a book about America, Alex."

"I intend to, Monsieur Zimri. I intend to."

"*The Maid of Beaufort*," Zimri read aloud. The orchestra began the prelude. "Sounds like a French melodrama."

"On the contrary," Alex said, "I believe it is by an American author."

Zimri looked up just as the curtain rose to reveal a scene that elicited a gasp from the audience. In complete contrast to the elegance of the theatre itself, the stage was littered with dilapidated furniture and work benches. The painted backdrop depicted scenes of domestic farm life, with barns, silos and barnyard animals milling about. A hazy sky permitted only the suggestion of a somewhat feeble sun. But most shocking of all, the actors on the stage, all clad in rags, were Negroes.

"Most interesting," Alex said, nodding his head.

Zimri moved forward in his seat to see better. The Negroes were at various farm tasks, it seemed, sewing, spinning, hauling firewood, pumping water from a well, and hammering away at a horseshoe on an anvil. Soon a white man appeared dressed in a corduroy jacket, gray riding pants, and high boots. He wore a broad-brimmed felt hat with a turkey feather protruding from the band and carried a riding whip curled in his right hand.

"Where is she?" the white actor said.

The Negroes did not answer, nor look up, but continued at their tasks.

"By heaven," the man said, slapping the whip against his palm, "where is she?"

One elderly Negro, white-haired and balding, looked up and said in a feeble voice: "Massa, who is you speaking of?"

"Tarnation, Willum. You know full well who I mean—Sophie, that's who."

"Ain't seen her, Massa." The old man turned to a younger Negro carrying a bucket of water. "You seen Sophie, Ned?"

"Nawsuh," Ned said. "Ain't seen Sophie no how."

"Now see here, you devious niggers," the Massa said, "there'll be hell to pay if you don't—"

Suddenly a young woman appeared from the wings on the opposite side of the stage. Zimri was struck by her beauty, but particularly her large, almond eyes. She was dressed in rags, like the others, but she appeared to be of a much lighter complexion.

"You lookin' for me, Massa?" she said.

'Massa' looked at her for a moment in consternation, then broke out into a broad grin. "You know I am, Sophie." He tapped his palm with the coiled whip. "You've been a bad, bad girl. You gonna have to come with me to the woodshed."

"Ain't goin' to no woodshed, Massa."

"Tarnation! You'll do as I say, or I'll—"

At this exclamation on the part of Massa, Sophie ran across the stage and disappeared behind a painted backdrop. Massa tried to follow, but was tripped up by the blacksmith who dropped a harness in his path, entangling his legs.

"Tarnation!" Massa said, trying to extricate himself from the harness. "Blasted nigger! There'll be hell to pay!"

As the play progressed, it became clear that the slave owner was as cruel and depraved as the slaves were pure and innocent. It was also clear very early on that Sophie, with the help of her fellow slaves, would succeed in protecting her virtue. Nevertheless, the cruel 'Massa' would get his just desserts in the end for even pursuing her, as his wife discovers his intentions and gets her revenge by calling in the sheriff to arrest him for abusing his slaves. The slave owner at last admits to the error of his ways, delivers an impassioned speech against the evils of slavery, and the curtain falls.

"Absolute nonsense," Zimri said. "A third-rate melodrama. But the girl who played Sophie—what a beauty! And she can act, too."

"I must say that I agree with you on both counts," Alex said, as both men rose from their seats. "Miss Rinaldi is capable of far greater things than this."

Zimri scanned the program. "C. Rinaldi. She's the leading actress and the author as well?"

"She's quite talented—would you like to meet her?"

"Meet her? Do you know her?"

"I became acquainted with her when I first came to New York. I was invited to a party which she attended—a very charming lady."

"And is she actually a Negro? A mulatto?"

Alex laughed. "Not that I know of. She is rumored to be the daughter of an impoverished Italian count. She came to America to seek her fortune."

"No wonder the characters in the play are so wooden. She has no experience of the South."

"Ah," Alex said, signaling a young woman selling flowers. "We'll purchase a bouquet for her in honor of her performance. I believe the audience was quite pleased with her in spite of the thinness of the material."

They reversed course, and proceeded towards the backstage area to the dressing rooms. There were numerous actors and stage hands milling about but they seemed to take no notice of them. They passed three doors with name plaques on them until they arrived at the fourth, which announced:

MISS CORA RINALDI

Alex held the bouquet of white carnations in one hand and knocked on the door with the other.

"Entrez, s'il vous plait," a feminine voice called from within.

Alex turned the handle and pushed the door open. The room was quite large, looking more like the parlor of a fine house than a dressing room. There was a Chippendale coffee table, a sofa in the Empire style, bronze sconces lighted by gas, vases filled with flowers, and directly ahead of them, Miss Rinaldi sitting before a large gilded mirror, removing cream from her face.

"Alexis!" She turned and rose from her chair, extending her arms towards Alex.

Alex went forward to meet her embrace, careful to protect the flowers.

"Mon ami." She kissed him on both cheeks. "Comment vas-tu?"

"Je vais bien," Alex said. "I see you have been practicing your French."

"Lessons," she said. "Every Tuesday with Madame Jordan." She laughed. "But I'm afraid that I've already exhausted my repertoire."

"That may well be," Alex said, presenting her with the bouquet. "But your accent is impeccable."

"Oh, Alexis, they're beautiful!" she said. "Where did you get them?"

"Aisle four," Alex said with a smile.

"Here? In the theatre? I would have thought that they would have been selling vegetables to throw at me instead. I'm afraid that 'Massa's speech at the end fell rather flat."

"Perhaps it was a little didactic," Alex said, "but no one could fault your performance."

"You're so kind to say that, Alexis, but aren't you going to introduce me to your friend?"

"Oh, forgive me, my dear," Alex said. "How rude of me. And to think I brought him here expressly to meet you. May I present Monsieur Zimri Rhodes, my shipboard companion from Georgia."

"Georgia?" Cora said. "So that's where you've been. How do you do, Mr. Rhodes?"

Zimri was at a loss for words. She looked even more beautiful at close quarters than she did from the sixth row of the theatre. And, after all, she was a Broadway star. "I am...quite well, thank you. Yes, quite well." He shook her hand awkwardly, then immediately withdrew it thinking he had squeezed it too tightly. "I must say...I was very impressed with your performance tonight."

Cora seemed to be looking around for a place to put the flowers. "Oh—thank you, Mr. Rhodes, but as much as I like being praised for my acting, I would much prefer that people take to heart the message of my play." She finally found a vase for the flowers and carefully placed them in it.

"Perhaps the message would be more palatable to the audience," Zimri said, "if it were implicit rather than explicit."

Cora stared at him for a moment. "Yes, I believe you are right. That's very observant of you, Mr. Rhodes—I'll have to rethink the ending."

Zimri stood staring back at her, unable to think of anything else to say.

Alex came to his rescue. "Mr. Rhodes owns a newspaper in Georgia."

"Oh?" Cora said. "How very interesting. Then you are a writer yourself, Mr. Rhodes."

"Of sorts. I only report facts. Rather easier than inventing characters and constructing a plot."

"I don't know about that—good writing of any kind is difficult, it seems to me. Won't you sit down, gentlemen?"

They all sat down, Cora in an armchair in front of the coffee table, and the two men on either end of the sofa.

Alex leaned forward, his hands resting on the head of his cane. "Monsieur Zimri is visiting his family in Connecticut."

"Connecticut? That explains the lack of a Southern accent. Would you gentlemen like some coffee?"

"Yes," Zimri said. "That would be…delightful."

"Mais oui," Alex said.

Suddenly Cora called out in a loud voice that could be heard all the way to the orchestra pit: "Rupert!"

Zimri was a bit taken aback, surprised at the power of her lungs. Presently a slight, elderly black man appeared at the door.

"Yes, Miss Cora?"

"My guests would like some coffee," she said in a soft but firm voice. "And I would like a glass of bourbon."

"Yes, ma'am." Rupert quickly disappeared down the hall.

Cora turned to her visitors and touched her fingers to her larynx. "It's the throat. It gets rather strained during a performance."

"Yes, I can understand that," Zimri said. "Actually, I think I'd prefer a glass of bourbon as well."

"Why not?" Alex said. "I don't want to be the odd man out."

"Rupert!" Cora bellowed.

After a few moments, Rupert appeared again. "Yes, ma'am?"

"Forget the coffee. Make it three bourbons."

"Yes, ma'am." He started again down the hall.

"Rupert!"

"Ma'am?"

"Bring the whole bottle."

Rupert didn't even bother to reply this time, and went off to fetch the bottle.

While Rupert was thus employed, Cora entertained her two visitors with a backstage anecdote of miscues on the part of the actors and malfunctions in the stage machinery. They all laughed at these peccadilloes and when Rupert arrived with the bourbon, they toasted to the health and vitality of the American theatre. After a second glass, Cora suggested they retire to a tavern on Broadway for a late supper. This they did, with Alex hailing a hackney in front of the theatre and Zimri climbing in behind Cora, where he found himself sitting in close quarters next to her.

"You must tell me, Mr. Rhodes," she said, "how you came to remove yourself from a place so genteel as Connecticut to the primitive wilds of Georgia."

"Oh, it's not so primitive as you might imagine," Zimri said. The cab lurched off towards Ann Street. "There are genteel people there as well as in Connecticut—or in New York, for that matter."

"But they still maintain the barbaric institution of slavery, do they not?"

"It is the unfortunate legacy of previous generations. It will eventually fade away."

Cora's jolly spirits seemed to dampen for the first time since they met in the dressing room. "But isn't it incumbent upon the more genteel people of the South such as yourself to hasten its demise?"

Zimri suddenly felt as if he were being cross-examined. "I don't know. There is only so much any one individual can do."

"But you are a newspaper editor." She shifted her position somewhat to the corner of the cab so that their bodies no longer touched. "You must have a great deal of influence in your community."

"Yes, I suppose I do. But Martinville is a small town and—"

Alex suddenly tapped the ceiling of the cab with the head of his cane. "La voici! We are at the supper club."

The cab stopped in front of a tavern lit by gas carriage lamps on either side of a door framed by fluted molding and an impressive cornice.

"I did not mean to put you on the spot, Mr. Rhodes," Cora said. "You cannot be held responsible for the manifold sins of slavery. Forgive me if I've overstepped my bounds."

"Not at all, Miss Rinaldi." Zimri helped her down from the cab. "It was a fair question." He managed a somewhat forced laugh. "It's just that as a newspaperman, I'm not used to being the one interrogated."

"Interrogated," Cora said, "is too strong a word, I should think." She looked directly into his eyes, making no effort to release her hand from his now that they were outside the cab.

Zimri blushed, but did not want to release her hand. He continued to stare back, almost mesmerized, and could think of nothing to say.

Alex rapped on the tavern door with his cane. "Come, let's be merry. I am absolutely starved!"

"I, too," Cora said, her eyes still intent upon Zimri's.

CHAPTER 7

Elizabeth lay in the swing on the front porch, gently swaying to and fro in a light breeze, her head propped up on an embroidered pillow, reading *Sense and Sensibility*. It was a fine Sunday morning, not too hot, and cumulous clouds billowed overhead, piling up like great fluffy balls of cotton. It would no doubt rain in the afternoon, but for now it was glorious, with huge expanses of cobalt blue stretching into infinity.

Maybelle, one of her father's cooks, labored in the kitchen at preparing a picnic lunch. She had been sent to her by Jamie, who said she would starve if she kept living on soup and vegetables from the garden, and besides, Patsy had been bored (and of little use, anyway) and wanted to return to Belle Oaks.

In a way, she was glad that Zimri was gone. Not that she didn't love him and want him near, but in the week or so that he had been gone, she had been able to relax, read, and reflect. And since Maybelle had arrived two days ago, she had hardly had to lift a finger. She had a way with Charlotte, too, so that she never had to worry about her.

She wondered why she had rushed into marriage with Zimri. After all, she was only sixteen and he twenty-eight. Perhaps she had only wanted to get out of the house, to escape the suffocating presence of her mother, who insisted upon controlling every aspect of her life, right down to the number of petticoats she wore and the debutante balls she would attend. Ah, yes, her debut! The coup de grâce, the final crushing blow to her mother's social ambitions for her eldest daughter. Well, perhaps she would someday regret it, but it all seemed so silly to her then, so…so adolescent. And the boys who were expected to be her escorts to these balls, they were hopelessly immature and provincial, unlike the beaux she had in Charleston. Zimri, on the other hand, was already a man of the world, in fact a man from another world, the world of New York, with its bustling commerce, its high fashion, its literary salons, its brilliant artists, its magnificent theatres!

For a time he talked of moving back to New York, where he had friends and business contacts. He would buy a small newspaper, perhaps that of his old employer, build it up, transform it into the premier newspaper of the city. But he had dropped the idea, decided that he wanted to be one of the founding fathers of a tiny provincial town, that it was a better place to raise children than New York, that in effect, it was better to be a big fish in a little pond than a small fish in a big pond.

And now he decides to go back to New York, not to scout for a newspaper, but to go to a friend's wedding, and to go at a time when he knew she could not possibly go with him!

Suddenly, it occurred to her that he might want to see some other woman there, some woman from his past, perhaps someone he had once been engaged to, someone who was far more sophisticated than she, and that he had grown bored with her, and was in fact shopping for another newspaper there, and would return only to sell this one and inform her that he was sorry, it had all been a mistake, it was all over.

"Elizabeth!"

She was startled at the sound of her name, it seemed that she was being shaken awake; in fact she had dozed off, the book lying open across her chest. She sat up and saw two men and a woman in a carriage at the front gate.

"Jamie?"

"Hey, Lazy Bones, wake up!" Jamie shouted from the carriage. "We'd better get going if we're going to beat the rain. It's already ten o'clock."

She sat up and put the book aside. Jamie was sitting in the driver's seat with the reins between his fingers, as if they didn't have a moment to lose.

Randolph stepped down from the open carriage and started down the path towards her. "Bon matin, Elizabeth!"

"Good morning, Randolph." She didn't know why he was suddenly lapsing into French, especially since he knew very little in the first place, but she did not wish to respond in kind for fear of appearing to be on too intimate of terms with him.

Randolph, dressed in an open shirt, scotch plaid waistcoat, and patent leather boots, strode to her like the chestnut stallion that he had been riding on his previous visit. "You look so very charming in your country calico!"

"And you look like you should be wearing a kilt." She stood up from the swing and pressed down the one thin petticoat beneath her dress.

Randolph laughed heartily. "I considered it, but then thought I might frighten the fauna—they wouldn't know what to make of me."

"Neither do I."

Randolph's face fell into a mock frown. "You can be so cruel, Elizabeth."

"Only when I intend it," she said. "Maybelle!"

No sooner had her name been called when Maybelle appeared at the front door carrying a basket. "Yes'um. Got yo' vittles right chere."

"We've got plenty of food, Elizabeth," Randolph said. "Bread, cheese, sausage, venison, tomatoes, apples, plums, oysters—even champagne!"

"But you ain't got no fried chicken and no corn muffins, neither, I'll bet," Maybelle said. She was a stout, middle-aged woman who favored red bandanas and hoop earrings.

"You're right, Maybelle," Randolph said. "We clean forgot."

"And bet you ain't got no shortbread, and butter, and molasses, and tapioca pudddin,' neither."

"Right you are again," Randolph said with a laugh. "You think of everything, Maybelle."

"It be my job," Maybelle said huffily, and handed Randolph the basket. "Now don't go spillin' nothin'—keep the basket in yo' lap, not on the flo' of the buggy where it'll get shook up and all mashed together."

"Yes, ma'am," Randolph said, taking the basket carefully.

"What are y'all yammerin' about?" Jamie called from the carriage, "Let's go!"

Randolph escorted Elizabeth down the path to the carriage where Jamie awaited with his lady friend. Elizabeth now recognized her as Fanny Cochran, a flame-haired girl who used to sometimes help her father in the feed store he owned in Clinton, the nearest town to Belle Oaks. She was about her own age and, like her father, somewhat coarse in speech and manner. It wasn't hard to figure out what Jamie saw in her.

"You remember Fanny, Elizabeth," Jamie said, as Randolph helped her up into the open carriage. "Fanny Cochran."

"Indeed I do," Elizabeth said, settling into the comfortable rear seat. "Cochran's Feed Store. Of course."

"I don't work at the feed store no more," Fanny said. "Me and my mama opened a dress shop in Clinton—just this spring."

"Why, that's wonderful," Elizabeth said. "I'll have to come and see it."

"We got all kinds of cloth—ordered it from Savannah. Sea Island cotton, flannel, wool, silk, satin. The satin comes all the way from Paris—Paris, France."

Elizabeth acknowledged a wink from Randolph, who had just finished securing the picnic basket in the compartment behind the seat. "I'll certainly come and visit you—after my confinement."

"Confinement!" Fanny said. "You're going to have a baby?"

"Eventually," Elizabeth said. "It's early yet."

Fanny clapped her hands together. "Oh, that's so exciting! Jamie, you didn't tell me your sister was going to have another baby!"

"Didn't ask," Jamie mumbled. He snapped the reins and clicked his tongue to get the horses moving.

They drove out the River Road, north towards Prescott's Ferry. Elizabeth and Randolph felt they were being chauffeured, as Jamie and Fanny occupied the driver's seat and they had nearly the whole carriage to themselves.

"Where are we going, Jamie?" Elizabeth asked.

"Prescott's Bluff," Jamie said. "Sets up high above the river there."

"Oh, it's a lovely spot," Fanny said. "You can pick daffodils and blue berries and watch the boats sail down the river. You can see them but they can't see you, you're so high up."

"Then you've been there before?" Elizabeth said.

"Oh," Fanny said, as if she had revealed something she shouldn't. "Once or twice."

They continued up the road, which hugged the river for the most part, and continued almost imperceptibly to climb to a higher elevation. Randolph seemed uncommonly taciturn, his long arms spread across either side of the richly upholstered seat. Elizabeth was very aware of his left arm, which was draped across the back of the seat, encircling her neck and shoulders, but not touching her at any point. He had fine hands, she thought, unlike Zimri's, which were somewhat coarse and scarred from working on his father's farm as a boy. It was clear that Randolph had never done any kind of physical labor, though he was well acquainted with horses and saddles and firearms.

"Daffodils," Randolph said. "I didn't know they were still blooming this time of year."

"Oh, they're all over the bluff," Fanny said. "I think they bloom late there because it's cool and shady."

"That's something we don't see much in the Low Country because of the heat and humidity," Randolph said. He tilted his head back and gazed at the sky.

> "I wandered lonely as a cloud
>   That floats on high o'er vales and hills,
> When all at once I saw a crowd—
>   A host of golden daffodils
> Beside the lake, beneath the trees,
>   Fluttering and dancing in the breeze."

Elizabeth turned and looked at Randolph in astonishment. "Why, that's beautiful, Randolph—what is it from?"

"Wordsworth," Randolph said.

"That's so pretty," Fanny said. "What's 'Wordsworth?' A book?"

"A poet," Randolph said.

Fannie seemed to consider this for a moment. "This Wordsworth fella—has he ever been to Prescott's Bluff?"

Randolph laughed. "I don't think so, Fanny. But there must be a place in England much like it."

"Oh," Fanny said. "England. I'd like to go there some time." She faced forward again, and remained silent for the next mile or two. Jamie seemed intent upon the road.

"Since when have you been reading poetry?" Elizabeth said after a few moments. "I remember you in Charleston as being preoccupied with nothing but balls and horses and gambling."

"My life has changed a great deal since I left Charleston," Randolph said. "My father's been ill and I've had to spend more and more of my time running the plantation. At the end of the day I find it relaxing to retire to the library and read poetry."

"I've been reading a great deal, too," Elizabeth said. "Jane Austen, mostly."

"Austen? Yes, she's a fine writer."

"You've read *Sense and Sensibility*?"

"Yes, of course. And *Pride and Prejudice*, too. But I prefer the poets—especially Wordsworth and Byron."

Elizabeth was ashamed to admit that she had not read Byron. But she had heard that he was a libertine and had strewn illegitimate children all over Europe. "Wasn't he somewhat…loose in his morals?"

"Depends on what you mean by 'loose,'" Randolph said. "Or by 'morals' for that matter. He was a free spirit who followed his heart wherever it led him."

"Sounds like a recipe for disaster," she said.

"Perhaps he went too far sometimes. But he lived life to the fullest, and when he fell in love, he loved completely."

They continued along the road in silence for some time. The river seemed to be receding farther and farther below them and the air became cooler. Elizabeth lay her head on the back of the seat and stared at the sky and the clouds. 'To love completely.' She wondered whether she loved Zimri completely, or he her. She wondered whether she had ever abandoned herself 'completely' to anything. She seemed to doze off again when she heard Jamie's voice.

"Here we are," Jamie said. "Prescott's Bluff—the highest point in the county."

Elizabeth opened her eyes and saw the clouds again. Then she became aware of Randolph's arm against the back of her neck and his hand upon her shoulder.

"You fell asleep," he said.

"I've been doing that lately," she said. "I don't know why."

"Look at those daffodils!" Jamie said, tying the horses to the trunk of a huge oak tree. "Thousands of them."

"There's a pretty spot on the bluff where you can see the river both ways," Fanny said. "And the daffodils run all the way down the slope to the water's edge. Let's pitch the table cloth there."

They all set about following Fanny's advice, and made their way to the edge of the bluff, carrying the baskets and the table cloth with them.

"Magnificent!" Randolph said.

"Look!" Jamie said. "You can see the ferry landing from here. And there's a sailboat coming up the river."

"I'll pick a basket of blueberries," Fanny said. "They'll be wonderful with the cheese."

"And champagne!" Randolph extracted a bottle from the hamper. "Not very cold, but the best of the cellar."

Fanny was off with her basket to pick the blueberries before Randolph was even able to pop the cork on the champagne. Jamie seemed preoccupied with unpacking the food and Elizabeth laid out the plates and utensils.

"Am I the only one to partake of the nectar of the gods?" Randolph held the bottle aloft with one hand and a champagne glass with the other, as if offering sacrifice on the high altar of the bluff.

"It's too early to be drinking, " Elizabeth said, admiring her arrangement of the place settings on the checkered table cloth. "Why don't we partake of the nectar of the gods after lunch? I'm sure the gods won't mind."

Jamie began slicing the venison into thin strips. "Hey, don't we want red wine with the meat? Champagne's for dessert."

Randolph sighed and then took a swig from the freshly opened bottle. "Condemned to be a Romantic among the Philistines."

"Randolph!" Elizabeth said. "Don't drink from the bottle. Now no one else will want to drink from it."

"No one else wants champagne, anyway. Besides, there's another bottle in the hamper."

Fanny returned from picking blueberries just as the full array of viands had been arranged. Jamie opened a bottle of the red wine, which he pronounced to be the best Catawba from the Carolinas.

"Vitis Labrusca," Randolph said, contemptuously.

"What?" Jamie said.

"An inferior grape altogether. I'll prove it to you." Randolph reached into the hamper at his side and extracted another bottle. "Bordeaux. From the Médoc." He inserted a corkscrew, extracted the cork, and poured the wine into a glass. "Here—try this and tell me which you prefer."

Elizabeth took the glass to pass to Jamie and brought it to her nose. "It does smell wonderful—like crushed violets."

"There's hope for you, yet, my dear," Randolph said. "You obviously have a sensitive nose—now try the palate."

Elizabeth glanced first at Randolph then at Jamie and again brought the glass to her nose. She inhaled deeply this time and brought the wine to her lips. "That is so luscious! It goes down like velvet."

"Now pass it to Fanny."

Fanny sniffed at the glass, wrinkled her nose and took a sip. "Lordy! It does taste like violets—maybe blueberries, too."

Jamie looked skeptical and took the glass from Fanny. He swirled the contents around the bowl, brought it to his nose, sniffed and swallowed. "It's all right. But I like the Catawba better."

"Ah, Jamie," Randolph said, shaking his head, "you're allowing your provincial prejudices to get in the way. We'll have to educate you out of them."

"Well, you've gotten high and mighty lately," Jamie said, returning the glass. "And you haven't even embarked on your Grand Tour yet."

"If I'm an insufferable snob now," Randolph said, "just wait until I get back!"

They all laughed at this comment and proceeded to drink the wine. Elizabeth, enjoying that 'velvety' feel of the Bordeaux rolling down the back of her throat, looked at Randolph in a new light. Not that he hadn't always been a charmer, with his fine Charleston manners and his precise elocution, but he seemed to have cultivated his finer sensibilities of late. Or was it all a ploy to seduce her? He, after all, had made his 'obscene proposal' only days before. Or had it been a week already? Somehow it seemed long ago.

They all sat on the table cloth and ate and drank and talked of food, wine, hunting, the difficulties of running a large plantation, the natural indolence of slaves, the advantages of living in the city versus the country, the latest fashions from New York and Paris, and the vulgarities of Andrew Jackson, though Jamie was quick to defend the president on this point.

After the meal, Jamie proposed that he and Fanny take a walk down to the river, where, he said, there was an old abandoned mill that he wished to explore. Fanny declared this to be an admirable adventure and invited Elizabeth and Randolph to join them, but the latter two, seeing Jamie's obvious displeasure at the idea, declined. And so they were left to gambol along the high bluff, where Elizabeth, though a bit giddy from the wine, picked some daffodils.

"Careful," Randolph said, taking her by the hand, "you don't want to go too close to the edge."

"Why," she said with an impish grin, "would you be tempted to push me?"

"Hardly. I'd be more tempted to throw you down and make love to you amongst the daffodils."

Elizabeth picked one and brought it to her nose. "I don't know which would be the greater crime—making love to a married woman, or crushing these beautiful daffodils."

Randolph laughed and pulled her gently towards him so that they faced one another. "The daffodils would grow back."

She saw that he was about to kiss her, and brought the flower between their lips. "But would my honor?"

"Honor?" he said:

> "Honor and shame from no condition rise;
> Act well your part, there all the honor lies."

"What does that mean?"

"I haven't the faintest idea—it just popped into my head."

They both laughed at this, and as Elizabeth dropped the daffodil to her side, Randolph leaned over and kissed her. She didn't resist, as it felt quite nice and the wine had lowered her defenses just enough to allow her to enjoy it for a few moments. But then she pulled away.

"That was for old times' sake, Randolph. Expect no more."

He pulled her to him again, this time a little more forcefully. "Expect no more? Elizabeth, that's like giving a child a taste of chocolate and denying him the rest of the dessert. Can you be so cruel?"

"Hardly cruel. A little mean, perhaps. But hardly—"

He kissed her again, harder this time and more passionately. At first she resisted, pounding her fists against his chest, but this had no effect. She then felt herself being pulled down into the daffodils, which, with their long stems, cushioned her fall like a soft down bed.

"Randolph, I can't—"

"Of course you can." He kissed her again on the mouth, the neck, the exposed shoulder.

"Oh, Randolph, you shouldn't have come. We shouldn't—"

"Hush, my darling. Just let yourself go..."

She felt his hand pull at the strings of her bodice and then slip between it and her breast. She pushed his hand away, but he relented only for a moment and she felt it again beneath her petticoat sliding up the inside of her thigh. She grabbed his wrist tightly this time and pushed against it, but he was much too strong for her and his hand continued to advance. She was angry at first, but the touch of his delicate fingers was light now, caressive rather than intrusive, and she could feel a sort of heat, a rising excitement that she had never felt before.

"Massa Jamie! Massa Jamie!"

She sat up suddenly and looked to the direction of the voice. A rider on a horse raced up the bluff to where the carriage was parked under the trees and stopped abruptly, spraying gravel in all directions. It was Carmichael, a house slave from Belle Oaks.

Elizabeth quickly pulled herself together and glanced at Randolph, who was now sitting up, looking annoyed. She stood and brushed what she imagined were leaves from her dress, though there were none. "What is it, Carmichael?"

"Where's Massa Jamie? He got to come quick!"

"He's down by the river. Why—"

"It's Luther—he done gone crazy!"

"Luther? What's he—"

"What is it, Carmichael?" Jamie suddenly appeared from the path to the river. "What about Luther?"

"He gone plum crazy, Massa Jamie. He done tried to kill Massa James."

"Daddy? He tried to kill Daddy?"

Elizabeth covered her mouth with her hand. "Oh, my God! Daddy? Is he all right?"

"He be hurt, Miz Lizbeth," Carmichael said. "But he gone be all right I think. Luther done run at him with a pitchfork, but Massa James jumped out the way and got stabbed in the side. Don't think Luther hit no vitals, but there's plenty 'nuff blood."

"Good God!" Jamie said. Fanny suddenly appeared behind him looking disheveled. "Did anybody fetch Doc Parcher?"

"Yes, suh," Carmichael said. "But he all the way to Wilkerson County deliverin' a baby."

"And Luther?"

"We done hog-tied Luther and locked him in the corn crib, Massa Jamie. He ain't goin' nowhere."

"Give me your horse, Carmichael." Jamie took the reins and swung his leg over the saddle. "Take the carriage and deliver Miss Elizabeth to her place in Martinville. Then bring Miss Fanny and Mr. Benson back to Belle Oaks. You got that?"

"Yes, suh."

Jamie seized the reins, and leaned down to give Fanny a kiss.

"Be careful, Jamie," Fanny said.

"Don't worry, Luther's not going to be any trouble from here on out." Jamie pulled on the reins and turned the horse around. "I'll cross at the ferry. And when I get home, I swear, I'll kill that nigger!"

CHAPTER 8

July 10, Saturday

Embarked on board the steamboat United States for New Haven. Pleasant weather and a calm sea all the way, but was much preoccupied with the events of the previous evening, especially Miss Rinaldi. She is a fascinating and most mysterious woman. I think I have never met a woman who exceeds her in both intellect and beauty. A rare combination! Certainly Elizabeth is beautiful, but in a wholesome, conventional sort of way. And she is often listless, moody, indolent. Miss Rinaldi, on the other hand, is not only possessed of great talent— especially for mimicry—but is brimming with energy. Not even a considerable amount of bourbon at Beal's Tavern seemed to diminish this energy. In fact, she seemed largely unaffected by the alcohol, while Alex and I fairly stumbled our way back to our rooms at the hotel after dropping her off at her lodgings in Pearl Street.

I will be much disappointed if I am unable to see her again.

Alex, by the way, sets sail for France tomorrow. He was met at the hotel today by his close friend, Monsieur Beaumont, who has been in Philadelphia doing research for a book that they intend to publish together. He is a droll fellow, somewhat shy, and in appearance and stature could easily pass for Alex's brother. They say they will send me a copy when it is finished.

Arrived in New Haven at 1 a.m. and went immediately to the Tantine, an excellent tavern, board $1.25 per day.

After breakfast the next morning, Zimri made the rounds to old friends and associates, including his mentor, Mr. Barber. He found Mr. Barber to be more prosperous than ever, having built one of the finest houses in the city, along with a large office building to house his flourishing newspaper. Zimri marveled at the size of the establishment, bustling with employees and equipped with the latest printing presses. The city itself, like New York, he found to be much improved, with new buildings, a canal, a new public square, and a new state house modeled on the Parthenon.

In the afternoon, after dining at the Tantine, he caught the stage to Brantley, the place of his birth.

Brantley, not much more than a village when he left it for New Haven and later New York, was only about eight or ten miles to the east. As the stage approached the town, his high spirits seemed to dampen, and finally to plunge into a gloomy abyss. The very trees seemed barren and struggling for survival. The road deteriorated, with the stage almost turning over at one point. The numerous varieties of birds that serenaded him upon awakening that morning seemed to have avoided this part of the country, as none were to be seen or heard. All was silence, decay, and desolation.

The stage stopped at the old Brantley Inn, which was still operating, but in obvious need of repair. No one came to greet him as he stepped down from the stage and the driver handed him his portmanteau.

"You sure you want to stop here?" the driver said.

"I'm sure," Zimri said. He handed the man a quarter. "You say you come through here to Middletown every Monday?"

"Sure do. Don't usually stop, though."

"Well, I trust you'll stop for me next week." He handed him another quarter.

"Sure. Sure, I will."

"I'll be standing right here. Monday. Four o'clock."

"Sure, give or take a half-hour, depending on my passenger manifest, and how much luggage they got. 'Course, there's more comin' to New Haven these days than goin.' Maybe that's why everything between here and Middletown is beginning to look like a ghost town,"

"Progress," Zimri said.

"Reckon so."

Zimri watched the stage drive off towards Middletown with a deep sense of melancholy. He hadn't really wanted to return to Brantley, but he felt that he must, that it might be the last time he would ever see his parents.

He deposited his portmanteau on the front porch of the inn, where there were a few rockers strewn haphazardly about, as if no one had sat in them for a long while. Paint was peeling off the shutters as well as the front door, which needed mending. He went inside and approached the desk, where he recognized Mrs. Clausen, the wife of the proprietor. Once an attractive, if not beautiful, woman, she had grown fat and had streaks of gray in her hair. She was poring over a ledger when she looked up and saw him.

"Zimri?" she said.

"Mrs. Clausen. You're looking well."

"Oh, Zimri, you always were a poor liar. I know I look terrible, but you are looking well—so grown up now—and with a beard! I almost didn't recognize you."

"I let it grow on the ship from Savannah. Rather difficult shaving on a pitching ship."

"Well, give me a hug, you rascal."

She came from around the desk where Zimri saw that she had gained more weight than he had supposed, and embraced him.

"Welcome home," she said, leaning back to get a better look at him. "What a man you've become! And Ned tells me you've got your own newspaper down in Georgia and gone and married a rich Southern girl!"

Zimri smiled. "Ned tends to exaggerate. Yes, I've got a small news-paper business, but my wife is hardly rich. We're getting by all right, though. Is Mr. Clausen about?"

Mrs. Clausen's face fell. "Didn't Ned tell you? He died last winter. Pneumonia."

"Oh, I'm terribly sorry, Mrs. Clausen. He was a fine gentleman."

"Yes, he was. It's been hard without him." She seemed suddenly about to burst into tears, but put her hand to her eyes for a moment and composed herself. "I'll tell Jerry to hitch up a gig for you—Ned said you're staying with him."

"Yes, for the first night, anyway."

Young Jerry—Mrs. Clausen's teenage son—brought the gig around and helped him load the portmanteau into the back. Zimri gave him fifty cents and drove off to Ned's place which, according to his letter, was the old fishing cabin on the lake that bordered the family farm. Ned had said that their father had broken his leg when a cow he was milking became agitated, stumbled and fell on him. Their mother, he said, felt that the house was too much in disarray while she tended to her husband's needs to put him up until later in the week.

He wondered whether this was an excuse to somehow punish him for his abrupt departure nearly ten years ago. Surely, his mother, though religiously devout, would no longer blame him for his outspoken de-nunciation of that itinerant preacher—what was his name—Gibson, and his brand of coercive evangelism.

Zimri brooded over these past events—'the pestilence,' he called them—all the way to the lake, a distance of three or four miles.

To his surprise, the 'old fishing cabin' was hardly recognizable as such, but appeared to be a large house made of birch logs, with an expansive front porch and a new fence that encircled the house. A small barn seemed to be in the final stages of completion.

Ned was pumping water from a well when he came riding up the path, his back to Zimri.

"Ned!"

Ned stopped pumping and turned around. "Zimri! Thought you'd be here Tuesday or Wednesday."

"Fast ship. Nothing much to do in New York. How are you?"

Zimri stopped the gig and got out. Ned came forward to embrace him.

"Nothing to do in New York? You must be getting to be an old man, Zimri."

They exchanged a hearty, warm-felt hug. Zimri had always liked his youngest brother. There was an innocence about him, a good-natured acceptance of others without precondition. He couldn't say the same about his eldest brother, Zeke.

"You've made a regular mansion out of this place, Ned."

"Hardly a mansion," Ned said. "It was all right for the first few years after I moved out of the main house, but then I got married."

"Married? You never mentioned that in your letters."

Ned glanced towards the front door of the house just as a young woman appeared with a baby in her arms. He turned back to Zimri and cupped his hand over his mouth. "You might say it was a bit rushed."

Zimri laughed. "Yes, that happens sometimes, doesn't it? Well, aren't you going to introduce me?"

Ned apologized, tied the horse to a hitching rail, and hurried Zimri up to the front porch.

"Honey, this is my brother, Zimri."

"Pleased to meet you, Zimri."

"And this is little Ned." Ned pinched the baby's cheeks, eliciting a squeal of delight from it. "But we call him Eddie, so's people know the difference."

Zimri offered his little finger to Eddie, who eagerly grasped it tightly in his tiny fist.

"He's got some grip, huh, Zimri? You got any luggage? I'll bring it in for you."

Zimri looked more closely at Ned's wife. She was actually rather pretty, not much younger than Ned, and had the same sweet innocence about her. Sandy blond hair pulled back in a pony tail, freckled cheeks, round face, baby blue eyes. "Aren't you going to tell me your wife's name? Or should I call her 'Mrs. Rhodes?'"

"What? Oh, hell—I mean heck. Didn't I say it? Samantha. This is Samantha."

"How do you do, Samantha?"

Samantha laughed and offered her free hand. "I'm fine, Zimri. Ned would forget his own name if he got excited enough. He hasn't talked about anything else since he got your letter."

Ned retrieved Zimri's portmanteau and showed him to a small guest room that had once been the storeroom of the cabin. It had a window overlooking the lake, lace curtains, and a whale oil lamp for reading. There were even a few books—a King James Bible, a Book of Common Prayer, the ubiquitous "Blue-Backed Speller" by Noah Webster, and an ancient copy of *Poor Richard's Almanack*.

At supper, Zimri caught up with the events of the last ten years in Brantley.

"Same old Brantley," Ned said, bringing a soup spoon to his mouth. "Mr. Ross still owns everything in town that ain't—that isn't—nailed down, except for the Inn, which is falling apart since Mr. Clausen died; Mr. Hinckley closed down his general store and started a new one in New Haven so's now we have to go there for supplies; the feed store's still run by the Witherspoons, but you can't get fresh oats there anymore, and Brother Gibson's still spoutin' fire and brimstone and eternal damnation over at the Congregational Church."

Zimri looked up from his plate. "Gibson? I would have thought that charlatan had been run out of town by now."

"He very nearly was," Samantha said. "About two years ago. Caught in the rectory with a thirteen-year-old girl. In a 'compromising position,' as they say."

"And?"

"Brother Gibson claimed he was merely teaching her the catechism," Samantha said with a smirk. "In his underwear."

"And he got away with it?"

"The girl's father didn't press the issue," Ned said. "He simply pulled up stakes and moved the family to Ohio. Brother Gibson denounced him the next week in the pulpit, calling him a liar and an extortionist. God would punish him, he said, by sending him into the hell of Ohio, where the Red Man would serve as His scourge."

Zimri sighed. "It's a shame that such a man could ensnare young girls' minds."

"From what I hear," Ned said, gesturing with his fork, "he pretty much ensnared everybody's mind around here until you exposed him as a—what is it?—a 'charlatan' in Mr. Barber's newspaper. I was just too young to have a mind then."

"And you've got one now?" Samantha said, with a supercilious grin.

Zimri waited for an explosion of anger from Ned, but instead he smiled and pointed his fork at his young wife.

"I've been working on it, Honey," he said, "and with all these books you've been buyin' from New Haven, I'm gonna be able to debate you pretty soon on everything from Abolitionism to Zen Voodism."

"That's Zen Buddhism."

"Boo, Voo—what's the difference?"

They both laughed, much to the relief of Zimri.

"Samantha went to the grammar school in New Haven," Ned said. "You'd think she went to Yale."

"I would have," Samantha said, "if they'd let women in."

"Maybe in another hundred years." Ned stabbed a piece of meat with his fork. "But what use is a college education to a woman 'cept to correct her husband?"

"That's reason enough," Samantha said.

"See?" Ned said. "Education just makes 'em uppity. Why, we've even got a lady school master now. Or school 'marm,' I guess you'd call her."

"Really? Here in Brantley?"

"Oh, yeah," Ned said. "I forgot—that's the one new thing that's happened in Brantley since you've been gone."

After supper, Ned took Zimri on a tour of the property and then they retired to the back porch where they sat on rockers facing the lake. Zimri pulled out a cigar and offered it to Ned, but Ned declined in favor of his pipe.

They sat smoking for a while, staring out at the lake in silence.

"Why didn't you bring your wife, Zim? Samantha and I were looking forward to meeting her."

"Five months pregnant," Zimri said. "Doctor says it would be bad for the baby."

"Oh. I guess the Doc knows best."

They remained silent for several more minutes.

"Zim?"

"Yes, Ned?"

"You happy down there in Georgia?"

Zimri smiled. "As happy as a man can be. It's beautiful country, Ned. Fertile—not exhausted like the soil here. And growing fast— new people, new farms, new businesses popping up like mushrooms everywhere you look. Cotton is what's driving it. The world can't seem to get enough of it."

Ned pulled on his pipe. "Zim...Can I ask you a question?"

"Fire away."

"You own any slaves?"

"No. My wife did, though. I sold them before I left."

"That's good."

Zimri glanced at Ned. "It was a practical matter. A business decision, that's all."

Ned puffed on his pipe. "There's a lot of abolitionist talk around here these days. Especially in New Haven, Boston."

"So I've gathered. Plenty of it in New York, too."

"Some people are even talking about seceding from the Union."

Zimri looked out over the lake where the light of the moon played gently on the water. "Some Southerners are talking about it, too."

"What do you think?"

"I think it would be disastrous if either seceded."

"Why?"

"War. War within, war without. We'd be more vulnerable to our enemies here and abroad." Zimri felt the blood rise to his cheeks. "Commerce would suffer. Tariffs would go up. And worst of all—the great idea of America would be destroyed."

Ned seemed satisfied with this answer, as he nodded his head in agreement. "Grandpa sure wouldn't like it."

"Not after leaving a leg at Yorktown." Zimri flicked away the ashes of his cigar. "What does Papa think about it?"

"Oh, you know Papa. He don't—doesn't—I swear, Samantha's got me thinking about my grammar so much I can hardly say a word for fear it's gonna come out wrong."

Zimri smiled. "She's good for you, Ned. Don't let her go."

Ned furrowed his brow. "Yeah, she is good for me. Probably better than I deserve."

"You were saying about Papa—?"

"Oh, yeah. Papa—doesn't—really care who secedes, as long as he can find a market for his milk."

"That's Papa. What about Zeke?"

"Zeke's fallen in with a bunch of abolitionists in Boston. Got a paper up there with a fellow named Garrison called *The Emancipator*, I think. They get pretty hot about it—Garrison's even been to jail for libeling some slave runner."

"Zeke tends to go to extremes. Is he going to John's wedding?"

"Sure is. He and John have gotten to be good friends since John moved to Boston and set up his practice there. His fiancée's from there, too."

"I'll look forward to meeting her."

The two brothers fell into silence again as the moon went behind a cloud and threw shadows across the porch. After a moment or two, Samantha appeared at the door carrying a candle lamp.

"You two caught up with reminiscing?" she said.

"Just about," Ned said. "First installment, anyway."

"Well, you just keep right on going if you like." She yawned and put her hand to her mouth. "I'm worn out, though. Good night."

"Good night, Samantha," Zimri said. "The mince pie was delicious."

"The rum's the secret. Makes you sleepy, though. 'Night."

"I'll be there in a minute, Honey." Ned seemed to make a great effort to yawn. "She's right about that rum." He winked at Zimri. "Didn't know I was so tired."

Zimri returned Ned's wink and said he'd stay out on the porch for a while and enjoy the breeze from the lake. Ned finally excused himself and Zimri found himself alone, contemplating his long journey from childhood to manhood, from Connecticut to Georgia, from farm boy to newspaper editor, from apprentice to master.

CHAPTER 9

By the time Jamie arrived at Belle Oaks, Doc Parcher had already been there for a half an hour.

Jamie stopped for a moment to see that Luther was secure in the corncrib, said nothing to him, and hurried into the house. He ignored the affectedly distant expressions of the house slaves in the kitchen, the great hall, the parlor, and finally at the door of his father's bedroom. He knocked, as he always did before entering his parents' inner sanctum, and heard his mother's voice.

"Yes?"

"It's me, Jamie."

"Jamie! Come in, come in!"

He pushed open the door and saw his father sitting up in the bed stripped to the waist and Doc Parcher wrapping his chest in bandages.

His mother rushed to embrace him, tears streaming from her eyes. "Oh, Jamie! Thank God, you've come!"

Jamie returned his mother's embrace, but hardly looked at her, so focused was he on his father. "You all right, Daddy?"

His father did not answer, but only stared back at him with sad, tired eyes.

"Daddy?"

"He's had a bit of a shock," Parcher said, securing the end of the bandage. "Best that he not talk for a while. And he may have a punctured lung. He'll have to be watched closely to see if any fluid builds up."

"Is he...he doesn't look good."

Doc Parcher chuckled. "You wouldn't either if you'd just been run through with a pitchfork. Fortunately, this particular pitchfork was only being used for its intended purpose—pitching hay. There was no dung on it, or rust either, for that matter. There shouldn't be any infection."

"But he's so pale..."

"I told you—shock. Don't worry, he'll be fine. It's only the lung I'm worried about, and it seems that Luther's aim wasn't so good."

"That blasted nigger!" Jamie turned on his heel and started for the door. "I'll flay his hide off and nail it to the barn door as a warning to the others!"

His mother intercepted him before he reached the door and latched on to his arm. "Oh, Jamie, don't make things worse—Luther's never done anything like this. Leon says his daughter's baby died last night, and your father wouldn't let him go to the funeral because he said it was full of that voodoo nonsense and he wouldn't tolerate it. Luther picked up the pitchfork and threatened him, but your father just laughed at him, and went to grab the pitchfork—it was a stupid thing to do—and Luther refused to let him, and the next thing anyone knew, two of the tines had gone clean through him. It was an accident, really."

"Accident!" Jamie jerked his arm away. "Attempted murder was what it was! And if we let him get away with it, all the others will start thinking that they can defy their masters, and the next thing you know they'll be picking up not only pitchforks, but axes and machetes and muskets and massacre every white person in the county. Accident! I'll give him an accident! I'll give him a hundred accidents!"

Jamie stormed out of the house and went to the stable, where he pulled a twenty-foot bull whip off of a wall containing a variety of harness equipment. He called to Leon, the head groom, who was brushing one of the horses.

"Leon! Get a couple of your niggers and pull Luther out of the corn crib. I want him stripped to the waist and tied to the whipping post."

"Yas, suh, Massa Jamie." Leon sighed and put down his brush. "Come on, boys, we got to get this thing over with."

Jamie took off his waistcoat and draped it over a bale of hay. Then he uncoiled the bull whip and practiced with it in the yard until the crackling that rent the air was loud and crisp. He watched as Leon and the others pulled Luther out of the corncrib and stripped his shirt off.

Luther was in his late fifties, only a little older than Jamie's father. They had grown up together on this same plantation, which was given to Grandpa Blake as a reward for service in the Revolutionary War. Luther had grown a bit fat, had lost most of his hair except for a bit of gray at the temples, and looked much older than he was. Unlike Leon and some of the other slaves, his back was smooth and free of scar tissue.

Jamie coiled the whip up and approached him as he was being tied to the post. Other slaves from the barn and the stable came outside to see, some leaning out of windows and doorways. A number of house slaves stood on the back porch.

"You never been whipped, have you, Luther?" Jamie glanced around the yard. There were about twenty slaves watching, and more coming up from the fields.

"Naw, suh," Luther said. "Ain't never give no cause to."

"Well, you've given plenty of cause this time."

"Yas, suh."

"You know I've got to do this."

"Yas, suh."

"Everybody's watching."

"Yas, suh."

Jamie glanced around the yard again. He was beginning to feel beads of perspiration form on his forehead. "I was thinking of giving you one hundred lashes."

"Yas, suh."

"But considering this is your first serious offense in a long life of service, I'm going to reduce it by half—fifty lashes."

"Yas, suh."

"You got anything to say for yourself?"

"Naw, suh."

"All right then. Let's get on with it."

Jamie rolled up his sleeves and walked to a spot about twelve to fifteen feet away, in the middle of the yard. He uncoiled the whip and let it lie loose on the ground, like a languid snake sunning itself, while he contemplated what he was about to do. He reproached himself for allowing his anger to subside and to give in to the sentimental attachments between Luther and his father, and Luther and himself. Not only had Luther and his father been playmates as children, but Luther had taught him, Jamie, how to hunt and fish. There had been many a time when Luther had baited his hook for him, told him where to drop his line, and admonished him for not being patient enough. He could remember when he shot a doe, missed the vital organs, and Luther forced him to track the poor animal into the thick brush so that they could finish her off and not allow her to slowly bleed to death or fall prey to other predators.

No, he must not allow these thoughts to deter him, to distract him from performing his duty, his responsibility as the heir to, and future master of, Belle Oaks.

The whip seemed to leap from his hands without conscious effort on his part. There was the familiar loud crack, followed by the appearance of a pink welt on Luther's back. Luther cried out in anguish, which surprised everyone, including Jamie, in sharp contrast to his stoic acceptance of his punishment at the outset. It was as if he hadn't expected it to be so painful.

Oh, Lord, Jamie thought. Forty-nine more? How would he be able to stand it? How would either of them be able to stand it?

Nevertheless, he slowly brought the whip around again through the red dirt like a slithering boa constrictor stalking its prey, lifted his arm high in the air, and threw his shoulder forward to launch the leather tip on its way to its target. Luther cried out again, and another pink welt appeared, this time lower down in the center of his back.

It became easier after this.

After ten lashes, the welts began to burst, and after twenty, Luther's back was covered in blood. After thirty, he no longer cried out, but began to slump against the post.

At forty, Jamie's shirt was soaked with perspiration, and he paused to catch his breath. He thought of stopping but he was afraid that the slaves, who now numbered around fifty, would consider him soft and irresolute.

"Leon!"

"Yas, suh?"

"Splash some water in his face. I think he's passed out."

"Yas, suh." Leon hurried over to Luther and looked at his eyes, which were closed. He propped the lids open and confirmed that he was unconscious. One of the others arrived with a bucket of water, and Leon splashed the contents onto Luther's face. He seemed to revive.

"All right, now," Jamie said. "Stand Back!"

Leon and the other slave quickly moved away, and Jamie sent the whip flying through the air again, this time ripping strips of flesh from Luther's back that had only been hanging by threads before. Even Leon winced at the sight of this, and the women covered their eyes or turned away. Luther let out a scream louder than any before.

"Count!" Jamie said.

"Suh?"

"I said, 'count.' You've stopped counting. That's forty-one."

Leon looked at Jamie as if amazed. But when the next blow struck, he resumed counting. " Fo'ty-two...fo'ty -three...fo'ty-fo'..."

By this time, Luther seemed to lapse into unconsciousness again.

"Fo'ty-five...fo'ty-six..."

At fifty, Jamie stopped. He was exhausted, and even his trousers were soaked with perspiration. He coiled up the whip. "Is he breathing?"

Leon went over to Luther, again propped open his eyes, and put his hand over his mouth and nose. "Yas, suh. He breathin.'"

"Cut him down then." Jamie tossed the whip to one of the stable boys, and picked up his waistcoat. "Take him to his cabin. I'll send Doc Parcher over to dress his wounds."

"Yas, suh." Leon complied, cutting Luther down from the post and ordering the others to help carry him to his cabin.

CHAPTER 10

Prepared for departure to Middletown after seven days in Brantley. Stayed at Ned's for most of that time, but spent one night at my parents' place and one at my Uncle Ben's. My mother received me warmly, even tearfully, and betrayed no feelings of the bitterness for what must have seemed to her my 'heresy' so many years ago.

Saw many of my childhood friends, many of whom did not recognize me, or I them. Most, however, upon renewing our acquaintance, showed much warmth and friendliness, and took an interest in my adventures in Georgia, which to them might as well be darkest Africa.

My last visit before returning to the Inn for the stage was to the old schoolhouse. This scene could not help but call up a thousand recollections of early days, of companions and scenes of boyish amusement. Standing in the center of the room, I scanned over every object, many of which had remained untouched and unmoved for these twenty years. On the walls and benches I could still trace some of the marks of my mischievous knife and pen. The armchair in which the master had sat still stood there in rather lame and faded majesty. The current school mistress, as I was to discover, turned out to be one of my former classmates, one who had often sat on the bench next to me and trembled, as I did, before the throne of the master as he dispensed his wisdom in stentorian tones. I was less humbled before this kind of majesty than I once was—now presuming myself its equal—bestowed on the arm of the chair a kiss, and withdrew.

At the Inn, Zimri chatted some more with Mrs. Clausen, who had begun to convert her establishment to a tavern rather than a way station for the scant travelers who stopped there. She was an excellent cook, and as a result, many of the local business people took their mid-day meal there.

The stage from New Haven arrived shortly after four o'clock, and soon Zimri was on his way to the wedding at Middletown. It was only a two hour jaunt, over fairly good roads, and Zimri, relieved at having fulfilled his obligations in Brantley, grew increasingly sanguine about the festivities that lay ahead.

He arrived at the Hoyt House in time for supper, and was delighted to encounter many of his oldest and best friends. These were the people who, like himself, had by industry and a sense of adventure, escaped to a larger world than the oppressive confines of Brantley.

In the lobby of the hotel, he immediately recognized his old friend from his early days of newspapering in New Haven, William Stow, now editor of his own newspaper, *The American Sentinel.* No sooner had he struck up a conversation with him, when another old friend, David Harris, appeared. All this reminiscing and back-clapping, while gratifying to the participants, only frustrated the desk clerk, who was doing his best to check the arriving guests in and assign them to their rooms.

The next morning Zimri shared a carriage with Stow and Harris to the bride's brother's house, where the wedding was to take place. Mr. Nichols, the brother, was apparently a man of some wealth and influence in Middletown, as the house was quite large with a long driveway and extensive gardens. Zimri found the latter to be most interesting and appealing, and took notes on the great variety of plants and flowers as they approached the house.

"Still a devotee of horticulture, I see," Stow said to him.

"I'm afraid it entered my blood when I was a small child," Zimri said. "I cannot look at a pastoral scene without wanting to know every variety, the condition of the soil, and the effects of the local climate."

"Ah," Harris said, ever the wit, "it must be the smell of manure that so filled your nostrils as a youth. Once a farm boy, always a farm boy."

Zimri bristled. "By that reasoning, Harris, you should be tanning hides now instead of loaning money to ship builders."

Harris grumbled. "The smell of my father's tannery when I was a boy was far more foul than horse manure. The stench was akin to that of decomposing bodies."

"Then perhaps you missed your calling as an undertaker," Stow said.

They all laughed at this, endeavoring to invent more similes and metaphors related to noxious smells as the carriage pulled up to the front portico.

A white gloved butler escorted them to the main drawing room, where rows of chairs had been set up at one end, and tables at the other with punch and hors d'oeuvres. There were Palladian windows along the rear wall, large enough in their open position for the guests to walk through to the rear gardens. Zimri estimated that there were seventy to eighty guests present.

He suddenly felt a hand on his shoulder and heard a familiar voice.

"Zimri!" It was the groom, and his best childhood friend, John Davies. He was dressed in full wedding regalia—morning jacket, white tie, carnation in his lapel. "I'm so glad you could make it. To think you came all the way from Georgia!"

Zimri embraced him, and followed it with a hearty handshake. "I would have come had I been living in the wilds of Borneo You're looking well, John."

"And you, also," John said, looking him up and down. "A little more weight, perhaps, and a thick beard. But it's the same old Zimri—I'd recognize you if you wore a bone through your nose. That's 'de rigueur' in Borneo, isn't it? Or perhaps even in Georgia."

"It seems that I have to educate you Yankees about the South," Zimri said with a combination of good humor and incipient irritation. "We have steamboats and gas lights and dandified wedding parties just as you do."

"Dandified?" Davies said with a laugh. "Well, I suppose I am dandified today. I'm most often found in a blood-stained smock and with a gleaming scalpel in my hand. Come and meet my bride-to-be."

The bride, Miss Nancy Nichols, was a very attractive blond, about twenty or so, with large blue eyes and a slightly up-turned nose that made her look even younger than she was. She seemed highly educated but, Zimri surmised, had led a somewhat sheltered life. She was bubbly and enthusiastic, and completely without artifice. She seemed worthy of his good friend in every way, and Zimri was assured that their union would be a happy one.

Just as he was getting acquainted with the bride, a servant rang a little bell, and the room fell silent. A clergyman appeared at a small altar at the head of the rows of chairs and announced that the ceremony was about to begin.

Zimri took his seat, the participants took their places, and a small group of musicians began to play a wedding march.

Zimri had just gotten comfortable in his seat when he heard someone whisper in his ear.

"It's a small world, Mr. Rhodes, I daresay."

The voice sounded very familiar, that of a woman, but he couldn't quite place it. Not wishing to be rude or disruptive, he continued looking straight ahead for a moment, then slowly turned his head. "Miss Rinaldi!"

"Shh!" a man in front of him said.

"Are you a friend of the bride?"

"Yes," Cora said. "and Dr. Davies as well."

"Shhh!" the man in front said.

The ceremony went very smoothly, as expected, and was over in fifteen minutes. There were claps and cheers and the musicians began to play again. The bride's brother, Mr. Nichols, invited everyone to partake of the refreshments, and Zimri found himself escorting Miss Rinaldi, as he still called her, to one of the tables laden with food and drink.

"How extraordinary to see you here." Zimri passed a cup of punch to her.

"Thank you," she said. "I must say it took me by surprise when I saw you talking to John and Nancy. You're a childhood friend of John's, I understand."

"That's right. We grew up together in Brantley, not far from here. But I was not acquainted with the bride until just a half-hour ago. She's a lovely girl, isn't she?"

Cora sipped her punch, which was half fruit juice and half champagne. "Yes, a lovely person. Very young, but very intelligent and like her husband very committed to the cause."

"The cause?"

"Yes the abolitionist cause."

"Oh," Zimri said, now reminded of their conversation in New York. "I didn't know he had become so involved, actually."

"Oh, they are quite involved," Cora said, standing on her toes to wave to a friend. "In fact, Dr. Davies has given very generously to Mr. Garrison's fund to start a new newspaper. Oh, see? There he is talking to Mr. Garrison now, along with another gentleman whom I don't know."

Zimri turned towards the windows and saw his friend John talking to a short, balding and rather unprepossessing man in a plain brown suit. And next to this man, standing quietly but attentively was his eldest brother. "My brother Zeke."

"Your brother? Why, you must introduce me."

"I'll probably have to re-introduce myself first. I haven't seen him in ten years."

"Ten years?" Cora looked again towards the three men at the

windows. "But surely you've written one another during that time."

Zimri handed his cup to the waiter for a refill. "No—we haven't. Would you like another cup of punch?"

"No, thank you. Champagne isn't really my libation of choice."

Zimri smiled. "Too tame, eh?"

"Let's just say that I like my refreshments to have a little more bite."

Zimri took the cup from the waiter. "Well, that bourbon in New York bit me and Alexis, all right. We both had a splitting headache the next morning."

"It doesn't agree with everyone." Cora seemed to want to change the subject, as if her penchant for bourbon was decidedly un-lady-like. "But tell me about your brother—you had a falling out?"

"Yes, I guess you could call it that. He used to own a newspaper in Brantley and I was his sole employee."

"Ah. You didn't like being ordered about by your older brother."

"Perhaps. Perhaps that was really at the bottom of it. That and Abigail."

"Abigail?"

Zimri looked to the windows. "My betrothed at the time. She broke off the engagement and married Zeke."

"Oh. I'm so sorry."

Zimri turned his eyes back to Cora's and forced a laugh. "Don't be. It happened a long time ago. I suppose I should be thankful to him now. Otherwise, I wouldn't have gone to Georgia and met Elizabeth."

"And started your own newspaper."

"Yes, that, too."

Cora smiled warmly. "Strange how events—however painful at the time—can sometimes lift us off one road of life and set us gently down on another, sometimes better one."

Zimri divined that she was speaking from experience. "And you, Miss Rinaldi? Have you found yourself lifted off one road and set down upon another?"

Cora's smile turned enigmatic. "I suppose I have. Events have thrust me into a world that I little knew existed when I was a girl."

"What sort of events?"

"I don't wish to bore you, Mr. Rhodes. I believe we were discussing your newspaper in Georgia. I suspect your political views differ markedly from your brother's. Am I correct in that assumption?"

Zimri smiled. "You are. At least in one important regard. He was a Constitutionalist, to be sure, but he believed that each state should remain aloof of the others. He was a kind of anarchist."

"And you?"

"I was—and still am—a Jeffersonian Republican. But I believe, like Hamilton, that a strong central government is necessary—without it, we would fall to cutting each other's throats."

"So he is a Constitutional anarchist, and you are a Jeffersonian Federalist-Republican."

Zimri laughed. "You make it sound as if we're both mad. I just believe that freedom of speech is the cornerstone of our democracy—and if one state is allowed to suppress that freedom, the whole fragile edifice will fall to pieces."

"And if one—or more—states choose to suppress the rights of the few in favor of the many...what then?

"Then the federal government must take punitive action."

"War, then."

"It need not be war, but merely—"

"What's all this talk of war?" It was the groom, who evidently had already had a bit too much punch. He put his arms around both Zimri and Cora. "This is supposed to be a wedding, not a funeral."

"Miss Rinaldi and I were just discussing politics," Zimri said.

"Politics?" John said. "Politics is for everyday, humdrum conversation. This is a very special day!"

"Indeed it is, John," Cora said.

"And I don't mean just for me, but for everyone! Drink and be merry!" John suddenly pulled Zimri closer to him. "But say, Zimri, I'm really glad that you've had the opportunity to meet Miss Rinaldi. Do you know what an extraordinary woman she is?"

"Oh, please, John," Cora said.

"No, no, no! It's true. Zimri, she is not only extraordinarily beautiful, as any fool can see, and not only an extraordinary actress, as any fool with the price of a theatre ticket can see, but she is an extraordinary soldier fighting for—"

"John, I think you'd better see about your bride," Cora said. "She needs rescuing from Judge Taylor."

"Judge Taylor?" John turned to see his wife standing before an elderly man who seemed to be delivering a lecture, his finger waggling before the bride's face. "Don't worry, I know how to handle him." And he wandered off to do as he was bid.

"You are a soldier?" Zimri said.

"He meant it metaphorically," Cora said. "I'm a soldier in the cause of abolition. I try to contribute in any way that I can."

"Then you give money?"

Cora laughed. "After the abysmal reviews of my play, I no longer can even do that. Mostly, I help send out circulars."

Zimri was dubious of this explanation, thinking that she was only being modest. He decided not to press the matter further, and suggested that they move outside where more and more people seemed to be taking advantage of the beautiful weather.

Along the way, they couldn't help but run into Zeke, who extended his hand. "How are you, Zimri?"

Zimri hesitated, then extended his own. "Quite well, Zeke. How is Abigail?"

"At home. Down with a bit of the ague, I'm afraid. But she sends her love."

Zimri tried not to betray his skepticism. "That's very thoughtful of her. Have you met Miss Rinaldi?"

Zeke bowed deeply at the waist. "I am a great fan of yours, Miss Rinaldi. I saw you in *Twelfth Night* in Boston last year."

"Thank you, Mr. Rhodes," Cora said. "I love doing Shakespeare—the language is so beautiful, and of course, the roles for women are many and varied."

Zeke glanced at Zimri. "May I ask how you became acquainted with my brother?"

"The theatre again," Cora said. "He came to a production of my most recent play in New York. A mutual friend introduced us, and we just happened to meet again today."

Zeke regarded Zimri with a suspicious eye. "A happy accident, no doubt. What have you done with your wife, Zimri? I was looking forward to meeting her."

Zimri did not like the insinuation. "She's at home—about to have our second child."

"Ah," Zeke said. "And in the meantime, you are to keep Miss Rinaldi amused."

Zimri suppressed an urge to paste his brother in the nose. "I'm sure Miss Rinaldi doesn't need me to amuse her. She has many friends here."

Cora suddenly looked as if she had fallen between two hungry wolves fighting over a piece of meat. "Oh—speaking of friends, I see an old acquaintance of mine from New York. If you'll excuse me, gentlemen—"

Zeke performed another deep bow as Cora made her exit. The two men then stood awkwardly together, each looking about them as if the other were invisible.

Finally, Zeke spoke. "I understand that you have your own newspaper in Georgia now."

"That's right," Zimri said.

A few moments passed.

"A Republican paper, is it?"

"Right again," Zimri said.

Zeke seemed to consider this. "How do you reconcile that with a wife who owns slaves?"

"She no longer does."

"But her family does."

"That's not her concern. She lives with me now."

Zimri was about to walk away when his brother suddenly grabbed him by the arm and drew him back. "Stay for a moment, Zimri— I'd like you to meet someone."

"Oh? Who?"

"A close associate of mine. Mr. William Garrison."

Zimri was not anxious to meet Mr. Garrison, but in the interest of at least making an attempt to reconcile himself with his brother, he consented.

The latter turned out to be a rather meek and quiet man, that is until the conversation turned to slavery. Then he suddenly became a firebrand, raising his voice and slapping the back of one hand into the palm of the other to make his points. Zimri could find little fault with his arguments, and admired his passionate commitment to the cause of abolition, but was uncomfortable with his religious fervor, which reminded him of the ranting of Brother Gibson in his youth.

"Will you join us, Mr. Rhodes?" Garrison said at last, as if everything he had said previously had been leading up to this one question.

"Join you?" Zimri said. "I find your position on slavery sympathetic to my own, Mr. Garrison, but I don't know what you mean by 'joining' you. I have a newspaper to run in Georgia."

"That's precisely what I mean," Garrison said, excitedly. "You can be of great value to the cause. Why, an abolitionist newspaper right in the heart of slave country! You could be of immense value to us."

Zimri looked into the bottom of his cup, which he realized now had been empty for half an hour. Then he looked into Mr. Garrison's fierce blue eyes again. "The *Mercury*, Mr. Garrison, is proud to be a Republican newspaper, but the term is used in the broadest sense of the word, not in the narrow partisan sense. Our only stated mission is to present our readers with the truth regarding the nation and the world—and to be subject to the control of no government, nor any partisan group, nor any individual, however powerful and influential. I'm afraid I cannot commit the editorial page to any cause, no matter how noble, though I will certainly publish opinions on that subject from time to time as they are submitted to me, or as they arise from my own thinking in reaction to events."

Garrison continued to stare at him for several moments, as if this little speech was wholly unsatisfactory. "Then your newspaper's policy is to be reactive, not progressive."

"Our policy is to report events, Mr. Garrison, not to shape them."

Garrison continued to stare at Zimri for several moments, as if expecting him to recant, then turned to speak to someone else. Zeke seemed to melt away.

Zimri, suddenly finding himself alone, began looking to the garden for signs of Cora. Not seeing her through the windows, he ventured outside and saw a large group of people, some standing, some sitting, on the grass before a small terrace containing a fountain and encircled by boxwoods. In front of the fountain stood Cora, singing a song:

> *The poor soul sat sighing by a sycamore tree.*
> *Sing all a green willow;*
> *Her hand on her bosom, her head on her knee,*
> *Sing willow, willow, willow:*

Zimri found an empty space on the grass and sat down to listen.

> *The fresh streams ran by her, and murmured her moans;*
> *Sing willow, willow, willow.*
> *Her salt tears fell from her and softened the stones;*
> *Sing willow, willow, willow;*
> *Sing all a green willow must be my garland.*

> *Let nobody blame him, his scorn I approve;*
> *I called my love false love; but what said he*

then?

Sing willow, willow, willow.

Cora bowed her head and performed a little curtsy, lifting the hem of her dress to signal that the performance was over. The crowd all clapped loudly and enthusiastically, with shouts of "More! More!"

Zimri found himself joining in, clapping till his hands reddened and felt as if they had been stung by bees.

CHAPTER 11

Started for New Haven. Our party consisted of myself, Miss Rinaldi, Messrs. Stow and Harris in one stage, Mr. and Mrs. Wilcox of Savannah in another, and the bride and groom leading the procession in a gig festooned with flowers and ribbons. Took tea at Mrs. Wilcox's daughter's in the afternoon, where Miss Rinaldi stayed for the night. While the others in the party dispersed to various homes and inns, each to pursue their own itinerary, I asked Miss Rinaldi if she wouldn't like a tour of New Haven, as I knew it well from my earlier days, and she consented.

The next day I let a carriage and after some dalliance in the town, we rode to the East Rock. Here one of the most beautiful prospects in the world was before us, and lying , as it were, at our very feet. The city and the bay, the ocean beyond, Long Island, a range of distant mountains to the northwest, the bold front of West Rock within two miles of the promontory on which we stood, immense meadows to the south and east through which two small rivers ran their winding course: these altogether formed a picture as various and beautiful as Fancy in her most romantic moment could draw to the mind's eye—a very paradise.

"Why, it's breath-taking," Cora said, as they both gazed out over the panorama before them. "I wonder at your ever leaving."

"Zeke had no small amount to do with it," Zimri said. "But I must say it wasn't all his fault. I was impelled by a sense of adventure and a desire to sever my roots to what I considered to be a puritanical and hypocritical society."

"And did you find less of that in Georgia?"

"In the beginning I thought so. Martinville was a frontier town—actually not even a town, but a military outpost—when I arrived, and I found the people there to be without social pretension or religious cant. As the town grows, however, I see more and more of both."

"Or perhaps it's always been there, and you are just beginning to see it."

"Perhaps." Zimri looked into Cora's liquid brown eyes. He was increasingly drawn to her, and wanted to know her, to know everything about her. Their lips were only inches apart.

"You're even more handsome without the beard," she said.

"I didn't wish to be mistaken for a country parson. Or a pirate."

Cora laughed. "A pirate, perhaps. A parson—no."

"Have you never married, Miss Rinaldi?"

"No, I haven't. And please stop calling me 'Miss Rinaldi.' My name is Cora."

"Cora, then. Forgive me if my question was impertinent."

"On the contrary, I wonder that you are not impertinent enough." Cora smiled and her lips seemed to part slightly, moist and expectant.

Zimri was somewhat taken aback, but collected himself enough to lean forward and bring his lips to hers. They stood on the precipice of East Rock, with the clouds drifting above their heads, and the breeze from the ocean rustling through their clothes for what seemed a very long time. At last Zimri withdrew his lips from hers and opened his eyes. "I don't think any other woman, aside from Elizabeth, could have made me do that."

"Elizabeth must be an extraordinary woman."

Zimri hesitated. "Yes, I think she is. But she's very young."

"Too young—to know who she is."

"Yes. I believe she's struggling with that at this very moment."

"And if, by the time you get home, she decides that she's someone else—someone who you perhaps don't care for as much as you had thought?"

"Then…I don't know."

Cora suddenly seemed agitated, uncomfortable. She looked around and spotted the basket they had carried up to the summit from the carriage. "The climb has stimulated my appetite. Are you hungry, Mr. Rhodes?"

"Mister Rhodes? So we are again on formal terms?"

"I'm not a home-breaker, Mr. Rhodes. I'm afraid you misconstrued my—"

Zimri suddenly seized her by the shoulders and pressed his lips again to hers. This time the kiss was passionate, violent, as Cora at first resisted but then returned his ardor in kind. They sank down into the grass, Cora on her back. Zimri's right hand reached for the buttons of her bodice, his fingers trembling in their eagerness.

Cora seized his hand. He was surprised at the strength of her grip.

"This must be a very popular place for lovers," she said.

"Yes, it is."

"Is there no place else more—private?"

"There's a cave about half-way down the rock. It was home to a hermit when I was a boy, but he's long since died."

"Take me there."

Zimri hesitated. "It may not be safe, Cora. It's been years since I've seen it, and—"

"You think too much." She put her hand to his cheek and caressed it softly. Then she kissed him. "Bring the basket."

Zimri rose to his feet and picked up the basket. Cora followed him to the edge of the rock and they soon found the overgrown path that led down to the cave. There was a great deal of undergrowth covering the entrance, and it took some cutting with a knife from the basket to clear it away. Once inside, they discovered some rudimentary furniture, chairs, and a bed with a rope suspension but no mattress. There was a kind of hearth with a kettle hanging from an iron hook driven into the wall and the charred remains of a wood fire.

"He invited me to share his supper once," Zimri said, examining the hearth. "There's a natural flue here that snakes its way up to an opening a few yards beneath the summit. He was entirely self-sufficient."

"How did he die?"

"Old age, I suppose. He was in his eighties or thereabouts even then."

"It's sad, isn't? I mean for an old man to die alone."

"Oh, I think he was happy enough in his own way." Zimri turned from the hearth to see a counterpane spread out on the floor and Cora unbuttoning the front of her dress.

"Take off your shoes, Zimri," she said. "Or you'll dirty the counterpane."

Zimri stood for a moment transfixed as Cora stepped out of her dress and began loosening her corset.

"There's plenty of light, isn't there?" she said. "And a beautiful view of Long Island Sound."

Zimri did not turn to look at the view. "Yes. Yes, it is beautiful."

Cora pulled off her petticoats and carefully laid them aside. Then she sat down on the counterpane and unbuttoned her shoes. Those set aside, she unhooked her garters, extended one leg in the air to remove her stocking, then performed the same task on the other.

"You look as if you've never seen a woman undress before. I'd wager you've never seen Elizabeth naked, in a clear light."

"No. No, I haven't."

She smiled. "Come here, Zimri. Come and let me undress you."

Zimri approached her as if a small boy to his mother. He noted that the corset was loose in front, partially exposing Cora's ample breasts. Her skin was the color of caramel, and smooth as butter. "Your skin is lovely."

"And yours is too pale. You must spend all of your time indoors."

"I suppose I do."

She unbuttoned his shirt and let it drop to the floor of the cave. Then she ran her hands over his chest and shoulders. "You're a very strong man—you have the physique of an athlete."

Zimri gave a nervous laugh. "I was never much of an athlete. But I did my share of heavy lifting on the farm until I was old enough to escape."

"Escape…yes, we all have escaped from something, sometime, haven't we? But then there's a difference between escaping *from* something and escaping *to* something. The former is often painful, while the latter can be…a new beginning." She turned up her chin and kissed him.

Zimri responded slowly at first, uncertain as to whether he should desist and put an end to this illicit dalliance, or allow himself to 'escape' this one time. After all, Elizabeth was a thousand miles away and would never know.

"You're thinking of her, aren't you?"

"Of whom?"

Cora laughed in a breathy way that emitted no sound except for the exhaling of air. "You are a poor dissembler, Zimri. We both know 'of whom.'"

"It apparently doesn't bother you."

She seemed to consider this. "No. No, it doesn't. Above, on the rock, I thought for a moment that it bothered you. But then you showed me that there's something missing in your relationship with Elizabeth."

"Missing? What's missing?"

Cora slipped off her corset and let it drop to the floor. "Passion. Adventure. The gratification of one's desires without guilt or remorse."

"And you? You can indulge your desires without guilt or remorse?"

"I can."

He watched as Cora pulled her remaining undergarment, a chemise, over her head, discarded it, and lay down on the counterpane. She then cocked her head to one side and gazed at him with lynx-like eyes.

"Come, Zimri. Come and show me what you know about making love."

He stared at her for a moment, then fumbled with the buttons to his trousers. Once he succeeded in removing them, he looked down at his erect penis and blushed.

She laughed. "Don't be embarrassed, Zimri. It's the most natural thing in the world. And I must say, you have nothing to be ashamed of.

Come here, darling—come to me."

Zimri felt almost paralyzed at first, with the small space between them appearing as a vast gulf, but at last he managed to move his feet, and followed her to the counterpane.

CHAPTER 12

Elizabeth lay on her back on the swing of the front porch, doing her best to recover from a bout of morning sickness. She felt drained, weak and depressed.

Maybelle had prepared some chicken broth for her and insisted that she get it down, but she pushed it away.

She thought of Zimri. What was he doing at this very moment? He was so serious, so practical, she imagined that he was noting every new building in New Haven, describing it in great detail in his journal, or else traveling through the countryside and cataloging every new species of plant life that he had somehow failed to notice as a young man, like a naturalist on an expedition into unknown country.

She thought of Randolph, who would soon arrive in France. What would he find there? Would he become homesick? Was he thinking of her? Would he write to her?

Speaking of writing, she had received scant correspondence from Zimri, who only described his trip to New York as 'uneventful,' and his stay in Brantley as 'akin to water torture.' At least, she hoped, he would enjoy the wedding of his good friend Doctor Davies.

How strange that she, still only eighteen, would soon be having his second child! Their own wedding had been so rushed. Yet it was not he, but she who couldn't wait. And all to prove that she was a young woman now, free and independent of her parents. How ironic! She was more dependent upon her parents than ever—Maybelle cooked all of her meals and nursed the child; Old George, also from her father's plantation, looked after the garden; Otis fed the horses and cows and chickens; and Jamie looked in from time to time to see that everything was running smoothly.

She really had very little to do even when she was feeling well.

At least her father seemed to be recovering well. In fact, Luther had had a longer convalescence than he after the whipping. How ghastly! She was glad she hadn't witnessed it. There were murmurings and whispers among the slaves that the punishment was too severe for the crime. But after all, he had tried to kill her father, or at least might have even if he didn't intend it. Jamie had done only what he had to do.

She had finished *Sense and Sensibility* and was now reading *Pride and Prejudice*. Somehow, *Pride and Prejudice* was more difficult to get into. She couldn't keep the characters straight. Nevertheless, she picked up the open book resting on her stomach and began reading again.

Though she shared the same name with the main character, she saw little of herself in this Elizabeth. She seemed rather a snob. And what did she see in this Mr. Darcy aside from the fact that he was rich?

After a few pages, she put the book down again and closed her eyes. She saw Randolph, with his chiseled features and Napoleonic curl on his forehead, staring intently at her, his lips pursed as if to kiss her. Oh, he did kiss well! And unlike Mr. Darcy, he had a lively sense of humor, a quick wit, and an unpretentious manner. Why did she refuse him when she was at school in Charleston?

She felt herself drifting, seemingly on a wave on the open sea. She had never been on a ship before, only a steamboat on the Ashley River in Charleston. But now she was not even on a ship, or vessel of any kind. She simply floated across the waves, her feet not even touching the water, clothed in a gossamer dressing gown that billowed in the breeze like a sail. Her head back, chest thrust forward, eyes closed (though seeing everything), it was if she were the figurehead on the prow of a ship. Yes, that was it. Only it wasn't an inanimate carved figure, but herself, a living breathing, sentient woman feeling the wind in her face, the salt air in her nostrils, and the splash of the waves against her breast.

And then she found herself standing on the deck of the ship. And there was Randolph, dressed as a naval officer, reaching out to her. For some reason, she did not take his hand, but continued to stare at him. He approached her, his hand still extended, as if to assist her, or no, rather to lead her somewhere. At the last moment he turned and offered his arm. But suddenly a fist slammed against the side of his head and he went sprawling to the deck.

The fist belonged to Zimri.

He was dressed from head to toe in black and glared at her before walking over to Randolph, who was struggling to get up, and hit him again, this time with some sort of club. She screamed and grabbed Zimri by the arm, pleading with him to stop, but he pushed her away, and continued beating Randolph until he sprawled face down on the deck again, his face in a pool of blood.

As she stood in horror at this scene, the blood began to spread out across the deck, gallons and gallons of it, far more than could have been contained in Randolph's body, until it covered the entire ship and even spilled over the gunwales, dyeing the sea red. She turned to look at Zimri, who was approaching her, his eyes glowing with a sort of fanatical fire, his lips mouthing angry words that she couldn't make out.

A mist, or more rightly a penetrating fog, began to envelop the ship, and Zimri's figure began to retreat into it, his eyes still glowing like hot coals.

"Miz Lisbeth, is you asleep? Lawd, it's two o'clock in the afternoon. You got to eat somethin, fo' the baby if not fo' yo' self."

She opened her eyes. "Oh, all right. I suppose I'll have some of that broth now."

"You need more than broth. I'll fix you mashed taters and lima beans and smoked ham and Maybelle's lighter-than-air biscuits. They'll melt in yo' mouth and slide right down and make yo' tummy feel as calm and satisfied as ol' bossy in the pasture over yonder. No, ma'am, you cain't tell me bout no mawnin' sickness. I done chased it away 'long wid the devil when he done got inside my own chillun. Now you just rest a mite longer and I'll rustle up them vittles in no time."

"Oh, Maybelle, I don't think I can keep any ham down."

"I'll chop it up in little pieces like fo' a chile—you'll never know it's there. Besides, you need red meat fo' yo' strength."

"Whatever you say, Maybelle."

Maybelle ambled off into the house and Elizabeth sat up in the swing. She felt a sudden dizziness, but it soon passed. Maybelle was right—she must eat something. Perhaps it was all this inactivity that was making her so sluggish, so weak. She needed something more than a silly English novel to occupy her time while Zimri was away.

She watched as Old George, nearing seventy now, worked in the garden, pruning back Zimri's rose bushes. Slightly stooped, heavy set, curly gray hair peeking out beneath his straw hat at the temples, Old George moved slowly but surely, as carefully and intently upon his task as Zimri might. How wonderful to be so absorbed in one's work, to have a sense of purpose! Even a slave could lose himself in his vocation once he had accepted his lot in life. But what was her vocation? To bear children? Surely an important function. But hardly a vocation. Even Maybelle had a vocation, one she was very skilled at, and yet she had borne ten children without missing more than a few weeks of work. But the darkies were of much hardier stock than she; they seemed to thrive on hard labor and adversity. She had heard that Luther, who had been demoted from groom to field hand, was working harder than ever since the whipping he received from Jamie.

As she continued to watch Old George move deftly about the rose bushes, she became aware of someone coming up the road in a gig. She shielded the sun's rays from her eyes and stood on her tiptoes. It appeared to be Jedediah, Zimri's assistant who had been left in charge of the newspaper.

The gig pulled up to the hitching rail in front of the house, and Jedediah got out. He was a young man, only a year older than she, tall and thin, and dressed like an undertaker. She hardly knew him since she had gone to school in Charleston while he attended the local grammar school. His father was a book dealer whom Zimri often purchased books from.

"Good afternoon, Mrs. Rhodes," he said as he came up the path. He took off his hat, which was a kind of bowler, too small for his head.

"Good afternoon, Jed," she said. "Is anything wrong at the office?"

"Well, not exactly wrong, ma'am. Just a little problem."

"And what might that be?" She sat back down and began swinging gently back and forth.

Jed stopped on the steps of the porch, his hat placed respectfully across his chest. "It's the new cylinder press that Mr. Rhodes ordered from New York. It's here."

"Why, that's good news, isn't it? Zimri didn't expect it to arrive until after he got back from New York."

"Well, yes ma'am. It's good that it's here and all, but there's a little problem."

"You already said that. What is it?"

"The teamsters from Savannah won't take it off their wagon until they've been paid."

"I see. And Zimri didn't leave enough money in the safe."

"No, ma'am."

"So what are we to do?"

"Mr. Patterson over at the bank says he can issue a bank draft, but you'll have to come and sign for it. I'm sorry to have to—"

"That's all right, Jed." Her hand went reflexively to her abdomen. "I'll have Otis bring me down after lunch. Won't you stay? Maybelle's preparing—"

"I'm afraid the teamsters won't wait, Mrs. Rhodes. They say they've got to go on to Milledgeville and deliver a cotton gin before dark."

"Yo' dinner's ready, Miz Lisbeth." Maybelle stood at the door, wiping her hands with her apron." "Oh, you got company. They's plenty fo' two."

"I'm afraid I'll have to go into town with Mr. Nesbit for a while." She rose unsteadily from the swing.

"Fo' a while?" Maybelle said. "It ain't gone be a while fo' the biscuits go stone cold."

"Sorry, Maybelle. It's a matter of business."

Maybelle put her hands on her hips defiantly. "Bizness? Ain't no bizness cain't wait til after dinner. Lawd, you been settin' here all mawnin' wid nothin' to do but stare at the clouds, and now you cain't wait to go on to town fo' bizness?"

"Sorry, Maybelle. It's important. Mr. Nesbit will bring me back in an hour. Just keep the biscuits warm in the oven."

Maybelle turned to go back into the house, muttering to herself. "An hour? Ain't gone be the same. Them biscuits will get hard as rocks settin' in the oven fo' an hour. And the lima beans will get mushy, and—"

Elizabeth allowed Jed to take her hand and escort her to the gig. She was beginning to show now, and she liked the attention that it elicited, especially from men. Jed, who wasn't bad looking, with a boyish face and an earnest politeness about him, was a suitable escort.

She hadn't been into town for a month.

CHAPTER 13

Thursday, 29 July

Landed in New York at sunrise and put up at Haydock's boarding house, North Pearl Street. Said farewell to Miss Rinaldi in New Haven after dropping her at Miss Wilcox's the previous evening. She said that she had business in New Haven for the next few days but that she hoped to see me again in New York.

I was obliged to call on my cousins, Mrs. Jane Selkirk and her daughter Emily, as they intend to join me on an excursion to Albany and Troy. I fairly consider this to be an ordeal that must be borne. Mrs. Selkirk, whom I hardly know, is a woman of some precision in her manners, and seems preoccupied with collecting prospective suitors for her daughter, who is , alas, rather plain of appearance and dull of mind.

Saturday, 31 July

Embarked with Mrs. Selkirk and Emily on the steamboat for Albany and Troy. The sublimity of the Highlands, the Palisades, and the Catskill mountain scenery almost make the constant chatter of Mrs. Selkirk bearable. The clichés she employs on every occasion to remark upon this unsurpassed natural beauty, however, could cause the most enthusiastic traveler to seek refuge in the ship's bar.

The mountains were 'majestic,' the Palisades 'like giants' footsteps,' and the fields of poppies 'precious.' Emily seemed impervious to these comments, and though her observations were a bit peculiar, I must admit were more original than her mother's. The Palisades, she said, reminded her of 'the wiggly hem of a broken doll's dress,' the mountains of 'bad teeth,' and the ship's paddle wheel of 'a cheese grater.'

In Albany we immediately boarded another steamboat for Troy, where Mrs. Selkirk and Emily had arranged to stay with a friend. Fortunately, I was advised that there was no room for me at this charming cottage, and put up for the night at the Troy House.

The next morning I hired a horse, crossed the river to the village of Gibbonsville on the Erie and Champlain Canal, followed the canal up to Waterford, and from there to the Cohoes Falls on the Mohawk. There is an immense quantity of water that cascades over these falls in a sheet about 300 feet wide. The few trees on the banks and grass have a singular green appearance, owing to their being constantly moistened by the spray from the falls. I can scarcely describe the effect this scene had on me, or the thoughts that it evoked of one who I longed to be with.

Pursued my way up the canal two and a half miles further to the Great Aqueduct on which it crosses the Mohawk. From Gibbonsville to this place there are nineteen locks, all beautifully built of rough-hewn marble. The Aqueduct is supported by twenty-five massive stone piers, and the water carried over in a trunk of wood.

I crossed the bridge over the Hudson to Lansingburg, a rather pretty but unremarkable place where only one object commanded my attention—a single shrub of the Rose Acacia which had been so trained as to nearly cover the front of a two story brick house.

Returned down the Hudson to Troy, and left there for Albany and New York.

The next morning Zimri ate a hearty breakfast at Haydock's and walked down Pearl Street in search of the address that Cora had given him.

The number on the card brought him to an imposing townhouse only a block south of Fraunces Tavern. It was a Greek Revival mansion that had been converted to a boarding house and was popular with actors, foreign diplomats, and visiting politicians. Zimri knew it well from his earlier days in New York as a reporter. He had once written a story exposing a ward boss' practice of keeping his mistresses here at taxpayer's expense.

The desk clerk informed him that Miss Rinaldi was not currently in residence, but had left an envelope with his name on it. Zimri thanked the clerk and sat down in the parlor to read the letter.

He examined the handwriting on the outside of the envelope before opening it. It was in a beautiful script, with sweeping curls at the end of the 'Z' and the 'R' and the final 's.' He brought the envelope to his nose. Perfume, but of what type he couldn't say. Violets? After much lingering and contemplation, fearing that the contents of the letter would put an end to their relationship forever, he reached into his pocket for his pen knife and slit the top edge of the envelope open. Upon extracting the letter an even stronger fragrance entered his nostrils, and this he savored before he finally unfolded it with great care and began reading:

My Dearest Zimri,
 It is with great regret that I must inform you—

Zimri dropped the letter in his lap, crestfallen, and turned his head up to the ceiling. It was over. Well, he should have known better in the first place. An actress, a woman from who knows where, with no real home and no family to speak of, and he a married man. What a fool he had been—no better than that ward boss, what's his name, O'Malley, whom he had exposed so many years before. He picked up the letter and resumed reading.

—I must inform you that I was obliged to leave New York before your return from Albany. This trip was not wholly unexpected, but events have made it necessary that I leave at once. There are a great many people depending upon me, and I cannot let them down.
 Zimri, you must not believe that I have taken our chance encounter in Middletown, and the subsequent events in New Haven, lightly, or as merely a frolic in a moment of summer delirium at the seashore. I was struck as if by lightning when our mutual friend Alexis brought you backstage at the Park Theatre that night after the performance. It was not only your handsome visage—of which I have never seen the like—but your manner, your every physical movement, and most of all, your lofty and sensitive intelligence.
 I will not insult your fine sensibilities by telling you that, after this short time of knowing one another, that I am deeply in love with you. No, that would be too facile, too ordinary, and too predictable. Only time will tell whether there will be—or can be—a deepening of the bond that already has taken hold of two beings so different, so far apart in background and temperament.
 I only know that I must see you again, though it threaten my most steadfast purpose. For though I will not shrink from these sacred responsibilities, I am not merely a vessel for the world's business to pass through. I am a woman, and as such, I must submit to the passions that nature has imposed upon me when those passions are strongest and most unyielding. Or else, in the end, I am nothing. So rest assured, my dearest, that we will meet again. It is only the time and place that are uncertain. Now I must bid you
 Adieu,
 Cora

Zimri read the letter over a second time, then a third. He folded it up, put it into its envelope, and placed the envelope in the inside pocket of his jacket. After a moment of staring out the window into the bustling traffic on Pearl Street, he removed the letter from his jacket and read it a fourth time.

He became aware that a gentleman sitting by the hearth reading a newspaper was staring at him. Surely, his behavior must have seemed peculiar. He put the letter back in his jacket, rose from his chair, and soon was swallowed up into the throng on Pearl Street.

He had gone only a block when he stopped at the corner, extracted the letter, and read it again. What could this 'steadfast purpose' be? And what were her 'sacred responsibilities?' He put the letter back into his pocket and continued walking toward Broadway.

Surely she was caught up in the abolitionist cause. Of that there could be no doubt—certainly she had not tried to hide it. But the language of the letter, 'steadfast' and 'sacred,' gave it a religious tone, a tone that he had not heard emanate from her lips until now. Of course, the abolitionists, like their most exalted leader, William Garrison, were often pious Christians. He chuckled as he was reminded of her sleek, curvaceous body stretched out on the counterpane at East Rock. She was hardly pious then.

As he turned up Broadway, he stopped for a moment to consider where, in fact, he was going. Oh, yes, to R. Hoe & Company to see if the new cylinder press had been shipped. Another four blocks.

No, Cora had none of the religious fanaticism about her that he so detested. But what was this 'steadfast purpose' she spoke of? It could be, of course, no more than the general goal of the abolitionists to abolish slavery. All well and good. He was against slavery himself. But the phrasing was more specific than that. Both more specific and vague at the same time.

Perhaps she was only alluding to some sort of convention or meeting in Boston. John had said something about that at the wedding. And perhaps she had been chosen as a delegate—that would explain her 'sacred responsibility.'"

The real question, though, was when would he see her again?

'R. Hoe & Co.' Ah, at last. He went in.

"Mr. Hoe?"

"The Mr. Hoe you are no doubt inquiring of is not in at the moment. May I help you?"

Zimri looked at the young man across the counter. He was about twenty-five, well-dressed, and looked more like a banker than a manufacturer of printing presses. "My name is Zimri Rhodes of Martinville, Georgia. I ordered a new cylinder press some two months ago, and—"

"Ah, Mr. Rhodes! Yes, your press was shipped on, let's see..." The young man across the counter consulted a large ledger. "On the fifth of July, a Monday. It should have arrived by now."

"So soon? Why, I thought it would be another month."

"Progress, Mr. Rhodes," the young man said. "Progress. We have a new, more efficient manufacturing system now and we ship only by express packet. That is, by steamship. From order to delivery in sixty days."

'Why, that's amazing."

"Isn't it, though. May I do anything else for you today, Mr. Rhodes?"

"No, no I don't think so. Thank you, Mr., uh..."

"Hoe. Richard Hoe. I'm the son of the founder."

"Pleased to make your acquaintance, Mr. Hoe. Give my regards to your father. Now you must excuse me for I have other business to attend to."

"Certainly. Good bye, Mr. Rhodes."

Zimri started for the door.

"Mr. Rhodes?"

"Yes?"

"I don't suppose you'd be interested in one of our new *steam* presses, would you?"

"Steam press? Well, I don't know. They must be very expensive."

"Oh, not so much more than a manual press, actually. And the price is always coming down. Would you care to take a look?"

"Well, ...yes, why not?"

"Come this way, Mr. Rhodes."

Zimri, suddenly absorbed in the possibilities of a steam-operated press, in spite of the fact that he had just spent most of the *Mercury's* operating funds on a manual one, followed the junior Mr. Hoe into a room that erupted into a cacophony of clanking iron, shouting men, and hissing vapors.

CHAPTER 14

Elizabeth was not intimidated by banks or bankers. She had accompanied her father several times while growing up when he was applying for loans or making deposits. And as one of Citizen's and Merchant's Bank's largest depositors, he often got a very favorable rate on the loans he needed for the capital improvements required to run a large plantation.

"You understand, Mrs. Rhodes," the bank's president, Mr. Hamilton, said, "that this is a loan secured by the value of the new printing press."

Elizabeth sat in a leather upholstered armchair looking across the immense desk of Mr. Hamilton. "Loan? You mean there's not enough in Zimri's account to cover the cost of the press?"

"That's precisely what I mean," Mr. Hamilton said. He was a middle-aged man, about forty-five or so, with gray sideburns, a gold watch chain draped over his belly, and a shiny, bald dome above his bushy eyebrows. "I don't mean to be disrespectful, but your husband, while a man of the highest integrity, is a poor money manager. He is often overdrawn here at the bank."

"How much is in the account?"

Mr. Hamilton consulted a ledger. "Nothing at the moment."

"Nothing? Nothing at all?"

"He is overdrawn three hundred thirty-eight dollars and sixty-two cents. I hasten to add, however, that when he returns from New York, we trust that he will cover the discrepancy."

"We have accounts receivable to cover the difference," Jed said. He was sitting in a chair only a few feet from Elizabeth's. "It's just that some of the advertisers are slow to pay their bills."

"A perennial problem, I'm afraid," Mr. Hamilton said with a chuckle. "It's one big cycle—the cattle rancher doesn't pay his bill with the feed store, the feed store proprietor can't pay his bill with the blacksmith, the blacksmith can't pay his bill with the merchant, and the merchant can't pay his bill with the newspaper to advertise his goods. But there has to be discipline, or the whole system breaks down."

"Discipline," Elizabeth said to no one in particular. "Yes, there must be discipline. You will have your money before my husband returns, Mr. Hamilton—you can count on that."

"I certainly hope so, Mrs. Rhodes. I do indeed."

Elizabeth rose and picked up the bank draft from Mr. Hamilton's desk. She noted that it was made out to R. Hoe and Co. She put it in her purse as the two men also rose. "You have my word upon it, Mr. Hamilton. I thank you for your cooperation. Jed, let's go to the office and take care of our business. Once the teamsters are paid, I want to see the books."

"Yes, ma'am," Jed said.

They took their leave of Mr. Hamilton and walked across Mulberry Street to the newspaper office where the teamsters were waiting with their wagon.

"That's for the press, ma'am," said one of the drivers, a burly man with red hair. "It don't include the shipping."

Jed led her inside where he extracted some petty cash from the safe to pay for the shipping and then directed them to the rear of the shop, where they unloaded the press. Elizabeth began poring over the books.

"This is a mess," she said, when Jed returned. "There are unpaid receivables dating back to February."

Jed peered over her shoulder at the account book. "That's Mr. Lewis, the milliner. Every time I go to his shop to collect, he's four sheets to the wind, starts telling me stories about his trips to Savannah and New Orleans, and ends up saying that all his cash is tied up in his inventory and he'll pay us the following week. But when I go back the next week, it's the same thing."

"I'll go see Mr. Lewis this afternoon. I want you to make a list of all the overdue accounts in a small notebook that I can put into my purse."

"Yes, ma'am."

"There must be thirty of them. I can't visit them all today, but I can make a good start."

"Yes, ma'am."

She looked around the office. There were newspapers stacked everywhere, some looking as if they were about to topple over. Zimri's desk, a large roll top, was bursting at the seams with various pieces of paper, unpaid bills she supposed, sticking out of every drawer. "Goodness. This place looks like a cyclone hit it. Don't you have any help?"

"Well, there's Peter in the back He's unpacking the new press right now. But he hardly ever comes into the front office. I know it looks bad, but Mr. Rhodes pretty much knows where everything is."

"I'm sure he does, but he doesn't seem to be doing anything about it." She extracted a piece of paper from one of the drawers. "Here's a bill for newsprint, dated May 22nd. It's never been paid."

Jed peered over her shoulder at the bill. "Oh, that's Mr. Colquitt's paper mill up in Milledgeville. Last time he came through Martinville, Mr. Rhodes was in a town council meeting and he said he'd be back. But I haven't seen him since."

"Well, the man should be paid," she said with an air of exasperation. "Doesn't Zimri give you the authority to pay his creditors when he's not available?"

"No, ma'am. He likes to do everything himself. I pay the delivery boys and such out of the petty cash, but that's about it."

Elizabeth turned abruptly around in the chair. "What *do* you do, Jed? I mean on a day-to-day basis?"

Jed tugged at his starched collar. "Well, I take care of the office here, write up the ads when they come in, go to the courthouse for any news of horse thieving and fights and such, and at the end of the week I set the type and put the paper to bed. Then on Friday–"

"All right, all right. I see that you keep busy. But Zimri needs more than one assistant. I can see that."

"Yes, ma'am. Especially now that we got the new cylinder press."

"The new press? Why will you need more help with that? Isn't it more efficient than the old one?"

"Yes, ma'am. That's just the point. With the old press, we couldn't print but one page at a time. Me and Peter would take turns at the lever and put out maybe ten pages an hour. With the new press, the pages feed themselves through the bed as fast as you can crank the cylinder—one man can print a hundred pages in an hour."

"A hundred? And only one man is needed? That sounds like you'll need one less man."

"No, ma'am. It means the second man will be freed up to bundle and deliver ten times as many papers. Actually, we'll need at least one more, maybe two, because I got to do other things besides delivering papers."

Elizabeth suddenly understood. "And with ten times as many newspapers, you'll have ten times as many subscribers."

"Yes, ma'am."

"And ten times as many advertisers."

"I don't know why not. There's merchants and planters all over the county that still don't get any paper at all. We just haven't been able to supply them up till now."

Elizabeth spent another hour in the office organizing the accounts receivable and payable, then had Jed drive her back home where they had dinner and discussed more efficient ways of running the business. She decided that she had been wrong at first about Jed's abilities. He was quite intelligent and industrious, but needed guidance.

Once back at the office, Jed made the list of accounts receivable she requested and she called on Mr. Lewis, the milliner.

She lingered for a moment outside the shop, admiring the hats and dresses, but reminded herself that she was on business and went in. Not surprisingly, she found Mr. Lewis to be less than completely sober.

"Ah, the lovely Mrs. Rhodes!" Mr. Lewis put down a coffee cup—which surely did not contain coffee—and came from behind the counter. "At last you've come to visit my emporium. Why, I was just saying to Mrs. Jenkins this morning—"

"I'm afraid I'm not here to shop, Mr. Lewis, though I must admit you have acquired some very pretty things since I was last here." She produced the unpaid bill. "I found this on my husband's desk today—it's dated February 19th."

Mr. Lewis seemed taken aback, but nevertheless reached for his reading glasses and examined the bill. "Oh, yes. I remember this. It was for an advertisement for new spring fashions from Charleston. Sold everything out in two weeks."

"Then why didn't you pay the bill?"

Mr. Lewis looked at her as if this were an odd question, then looked at the bill again. "I don't know. Are you sure I didn't pay it?"

"Quite sure. Jed said he came to collect more than once and you said that all your funds were tied up in inventory."

"I did? Well, yes, that could be. By the time the spring things were sold out, I had to go to Savannah and buy a whole new line of summer things. And now that summer's almost over—"

"Mr. Lewis, this is an endless excuse that has to stop somewhere. If you don't pay this bill now, I'm afraid the *Mercury* will not be able to accept any further advertising from you."

"But the fall line is coming out next month—"

"Then you'll want to be sure your account is up to date so that you can sell all of those warm sweaters and wool dresses, won't you?"

Mr. Lewis looked at her as if he had somehow misjudged her on previous meetings. And indeed he had. "All right, Mrs. Rhodes, I'm sure I've got the money lying around here somewhere. I'll send it over tomorrow with—"

"I must have it now, Mr. Lewis, and I am not leaving until I get it."

Mr. Lewis's eyes seemed to glaze over. "Now...I see. Well, I'm sure I must have it—Marth Ann! Where is that girl? Oh, I suppose she's gone home already. I'll have to get it myself." He went behind the counter, picked up his coffee cup, and drank from it. Then he put it down and pulled out a box from beneath the counter. "Ah, here it is! You never know where Marth Ann is going to put things. How much was that bill?"

"Twenty-eight dollars and seventy-nine cents."

"That much?"

"Apparently the ad ran for six weeks."

"Oh, yes. That's right. February, March, into April—twenty-eight seventy-nine. Here you are, Mrs. Rhodes. Just so happens I sold several hats today. Would you be interested in one for yourself? These bonnets from Charleston are all the rage right now—"

"They're very smart, Mr. Lewis, but I'm afraid I'll have to do my shopping another day." She folded the money and put it in her purse. Then she marked 'paid' on the bill and handed it to him. "Thank you."

"You're welcome, Mrs. Rhodes." He glanced down at her belly. "You know, we have some lovely maternity clothes—just came in from New Orleans."

"I'll put that on my shopping list, Mr. Lewis, but now I have to get back to my husband's office." She started for the door and Mr. Lewis rushed to open it for her.

"Oh, yes, of course. Someone has to mind the store. But doesn't that young man, what's his name—"

"Jed."

"Yes. Jed. Doesn't he take care of things all right?"

"He's learning," she said as she passed through the door to the street.

Mr. Lewis watched her for a few moments and then called after her. "Tell Zimri I'd like to see him when he gets back."

"I certainly will, Mr. Lewis. I'm sure he'll be full of stories to tell."

"Yes, yes, he'll have lots of stories..." He watched her walk across the street, gingerly avoiding mud puddles and horse manure, until she was safely out of hearing range. "And I'll have a story to tell him—women ought not be sent to do a man's business!"

He slammed the door hard enough to rattle the glass, went back behind the counter, and poured a generous portion of whiskey into his cup.

CHAPTER 15

Friday, 13 August

Embarked in the schooner Oregon for Savannah. Sailed with a very light wind and in the afternoon was becalmed near Sandy Hook, landed with the captain, and went to the lighthouse. The land here is entirely a bed of sand composed of dunes and small hills covered with sedge grass, and here and there patches of small bushes and a few stunted plum and willow trees. Near the keeper's house are a considerable number of Lombardy poplars of small size. He has a small garden of artificial soil and a well of tolerable water. Upon the whole, it is a desolate, dismal place...sailed again at 6pm Sunday.

Tuesday, 17 August

Cloudy, wind more favorable and fresh, at noon wind increasing and rainy; by one o'clock a severe gale had set in with dreadful violence and a heavy sea which continually broke over the vessel. The spray, with a heavy rain, seemed almost to render the atmosphere an entire sheet of water so that objects could scarcely be discerned at any distance. Between four and five, the foretopmast broke at the cap and fell between the masts, supported by the rigging. Two men were on the yards clewing up one of the topsails, which had blown loose when the mast gave way. One man fell to the deck, striking it on his head and shoulders. The other clung to the falling rigging and managed to climb down, but was very badly bruised, and both were carried below into the cabin. The jib boom was carried away with the topmast, the flying jib and the foresail were split and torn in two, the gaff topsail blown into tatters.

The wreckage was cut from the mast by the first mate after very great and dangerous exertions, and it fell overboard. One spar stove a hole through the main deck as it fell.

Night set in, and the gale continued in all is fury till eleven o'clock when the wind gradually lulled and became nearly calm. The next morning the decks were cleared, the jib and the mainsail, double-reefed, were set, the vessel got under way, and we steered for Norfolk to repair the damages and deliver the disabled sailors to a hospital.

Once in port at Norfolk, Zimri and the other passengers were directed to a hotel where they were informed that they would continue their journey by stage. The next morning Zimri took a stroll around the town, which he found to be in somewhat of a state of decay, but nevertheless seemed bustling with commerce. The most noteworthy characteristic of the place, in his view, was that fig trees seemed to flourish as in no other place he had visited.

That evening he took supper in the hotel. Several of the passengers were from either Georgia or South Carolina, while most were headed to their homes in Virginia and North Carolina.

As he sat down at a table along with a Mr. Heekins of Twiggs County, Georgia, and a Mr. Demarest of Saint Simons Island, a well-dressed black man entered the main lobby, and approached the desk. This event attracted a certain amount of attention from the patrons, including Zimri, but was unremarked upon until the man asked for lodging, as he was traveling to Savannah to see his niece.

"Sorry, no vacancy," the desk clerk said.

"But I was referred to you by the manager of the Norfolk Inn, who said you certainly would have a room available."

"Ship just came in from a storm. All busted up. Seems like most of the passengers came here."

"He said most of them came to *his* place."

"Don't know about his place. We're full up."

"I see."

The black man, who looked to be about thirty-five and of medium build, looked about him in despair. "Can you recommend another establishment?"

"There's the Boatswain's Tavern down by the wharf. They take mostly sailors, though. Kind of a rough crowd."

"Oh, no, I don't think that would do. Isn't there some kind of boarding house nearby?"

The desk clerk scratched beneath his chin. "Well, there's ol' Hattie Crawford's place. Colored lady. She might have room."

"Can you direct me there?"

"It's on the other side of town. Don't rightly know how to get there myself."

The black man sighed. "All right. I suppose I'll have to ask someone else along the way. I'm a bit thirsty, though. Any objection if I have a drink?"

The desk clerk looked at him skeptically for a moment, then nodded his head towards the bar. The black man proceeded into the dining area, where he nodded towards Zimri and his companions, but receiving no acknowledgment, continued on to the bar.

"I'll have a whiskey and soda," he said to the bartender.

The bartender looked at him as skeptically as had the desk clerk, and continued drying a glass without saying a word.

"I'm sorry, you must not have heard me," the black man said. "I said I'd like to—"

"We don't serve no niggers here, Mister," the bartender said. "Now, do like Mr. Jeffers said and get on over to Hattie's where you belong."

The black man started to protest, seemed to think better of it, and turned to leave.

"It's on me," Zimri said.

All eyes turned Zimri's way, including those of his startled companions.

"I said it's on me. The man's come a long way and he's thirsty."

The bartender seemed frozen to the spot. The black man looked at Zimri in wonderment, then at the bartender as if curious to see whether he would comply.

"You a guest here, Mister?" the bartender said to Zimri.

"I am indeed," Zimri said.

"Room number?"

"Fourteen."

"You'll have to sign."

"Glad to."

The bartender set about preparing the whiskey and soda and the black man once again approached the bar. But he hesitated a moment, then turned to Zimri.

"Thank you, sir. Thank you, Mister—"

"Rhodes. Zimri Rhodes. It's my pleasure, sir. Enjoy your whiskey,"

"Yes. Yes, I will."

Zimri thought of joining the black man at the bar, but caught the censorious looks of his dinner companions and thought better of it. It wasn't that he was afraid for himself, but that he might push things too far and create a disturbance that could careen out of control.

"These Northern niggers are different," Mr. Heekins said in a low voice. "They don't seem to know they're not like white people."

"He seems to have a certain amount of refinement about him,"

Mr. Demarest said. "Unfortunately, that makes little difference to these crackers. If anything, they detest them for what they consider to be their superior airs."

Zimri was surprised at this insight on the part of Mr. Demarest, who owned a large plantation and was said to be master of over three hundred slaves. "He's a free man. And an American citizen. He has the same rights under the Constitution as the rest of us."

Mr. Demarest smiled. He was a much older man than Zimri, perhaps sixty, with white hair and a goatee. "I see now that you are an idealist, Mr. Rhodes. That's a very good thing. But you should not imagine that you can overturn an institution that has lasted for two centuries by citing words from a piece of paper that was written less than fifty years ago."

"I don't imagine that I could, Mr. Demarest. I just thought that the man was thirsty and entitled to a drink."

"Sure he is," Heekins said, looking uncomfortable with the drift of this conversation. "Sure he is. I just hope he don't come over here and set down and think he's as good as we are. Nothing wrong with being kind to a stranger, Zimri, but these Yankee free blacks got to know their place just like their Southern brethren. No veneer of fancy clothes and high falutin' manners is gonna change that."

Zimri didn't think this argument was worth refuting, and changed the subject. Their supper arrived and while they ate, the black man finished his drink and left without saying another word. Zimri wondered what would become of him.

The next morning Zimri awoke early, packed his portmanteau, and carried it to the front of the hotel where he was told that the stage would pick him and the other passengers up for Fayetteville and other points south.

Upon climbing into the stage he was surprised to see the black man from the night before sitting in one corner of the vehicle dressed in a freshly pressed suit, while he had on the same clothes as he wore the night before.

"Good morning, Mr. Rhodes. I trust you slept well."

"That I did, Mr...."

"Sparks. Augustus Omri Sparks. My friends call me Omri."

Mr. Heekin, who had immediately followed Zimri into the stage, looked at Mr. Sparks as if he were a particularly persistent rodent that resisted all means of extermination.

"Omri, then," Zimri said, extending his hand. "My friends call me Zimri."

"Zimri?" Sparks said. "Why, our biblical namesakes were deadly enemies. I hope that won't prove to be the case for us."

Zimri chuckled as he settled into the seat next to Mr. Sparks. "I certainly hope not. If I recall correctly, Omri besieged Zimri in the citadel at Tirzah and set fire to his palace."

"And Omri became King of Israel," Mr. Sparks said.

"And reigned for seven years, I believe," Mr. Demarest said, taking his seat. "While poor Zimri reigned for a mere seven days."

"My father gave me that name," Zimri said, "as a warning to stay out of politics."

Even Mr. Heekins seemed to find this amusing, and all three laughed heartily as two other passengers entered the stage. One introduced himself as George Blanchard, of Edgefield, South Carolina, and he in turn introduced his wife, a plump, middle-aged woman who admonished her husband for not mentioning that he was the Chief Circuit Judge of Edgefield County.

After the stage started moving, Zimri couldn't resist finding out more about this well-spoken black man. It turned out that he was from Philadelphia, where he owned a book-binding business. His parents had both been slaves on a plantation near Savannah and had each bought their freedom before he was born. They moved to Philadelphia, where his father established his own harness shop and earned enough money to send all of his children to parochial schools. After working for a short time in the harness shop, Omri was apprenticed to a local printer, and combining his love of books with a good sense for business, started his bookbinding manufactory.

All the passengers seemed to listen attentively to this discourse.

"I seem to recall hearing you tell the desk clerk last night that you were going to visit your niece in Savannah," Zimri said. They were approaching Suffolk, about thirty miles south of Norfolk, and the road was proving to be rough.

"That's right," Mr. Sparks said. "She's my older sister's daughter. She's the last one."

"Last? What do you mean," the judge said.

"To be held in slavery. I'm going to buy her freedom."

The rest of the passengers fell silent at this revelation. Mr. Heekins looked out the window and upon the low, swampy soil in this part of the state. Mr. Demarest seemed preoccupied with the card game he had struck up with Mrs. Blanchard. Mrs. Blanchard seemed oblivious to the whole conversation.

"And may I ask," the judge said, "how much the purchase price will be?"

"Six hundred dollars," Mr. Sparks said. "Her owner agreed only after a kitchen fire left her crippled. She's lost all the feeling in her right hand."

"I would say you were cheated, Mr. Sparks," Mr. Demarest said without looking up from his cards. "A house slave who can't lift a kettle or stir a pot isn't worth half that. She's not even good for serving."

Mr. Sparks looked at Mr. Demarest with the deepest resentment. Then he looked out the window at the passing scene of woods, swamp, and decaying foliage. "She's worth twice that to me."

Another veil of silence fell over the passengers. Zimri could think of nothing constructive or helpful to ease the tension, which was palpable. Finally, the stage rounded a bend and they could see the town of Suffolk looming into view.

"Not much of a town, is it?" Mr. Heekins said.

"It's the county seat," the judge said. "There's more going on here than one might suppose."

"Corn, hogs, peanuts," Mr. Demarest said. "Tobacco to the west. Some of the largest plantations in the state just a few miles from here."

"I win!" Mrs. Blanchard said "You haven't been paying attention, Mr. Demarest. You missed the last two tricks."

Mr. Demarest looked down at the cards and sighed. "You're too clever for me, Mrs. Blanchard. But I shall be rejuvenated after dinner and sure to give you a run for your money."

"Harriet," the judge said, "must you be so mercenary?"

"Pooh, Judge." Mrs. Blanchard picked up the cards from the makeshift game board. "Don't you know that Mr. Demarest is one of the richest planters in Georgia? This may be our only chance to profit at his expense."

All the passengers laughed at this comment except Mr. Sparks, who continued to stare out the window at the little town of Suffolk.

CHAPTER 16

By the end of the week, Elizabeth had collected twenty-eight of the thirty outstanding debts owed to the *Mercury*. Of the two remaining unpaid, one of the merchants had gone out of business and the other, Mr. Friedland, the haberdasher, was out of town on a buying trip. His wife, Mary, who Elizabeth knew as an avid supporter of the Committee to Establish a Lending Library, claimed that her husband did not allow her to either write checks or enter the cash box, which he kept padlocked and retained the only key. He would return on Monday, she said.

After depositing seven hundred and eighty-four dollars with Mr. Hamilton at the bank (who was astonished to see the bills neatly stacked on his desk and banded into denominations of 1, 5, 10, and 20 dollars), Elizabeth returned to the office, where she worked into the evening organizing the books. At seven, she was persuaded by Jed to leave the few remaining entries for Monday, and she went home for supper.

"Lawd," Maybelle said as she served her a bowl of Brunswick stew. "You working as hard as any nigger out in the fields, Miz Lisbeth. Ain't you skeered the baby gone drop out fo' its time?"

"The baby's just fine, Maybelle. In fact, the appetite I've had this week has probably done more to nourish the child in one week than everything I put in my stomach for the previous twenty."

"You ain't lyin' 'bout that. Lawd, I never seen such a change in a woman. From lyin' on the swing all day hardly eatin' nothin,' to ridin' all over town squeezin' money outa peoples like they was turnips with one last drop of blood in 'em. And then workin' wid the books till midnight, just like Mr. Rhodes."

"Mr. Rhodes works long hours all right, but he apparently has paid scant attention to the books. Have we got any more of those delicious biscuits?"

"I reckon so." Maybelle started for the kitchen. "I reckon we gone have to buy another ten-pound sack of flour tomorrow, the way you been packin' them things away."

Elizabeth smiled, ingested another spoonful of her stew, and spread the latest issue of the *Mercury* out on the table. She hoped Zimri would like her idea of placing little rosettes at the end of each article to separate it from the next. Jed had resisted the idea as being too feminine, but she had pointed out that Zimri was a lover of roses and all beautiful things, and there was no shame in that. Besides, the *Mercury* logotype, which appeared at the head of each page was masculine enough, even if Mercury did look a bit like a cherub from a painting by Rubens.

What a fascinating business! There was news from other news-papers in other states, including New York, and even from the capitals of Europe. To be sure, the news from London and Paris was at least four months old, but that was better than no news at all. And the fashions! What provincial boobies the women of Paris must think American women are. Did they still wear powdered wigs piled high on their heads like Madame Pompadour?

She thought of Randolph. Odd that she hadn't thought of him all week. Was he in Paris now? She pictured him at an elegant ball at Versailles kissing the hand of a courtesan complete with penciled-in beauty mark on her cheek. No doubt the beauty mark would shift its position for each new ball, depending on the time of day and the occasion. And no doubt Randolph, who must be improving his French at a rapid rate, would say all the right things to this contemporary Madame Pompadour, even reciting poetry in her ear as she blushes and giggles.

"Lawd, you done swallowed all that stew fo' I could fetch the biscuits out the oven." Maybelle stood at her side with a plate of biscuits in one hand and a ladle in the other. "Plenty mo,' though. It good to see you eatin' right."

"Thank you, Maybelle. I think I will have a biscuit or two."

"Sho.' Eats all you want." Maybelle peered cautiously over Elizabeth's shoulder. "What all that writin' say?"

"It says that there are revolutions going on all over Europe."

"Rebolutions? What kind of rebolutions?"

"Well, the French, the Italians, the Russians—they all want more democracy."

"Mo' democracy—you mean like the kind we got here?"

"Yes—American democracy is the envy of all the world."

"They got slaves over there in France and It'ly?"

Elizabeth was beginning to feel uncomfortable with the drift of this conversation. "Well, not exactly. They have serfs, which is almost the same thing."

"Then these 'serfs,' you call'em, they want the democracy?"

"Yes. I think so. But mostly it's just ordinary people. They don't have the right to vote, they're taxed too much without their permission, they—"

"They want to be free."

Elizabeth hesitated. "Yes, that's right. They want to be a free people. To determine their own affairs."

Maybelle seemed to be struggling with this explanation. "These 'serfs'—they gone be free, too?"

"I don't know. I suppose some of them will be."

"Then democracy ain't fo' ever'body."

Elizabeth closed the paper and folded it into a neat packet. "I think it is for everybody—eventually. But it has to take place in stages. Not everyone is ready for it."

Maybelle seemed to consider this for a long time "You want any mo' biscuits?"

"No, thank you, Maybelle. I'm stuffed. That was delicious."

"I'll make you a mess o' eggs and bacon in the mawn'in. You'll need it if you gone keep workin' like this."

"Tomorrow's Saturday. I don't think I'll go into the office to-morrow—though I expect Jed will be there."

"I'll make you the eggs and bacon anyhow. You eatin' fo' two now."

As Maybelle returned to the kitchen to clean up, Elizabeth sat at the table staring into a candle flame. She had never had such a conversation with Maybelle before and she found it disturbing. There was a contradiction in our democracy, wasn't there? How could slavery be justified? And yet she found it hard to imagine Maybelle or Otis, or Old George behaving as responsible, free adults. Why they couldn't even read! They were more like chil-dren than adults for all of their experience and wisdom. Wisdom…yes, she had to admit that they were wise in some ways. But it was more a kind of animal cunning than wisdom. And if all the Negroes were suddenly free, what would happen to the planta-tion system? How could planters like her father survive if they had to pay wages like the factory owners up north? It took hundreds of slaves to extract a modicum of wealth from the soil. And unlike a factory, which could run twenty-four hours a day, seven days a week through all kinds of weather, an agricultural enterprise was subject to everything from winter storms, to floods, to parasites, to total crop failure. What if the planter had to pay his laborers during those times when the land was unproductive?

Charlotte was awake. "I'll see about her, Maybelle." She rose from the table and went to the bedroom. It was still light outside, but long shadows were cast across the room from the last rays of the sun. She picked the baby up, put her over her shoulder and patted her on her back. Then she sat in a rocker and began singing a lullaby and Charlotte seemed to go right back to sleep again. A remarkable child! Sleeps most of the day, rarely cries, sleeps again through the night as if it would take a bolt of lightning to get her attention. She wondered if, in fact, something were wrong with her. She was slow to learn to walk, and she seemed to avoid it whenever possible. She seemed to prefer exploring rugs, furniture, fire tools, and even books on all fours to any upright adventures whatever. Well, at least it kept her out of the cupboards.

As she rocked back and forth, nearly falling asleep herself, she suddenly became aware of someone at the front door. Then she heard Maybelle trudging from the kitchen through the hearth room. Who could that be at such a time?

"Where's Miss Lisbeth?"

"She in the bedroom wid Charlotte, Massa Jamie."

"Tell her I'm here to see her."

"Yas, suh."

Elizabeth put Charlotte carefully back into her crib, left the room and closed the door behind her.

Jamie looked tired and haggard, as if he had been laboring in the fields all day himself.

"What is it, Jamie?"

"You got any whiskey?"

"Of course. Maybelle, fetch that bottle of whiskey that Master Zimri keeps in the sideboard there."

"Yes'um."

"Sit down, Jamie, and tell me what's happened." Jamie hung his hat on a peg by the door and made his way to Zimri's favorite armchair, where he slumped down into it like a sack of corn meal. "You better sit down, too, Elizabeth. This is hard news."

She sat down on the sofa opposite the armchair and waited expectantly.

"It's Daddy," Jamie said. "He passed away this morning."

Elizabeth gasped and brought her hand to her mouth. "How?"

Maybelle, who showed no reaction to the news, put the bottle of whiskey along with a glass down on a small table next to the armchair.

Jamie poured some whiskey into the glass. "Doc Parcher says his lungs filled up with fluid during the night. He drowned."

Elizabeth was stunned. A flood of memories associated with her father raced through her mind. He always seemed so young! He couldn't be gone—just like that. "How could it happen, Jamie? He seemed to be doing just fine. Doc Parcher said—"

"Apparently Luther's pitchfork penetrated one of his lungs after all." He downed the whiskey and poured some more. "Maybe both lungs. He had been complaining about shortness of breath for the last week or so. Parcher says the puncture could have sealed itself and then broke loose later when he was out riding."

"Oh, Jamie, you shouldn't have let him—"

"Now don't go blaming me! You know how Daddy was about being sick or injured. He got on his feet as soon as he possibly could and acted like nothing was wrong at all."

"I'm not blaming you. Of course you couldn't have stopped him. How's Mother taking it?"

"Not well." Jamie threw down the second shot of whiskey and poured another. "This is good stuff—I didn't even know Zimri drank whiskey."

"He doesn't much. But he says that his guests have a right to expect the best."

"I might have to revise my opinion of him. When's he getting back from New York?"

"Next week, I think. Maybelle, I think I'll have a glass, too."

"Yes'um." Maybelle retrieved a second glass from the sideboard and poured some whiskey in it. She handed it to Elizabeth. "Now you just sip it—like a lady."

"All right." Elizabeth took a sip and frowned. "Oh, it tastes awful!"

Jamie smiled. "Always does the first time. Put some water in it, Maybelle. Take a little hair of the dog out of it."

"Yes, suh. That a good idea." Maybelle went to the sideboard for the water.

Elizabeth ventured another sip. "Actually, it's not so bad as that. Just bitter." She set the glass down on the coffee table. "When's the funeral?"

"Monday. At the Clinton Presbyterian Church."

Maybelle returned with a pitcher of water and filled the glass.

"Thank you, Maybelle."

Elizabeth watched as Maybelle returned to the kitchen, and then said to Jamie in a whisper: "What will happen to Luther?"

"I just turned him over to the sheriff. He'll be tried for murder next month when the circuit judge comes through."

"Murder? Oh, Jamie—they'll hang him!"

"Of course they will. I would have strangled him with my own hands if Mama hadn't reminded me of my Christian upbringing. At least this way, it's legal."

"But Jamie, I don't think Luther meant to kill him. Besides, we don't even know if that's what caused Daddy to suffocate."

Jamie emitted a snort of derision. "It ain't hard to figure out, Elizabeth. Doc Parcher says his lungs filled with fluid from a puncture. What else could it be?"

"I don't know. But what good will it do to hang Luther? He's getting to be an old man, and according to the reports I get, he's worked harder than ever since...since the incident."

Jamie threw another shot of the whiskey down. "You've gotten soft in the head since you married Zimri, Elizabeth. It's that Yankee sympathy for the niggers. The Yankees don't know them the way we do. They're fine in their place, but once they think they can get away with anything, they'll steal you blind and cut your throat on the way out. Imagine what the other niggers would do if they thought Luther had gotten away with killing Massa James. Why, they'd go hog wild! And you and me would be next on the list."

She considered this for a moment. "I suppose you're right. But hanging Luther's not going to bring Daddy back. And all the darkies will think it's unjust. They do have a sense of justice, you know."

Jamie smiled sardonically. "And I suppose they have a sense of double-entry bookkeeping, too. Do you think they could run a plantation for five minutes without someone telling them what to do?"

"They're just not ready to manage their own affairs." She wondered why she was suddenly defending the rights of black slaves. Was she just being contrary to irritate Jamie? "Even Zimri is muddle-headed when it comes to accounting."

"That's not all he's muddle-headed about." Jamie put down his glass and rose from his chair. "I didn't come here to argue about the delicate feelings of black folks, Elizabeth. I came to tell you about Daddy. Now that I've done that, I'll be on my way."

She rose and put her arms around him. "Oh, Jamie, I'm sorry. I didn't mean to argue with you, or to criticize anything you've done. I know you're doing what you think is right."

"Doesn't sound like you think so. I don't know where you're getting these ideas, unless it's from Zimri."

"Zimri's not even here. Don't you think I have thoughts of my own from time to time?"

Jamie glanced at the newspaper lying on the table. "Sure I do. You get'em from...sure I do. I've got to go, Elizabeth. Mama's in a pitiful state. And Patsy's retreated into a make-believe world where she thinks Daddy's off on some mission to awaken Sleeping Beauty. She won't come out of her room."

"Poor Patsy—Daddy was such a swash-buckling hero to her. I'll have Otis drive me out to Belle Oaks tomorrow. You need a woman to put the house in order."

"That's the best news I've heard since I've been here. Thanks for the whiskey. I'll see you tomorrow."

Elizabeth accompanied him to the front door and watched as he walked down the path to the road and got into the carriage. As he drove off she was aware of Maybelle standing behind her.

"Is they gone hang Luther, sho' nuff?"

She turned to look at Maybelle. She seemed older than ever, with deep creases in her coal-black forehead, and rheumy brown eyes. "I don't know, Maybelle. It'll be up to a jury to decide."

"Jury?" Maybelle shook her head. "Ain't no black man gone get no fair trial from no white jury. Luther might as well hang his own self right now."

Elizabeth started to protest, but knew that Maybelle was right. She watched as she walked back to the kitchen, wringing her hands in her apron even though her hands must have been dry.

She went back out onto the porch and sat in the swing. The air was warm and humid, though there was a bit of a breeze from the southeast. She thought of her father. She had idolized him as a young girl, just as Patsy did, and like Patsy, she was always made to believe that she was his favorite. When she defied him on the issue of her marriage to Zimiri, there was naturally an estrangement for a while, but in the years since the wedding he had accepted this state of affairs, and even praised Zimri as a model husband and citizen.

What would become of her mother? She could barely make a decision about her own wardrobe without her husband's advice. Would she remain at Belle Oaks? Ah, Belle Oaks. It belonged to Jamie now. She suddenly realized that her brother was a rich man. Would he marry? And if so, would it be to that feather-brained Fanny Cochran?

She plumped up two of the cushions, set them in a corner of the swing, and lay her head on them. She was seized with a panicky feeling of abandonment. Her father dead, Zimri in New York—

how did she know he would come back? He must have already encountered scores of women who were far more sophisticated than she...she was still hardly more than a girl, after all, a teenager from rural Georgia who had never been farther than Charleston...Did Zimri really love her? Did Randolph?

Randolph...she saw him dancing at a soirèe with a beautiful Parisian woman and then languidly floating down the Seine with this same woman in a open boat, the bright torches along the embankments casting flickering shadows across the young couple's faces. And as the young woman's face came more clearly into view, she saw that...it was herself.

CHAPTER 17

The stage pulled up to a tavern on the outskirts of Suffolk and disembarked its passengers for the mid-day meal. The air was humid and still, and dark clouds gathered to the north.

"Storm coming," Mr. Heekins said. "This place looks like it gets plenty of rain."

"Rich soil," Mr. Demarest said, picking up a handful and examining it. He let it fall between his fingers and brushed his hands off. "Not much else to amuse the traveler it seems."

No one disputed Mr. Demarest's assessment of the town's entertainment potential, and the six passengers entered the tavern, where they were met by the owner, a swarthy man in his thirties with his hair pulled back in a ponytail.

"What can I do for you folks?" the owner said.

"We're on our way south," Judge Blanchard said. "The bridge into Suffolk was washed out and we had to detour to your charming little village. We had hoped to revitalize our spirits with some home-cooked food."

"You came just in time, Mr.—"

"Blanchard."

"*Judge* Blanchard," Mrs. Blanchard said.

"Judge? Well, yes sir, we've got a table over yonder by the winder that ought to accommodate your party. Got fresh country ham today with mashed potatoes and corn on the cob. And your servant there can eat in the kitchen."

The judge glanced at Mr. Sparks, as did the others. "This gentleman is not my servant, sir, but a fellow traveler from Philadelphia. I trust he'll be able to sit with us."

The hotel owner looked at Mr. Sparks again with closer scrutiny, and then turned his eyes back to the judge. "We don't get many free blacks here, Judge. People 'round here wouldn't know what to make of him settin' at the same table with white folks."

"If they ask, you can simply correct their misconceptions."

"Ain't that simple, Judge. Me, I don't mind. Used to work in a seafarin' restaurant in Boston. But the folks here, they wouldn't understand."

"What about outside?" Zimri said. "You've got several tables out there and no one seems to be using them."

The owner turned and looked out through the open windows. "You'd have to use two tables. One for yourselves and one for Mr., uh—"

"Sparks," Sparks said.

"Oh, it's so hot outside," Mrs. Blanchard said, fanning herself. "Can't we all just sit inside by the window at one table?"

"No, ma'am," the owner said. "I just explained—"

"We'll take two tables," Zimri said. "One inside by the window and the other outside next to the brook. I could use the fresh air."

The owner seemed to be on the verge of protest, but turned abruptly and led them to the table by the window, where he pulled out a chair for Mrs. Blanchard. As Zimri and Sparks approached, he indicated the open door to the garden with a curt movement of his hand. Sparks passed through the door and Zimri followed. Mrs. Blanchard sat down in her chair, and the judge followed suit, as did the others.

"Damn nigger's a lot of trouble," Mr. Heekins said, tucking a napkin into his collar.

Mr. Demarest looked around the dining room at the other guests, who were still looking at them with curiosity. "It seems that the general populace is not ready for this."

"Mr. Sparks is a free man," the judge said, spreading his napkin across his lap. "He has a right to dine where he pleases."

"You may know the law, Judge," Heekins said, "But that just ain't the way it is here in the South. Like Mr. Demarest said, the people ain't ready for it."

Zimri and Sparks made their way to a table beside the little brook that Zimri had spotted from the foyer, and sat down. It was actually a picnic table, constructed of long, broad planks nailed to a frame, with bench seats and no table cloth.

Zimri noted the perennials on either side of the brook. "Primroses."

"We call those 'Quaker's Bonnets' in Philadelphia," Sparks said. "They do better in light shade. The soil here, though, looks rich in humus."

"You have a garden?"

"Just a small one. Out back of the house." Sparks laughed for the first time since they'd met. "Hardly bigger than a hog pen. But the soil's good."

"Any vegetables?"

"Sure. Tomatoes, mostly. But apples and pears, too."

"Pears don't seem to do that well in Georgia. Same with apples. At least not the succulent kind you get in New England."

"That where you from?"

Zimri smiled. "How'd you guess?"

"Got a good ear for accents. I'd say...Connecticut."

"Right you are, Mr. Sparks. I—"

"Omri."

"Omri. But it's been ten years since I lived there. Thought I'd picked up a bit of the Southern drawl in that time."

"You got 'Yankee' written all over you."

They both laughed at this when a black woman of about nineteen or twenty approached them. "Y'all gonna have the ham and 'taters?"

"Is there a choice?" Omri said.

"Sure. You can have grits instead of 'taters, or yams instead of corn."

"I'll have potatoes and corn," Sparks said.

"And I'll have the yams," Zimri said.

"Yams and 'taters, or yams and grits?"

"Potatoes, yams and corn."

"Can't have no three vegetables. Got to be two."

"Why?"

"It's the rules. But if you want—"

"What if I dispense with the ham?" Zimri said.

The girl put one hand on her hip. "What if I just bring you a whole mess of food and you can pick what you like?"

"You sure it's not against the rules?" Zimri said.

"I just tole you it's against the rules. But for certain gentlemen of certain means, I can break the rules—just this once."

Zimri smiled. "There's an extra two bits in it for you."

The girl looked over her shoulder. "I'll see what I can do. Now you just set there and watch the babblin' brook, and I'll be back directly with your vittles."

Their eyes followed her as she returned to the tavern.

"She's a saucy one, isn't she?" Zimri said.

"Got a wiggle in her walk that gets your attention," Sparks said. "That she does."

Sparks suddenly turned contemplative. "I wonder if she's free?"

"What do you mean?"

"Oh, I don't mean that. I mean, is she a free soul?"

"You'll have to ask her."

When the young woman returned with several plates of food and set them down, Sparks put the question to her.

"I be free in seven years," she said.

"You're an indentured servant?"

"That's right. My massa done sold me and my husband to Mr. McCabe here last spring. Mr. McCabe say he need a cook and a houseman, and if we works hard, and don't give him no trouble, he set us free at the end of our time. Got the papers to prove it."

"That's mighty generous of Mr. McCabe," Zimri said. "Why wouldn't he just keep you if he paid good money for you?"

"Mr. McCabe say he was an indentured servant hisself—that how he got to Boston from Ireland. Besides, he say slaves ain't got no reason to work hard—they got nothin' to look forward to."

"And what do you think?" Sparks said.

She shrugged. "Seven years a long time. But at least we knows we be free then."

"Hey, Gwen!"

All three of them turned and saw two young white men sitting at a table nearer the tavern. They were wearing the aprons of their trade and obviously drunk.

"You gonna keep yappin' with the Yankees, or you gonna get your pretty little tail over here and bring us some more grog?"

Gwen hesitated. "I got to go." Then she moved quickly to do the other men's bidding.

"White trash," Sparks said.

"Oh, I wouldn't characterize them as 'trash,'" Zimri said. "They're just apprentices whose master has neglected to keep an eye on them."

Sparks picked up his knife and fork and began cutting into his ham, all the while keeping his eyes fixed on the two white men. "We'll see."

Zimri likewise began eating and the two said little to each other until they were finished. They saw Mr. Heekins lean out of the door to the tavern and signal that the others were finished and ready to go. Gwen returned and collected their empty plates and started for the kitchen, but not before being pinched on the bottom by one of the apprentices. They roared with laughter as Gwen dropped a plate, bent over to pick it up, and was pinched again.

Zimri and Sparks rose and started for the tavern, with Sparks ahead. As he passed by the table of the young apprentices, one of them stuck his boot out and caused Sparks to fall face forward. He caught himself with his hands and knees, but mud from recent rains spattered his suit.

The young men again roared with laughter.

"Ain't that a shame," the one who tripped him said. "The poor Yankee nigger went and tripped over himself and got his checkerboard suit all muddy."

Sparks said nothing, but slowly rose to his feet and brushed himself off.

"I'd say you owe the gentleman an apology," Zimri said.

"Forget it, Zimri," Sparks said. "Let's go."

"Just a minute, Omri," Zimri said. "These boys need to learn something about good manners. On your feet, young man."

The young apprentice who had tripped Sparks wiped his mouth with his napkin and seemed to consider Zimri's size and bulk. He was no more than sixteen, but of a stout build. "Ain't gettin' up to apologize to no nigger."

"I see." Zimri, in one quick motion grabbed the boy's right ear, twisted it so that he cried out in pain, and jerked him to his feet. "Now tell Mr. Sparks you're sorry, or I'll have to report you and your friends to your employer. I'm sure he doesn't know you're out drinking when you should be minding the shop."

"Ow!"

"It's easy," Zimri said, twisting the ear even tighter. "Just say, 'I'm sorry, Mr. Sparks—it won't happen again.'"

"Leggo! All right, I'll say it!"

Zimri relaxed his grip slightly.

"I'm sorry, Mister, uh—"

"Sparks."

"Sparks. It won't happen again."

Zimri released the boy's ear. "I suggest you boys curtail your holiday and get back to the shop before your employer discovers what you've been up to."

"Yes, sir. We was just leavin.'"

Sparks walked briskly ahead and Zimri followed as several of the guests stared. Once they had paid their bill and emerged from the front of the tavern where the stage was waiting, Sparks spoke to Zimri in a low whisper:

"I appreciate what you did, but the whole thing could have gotten a lot uglier."

"It was pretty ugly from the start. I didn't think those boys should have gotten away with it."

"Sometimes it's better to let sleeping dogs lie." Sparks climbed into the stage where the others were waiting.

Zimri stood in the road for a moment, somewhat disturbed by Sparks' censure. To what lengths should a man go to defend one who does not wish to be defended?

"Let's go, Mister," the driver said. "We got to make up for lost time."

Zimri climbed into the stage, pulled the door shut, and took his seat.

"Idealism," Mr. Demarest said as the stage moved off, "is a very good thing—in its place."

Zimri looked at Mr. Demarest, then the others, who all seemed to agree with the statement. He suddenly felt foolish, like a young man who has intervened in a family quarrel only to be chastised by all its members.

CHAPTER 18

The one hundred year-old oaks that flanked the drive to the main house always gave Elizabeth a sense of serenity and peace. The trees, planted by her great grandfather, were spaced at precise intervals so that they formed a corridor nearly a mile long. The gaps between the trees offered a view of the fields, planted mostly with cotton, and were being picked by hundreds of slaves, many of them children.

The presence of children in these fields had never given her cause for concern before, but now she wondered if some of them might belong to Luther's grown children.

"Otis?"

"Yessum?" Otis was driving the gig with his usual aplomb, staring straight ahead and apparently thinking of nothing more than the job of keeping the horse moving at a steady gait.

"Does Luther have grandchildren?"

"Oh, yessum. He have…let's see…there be Cory and Ada and Thomas by his daughter Jessie. Then there be Michael, Teresa, Mary, Annie May, and Henry by his second eldest, Bertie. Then there be—"

"And do they work in the fields?"

"Oh, this be pickin' season, Miz Lisbeth. I 'spect most of 'em out in the fields 'cept the youngest."

Elizabeth considered this for a few moments as they approached the grand brick façade of the house, with its six Corinthian columns surmounted by a frieze depicting figures from Greek mythology.

"Do they know their grandfather is in jail?"

Otis looked askance at her. "Don't rightly know, Miz Lisbeth. I 'spect they too young to understand what it all about."

They pulled into the gravel drive and rounded the marble fountain that spewed forth hundreds of gallons of water per hour from the mouths of dolphins, splashing the feet of Artemis, goddess of the hunt.

"What do you think, Otis? About Luther and Master James, I mean."

Otis pulled up to the front steps and one of two liveried slaves moved quickly to take charge of the horse while the other offered to help Elizabeth down from the gig. "I don't rightly know, Miz Lisbeth. Seem like Luther be out of his head that day. But then he and the Massa done got into spats befo' and nothin' come of it. Seems to me, it was some kind of accident. Luther never meant no harm to nobody."

"Well, we'll have to wait for a jury to decide."

"Yessum."

Otis' skepticism on this point did not escape Elizabeth's attention as she was helped down from the gig.

Jamie appeared at the huge oaken front doors. "At last you're here." As Otis moved off in the gig, he came down the steps and took her hand. "You can go right in to see Mama. She's in her bedroom staring at a portrait of Daddy and refusing to eat."

"Has Doctor Parcher been here?"

"Yesterday. He says the only cure for her is time. Meanwhile, she could starve to death."

Jamie ushered her into the bedroom where she found her mother in bed, her head propped up on pillows and still in her nightgown. She seemed not to notice that her daughter had just entered the room.

"Oh, Mama, I'm so sorry about Daddy." She rushed to the bed, kissed her mother on the cheek and took her hand in hers. "We all are. But you mustn't stay in bed all day. And you've got to eat something."

Her mother continued to stare at the portrait above the mantelpiece. "He was such an odd man."

"Odd?" Elizabeth sat down on the bed. "What do you mean?"

"He refused to wear pajamas in bed."

"Pajamas?"

"He said it was unhealthy. Whenever you children would come in to wake him when you were little, or ask of some favor, it was all I could do to prevent his getting out from beneath the covers and taking you in his arms. He had no sense of shame."

Elizabeth stifled a giggle. "Shame? There was no shame in that. I always thought he just wanted to stay in bed. And Jamie and I would leap on top of him and pull at his whiskers."

Her mother looked at her for the first time since she had entered the room and smiled. "And he would cry out in mock pain. He liked that."

After an hour of reminiscences about her husband, Mrs. Blake was finally persuaded to eat some breakfast. Elizabeth had some coffee with her and then took her leave to attend to the household. She visited Patsy, who seemed to have emerged from her 'fantasy world,' as Jamie termed it, on her own accord.

"You know that Papa's gone to Heaven now, don't you?" Elizabeth said to her.

"Oh, I don't think so."

"You don't? Why not?"

"He always said that he wouldn't want to go to a heaven that would let him in."

Elizabeth smiled and recalled that he had said the same thing to her when she was a child. She kissed Patsy on the forehead. "You're probably right. He'd rather be out hunting."

"Like Orion."

"Orion?"

"Yes. The constellation. Papa would be much happier as a constellation in the sky than in some place boring like Heaven. And he could probably persuade God to let him have a spot near the Big Dipper—there's plenty of room."

"Yes, I suppose there is."

Elizabeth came away from this conversation not altogether convinced that Jamie was wrong in his assessment of Patsy's mental state, but she was at least reassured that the girl had emerged from her initial shock.

She spent the rest of the day putting the house in order, instructing the servants to continue with their regular duties regardless of the erratic behavior of their mistress and the absence of their former master, to whom they were accustomed to giving instant obedience. Jamie had already asserted himself as the de facto manager of the estate, but he spent most of his time in the fields and stables. Many of the household slaves still regarded him as a boy, albeit an obstreperous and volatile one. So she appointed Carmichael as the head steward, a position that he accepted with enthusiasm.

"You will answer only to Master Jamie," she said to Carmichael.

"Yessum."

"And don't say 'yessum' anymore. A head steward must speak properly or he won't be respected. Say 'yes, ma'am.'"

Carmichael looked hesitant. "Yes, ma'am."

"Good. And to unmarried young ladies like Patsy, you must say 'Yes, Miss'—not 'Miz.' Do you understand?"

"Yes, ma'am. It's 'Miss' Patsy now."

"That's correct. And the other servants will now call you 'Mr. Carmichael.'"

Carmichael grinned from ear to ear. "Yes, ma'am."

"Don't let them get away with anything less."

"No, ma'am."

She then called a meeting of the household servants to inform them of this development, with Carmichael at her side. There were many sidelong glances, but as they liked Carmichael for the most part, and as he was the son of Maybelle, who they all respected, the appointment seemed to be an agreeable one. Her only concern was that Maybelle, on returning to Belle Oaks when Zimri arrived, might balk at being required to call her son 'Mr. Carmichael.' But on second thought, she was sure that Maybelle would be so proud of her son that she would gladly comply.

Late in the afternoon, Jamie returned from his rounds out in the fields to find the house running smoothly and his mother, along with Patsy, preparing for dinner.

"My God, Elizabeth—how did you do it? Carmichael's even calling me 'Master James' now."

"Delegation of authority," she said.

"What?"

"Delegation of authority. You give your servants a little authority and it gives them a sense of pride and responsibility. It's better than issuing draconian decrees from above and threatening them with mortal punishments if they don't comply."

Jamie looked at her curiously. "What's 'draconian' mean?"

"Extreme."

"You think I'm extreme?"

"Only when you lose your temper."

Jamie flopped down in a chair in the drawing room and put his muddy boots on an ottoman. A young house slave, a boy of about twelve, rushed to pull them off. "What do you think you're doing?"

The boy stopped suddenly and looked at Elizabeth.

"He's about to pull your boots off," she said.

"Why? I can do it myself."

"Carmichael's apparently taking his duties seriously. He's instructed him to treat you as the lord of the manor."

Jamie pulled at his moustache and eyed the boy with curiosity. The boy looked terrified. "Well, I guess I *am* the lord of the manor now. Boy, what's your name?"

"Cory, suh."

"Cory. That's a good name. Well, Cory, go ahead and pull my boots off, take them to the tack room and tell the stable boy to clean them off. Then bring them back, and if they're nice and clean, I'll tell Sissy to give you a piece of her lemon meringue pie after dinner."

"Yes, suh." The boy smiled with satisfaction at this prospect and pulled first one boot off, then the other. He hurried out of the room with them.

"How's that?" Jamie said.

"Very admirable," she said.

"Won't you stay for dinner?"

"I've got to get home to see about Charlotte. I've been so busy with collecting the *Mercury*'s overdue bills that I'm afraid I've neglected her. She's going to start thinking Maybelle's her mother."

"Speaking of Maybelle, I wish your husband would return so that we can get some good cooking around here. Sissy's efforts ain't anywhere near her standards."

"Like the others, she's learning."

Jamie sighed and slumped back into his chair, exhausted. "Like all of us, I guess. Even you."

She smiled. "Even me."

CHAPTER 19

Wednesday, 25 August

Put up at the Lafayette Hotel in Fayetteville, North Carolina. A very fine house, kept in the best manner, but the town has considerably declined in business and population in the last few years. Overall, however, it is a pleasant place with a few good buildings, supplied with water by aqueducts. Two creeks pass through the center of the town.

Said farewell to Mr. Sparks, who was pleased to be put up at the hotel without protest on the part of the proprietor. At previous stops along the way he had been obliged to either sleep in the stable or stay at a colored boarding house, often with inferior accommodations. In accordance with his wishes, I did not intercede in these instances, and he seemed resigned to the inconvenience and inevitable racial slurs.

I wished him well in his quest to purchase the freedom of his niece in Savannah, and he promised to write once they were settled in Philadelphia. I suggested that the trip home, by ship, would be far more comfortable and accommodating to both his and his niece's needs. He laughed and said he didn't know which he preferred— the discomforts and indignities of traveling overland through the South, or the treacherous storms off Cape Hatteras.

We parted as friends.

Tuesday, 30 August

Uneventful journey through South Carolina; stopped in Camden, where the innkeeper was hospitable enough, but the food very poor. Thunderstorms and some flash floods greeted us at Augusta, where we were delayed nearly a whole day. Stopped briefly in Milledgeville, where I paid a visit to Senator Ambrose Baker, who I had been acquainted with during his early days in Martinville and implored him to persuade his colleagues to approve the funds for the new bridge across the Ocmulgee. He seemed disposed to do so, saying that he shared my enthusiasm for the project.

Wednesday, September 1

Arrived in Martinville at noon.

The trip from Milledgeville to Martinville being the shortest leg of the journey, Zimri alighted from the stage feeling refreshed and full of energy. He took his portmanteau from the driver, who then scrambled over the top of the stage, tossing luggage down to the passengers as if he were flinging cargo from a sinking ship.

"Careful there!" one man shouted. "I got some very valuable items in that wardrobe."

"Got to get to Hawkinsville a'fore sundown," the driver said.

"I don't care if you got to get to Tallahassee. You bust one of my samples and I'll climb up there and wring your neck!"

"Easy, Mister," the driver said. "I ain't never broke nothin' yet."

Zimri ignored this colloquy and walked the two blocks to the *Mercury* carrying his portmanteau. He assumed Jed would be in the office and could drive him home in the gig for dinner. He had been thinking much of Elizabeth since he left Fayetteville, and felt somewhat ashamed of his brief affair with Cora. It now seemed to him to have been a dream, and like a dream, he expected little or nothing to come of it. It would best be forgotten.

As he approached the office, he suddenly remembered the new cylinder press. According to Mr. Hoe, it should have arrived by now. Of course, Mr. Hoe, being a good salesman, had talked him into ordering one of the new steam presses, which would require sending the mechanical press back to New York. And the steam press was nearly twice as expensive. But certainly he would find the money somewhere.

As he stepped up onto the sidewalk in front of the office, he stopped for a moment to read the headings to the latest edition of the *Mercury* posted in the window:

> *Violent storm off Hatteras sinks British frigate.*
> *General Sanchez Executed in Madrid.*
> *Anarchists Riot in Paris.*
> *Murder Trial of Plantation Slave Set.*

Zimri skimmed quickly through these, noting only the format and positioning of the stories. There seemed to be more advertising than usual, a very good thing. Jed must have been more enterprising than expected during his absence. At the bottom of each article, however, he noticed a curious thing: instead of the usual thin line separating the end of one article from the beginning of the next, there was a border composed of three little rosettes. Unusual, but not a bad idea, really. It would distinguish the *Mercury* from its competitors in format as well as substance.

He opened the door and stepped inside. He could hear someone running the new press in the backroom. He knew the sound now of the whirling cylinder and its grippers releasing one sheet of paper and grabbing the next from the demonstration given to him by Mr. Hoe. And the steam press would be even faster!

"Jed?"

The noise from the press seemed to drown out the sound of his voice before it reached the back room. Then, to his astonishment, Elizabeth appeared from behind the partition to his office.

"Zimri! You're here!"

She rushed to embrace him, moving agilely in spite of her considerable increase in girth since he left for New York two and a half months ago.

He dropped his portmanteau to the floor and embraced her, kissing her on the mouth, the cheeks, the neck. He *had* missed her, terribly.

"Oh, Zimri." She took his hat from his head and dusted off his clothes. "You look as if you've been on a cattle drive. And you stink like a cowboy! Didn't you have your clothes laundered?"

"Only in New York. Laundresses seem to be scarce in provincial towns. How's the baby?"

"Growing like a weed in your rose garden. Sometimes I think there's two of them."

"Two? Twins?"

"I'm not sure, but Doctor Parcher says it's quite possible. We'll have to wait and see."

"I hope they're both girls."

"Girls? Don't you want a boy to carry on the family name?"

"The family name will always be on the masthead of the *Mercury*. Boys are too troublesome."

Elizabeth laughed and kissed him again lightly on the lips. "You are a strange man, Zimri. Almost as strange as—Oh, Zimri, so much has happened since you've been gone."

The whirring of the press in the back room suddenly ceased.

"Apparently," Zimri said. "Sit down, Elizabeth, and tell me what has happened. First of all, what are you doing here instead of at home?"

Jed appeared at the doorway wiping grease from his hands. "Welcome home, Mr. Rhodes! I thought I heard your voice."

"Thank you, Jed. It seems you've been very busy."

"Yes, sir. Between me and Mrs. Rhodes we've been fairly swamped."

Zimri looked incredulously at Jed, then with the same expression at Elizabeth. "Between the two of you? You've been working here, Elizabeth?"

"There was no alternative. The new press arrived and there wasn't the money to pay for it."

"No money? Why..." He looked to Jed. "Couldn't you get a line of credit from Mr. Hamilton?"

Jed looked uncomfortable. "That's just what we did do, Mr. Rhodes. But we already owed more than the cost of the press, and Mr. Hamilton wouldn't advance the money without Mrs. Rhodes' signature."

Zimri turned to Elizabeth. "*Your* signature?"

Elizabeth flushed. "Perhaps it was because of Daddy—he thought he would make good on it if you couldn't—"

Zimri slammed his fist down on the desk beside him. "Dammit, Elizabeth! You know I don't ever want to have to go to your father for money!"

"We didn't go to him, Zimri," she said. "His name was never even mentioned."

"Still, that was the implication."

"She collected all the bad debts, Mr. Rhodes. Even from Mr. Lewis."

Zimri gaped at his wife. "You collected from Lewis?"

"It just took some persistence." She smiled coquettishly. "And a little flattery."

Zimri continued to stare at her in amazement for several seconds and gradually a smile came to his lips. "Then how can I be angry with you, darling? You did what had to be done. What other shocks, natural and unnatural, are in store for me, my dear?"

Elizabeth embraced him. "A number of them, I'm afraid, darling. But let's not discuss them now. Jed, can we borrow your gig? My husband and I would like to go home and have the first dinner we've had together for two and a half months."

"Yes, ma'am. I'm not going anywhere."

"Thank you, Jed." She turned again to Zimri. "Of course, you'll need a thorough scrubbing if you are to be presentable for dinner." She pinched her nostrils together in mock disgust. "That smell! Even Maybelle would refuse to be in the same room with you until you've had a bath"

Zimri laughed. "I'll try to stay downwind of you on the way home, though it'll be difficult in a two-seater. Where's your gig, Jed?"

"Out back, Mr. Rhodes. But don't you want to see the new press before you go?"

"The new press? Well, yes, I suppose so."

Elizabeth took his hand and eagerly escorted him to the back room. "Oh, Zimri, it's so exciting. Jed says it's ten times as fast as the old one and now we can increase the circulation by the same amount."

Zimri allowed himself to be pulled into the room, where he beheld the gleaming new machine in all its mechanical glory.

"And it's a whole lot easier to operate," Jed said. "I can tell you that. Here, let me show you." He manned the crank on the cylinder and began turning it rapidly. Several sheets of printed paper shot out from the bed and fell into a bin. "See?"

"It's quite an improvement. But we'll have to send it back."

"Send it back!" Elizabeth was stunned. "But Zimri. It's all paid for. And it's marvelous!"

Zimri nodded. "Yes, it is marvelous. But the steam-powered version is even faster. Five hundred pages an hour."

"Steam-powered?" Elizabeth said. "Five hundred pages an hour? Why, I don't even know if we need a press that fast. And it must be very expensive."

"Not so expensive, really."

Elizabeth stared at him for a moment.

"Zimri! You didn't order a steam press while you were in New York!"

"Mr. Hoe himself demonstrated it for me. He said that it would more than pay for itself in a few months. And he would give me a credit for this one."

"A credit," she said. "And how much is the steam press?"

Zimri pulled at his collar. "Two thousand dollars."

"Two thousand! Oh, Zimri, we've just gotten out of debt. You'll just have to cancel the order."

"But it's on its way, darling. It's too late to stop it."

"When it gets here, we'll just put it back on the wagon and send it back. We can absorb the shipping costs."

"But Elizabeth—"

"She's right, Mr. Rhodes. We'd go broke with that steam press before the end of the year. We need time to build up our circulation and advertising with this one first."

Zimri looked at Jed as if he had betrayed him, then to Elizabeth, who folded her arms across her chest.

"Then we can sit down again and decide whether the steam press will be economical," she said.

Zimri sighed. "All right. You're both right. We'll have to send the steam press back. But the thought of the *Patriot* getting one of the new steam presses before we do makes me ill."

"The *Patriot* is still using the old platen and lever press, Mr. Rhodes. And we've already passed them in both circulation and advertising."

"We have? Well, that's good news, at any rate."

Elizabeth took Zimri by the hand and led him to the back door. "Come on, dearest, let's leave the shop to Jed and surprise Maybelle and Charlotte. Charlotte has been calling your name out in the middle of the night and waking us both up."

"Wait till she sees what I've brought her from New York."

"You've brought her something and not me?"

"I might be able to find something in my portmanteau for you as well."

She glanced down at the portmanteau. "Oh, Zimri—what is it? A dress? But you know I can't wear anything but maternity clothes now. You didn't —"

"Wait till we get home, dear, and I've had my bath."

She tugged at the straps to the portmanteau. "Oh, Zimri, tell me what it is. I don't want to wait till we get home!"

Zimri pulled the portmanteau away from her and escorted her to the door. "You're worse than Charlotte. At least I know she can wait. I'll be back after dinner, Jed."

"Yes, sir, that'll be—"

"No!" Elizabeth said. "He won't be back after dinner. He'll be back tomorrow morning at seven o'clock. You can do without the gig until then, can't you, Jed?"

"Yes, ma'am. I can walk home."

Zimri shrugged his shoulders. "Don't ever get married, Jed. A woman will sap your ambition."

"Yes, sir. I mean, no sir. I mean, I'll have to think about it a lot first, I'm sure."

"Don't listen to him, Jed," she said, pulling Zimri towards the door. "Like all old men, he's an incorrigible liar."

"Old?" Zimri said. "Liar?"

"Both of which I can put up with," she said. "But the odor is overwhelming. Come on, dearest—your bath is waiting."

They passed through the door and found Peter waiting with the gig.

Jed remained standing in the middle of the room, watching as they drove off, and after a shake of his head resumed cranking the handle on the cylinder. "Actually, I didn't think he smelled *that* bad."

CHAPTER 20

Zimri sensed that a change had come over Elizabeth, but he could only speculate as to what had caused it. Certainly she had always been a very intelligent and practical young woman, and those qualities, standing out as they did in contrast to those of other young women of his acquaintance, were a large part of why he married her.

But whereas before he left for Connecticut she had been moody and listless, often lying on the swing half the day reading some romance or other, now she seemed intent on not only working long hours at the newspaper, but on running it! This produced mixed feelings in him, for while it seemed somewhat improper for a woman, especially a well-heeled one to work in her husband's office, she was quite obviously well-qualified to do so. In fact, she was more than well-qualified, she showed a real talent for it. And that freed him up to focus on the editorial side; he could even do a little more reporting, especially on the more complex political issues, and leave the 'soft' news to Jed.

These thoughts ran through his mind as he watched Elizabeth undress. It was about nine o'clock, and they had both had a full day. The news about her father's death had come as a shock, though he had never really cared much for James Sr. Not that there had been any real hostility between them, only a distance created by very different temperaments and upbringing. After some initial friction, they had grown to trust and respect one another.

The truly shocking thing, of course, was the manner of his death. That is, if Jamie's version of events was to be believed. He would have to interview both Luther and Dr. Parcher to get other perspectives.

Elizabeth, as usual, had extinguished the candles in the room before undressing. But there was enough moonlight streaming in through the window that he could see her figure as she shed first her dress, then her petticoats, and finally her underclothes. She was now about seven or eight months pregnant and her belly was enormous, much larger than it had been with Charlotte. And yet Elizabeth seemed intent upon love-making.

He thought of Cora, and her beautiful skin, her full breasts and slim waist, and of course her almost complete lack of sexual inhibitions. She seemed to revel in her body and to be as comfortable without clothes as with. He mused that she could probably appear on stage naked before a thousand people and not betray so much as the suggestion of a blush.

Elizabeth slipped on her nightgown and carefully put her undergarments away. Then she approached the bed, which was of elaborately carved mahogany said to have been imported from Honduras by her grandfather especially for her. She had always slept in this bed, and it was almost like a second skin to her. She put her hand on one of the posts and swung around it in a half circle as she must have done a thousand times as a child.

"What are you thinking?" she said.

"Why do women always want to know what a man is thinking?" He clasped his hands behind his head, which was high against a pillow. "I hardly know myself. A number of things. A confusion of images."

"What images?" She sat on the bed beside him and placed one hand on her belly for support, as if it would roll off the bed like a melon if she didn't.

"Images of New York, of Connecticut, of my younger brother and his wife, of the great aqueduct across the Mohawk, of a rose acacia covering the entire wall of a house in Lansingburg, of the foretopmast of the *Oregon* splitting in two and sailors falling fifty feet to a deck awash in sea water and tangled rigging, of my roses that Old George has so tenderly cared for in my absence, of Charlotte's face when she saw the doll I brought her from New York, of yours when you saw the diamond brooch."

She kissed him on the lips and lay her head against his chest. "It's beautiful, Zimri, but you're too extravagant. Why, the brooch must have cost as much as the new cylinder press!"

Zimri laughed. "Not so much as that. But the new press will soon be replaced by another, and then another, while the brooch will last all of your life."

"And then some. I intend to leave it to Charlotte."

"And Charlotte to her daughter. I'd say it was one of my better investments."

She raised her head and looked into his eyes. "You're a fine man, Zimri. The best I've ever known."

"How many have you known?"

She cocked her head impishly. "More than you think."

"Well, this is getting interesting. I don't believe we've ever discussed your previous lovers before. Let's see...the only one I know of is the fellow from Charleston who came to the wedding and had the audacity to ask you to break it off with me and run off with him!"

She lay her head back on his chest. "He was just a boy. Randolph doesn't know what he wants."

"Apparently he knew he wanted you."

She sighed. "Not really. Not in any deeper sense. I was just a bright toy that caught his eye. He's probably already forgotten me." She raised her head and put her arms around his neck. "But let's not talk about Randolph. In fact, let's not talk—that's all we've been doing today."

"Well, I—"

She pressed her lips to his with a passion that surprised him. She seemed more aggressive since he returned, more aggressive in every way. But it was a welcome change, and it excited him more than anytime since their wedding night in spite of her enormous belly.

She slipped off her nightgown and pulled back the covers to reveal his erect penis. She seemed intrigued, as if it were the first time she had seen it. "Why were you never circumcised?"

"They didn't seem to think it was necessary in Brantley. At least not at the time."

"If it's a boy, I'd want to have him circumcised."

"Why?"

"Because it's ...the Christian thing to do."

He laughed. "I didn't know that you took religious rituals so seriously."

"Well, I don't...actually, I guess I thought that all boys were circumcised. Like Jamie."

"I'll have it done if you insist."

"Oh, no, I don't insist. I like it...like this."

"You're sure?"

"I'm sure." She leaned forward and kissed him. "I learned everything I know about sex from Maybelle."

"And what did Maybelle teach you?"

She nestled against his shoulder. "Well, she said that men were only interested in getting what they call 'toonkie.'"

"Toonkie?"

"A woman's vagina."

"Oh."

"And that a woman's job was to keep the man from getting any of her toonkie until she secured a promise from him to marry her."

"And then what?"

"And then, if he didn't keep his promise and she got pregnant, she was absolved from sin."

"Not her fault then."

"No."

"Anything else?"

"Yes. Lots more. Do you want to hear it?"

"Just give me a sample."

"All right. She once said that if a woman became pregnant and the man wouldn't marry her, she could go to a root doctor and get her to cast a spell on him."

"Voodoo."

"Of course. And if she didn't want to have the baby, she could get the root doctor to give her a magic potion and when she drank it, the baby would dissolve into a kind of jelly that would be flushed out the next time she had her period, but that its soul would go straight to heaven."

"Very convenient."

"I thought so, too That's why I never worried about getting pregnant."

They both laughed until Elizabeth became alarmed that they might wake Charlotte and put her forefinger to his lips. "Shh!"

"Well, you don't have to worry about it now, either," he said.

"No, and we won't even need a root doctor."

They both giggled, trying not to wake Charlotte. And then they made love as if for the first time.

CHAPTER 21

The next morning, Zimri had a hearty breakfast, inspected his roses, and drove Jed's gig back to the office. He advised Elizabeth to stay home and rest, advice which she reluctantly agreed to.

He spent half the morning going over the new accounts that she and Jed had secured in his absence, and after reviewing the books, which seemed to be in the best order since the *Mercury* was founded some ten years earlier, he walked over to the jail to interview Luther.

The jail was a temporary annex to the old courthouse, which was soon to be replaced with a new one. It had been built during the Indian wars prior to Zimri's arrival, and at first served as the fort's stockade. It consisted of wooden stakes driven into the ground and lashed together with leather straps, the spaces between them later filled in with caulking. A low-pitched roof had been added since the decommissioning of the fort, and an office of sorts built onto the front of the building to accommodate the sheriff and his deputies.

"Hello, Zimri." The sheriff rose from his desk and adjusted the pistol belt that encircled his ample belly. He extended his hand. "I reckon you'll be wanting to see Luther."

"That's right, Aaron. It seems he's gotten into a bit of trouble since I've been gone."

Sheriff Beasley laughed, the big barrel-chested laugh of a man accustomed to eating more at breakfast than Zimri did the entire day. "Trouble? I'll say he's in trouble. A black slave killing his master? He's lucky he didn't get strung up by a mob on the way in from Belle Oaks."

"How's he handling it?"

"Quiet. Real quiet. He ain't give me no trouble at all. You want to see him now?"

"Please."

"Open the door, Harold. You got the key to number six?"

Harold, the deputy, opened the door to the cell block and picked a key off of a peg next to it. Sheriff Beasley took the key and led Zimri into the block, which consisted of one large room divided by iron cages, twelve in all, six on each side of the boarded walkway between them. The cell floors were of dirt, with a hole in the center for the prisoners to relieve themselves. Each contained anywhere from one to four bunk beds, all left over from the fort. A few stools were scattered about. Most of the cells were empty, while others were crowded with prisoners, mostly white. Two black men occupied a cell opposite Luther's, while Number Six contained only Luther himself. He sat on a stool, his clothes ragged, and his head down, 'reading' a Bible. He didn't look up until the sheriff unlocked the cell door.

"Hello, Luther," Zimri said. "Remember me?"

Luther raised his gray head slowly and studied Zimri for a moment. "Sho' do. It's Mr. Zimri, Miz Lizbeth's husband."

"I'm here to talk to you about what happened out at Belle Oaks."

"'Spect so," Luther said.

Zimri turned to the sheriff. "Can we have some place more private?"

"The washroom," Beasley said. "'Long as you keep an eye on him. Not that he's goin' anywhere, but so's nobody grabs him and strings him up on a lamp post."

"I'll see that he's safe."

"No, *I'll* see that he's safe. You just make sure that he don't wander out the back door of the washroom so's me and Harold don't have to go after him."

"Agreed."

Sheriff Beasley led them both to the rear of the building, where a small room was attached to the larger one. It consisted of two wooden benches parallel to one another, each with copper water basins for washing. There was indeed a back door for carrying water into the room, but it was secured from the outside with a wooden crossbar and latch.

Luther sat down on one bench, Zimri on the opposite one with a pad and pencil on his knee.

"Start from the beginning, Luther. And don't leave anything out."

"Ain't much to tell, Mr. Zimri. Me and Massa James got in a spat over my grandbaby's funeral...I got so mad that he wouldn't let me go that I picked up the pitchfork and kind of jabbed it at him, he grabbed it, and the next thing I knows he be laying on the ground grabbin' his belly and hollerin' that I done kilt him."

"Did you intend to stab him with the pitchfork?"

"Naw, suh."

"Just to threaten him?"

"I reckon so. I just wanted to show him he couldn't do me that way. I would've stopped right there, but he grabbed the pitchfork and tried to twist it out of my hands."

"And you twisted back?"

"I reckon I did."

"And then you struggled."

"Yes, suh. We each started pullin' first one way, then t'other."

"And he fell?"

"I reckon so. I can't rightly remember how it was he got stuck. Next thing I knows, he be hollerin,' 'You done kilt me, you black bastid, you done kilt me!'"

"And did you think that you had killed him?"

"Naw, suh. He warn't bleedin' that much, and he was hollerin' at me just like he do sometimes when I ain't moved fast enough to bring his hoss round to the front do'."

"What did you do then?"

"Well, I told Leon to get some bandages and liniment 'cause he done hurt hisself."

"You didn't try to run away?"

"Naw, suh. Why would I do that?"

"Most men would if they had just tried to kill someone."

"That's what I'm telling' you, Mister Zimri. I warn't tryin' to kill Massa James no how. We been in worse spats than that since we was both chillun.'"

Zimri put his pencil down and studied Luther carefully for a moment. He was a small man, perhaps only five feet six or so, and couldn't weigh more than 140 pounds. His almost completely gray hair was receding but still thick and curly. His brow was deeply furrowed, and his eyes were large and inquisitive, with that brown filmy look that Zimri had noticed in the eyes of many older blacks. There was an earnestness in his expression that made one want to trust him. "You grew up with Master James at Belle Oaks?"

"Yas, suh. We was the same age and my mammy nursed him jest like she nursed me."

"Then you must have played together as children."

"Sho.' We was best friends, gettin' into all kinds of mischief together till about the age of twelve or so, when he suddenly started puttin' on airs and sich, like he didn't know me no more."

"That's not unusual is it? I mean among the slave children and the master's children?"

Luther sighed and hung his head. "Naw, suh. That the way things be. I jest had a harder time gettin' over it than most nigger chillun, I guess."

"Because he was your best friend."

"Yas, suh. But that be a long, long time ago."

The room was getting hot and beads of perspiration began to run down Luther's forehead.

"How did you feel, Luther, when Master James died?"

"I be sorry, Mister Zimri. I be sorry that he dead even though he don't do me right."

"Why? He had you whipped, didn't he?"

Luther looked up, showing the first sign of anger since the interview started. "Naw, suh. It warn't him that had me whipped. It was Jamie—he took it on hisself."

"And how did you feel about that? I mean, of course it was painful, but did you think it was a fair punishment?"

"Naw, suh. Twarn't nothin' fair 'bout it no how. Maybe I shouldn't had poked Massa James wid the pitchfork, maybe I shoulda jest throwed it down and let him cut me once or twice wid his ridin' crop like he do sometimes, but I didn't mean to kill him. Jamie jest had to prove hisself in front of all the other slaves. I could see it in his eyes—he was more scared than I was."

Zimri put his notepad and pencil in his pocket. "All right, Luther. I suppose that's all I need to know for now. Has anyone else come to see you since you've been here? An attorney?"

"Attorney?"

"A lawyer. Has the court appointed a lawyer for you?"

"Nobody's said nothin' 'bout no lawyer to me, Mister Zimri. You the first body to come see me 'cept my chillun t'other day, and the sheriff ain't let them see me but five minutes."

Zimri stood. "I'll speak to the judge. You'll need a lawyer."

"Ain't got no money for no lawyer, Mister Zimri."

"Don't worry about that, Luther. I'll see that you get one."

"Thank you, Mister Zimri, but I don't think it'll do no good."

"Maybe not, Luther, but without one you'll have no chance at all."

"Yes, suh."

Zimri allowed Luther to walk ahead of him and delivered him back into the custody of the sheriff. Then he went back to the office where he found Jed about to go home for dinner, and asked him to drive him back home and have dinner there instead.

After dinner, Jed drove back to the office and Zimri took one of the horses from the stable and rode out to Clinton to interview Dr. Parcher. He found him in his office, packing his stethoscope and some rather frightening-looking medical instruments into his valise. He seemed to notice the alarm on Zimri's face, and laughed.

"I'm playing veterinarian today," he said. "Old Mrs. McKinney's mare is foaling."

"That's a relief," Zimri said. "I thought you had offered your services to the Spanish Inquisition."

Dr. Parcher laughed again and snapped his valise shut. Then he sat down, put his feet up on his desk, and motioned to a chair. "Have a seat, Zimri. What can I do for you today?"

"I don't want to hold you up."

"Nonsense. The mare can wait. She may not be ready till nightfall."

Zimri sat in the chair. "I'm doing a piece on Luther Caldwell. You know him?"

"Luther? The slave that ran Jim Blake through with a pitchfork?"

"That's part of what I'm trying to determine. Did you see it happen?"

"No, no. I didn't see it. Leon—one of the other boys who was there—came running to get me. I arrived about an hour later."

Zimri took out his note pad and laid it on his knee. "An hour? And where did you find Mr. Blake?"

"He was in his bedroom. A couple of the boys wrapped him in make-shift bandages to stop the bleeding and carried him there."

"And how did he look when you got there?"

"Pale. He'd lost a fair amount of blood even though Luther apparently missed most of the vital organs."

"Most of them?"

"Except for the lungs. At first I thought he—Jim—might have gotten lucky and been spared that organ as well. But as it turned out, at least one of the tines on the pitchfork must have punctured the lung."

"How do you know that?"

"Because his lungs began to fill up with fluid. That's what killed him—drowning."

"But isn't it unusual for that to happen so long after the initial wound? He didn't die for another three weeks. And in the meantime he seemed to have fully recovered, riding everyday to inspect the property or to go hunting."

"That's just it. The riding must have caused a rupture, a re-opening of the wound in the lung. If Jim had only listened to my advice and stayed in—"

"But it's possible that there could have been some other cause for the fluid build-up, isn't it?"

Dr. Parcher frowned. "It's possible, but not likely. Say, Zimri, I thought you were a newspaperman, not a detective."

Zimri smiled. "A little bit of both. Just trying to get the facts."

Dr. Parcher swung his legs off of the desk and grabbed his valise. "Well, you've got'em. Now if you'll excuse me, Zimri, I'd better get going. Mrs. McKinney is a lonely old widow and she's probably out on her front porch right now expecting me for tea before I plunge into her mare's innards."

Zimri put his pad and pencil in his coat pocket and rose from his chair. "One more thing, Dr. Parcher."

"Yes?"

"Is it possible that Mr. Blake had some sort of influenza?"

"Again, it's possible, but there were no symptoms of influenza. And you said yourself that he was out riding every day before he was suddenly struck down." Dr. Parcher walked to the door and donned his hat. "No, Zimri, I can see what you're up to—you want to save poor Luther from hanging. I don't blame you—he seems a nice old fellow. But I'm afraid all the evidence is against him— I've seen white men hanged on less. Good day to you, sir."

Zimri rode on to Belle Oaks where he owed Mrs. Blake a condolence call in any case. He found her to be somewhat distracted while he spoke to her in the drawing room, seemingly willing to talk about anything and everything but her husband.

"Elizabeth tells me you bought her a diamond brooch in New York, Zimri. That was rather extravagant of you, wasn't it?"

"Well, Mrs. Blake—"

"Especially for a newspaperman like yourself. Would you like some tea?"

"No, thank you, Mrs. Blake. I—"

"And a pretty little doll for Charlotte. That would be more within your budget, I would think. I'm sure Elizabeth would have been just as happy with a new dress. Of course she wouldn't be able to wear it until she's had the baby—do you know that Dr. Parcher says she might have twins?"

"Yes, I—"

"Twins! Think of it—you'll have twice as many mouths to feed then, Zimri. You shouldn't be throwing money away on diamond brooches. Besides, when I pass on to join my poor James in the Final Reward, Elizabeth will inherit all of my jewelry anyway. And

I can tell you—"

Zimri saw little point in continuing this interview and looked for an opportunity to take his leave as soon as he was able to get a word in. Mrs. Blake accommodated him by announcing that she felt very tired and rang for a servant to escort her to her bedroom for a nap. Zimri then went to the stable where he found Leon, who pretty much corroborated Luther's version of events. When this interview was completed, Leon brought his horse around to the front and Zimri headed for home.

CHAPTER 22

Fall came a bit early to middle Georgia that year and Elizabeth enjoyed watching the leaves turn to red, then to yellow and gold. The weather was clear most days, with cobalt cloudless skies and crisp, cool temperatures. Sweaters and overcoats were brought out of storage, and Zimri could be found on a Saturday morning out chopping wood for the hearth.

Both Otis and Old George returned to Belle Oaks, where they were needed for the peanut harvest. Maybelle remained, in spite of Jamie's protests, to make things easier for Elizabeth as she approached her delivery date. Once again, Elizabeth found herself with little to do, and spent much of her time on the front porch reading. A shawl kept her shoulders warm, and Maybelle brought her hot chocolate and pralines.

On this particular morning, she was reading *Northhanger Abbey* when she saw a rider approaching the house. It was Jamie. He dismounted and flung the reins over the hitching rail in his usual cavalier manner and bounded up the path. "Elizabeth!"

"Hello, Jamie." She struggled to get up from the swing.

"Don't try to get up," Jamie said. He gave her a kiss.

"All right. What are you so excited about?"

"News!"

"What kind of news? What is it?"

He seemed to be holding something behind his back. "First—I am going to get married."

"Married! Oh, Jamie, I'm so happy for you. Who is the—"

"Fanny, of course."

"Of course." She reached up to give him a hug. "She's a lovely girl. When is the wedding?"

"In the spring. I don't like the idea of a long engagement, but Mama thinks it's best."

"Well, of course. You don't want to have it during the Christmas holidays, and every bride loves a spring wedding so that there will be flowers everywhere."

"That's what Mama said. Not that Fanny cares about being covered with oceans of flowers, but it will show off Belle Oaks to its best advantage as well."

"It will be gorgeous then. Now, what do you have behind your back?"

Jamie looked around towards the side yard and then to the front door. "Where's Zimri?"

"Out by the barn, chopping wood. Why?"

He slowly brought his hand from behind his back to reveal a letter. "I don't think that this is really any of his business, that's why."

"A letter? From whom?"

"Why don't you see for yourself?"

She took the letter, which was of a fine blue paper. It was addressed to 'Mdme. Elizabeth Rhodes, c/o J. Blake, Belle Oaks, Georgia, USA.' She turned it over, and on the back was a red seal bearing the initials of the sender: JRB. "Randolph!"

"Shh!" Jamie looked around again conspiratorially.

"Oh, Jamie—I don't care if anyone sees it. Zimri knows that Randolph is a friend of both yours and mine."

"Maybe he wants you to come to Europe."

"Don't be silly. He's just sending news of his adventures there." She slit open the envelope with a butter knife from her breakfast plate and began reading:

Thursday, 9 Sept.

My Dearest Elizabeth,

I am writing you from the very villa that Byron lived in for a time near Livorno, where he met with Shelley before the latter's tragic drowning only eight years ago.

Oh, the very walls here are alive with poetry! I can almost hear the immortal lyrics of Don Juan emanating from every crevice in the ancient masonry. I can hardly sleep at night, so excited am I by the presence—yes, it is an almost palpable presence—of the two greatest poets of our age.

I am afraid my pitiful pen cannot convey to you the transformation that I have undergone since coming to Europe. But I will try.

In Paris, I was introduced to the highest levels of French society and attended the salons of the aristocracy on an almost daily basis. And yes, I was even invited to a grand ball at Versailles attended by the new king, Louis-Philippe himself. He has formed a new government that has restored most of the rights of the common people, and appears to be very popular with both the people and the nobility. The Marquis de Lafayette, a hero of our own revolution, was also in attendance.

But Elizabeth, I must tell you that aside from Lafayette, I was not impressed! Granted my French was very poor but many of the guests spoke English quite fluently, and whenever I stumbled, a translator seemed to be always whispering in my ear. For all of their recent advances, these French are hopelessly mired in the most appalling snobbery and decadence. They espouse 'liberté, egalité, and fraternité' out of one side of their mouths and simultaneously speak of the middle and lower classes ('the bourgeoisie') with the utmost contempt out of the other.

I far prefer Italy, which is undergoing a similar struggle for republican freedoms at this very moment, under the direction of Mazzini. No one knows whether he will be successful or not at this point, but the Italians, unlike the French, seem to have a genuine love of freedom and of life. To be sure, the aristocracy here is very much alive and well, but they seem not to have the contempt for the middle classes that the French do, nor do the common people seem to resent their presence as long as they support the ouster of the Austrians.

Forgive me for rambling on so about politics and class antagonisms and the eternal quest for human freedom. But they are so much a part of the air here that one can hardly take a breath without their seeping into one's very pores. The great irony, of course, is that the Europeans ape the ideals of our own revolution without the slightest respect for their substance.

But this, my dearest Elizabeth, is not what I meant to say to you. And again, my pen, but not my heart, fails me. Since I arrived in Europe and have partaken of those Epicurean delights of which the higher circles of the aristocracy, particularly in France, are renowned for, I have become more and more dissatisfied with myself, even disgusted. I have learned , if nothing else, that there is no pleasure in life greater than true love, and that there can be no true love without mutual respect. And it is this last quality of which I have been so lacking all of my life. As I think on it, I can hardly conceive that you had any respect for me whatever, either in Charleston, or more lately in Martinville. As I said, however, I have begun a great transformation of myself, and God only knows if I will succeed.

It would be the height of impertinence for me to suggest that you return the love that I feel grows stronger in me every day, my darling. I know that I am not worthy of you. And I know, alas, that you are wed to another and by now are about to have his second child. But what can I do? I have met no other woman who is worthy to kiss the hem of your dress either in Europe or America. My first impulse is to return home immediately and rush into your arms. How is Zimri with dueling pistols? I would as soon have him kill me and put me out of my misery.

But no. I will remain in Europe until I am a better man. I will assist the republicans in any way that I can, and I assure you, I have considerable resources to do so. I may even go to Greece, where the noble Byron fell, and further the cause of which he was so passionate.

Adieu, my darling. I will write again when I have the courage.
Randolph

Elizabeth put the letter down and gazed off towards the low hills that receded into the distance.

"Well?" Jamie said. "What does he have to say?"

She did not answer at first, as if Jamie's voice rose from within a deep well and was barely audible. Then she looked at him oddly, folded the letter, and placed it back in its envelope. "He says he is enjoying Italy."

"Is that all? Just that he's having a good time?"

"No...he says that he is undergoing some sort of spiritual transformation."

"Spiritual transformation?"

"At least that's what he would have us believe. I seriously doubt that Randolph will ever change."

"I doubt it as well. Why should he? He's already got everything a man could want."

"Yes. Most everything."

Jamie sat down on the swing beside her. "Most everything but you."

"I would appreciate it, Jamie, if you didn't encourage him."

"Me? What have I done to encourage him? He's always been sweet on you. And besides, he's not the sort of man to be easily influenced. He knows what he wants."

"Yes. And he usually gets it. Like the spoiled child that he is. Unfortunately, he thinks rules are for other people."

"Rules? What rules?"

"Don't be obtuse, Jamie. You know what rules I'm talking about. The rules of marriage, of social decorum, of common decency."

Jamie threw his head back and laughed. "Oh, those rules. Well, he's just a free-thinker. For now. But just wait till he returns from Europe and sees that he will have to settle down. Then all the liberal ideas and the passion for equality and brotherhood will go out the window. He'll stop reading all that damn tomfoolery he calls poetry and face the practical business of running a large plantation. I don't have to read the letter, Elizabeth. I know what it says, because I know Randolph."

"Do you?"

"Yes. Correct me if I'm wrong. He says that he's disgusted with all the excessive wealth and snobbery of the European aristocracy, that he merely wants to live the life of a simple peasant, and that he intends to throw himself into the republican struggle for freedom. Am I right?"

"All except the part about living the simple life of a peasant."

"And further more, he wants you to abandon your husband—who's already a republican of the most extreme sort—and join him in Europe, perhaps Greece, where you'll live together in a stone hut on the shores of the Mediterranean. After the revolution, of course."

"Jamie, if you know all this about Randolph, why do you insist upon goading him into making improper advances towards me? If Zimri knew, he'd—"

"Because Zimri is unworthy of you, Elizabeth. I've told you. And I don't want to see you struggling to make ends meet for the rest of your life just to please a damn Yankee abolitionist."

"He's not an abolitionist."

"Then he's doing a pretty good imitation of one. I've been told that he has you working in his office day and night because he's either too stupid or too lazy to keep his own books straight."

"That's enough, Jamie! He's not stupid, he's not lazy, and he never asked me to lift one finger to help him at the office. I volunteered to do it while he was in New York."

"Then he left you a mess to clean up while he gallivanted around New York, looking up all his old girlfriends."

Elizabeth had no answer for this because she believed it was true.

"I'm sorry if I've upset you, Elizabeth," Jamie said. "I just want the best for my baby sister."

"I'm not your baby sister, Jamie. Patsy is."

"You're both babies to me. Especially now that Daddy's gone. I'm responsible for you."

"That's very sweet of you, Jamie, but I'm a married woman. Direct your paternal impulses towards Patsy—she needs you more than I do. Besides, you'll be having children of your own soon."

Jamie sighed. "Fanny can't have children."

"What? How do you know?"

"For one thing, she's already had a miscarriage. For another, Doc Parcher's examined her and said she's got something wrong in her—inside her. Says she'll never be able to carry a child to term."

"Doc Parcher seems to know everything."

"He knows enough."

They remained silent for several moments.

"Your children will be my only heirs, Elizabeth. At least until Patsy gets married. And who knows? She's such a strange child, she might never get married."

"Oh, Patsy's not so strange. She'll be all right." It suddenly dawned on her what Jamie was driving at. "Jamie! You want me to marry Randolph so that his children will be your heirs?"

Jamie looked sidelong at her, and began gently rocking back and forth in the swing. "You could do worse. We both could do worse. Suppose those twins you're carrying are both girls? We'd still need a male heir."

"Suppose I never speak to you again? Thank you for bringing the letter, Jamie. But I think it's time for you to go home now."

"Time to go home?" It was Zimri. He was at the front door drying off his hands. "But he just got here, darling. What's this talk of his going home? Stay and have dinner with us, Jamie. Maybelle's cooking up some—"

"Thanks anyway, Zimri." Jamie rose from the swing. "But Elizabeth's right. I've got to get back to Belle Oaks. Mama's expecting me and Fanny to dine with her in the upstairs dining room."

"Upstairs dining room?" Zimri laughed. "I didn't even know there was an upstairs dining room at Belle Oaks. But then I've never been upstairs there, either."

"It's Mama's private dining room," Jamie said. "She never eats downstairs anymore since the day Daddy died."

Zimri's hearty mood evaporated. "Well, yes, I can understand that. Perhaps you will join us another time."

"Perhaps." Jamie gave Elizabeth a kiss and stepped down from the porch into the pathway. "Goodbye, Elizabeth. I'll send Doc Parcher out to see how you're doing."

"No need, Jamie," she said. "The baby—or babies—won't make their grand entrance for at least another month."

"I'll send him, anyway. Just to be safe." He turned to Zimri. "I don't want to hear of her working down at the office, Zimri, you hear?"

Zimri was somewhat taken aback. "Working? No, no, of course not. That was some time ago. While I was in New York." He smiled at Elizabeth. "Apparently, she was bored to tears and luckily for me, could find nothing better to do than to collect the outstanding debts and balance the books. Your sister's got quite a head on her shoulders, Jamie."

Jamie scowled at him. "Yes—luckily for you." Then he turned and walked briskly to his horse, swung into the saddle, and galloped off.

Zimri watched him for a moment as he grew smaller in the distance. "What's he so upset about?"

"He just found out that Fanny can't have children."

"Oh, no wonder he's in a foul mood. What a shame."

She pulled him down into the swing. "At least that's what Doctor Parcher says. He could be wrong, though, couldn't he?"

Zimri caressed her hand and turned his eyes to his roses. "Yes, I suppose Dr. Parcher could be wrong. He could be wrong about the way your father died."

"The way Daddy died? What do you mean?"

"I mean that...well, I suppose it's a matter of diagnosis. I'm afraid that I don't know enough about medicine to be sure of whether he's right or not."

"You mean about Luther's puncturing his lungs?"

"Yes. Or even if he did, whether that was the cause of death."

She put her head against his shoulder. "Poor Daddy. Poor Luther. You know they were the best of friends when they were little boys."

"That's what Luther said."

"Luther even helped nurse Daddy when he was sick."

"Sick? What was wrong with him?"

"Pleurisy. He almost died from it when he was about ten or twelve."

"Pleurisy? He had pleurisy as a child?"

"Yes. But he got over it. The doctor, Dr. Houghton I think was his name, cured him somehow and—"

Zimri stood.

"Zimri! What is it?"

"I need to find this Dr. Houghton. Is he still alive?"

"I think so. He's an old man, though. He lives in Milledgeville, I think."

"I've got to see him."

"What about dinner?"

"Tell Maybelle to keep it warm for me. I'll be back by dark." He gave her a kiss and started for the barn.

"Zimri!"

"Don't wait up for me if I'm late. And make sure you get enough to eat. The twins are counting on you!"

She laid her head back on the pillows. "Oh, Zimri…if Dr. Parcher is wrong about Luther, then maybe he's wrong about the twins." But Zimri was out of hearing range by now. "Maybe I'll have a sixteen pound boy!"

CHAPTER 23

Zimri arrived in Milledgeville late in the afternoon, just as the sun's rays were beginning to slant in from the trees and give everything an amber glow. He decided that his good friend and former associate, Marcus Slade, editor of *The Georgia Journal*, would know practically everyone in town, and therefore the whereabouts of Dr. Houghton, if indeed he was still alive.

Slade informed him that Dr. Houghton was very much alive, though getting on in years, and still practicing medicine. He directed him to a small office building just off of Main Street, where Zimri found an outside stairway with a sign attached to it that read, 'M.M. Houghton, M.D. One flight up,' with the dim outline of a forefinger pointing in that direction.

Zimri entered and found himself in a small waiting room with a few empty chairs and a coffee table on which rested stacks of newspapers. He closed the door, which had a bell attached, placed his hat on the clothes tree opposite the door, and picked up a copy of the *Journal*.

"Be with you directly," came a voice from the next room. "Now don't go bustin' that new cast up like you did the last one. Otherwise, that ulna will never heal right. And take a little elderberry wine at night before you go to bed. That'll help you to sleep without too much pain."

"Okay, Doc."

A burly man of about forty with his arm in a sling appeared at the door to the next room. Standing behind him and escorting him through the door was a diminutive old man wearing a white smock and a stethoscope around his neck. When the man with the broken arm was gone, he adjusted his glasses and addressed Zimri.

"What can I do for you, young man?"

"My name is Zimri Rhodes. I'm a newspaper reporter."

"Reporter? You work for Marcus Slade?"

"No. I've got my own paper now in Martinville. Marcus and I used to be partners."

"Martinville? The *Mercury*?"

"That's right."

"I read your editorials just like I do all the others. You're a Unionist."

"I have to confess that I am indeed."

"And a Republican."

"That, too."

"That's illogical."

"How so?"

"Because a Unionist doesn't believe in states' rights, and a Republican believes in maximum freedom for the individual."

"I don't see the contradiction."

"Then you are a horse's ass. Now, Mr. Rhodes, what can I do for you?"

This was said without malice and Zimri found the old man rather amusing. "I just have a few questions about your treatment of James Blake."

"Blake? I don't recall—"

"It was years ago, Dr. Houghton. At Belle Oaks."

"Belle Oaks? Oh, yes. I used to have a practice in Clinton, not far from there. Belle Oaks...the Blake family...Now I remember. Little James had a bout with tuberculosis in his early teens, I believe. He pulled through, as I recall."

"That he did, Dr. Houghton. But I think he might have had a relapse recently. He died last month."

"Died? That's too bad. Come into my office, Mr. Rhodes. We'll be more comfortable there."

Dr. Houghton led Zimri into the examining room where the most prominent feature was a complete human skeleton suspended from an iron hook attached to a wall. There was an examining table, a wash basin with various medical instruments laid out neatly beside it, and bookcases full of medical books.

"Sit down, Mr. Rhodes, sit down. Now what's this all about?"

Zimri took his seat in a cane chair not far from the skeleton, which he eyed with curiosity. "Mr. Blake was my father-in-law."

"I see. Now tell me what's happened."

Zimri explained to him the circumstances of James Sr.'s death, as well as his suspicions that the cause of death was due to a recurrence of his childhood disease.

"That's quite possible," Dr. Houghton said. "Of course, when consumption occurs in childhood, it sometimes serves as a vaccination and it therefore never recurs. But as I recall, young James' case was complicated by pleurisy."

"Pleurisy?"

"Yes. An inflammation of the pleural membrane that wraps around the lungs. Pleurisy is recurrent, and can flare up again even after forty years."

"What are the symptoms?"

"Shortness of breath, painful breathing. Sometimes a build-up of fluid in the pleural cavity or even in the lungs themselves."

Zimri focused his attention on the chest cavity of the skeleton. "Could the puncture from the pitchfork have caused a similar build-up of fluid?"

"Possibly. But once scar tissue has formed over a period of several weeks it would be unlikely."

Zimri jotted all this down in his notebook and then looked up. "Would you be willing to testify at Luther's trial to that effect?"

Dr. Houghton sighed. "I'm an old man, Mr. Rhodes. I'm blessed with good health, but I can't get around as well as I used to."

"The trial would only last a day or two. You could put up at the Central Hotel."

"At whose expense?"

"Mine."

"Well, that's very generous of you. Mr. Rhodes. I'll have to check my calendar. When is the trial?"

"Next month. Probably on the fourth, or thereabouts."

Dr. Houghton went to his desk and leafed through his calendar. "The fourth, the fourth. A Monday. No appointments that day so far, or the next. All right, Mr. Rhodes, I suppose I can accommodate you. I'll need someone to fetch me, though, and bring me back to Milledgeville. My eyesight isn't so good anymore, and horses tend to ignore me when I say 'giddy-up'!"

Zimri laughed. "I'll send a driver for you." He rose from his chair.

"One more thing before you leave, Mr. Rhodes."

"Yes, Doctor?"

"Why are you doing this? Isn't it a bit beyond the call of your profession to be tracking down witnesses from forty years ago?"

"I suppose it is. But I hate to see a man hanged for something he had no part in."

Dr. Houghton seemed to consider this for a few moments. "If this boy Lucas—"

"Luther."

"If Luther is acquitted, then a lot of white folks, not just around here, but all over the state, are going to be upset."

"That's a distinct possibility."

"And they might be just as upset with your Unionist newspaper."

"That's also a distinct possibility."

"And after they drag poor Luther out of his jail cell and string him up from the nearest oak tree, they just might come after you."

"I'm prepared for that."

"Are you? Well, then, you're a brave man, Mr. Rhodes."

"Not especially, Dr. Houghton. But it seems to me that any republic will stand only as long as its citizens are willing to stand up for what is right and just."

Dr. Houghton smiled. "Ah. That's the Unionist in you. Of course, there's nothing that says that a state can't dispense justice just as well as the federal government."

"I certainly hope so, Dr. Houghton. But your own characterization of the local citizenry just now doesn't seem encouraging."

Dr. Houghton chuckled. "Touché, Mr. Rhodes. You remind me of my son-in-law. He would stand and argue with Fred there until poor Fred's bones turned to powder. Doesn't know when to give up."

Zimri glanced at the skeleton. "Fred will be around a lot longer than either of us, Doctor. And maybe he'll see the day when a conversation like this won't be necessary."

"So you're an abolitionist, too."

"I've been accused of that lately. But I'd rather think that I'm a man who wants to see simple justice done."

Dr. Houghton shook his head. "Justice is never simple, Mr. Rhodes. That's what eighty-eight years of life on this earth has taught me if nothing else."

"But you're still willing to testify."

"Of course. I want to see what happens."

Zimri smiled and now felt confident that Dr. Houghton would be as good as his word.

By the time Zimri got home, it was well after dark and he found Maybelle cleaning up in the kitchen.

"Where's Elizabeth?" he said.

"She done gone to bed, Massa Zimri."

"Bed? This early?"

"She sleep a lot these days, Massa Zimri. It be natural in her condition."

"I suppose so, though I was looking forward to having supper with her. Anything left to eat?"

"Oh, yes, suh. You jest set down at the table there and I'll whip you up some yams and collards and roast chicken."

"Sounds good to me. I can catch up with the latest edition of the *Mercury* in the meantime."

"Yes, suh. Massa Zimri—"

"Maybelle—"

"Yes, suh?"

"I'm not your master. 'Mister' Zimri will do."

"Yes, suh, Mass—Mister Zimri. I know that. I belong to Massa Jamie now that his daddy done passed away. It's jest that I been here helping Miz Lisbeth so long now, I done started thinking this be my home now."

"Well, we're delighted to have you here, believe me. In fact, I don't know what we'll do without you after the baby is born."

"Doc Parcher say it may be twins."

Zimri sighed. "I'm well aware of that. It just means we'll need all the more help. Do you know a free colored woman that I could hire?"

Maybelle seemed to think hard as she pulled some biscuits out of the oven. "I don't rightly know, Mister Zimri. They's a few womens that work for Mr. Thompson on his farm near Belle Oaks. And they's Boone Carter that has a blacksmith shop on the outskirts of town. Yeah, I think he got a daughter or two may need work."

"Boone Carter? That's right. I'd forgotten that he had a couple of daughters. I'll ask him about it on Monday. Thank you, Maybelle. That's an excellent idea."

"Yes, suh."

Zimri went to the bedroom door which was cracked open and peered in. He could see Elizabeth sleeping on her side beneath a thin blanket. Charlotte was in her crib next to her sleeping in nearly the same position. He closed the door carefully and then sat at the table, where he perused a few back issues of the *Mercury* while Maybelle served him his supper.

After supper, he went out onto the front porch and sat down on the swing. It was a clear, crisp moonlit night, and he enjoyed the feel of cold air entering his lungs. But this simple act of inhaling fresh air made him think once again of James Sr. Was it merely a coincidence that he died shortly after the stabbing, or did the pitchfork really do him in? And what do doctors really know about these things? Dr. Houghton certainly sounded convincing in his explanation this afternoon, but then how could he be sure?

Zimri stretched and yawned. It had been a long day, and he suddenly realized that he was quite tired. As he rose from the swing to turn in, he tossed one of Elizabeth's embroidered pillows aside. Beneath it was a letter. He sat back down and examined the envelope, which was addressed to Elizabeth in care of Jamie at Belle Oaks. None of his business, he thought. He started to put the letter down but was intrigued by the numerous postmarks. Genoa, Marseille, Paris, Savannah. He turned it over. On the back was a seal of red wax with the initials 'RJB' imprinted upon it. Now who could that be? He put the letter down again on the swing, stood up, and stretched again. Elizabeth would get it in the morning. On second thought, why leave it out on the porch where it might get wet or blow away? He decided to take it inside and put it on Elizabeth's desk.

As he stepped inside the house, he heard nothing from the kitchen and assumed that Maybelle had gone to bed as well. He then went about the hearth room to extinguish the candles. But at the first candle he brought the envelope closer to the light and examined it again.

Who did Elizabeth know in Europe? One of her French relations? Ah, that must be it. He again started to extinguish the candle with his fingertips. But she's never corresponded with any of her cousins in France, nor even mentioned them, for that matter.

His curiosity having got the better of him, he extracted the letter from its envelope and began reading:

My dearest Elizabeth...

He found the description of the political situation in France and Italy quite interesting, all of which seemed innocuous enough. But then he came to the writer's declaration of love for his wife. Elizabeth has a secret lover! He skimmed the rest of the letter and noted the signature: Randolph. Oh, yes, that young man from Charleston that came to the wedding and tried to persuade Elizabeth to break it off and elope with him. Elizabeth had flatly refused him. But apparently he has been persistent. Did he come around while he, Zimri, was in New York and Connecticut? He was a friend of Jamie's. A visit to Belle Oaks would serve as a good pretext to see Elizabeth again. Yes, he most certainly visited Elizabeth while he was gone. And now, thank God, he was in Europe.

Zimri put the letter back into its envelope and extinguished the candles in the room one by one. He suddenly felt guilty about having read it at all. And he thought of Cora. What a hypocrite he would be to condemn Elizabeth for simply receiving a letter from a foolish and romantic young man whom she had twice rejected before! And what if he should someday receive a letter from Cora? Would Elizabeth pick it up and read it if she happened upon it? Possibly. He shuddered at Cora's alluding to their tryst in New Haven.

He cracked open the door to the bedroom and saw Elizabeth still sleeping in the same position on the bed. Likewise Charlotte. He entered and carefully closed the door behind him, his eyes growing accustomed to the darkness. Elizabeth at last turned over and opened her eyes.

"Zimri?"

"Yes, darling. I'm home."

"Did you get something to eat?"

"Yes. Maybelle served up some of her roast chicken. It was delicious."

"Oh, good. Come kiss me good night."

Zimri hesitated for a moment, wondering what he should do with the letter. Then, seeing that her eyes were closed again, he made a detour to her desk, placed the envelope in her letter box with the others, and went over to the bed. He leaned over and kissed her on the cheek.

"Forgive me for not staying up, Zimri." Her eyes opened half way. "I'm so tired. I don't know why."

"As Maybelle says, 'it be natural.' Sleep well, darling."

"Umm," she said, and rolled back over onto her side.

Zimri sighed, partly with relief and partly from weariness himself. He pulled off his boots, lay on the bed without removing his clothes, and fell asleep.

CHAPTER 24

On Monday Zimri dropped by Boone Carter's blacksmith shop on the way into town and inquired about his daughters. Boone replied that at least one of his daughters would certainly be interested in doing some domestic work and that he would mention it to them.

From Boone's shop, he went to the office and read the galleys that Jed had prepared for the next issue. In the afternoon, he visited the courthouse and found Judge Henry Kincaid in his chambers.

"I've appointed Abner Flewellen as the defense attorney in the case, Zimri. He's new in town, a young fellow, but he's a hard worker, I'm told."

"What experience has he had?"

Judge Kincaid, a man in his sixties with salt and pepper hair receding at the temples and mutton chop whiskers of the same hue, leaned back in his chair and gazed at the bust of Cicero that occupied a prominent spot on his bookshelf. "This will be his first case."

Zimri said nothing.

The judge leaned forward and rested his heavy forearms on the desk. "You know as well as I do, Zimri, that there's little money in the county treasury to spend on lawyers for indigents. Particularly for slaves accused of killing their masters. I'd say the defendant is pretty lucky to have any representation at all. And this boy is smart as a whip, according to Mac Brady in Milledgeville. He's clerked for Mac, and read law with his old firm for three years before that. He'll do a fine job."

"I didn't say he wouldn't."

"But I could see the veil of doubt descend over your eyes when I told you about him."

"It's not my job to second-guess your appointments, Henry. I'm just a reporter."

The judge laughed and leaned back in his chair. "You're just a reporter like Andrew Jackson is just the president. You've got a lot of influence in this town, Zimri, and you know it. People read your editorials like they're the sermon on the Mount."

Zimri smiled. "I'm flattered, Henry, but I can think of more than a few people who take the *Mercury* with them to the privy. And not to read."

The judge laughed loudly and slapped his hand on his desk with a resounding bang. "I can't say that I haven't done it myself, Zimri. But I usually read it first."

"That's a relief."

The judge roared with laughter. "I'll say! It always is."

Zimri didn't mean for his last comment to be taken as a double-entendre. But he was content to let the judge think so.

"I'll tell you what, Zimri," the judge said. "You come back to-morrow for the jury selection—early—and I'll introduce you to Mr. Flewellen. Then you'll get to see him in action."

"I'd like that, Henry. Has he met with his client yet?"

"I suppose Sheriff Beasley could tell you that. Maybe you should drop by and see him."

"I intend to." Zimri rose. "Thanks, Henry. I know your time is valuable. I hope I haven't—"

"Two more cases this afternoon. One's a horse-stealing, the other an assault. Pretty cut-and-dried. But this trial of the slave—what's his name?"

"Luther."

"Right. Luther's trial is going to attract a lot of attention. And I don't want any lynching." The judge sat back down in his chair and seemed to brood. "I'm not worried about you and the *Mercury*, Zimri. But Anderson over at the *Patriot* seems to want to stir people up at every opportunity. If this boy Flewellen gets Luther off— even with a manslaughter charge—we could have big trouble here in Martinville."

"I'm aware of that, Henry. And I'm prepared to meet any racist invective with the derision it deserves."

The judge raised an eyebrow. "Are you speaking as a reporter or as an editorial writer?"

"You should know better than to ask a question like that, Henry."

The judge's frown turned to a smile. "I suppose I should, Zimri. I'll see you here tomorrow morning at quarter till nine."

Zimri left the courthouse and stopped at the jail where Sheriff Beasley informed him that Mr. Flewellen had indeed visited the prisoner.

"Twice," he said. "The second time, he stayed over two hours. Beats me what an educated man like that would have to talk about with an ignorant nigger for two hours, but that's what he did."

Zimri then went back to the office for a couple of hours and finally returned home about six o'clock.

At supper, Zimri seemed to be playing with the chunks of potato and celery floating in his soup.

"What's bothering you, Zimri?" Elizabeth had spent the day knitting a blue dressing gown, hoping that if it were twins, at least one would be a boy. "Your soup will get cold."

"What? Oh—it's Luther's trial, I guess."

"Don't you think it'll be fair?"

Zimri brought a spoonful of the soup to his mouth and put it down again. "Fair? Why, yes—I think the trial itself will be fair. Judge Kincaid, for all of his coarse humor, is a fair man and a conscientious judge. But it's not him I'm worried about, or even this novice of a lawyer. It's the jury."

"They haven't even picked a jury yet."

"I know. But it's going to be all white."

"Of course it is. That's the law, isn't it?"

Zimri stared at his soup for a moment and pushed the bowl aside. "Yes, and a bad one, in my opinion. A man—even a black man—ought to be judged by a jury of his peers."

"What about witnesses? Can't they be colored?"

"Yes. But the only two witnesses are Carmichael and Leon. And they will be seen as biased."

"Jamie was there."

"Jamie wasn't there. He was with you at Prescott's Bluff on a picnic."

"Oh—that's right."

Zimri thought that Elizabeth remained strangely silent after this last remark. He waited until Maybelle had taken the soup bowls away before he spoke again. "Is that where you entertained Randolph?"

Elizabeth looked at first surprised, than angry. "You've been reading my mail!"

"I couldn't help it. I sat down to rest on the swing Saturday night and when I got up to go to bed, there it was."

"But you shouldn't have read it—it was addressed to me!"

"Ordinarily I wouldn't have. But the postmarks, the wax seal with a man's initials on it—"

"How would you know it was a *man*'s initials? They could have belonged to a woman!"

Zimri wiped his lips with his napkin, his eyes fixed on hers. "That's enough, Elizabeth. I'm your husband. I have a right to read *all* of your mail if I've a mind to."

"That's another bad law! Besides, it doesn't compel you to read my letters, it only—"

"I said that's enough, Elizabeth."

She started to speak again but fell silent. Maybelle came in with the main course, a filet of catfish with stewed tomatoes, set the plates down and retreated to the kitchen. When she was gone, Zimri eyed the catfish with some distaste and continued:

"I will assume nothing untoward happened between you. The letter has the sound of a love-sick calf pining away for an unattainable object. Let's forget that it ever happened."

Elizabeth stared at her fish for a moment, then raised her eyes to meet Zimri's. "I will not forget that an old friend thought enough of me to write all the way from France to tell me of his impressions of that country, the country of my ancestors. Nor will I forget that you, a writer and supposedly a champion of individual liberty, stooped to reading his wife's mail!"

"Elizabeth, I—"

"And don't tell me 'that's enough, Elizabeth.' I am a woman now and your wife. I have helped save your newspaper from ruin."

Zimri found this last statement to be amusing. "I hardly think that you single-handedly saved the *Mercury*. Yes, you did collect the outstanding debts, for which I am grateful, but—"

"And most of all, I have never pried into your adventures in New York."

This stung Zimri. At first he was speechless, as memories of his encounters with Cora came rushing to the forefront of his mind. At last he formulated the most innocuous and non-committal response he could think of:

"I didn't think you were interested."

"Of course, I'm interested. I'm interested in everything you do. I could think of nothing else while you were gone, but who you were with, where you were on a given day, who you dined with, whether you went to the theatre—"

Zimri lowered his eyes and cut into his fish.

She stared at him intently. "You did go to the theatre, didn't you?"

"Yes, I went to the theatre."

"With whom, may I ask?"

"With a Frenchman I met on the ship. It was a poor entertainment."

She watched him carefully as he chewed his food and seemed to avoid her gaze. "The two of you? Alone?"

"Yes, just the two of us."

"And then what did you do?"

Zimri put his knife and fork down on his plate with a clatter. "We had a late supper and went back to the hotel. Elizabeth, I will not sit here and be interrogated about my—"

"Then you will not read my mail in the future?"

Zimri considered this for a moment and picked up his knife and fork again. It seemed a reasonable compromise. "No. I will not read your mail. Ever again."

"I have your word?"

"You have my word."

Elizabeth picked up her own knife and fork. "And I will not pry into your....adventures in New York. Agreed?"

"Agreed. Could you pass the salt, dear?"

CHAPTER 25

More than a week passed, during which time Zimri met Mr. Flewellen, who he found to be quite competent in spite of his inexperience; the jury was empanelled and the trial date was set.

On the morning of the fourth, the courtroom filled up very quickly, with members of the white community occupying all the first floor gallery seats, and the blacks, mostly relatives of the accused, filling the balcony on the second level.

Zimri, along with Isaac Anderson of the *Patriot* and Marcus Slade of the *Journal*, as well as reporters from as far away as Augusta and Savannah, sat in the first row nearest the judge. There were two opposing tables set up for the defense and the prosecution. The jury sat opposite the reporters and consisted of twelve men of various occupations. Zimri was acquainted with all but four of them. Among the jurors he did know were John Lewis, the milliner, and Mr. Herzen, the German immigrant who purchased Betty.

Luther sat quietly at the defense table, his ever-present Bible in front of him. He looked thinner than when he was incarcerated, and a bit more gray around the temples. His attorney, Mr. Flewellen, sat beside him, looking over some documents. Flewellen was about twenty-three, somewhat less than medium height, and of an athletic build. He was clean-shaven, with relatively short auburn hair that he parted in the middle and brushed back over his ears.

Opposite Mr. Flewellen at the prosecution's table sat the clerk of the court, Mr. Joshua Bates. It was his job to serve as the court's prosecutor. He was assisted by a junior clerk from his office, Mr. Stanley Ingram.

Judge Kincaid made his usual grand entrance with his black robe streaming behind him, surveyed the courtroom with a penetrating gaze, sat down, and banged his gavel on the bench.

"The court will come to order."

The trial had begun.

Mr. Bates rose and explained to the jury that this was a cut-and-dried case of a slave murdering his master. He further explained that under Georgia law, it made no difference what the defendant's intent was; he, as prosecutor only had to prove beyond a reasonable doubt that the defendant's actions were likely to produce death. Even if, he said, the victim had died of some unrelated cause at a later date, the mere fact that the assault with the pitchfork resulted in grievous bodily harm to the victim was enough to require the death penalty. Nevertheless, he would prove that the defendant's unprovoked assault was the proximate cause of the victim's death.

After Mr. Bates sat down, Mr. Flewellen rose and addressed the jury. He started by dismissing Mr. Bates' interpretation of Georgia law, saying that the defendant's intent was highly pertinent to the case, though not crucial. And while he would show that his client had no intention of harming his master, much less of killing him, he would show that Mr. Blake's death had not resulted from the 'accidental' penetration of the pitchfork—where it passed through no vital organs—but from the recurrence of a childhood disease several weeks after the incident in question. During this time, he said, Mr. Blake had recovered fully from the 'accident,' and gradually began to show symptoms of his childhood disease—fever, coughing, and shortness of breath. And it was this disease—consumption complicated by pleurisy—that finally killed him.

After Mr. Flewellen sat down, Mr. Bates rose again and called his first witness: Dr. Robert Parcher.

All this time, Zimri scribbled furiously in his own idiosyncratic shorthand, trying to get every word down as accurately as possible. It seemed to him that the nuances of Georgia law, while not especially fine in regard to slaves charged with capital offenses, nevertheless were crucial to the outcome of the case.

But he had no time to reflect upon this. He looked up from his notes and saw Dr. Parcher lowering his right hand and taking his seat in the witness stand.

"Dr. Parcher," Mr. Bates said, "you are a physician duly licensed to practice medicine in the state of Georgia?"

"Yes, sir, I am."

Mr. Bates, a tall, thin man of about fifty, paced in front of the jury box with his hands folded behind his back, "And how did you come by your training?"

"I attended the College of Charleston for three years and immediately went into the office of a prominent physician there, Dr. Jeremiah Brooks."

"Ah, yes. Dr. Brooks. A renowned surgeon, I understand."

"Yes, sir. He studied at Harvard before returning to Charleston to practice."

Mr. Bates stopped pacing and faced the jury. "Harvard. And did he have a specialty?"

"Yes, sir. He focused primarily on diseases of the lungs—consumption, pleurisy, pneumonia, that sort of thing."

"Consumption and pleurisy. So you learned a great deal about those diseases during your apprenticeship under Dr. Brooks, I would assume."

"Yes, sir. I would say so."

Mr. Bates went on to elicit from Dr. Parcher his opinion upon examining Mr. Blake shortly after the incident occurred.

"Did you determine at that time that Mr. Blake's lungs had been penetrated by the tines of the pitchfork?"

"No, sir."

"No?"

"No. I couldn't be certain. But I concluded that it was highly likely."

"And what brought you to that conclusion?"

"The difficulty he had breathing. Also, with my stethoscope, I thought I could detect a slight hissing sound—like air passing through a small hole."

"Like a whistle?"

"Something like that."

Dr. Parcher went on to describe Mr. Blake's' condition over the following three weeks and finally offered his opinion that Mr. Blake's vigorous outdoor activities ruptured the hole or holes in his lung and caused both lungs to fill up with fluid, thus drowning him.

"And this drowning, in your opinion, was a direct result of the defendant's stabbing Mr. Blake with the pitchfork?"

"Objection!" Mr. Flewellen rose to this feet.

"Overruled," the judge said. "The witness is an expert in his field. He may offer his opinion."

"Dr. Parcher?"

"Yes—I would say that the stabbing led directly to Mr. Blake's death."

"No further questions of this witness, Your Honor." Mr. Bates sat down.

"You may cross-examine the witness, Mr. Flewellen."

Mr. Flewellen rose from the defense table. "Thank you, Your Honor." He then approached the witness stand. "Dr. Parcher, you say you attended the College of Charleston for three years. Isn't that a four year program?"

Dr. Parcher glanced furtively around the courtroom. "That's correct."

"But you left after only three. Why?"

"My funds ran out. I needed to earn a living."

"I see. So you went to work for Dr. Brooks."

"That is correct."

"And that's where you learned about such diseases as consumption and pleurisy."

"Yes."

Mr. Flewellen looked at the jury. "Then I suppose you spent many a night pouring over Dr. Brooks' treatises on the subject."

Dr. Parcher appeared to be surprised at this statement. "Well...yes. Whenever I could."

"Of course you did. You were young and ambitious and wanted to rise in your profession. Isn't that right, Dr. Parcher?"

"I suppose so."

After a lingering gaze at the jury, Mr. Flewellen went on to ask Dr. Parcher why he assumed that the pitchfork had penetrated Mr. Blake's lungs.

"I've already said why. He was short of breath and I could hear a whistling of air with my stethoscope."

"But he could have experienced shortness of breath for any number of reasons, couldn't he? Because of a recurrence of his childhood disease, for example."

"Not likely. It would have been too much of a coincidence to have occurred precisely at that time."

"But what if he had experienced shortness of breath prior to the incident in question? Mrs. Blake, in her deposition says that she noticed that her husband was short of breath for a week or more prior to that."

"Well, I don't know about that. She never mentioned it to me."

Mr. Flewellen didn't respond, but gave the jury another meaningful look. "And this whistling, Dr. Parcher. Couldn't that have been caused by something other than a hole in Mr. Blake's lungs?"

"No, I don't think so."

"Have you ever held a shell up to your ear, Dr. Parcher? Maybe while you were walking on the beach near Charleston?"

"No, I don't think I ever did."

"No?" Mr. Flewellen cupped his hand over his ear. "Well, I have, Dr. Parcher. I used to spend summers with my family on St. Simon's Island. When you bring a big conch shell up to your ear, it sounds just like the ocean."

"Well—what of it?"

"There's no ocean or even a sea breeze in that conch shell, Dr. Parcher. It's just a cavity that plays tricks with your ear. It mimics the sound of the ocean. Couldn't that happen with your stethoscope?"

"That's preposterous. A physician is trained to detect the slightest sound in a patient's chest. There are no tricks to it."

"But isn't the chest also a cavity, Dr. Parcher?"

"Yes, that's true, but—"

"And it has just as convoluted a chamber as a conch shell, wouldn't you say?"

"Again, what you're saying is preposterous. There is no relationship between a—"

"Thank you, Dr. Parcher. I have no further questions, Your Honor."

After a short recess, during which Zimri stretched his legs and caught up with his colleagues from the other papers, Mr. Flewellen called Dr. Houghton to the stand. Dr. Houghton appeared to be as old as his years as he ascended to the witness chair; that is, slowly and steadying himself with a cane. Once seated, however, he looked about the courtroom with an alert curiosity in his eyes. He placed both hands on the head of his cane in front of him and focused on Mr. Flewellen, who came quite close to the witness chair.

"Dr. Houghton—"

"Stand back! I need air to breathe."

The spectators seemed to find this comment amusing.

Mr. Flewellen took a couple of steps backward. "Sorry, sir. I just wanted to make sure that you could hear me."

"I can her a pin drop in the next room. The hearing's fine. The eye sight is a little fuzzy at distances, though. Stop there."

"Here?"

"Right there. That's just right. And don't shout."

"No, sir. I wouldn't think of it."

"All right then. Now, you were about to ask a question."

"Yes, sir. Several questions."

"Fire away. I haven't got all day."

Mr. Flewellen acknowledged the spectators' laughter with a smile and crossed his arms over his chest. "How long have you been practicing medicine, Dr. Houghton?"

"About sixty years."

"And where did you get your training?"

"In medicine?"

"Yes, in medicine. Start with your formal education."

"I attended William and Mary College in Williamsburg, Virginia."

"And what year was that?"

"Well, let's see." Dr. Houghton turned his eyes to the ceiling and scratched beneath his chin. "I was in the class of '64, so I must have entered about 1760."

"1760? Then you must have been a classmate of Thomas Jefferson's."

"That's right. A highly opinionated fellow."

There were murmurings of laughter.

"And did you study medicine at William and Mary?"

"Not much. We had some anatomy classes. But there was no medical school there at the time."

"So how did you acquire your knowledge of medicine?"

Dr. Houghton returned his free hand to the head of his cane. "An opportunity came up."

"What kind of opportunity?"

"The opportunity to study medicine at Edinburgh University."

"In Scotland?"

"I don't know of any other Edinburghs, do you?"

"No, sir, I do not. How did that opportunity come about?"

"One of my professors came from there. He arranged for a scholarship for me."

"Then he must have had great confidence in you as a promising physician."

"I suppose so."

"And so you attended Edinburgh University?"

"Yes."

"And how long did you spend there?"

"About four years."

"And did you graduate?"

"Oh, they gave me a certificate of some sort. 'Doctor of Physick,' I think they called it. An out-of-date term these days."

"And where did you go from there?"

Dr. Houghton looked up in surprise. "Where? Why, home. You'd want to come home, too, if you spent four winters in Edinburgh."

The gallery tittered with laughter.

Dr. Houghton continued. "A bone-chilling climate. Cold and damp and the sun never comes up—peeks out sometime about noon for about twenty seconds."

"You came home to Georgia, Dr. Houghton?"

"What? Oh, yes. Home to Milledgeville. Only it wasn't the

capital then. Hardly even a village."

Mr. Flewellen began pacing in front of the witness stand. "And did you find plenty of patients there?"

"Oh, yes. Stop that pacing! Stand still where I can see you."

More laughter from the gallery.

"Sorry, doctor." Mr. Flewellen stopped and faced the witness again. "You say you found plenty of patients in Milledgeville?"

"Oh, yes. I was the only doctor there, for heaven's sake. I did move for a while to Clinton as there were a number of wealthy planters there who paid higher fees. But as Milledgeville grew, I came back."

"So you became very established there as a physician."

"Oh, yes. Everyone knows me there."

After noting that the witness had in fact written a book on pleurisy, Mr. Flewellen elicited from Dr. Houghton a description of the disease that afflicted Mr. Blake in childhood and how he had treated him.

"And in your opinion, Dr. Houghton, could Mr. Blake have died from the wound caused by the pitchfork?"

"Objection!" Mr. Bates stood up. "The witness has not examined the victim in over forty years. He cannot possibly—"

"Sustained."

"I'll rephrase the question, Your Honor." Mr. Flewellen began pacing again. "In your opinion, Dr.—"

"Stand still," Dr. Houghton said.

"Sorry. In your opinion, Dr. Houghton. Could the tines of a pitchfork puncture a man's lung, cause it to fill up with fluid, and subsequently drown the man?"

"That's possible."

"Even if the—let's call him 'the patient'—even if the patient seemed to recover fully from the wound to the point of going out riding and hunting every day for a period of three weeks?"

"That's not likely."

"Why not?"

"Because the wound would have been closed with scar tissue and therefore plugged the leak."

"But couldn't the scar tissue have broken loose from all that horseback riding?"

"That's possible, but it would have had to have happened fairly early on, and then the fluid would have built up very quickly—not over a period of weeks."

"But a recurrence of pleurisy could have occurred at any time?"

"Oh, yes. Anytime."

"And what would be the symptoms if indeed pleurisy returned?"

"Shortness of breath, painful breathing, possibly a fever."

"And would there be a build-up of fluid in the lungs?"

"Depends. If it were an effusive pleurisy, yes."

"Effusive pleurisy?"

"That means 'wet,' or 'fluid.' There's a dry pleurisy where no such fluid is present."

Mr. Flewellen brought his forefinger thoughtfully to his chin, "And what would be the symptoms of a 'dry' pleurisy?"

"Well, the patient would find breathing to be considerably more painful, because there would be no lubrication between the lungs and the pleural membrane, you see."

"So that if the patient didn't complain of painful breathing—"

"It would most likely be an effusive, or 'wet' pleurisy."

"Thank you, Doctor Houghton. Your testimony has been most helpful. No further questions, Your Honor."

Mr. Flewellen sat down and Mr. Bates was allowed to cross-examine the witness. But to everyone's surprise, he asked the witness only one question.

"Have you laid eyes on the deceased these last forty years, Dr. Houghton?"

"No, I have not," Dr. Houghton said.

"Thank you, sir. No further questions, Your Honor."

After an hour break for lunch, the participants returned to their places and Mr. Flewellen called several witnesses, the most important being Leon, the stable hand.

Leon took the stand reluctantly, as if it were he who were on trial. He was a young man, hardly more than a boy, and like Luther, had been born at Belle Oaks. He had a way with horses, and James Sr. recognized his talent early, promoting him above his older peers. He was rather short but powerfully built, and black as coal. He wore the green and white livery of the house slaves, but he was rather negligent in keeping up his uniform, and often appeared to be disheveled.

"How long have you been the head groom at Belle Oaks, Mr. Stokes?" Flewellen looked at his lapels as if comparing his own coat unfavorably with Leon's.

"Don't rightly know, suh. Maybe two, three years."

"How old are you now?"

"Don't know 'zactly. Maybe nineteen."

"Nineteen. So you've been head groom since you were sixteen. Mr. Blake, your master, must have had a lot of confidence in you."

"Reckon so."

Mr. Flewellen turned towards the defendant's table and indicated Luther with a gesture of his hand. "Do you know the defendant there, Mr. Caldwell?"

Leon leaned towards the defendant's table as if seeing Luther for the first time that day. "Sho' do."

"And what is your relationship to Mr. Caldwell?"

"Suh?"

"What is your connection with the defendant?"

"Oh. Well, he be a house slave sometimes, and sometimes he work in the stable wid me."

"So he had no assigned job?"

"Not 'zactly. He knowed Massa James since they was boys together, and Massa James jest let him roam about, I guess you'd say, doin' whatever needed to be done."

Mr. Flewellen seemed to study a tobacco stain on the floor. "Were you in the stable the day of the incident in question?"

"Yes, suh."

"And you were there when he had an argument with Mr. Blake?"

"Yes, suh."

"I see. Now, Mr. Stokes, can you tell us in your own words what you saw?"

Leon slumped down into the witness chair and rubbed his chin. He looked at Luther for a moment, who did not look up from his Bible, and then to the balcony where the blacks sat expectantly. Then he turned back to Mr. Flewellen. "I seen Massa James come in to get his hoss, 'cause he was goin' huntin' that day. Luther was there hepin' me brush ol' Cinnabar down and puttin' the saddle on him."

"And were there words exchanged between Luther and Master James?"

"Yes, suh. Ol' Luther, he was upset that Massa James wouldn't let him attend his grandbaby's funeral. Massa James say he wouldn't put up wid none of that voodoo foolishness, and that no nigger of his was gone 'ticipate in it."

"And how did Luther react to that?"

"Oh, he plenty mad. He be cryin' and—"

"He was crying before Master James came into the stable?"

"Yes, suh. His grandbaby's death done tore him up."

"And then what happened?"

Leon rubbed his chin. "Well, Massa James started to get on his hoss, got one foot in the stirrup, and Luther, he picked up a pitchfork and kinda point it at him and say, 'you ain't goin' nowheres till you give me permission to go to that funeral.'"

"And what did Master James do?"

"Massa James get down from ol' Cinnabar, look Luther in the eye, and say, 'Gimme that pitchfork, you ol' fool.'"

"And did Luther give it to him?"

"Naw, suh. He jest stand there wid it pointin' at him."

"Did he lunge at Master James with it?"

"Suh?"

"Did he make a move in Master James' direction as if to stab him with the pitchfork?"

"Naw, suh. He jest stand there wid it."

"And what did Master James do then?"

"Massa James reached out to grab it from him."

"Then what?"

"Massa James grab the handle of the pitchfork and try to twist it out of Luther's hands."

"And did he succeed?"

"Naw, suh. Luther hung on tight."

"And then what?"

"Then they both kinda tumble onto the ground and the next thing I knows, Massa James is hollerin,' 'Luther, you damn nigger, you done kilt me!'"

"And did you think Luther had killed him?"

Leon smiled. "Naw, suh. That was jest Massa James' way."

Mr. Bates leaped to his feet. "Objection!"

"Sustained," the judge said. "Just tell us what you saw and heard, Mr. Stokes."

"Yes, suh."

Mr. Flewellen continued. "Did you see the pitchfork penetrate Master James' side?"

"Not 'zactly."

"What did you see?"

"Well, I saw some blood on Massa James' shirt."

"How much blood?"

"Jest a speck at first. Then more as Massa James kept squeezin' his side."

"Was the pitchfork actually sticking in Master James' body?"

"Naw, suh. Not that I could see. It be layin' on the ground."

Mr. Flewellen turned to Luther. "What was Luther doing all this time?"

"He be kinda crouched on the ground and sobbin.'"

"He was still crying?"

"Yes, suh."

"Did he try to help Master James at all?"

"Naw, suh."

"Did he pick up the pitchfork again and try to stab him with it?"

"Naw, suh."

"He just remained in that crouch, sobbing."

"Yes, suh."

"Then what happened?"

"Well, Massa James be tryin' to get up, and holdin' his side and I be tryin' to hep him, and that when Carmichael come runnin' in."

"And what did Carmichael do?"

"He tell me to get some liniment and bandages and sich, so's we could stop Massa James from bleedin.'"

"And did you do so?"

"Yes, suh."

"What about Luther? Was he still sobbing on the ground?"

"Naw, suh. He run off into the yard."

"Did he try to run away from the premises altogether? That is, did he try to hide or escape?"

"Naw, suh. He jest run out into the yard and throwed hisself on the ground and started sobbin' some more. Then, after me and Carmichael carried Massa James to the house, we come back out and truss him up and put him in the corn crib till we figger out what to do wid him."

Mr. Flewellen turned to Jamie, who was sitting in the first row of the gallery. "But you didn't have to figure out what to do with him, did you? Master James's son, Jamie, came home and promptly administered fifty lashes across his back with a bull whip, didn't he?"

"Objection!"

"Sustained."

"I have no further questions." Mr. Flewellen sat down.

At this point, there were murmurings among the spectators, both black and white. The judge banged his gavel. "Quiet in the court-room! Mr. Bates, you may cross-examine the witness."

"I have no questions, Your Honor."

The judge stared at Mr. Bates for a moment. "All right, then. We will adjourn until tomorrow morning at nine o'clock sharp." He banged his gavel, all rose, and when he had disappeared behind his chamber door, the courtroom seemed suddenly transformed into a county fair.

Amongst the tumult, Zimri watched as Luther was led away in shackles, clutching his Bible.

CHAPTER 26

Elizabeth and Zimri sat on the sofa before a roaring fire after supper that night, the first day of Luther's trial. It was getting too cold to sit outside on the porch and besides, Elizabeth was concerned about catching cold—or worse—and passing it on to the baby. She snuggled closer to Zimri and stared into the fire.

"Do you think this Mr. Flewellen—Flewellen—what a funny name. It sounds like a chimney sweep."

Zimri laughed. "His ancestors may well have been."

"Do you think this Mr. Flewellen can actually get Luther acquitted?"

"I don't know about his being acquitted, but if anybody can save him from the gallows, I think it's Flewellen. He was absolutely brilliant today!"

"He must be very smart."

"Yes, and he has a flair for the dramatic. He had the jury—and the spectators—eating out of his hand."

Elizabeth continued to stare into the fire, watching the flames licking the underside of the logs like dancers performing a primitive ritual. "Jamie would be furious if Luther were to be acquitted."

"No doubt. He needs to be vindicated for that whipping he gave him." They both remained silent for a few moments.

"Do you know what Maybelle told me today?" she said.

"No. What?"

"She said that if they hang Luther, the root doctor will put a hex on Jamie. Just like she did on Daddy."

Zimri looked at her in surprise. "She put a hex on your father?"

"That's what Maybelle said. She said that's what killed him, not the pitchfork or the pleurisy, either."

"That's ridiculous."

"Of course it is. But Maybelle believes it, and so do most of the darkies out at Belle Oaks."

Zimri considered this for a few moments. "Why did the root doctor place a hex on your father?"

"Because he wouldn't let Luther go to the funeral of his grandbaby. She—the root doctor—says he insulted the loa by preventing Luther from going."

"What in heaven's name is the 'loa?'"

"The spirits of Luther's ancestors."

Zimri chuckled. "Elizabeth, I think you've been spending too much time talking to Maybelle."

She gave him a kiss on the cheek. "Well, I don't have anyone else to talk to all day. You're either at the office, or the trial, and Charlotte's still too young."

"You'll soon have your hands full enough. When does Dr. Parcher think you're due?"

"Perhaps as early as next week, he said."

"Hmm. I can't say as I have the confidence in Parcher's judgment that I once had. Not after the way Flewellen carved him up today."

She snuggled again against his chest. "He may not know much about pleurisy, but he's a good doctor. He's delivered thousands of babies, including Charlotte."

"Yes, I suppose he's a good baby doctor. And maybe he was right about the pitchfork puncturing your father's lungs. Who knows? The only thing that matters is what the jury believes."

"Oh, darling, let's not talk anymore about Daddy and Luther. I want to enjoy the little bit of time I have with you."

Zimri pulled her closer. "I hope it's a girl."

She sat up and looked into his eyes. "Boy."

"Girl."

"Boy and girl."

Zimri laughed. "All right. If it's twins, it shall be one of each."

"Kiss me."

"I was just thinking of that."

The next morning Zimri watched from his seat as the jurors filed out of the jury box and into the deliberation room. The judge instructed the attorneys to remain close by so that the bailiff could summon them once the verdict came in.

Zimri stretched his legs, spoke briefly to colleagues from the other papers, and walked out into the hallway, where he found Jamie smoking a cigar.

"Well, Zimri," he said. "Won't be long now. I'm sick of this whole thing."

"It's been a brief trial," Zimri said, glancing at his notes. "Much shorter than I anticipated."

"Seemed like an eternity to me. All that testimony about pleurisy and 'effusion' and God knows what all. Who can make anything of what these doctors say? It's cut-and-dried as far as I'm concerned. Luther stabbed Daddy with a pitchfork and he died. That's it. And even if he hadn't died, according to Georgia law, a slave raises his hand against his master and—zzzt!"—Jamie drew his forefinger across his throat—"he's a dead man. Capital offense."

Zimri started to take issue with this oversimplification, but saw that it was useless to argue with Jamie about anything that required subtle distinctions. "The judge has a certain amount of discretion in these cases."

Jamie glared at him. "Kincaid can exercise all the discretion he wants—as long as the verdict comes back 'guilty,' he's got to hang him."

"We'll see."

"Damn straight we will. Look, here comes the bailiff now."

"Attorneys return to the courtroom," the bailiff said.

Zimri took his watch out of his vest pocket. It had only been ten minutes since the jury went out.

Suddenly there was a crush to get back into the courtroom. The attorneys took their places, the reporters perched on the edge of their front row seats, and the spectators, black and white, clamored for any seat they could find.

Judge Kincaid banged his gavel for silence and instructed the bailiff to open the door to the jury room. Each juror, stone-faced, entered the jury box in single file and when all were seated, the judge asked if they had reached a verdict.

The foreman stood up. "We have, Your Honor."

"Please hand the verdict to the bailiff."

The foreman did so.

"You will read the verdict, Mr. Donaldson."

"On the charge of a slave or free person of color assaulting a free white person with intent to murder, or with a weapon likely to produce death, we, the jury, find the defendant guilty."

A black woman in the balcony swooned and others rushed to assist her.

"Continue, Mr. Donaldson," the judge said.

"On the charge of a slave or free person of color murdering a free white person, we, the jury, find the defendant guilty."

There were more shrieks and moans in the balcony, and a second woman swooned followed by a third.

"You're going to die, nigger!" Shouted a young white man in the first floor gallery. Zimri recognized him as the same young man that disrupted the auction at which he sold Betty and Solomon.

Judge Kincaid banged his gavel several times in succession. "Order in the court! There will be order in the court! Any more outbursts like that, young man, and you'll be a guest of the sheriff tonight! Order!"

The noise from the gallery was considerably reduced, though there was still much moaning and crying in the balcony. Having restored order, the judge banged his gavel and said:

"The defendant will rise."

Both Mr. Flewellen and Luther rose to their feet.

"Under Georgia law I am required to pass sentence on all capital cases involving people of color without delay. The defendant, Luther Caldwell, is hereby sentenced by this court to be hanged by the neck until dead on the fifteenth day of this month."

There were more shrieks and cries from the balcony.

The judge banged his gavel. "Order! Order!" The balcony again quiet, he turned to the defense table. "Mr. Flewellen you may apply to the Superior Court in Milledgeville if you wish to appeal the verdict on behalf of your client. If so, the execution date may be postponed or rescinded, depending on the decision of the Superior Court."

"We will appeal, Your Honor."

"Very well," the judge said. "Mr. Donaldson, return the defendant to the jail. Mr. Flewellen, please see me in my chambers." He banged his gavel three times. "This court is adjourned!"

Zimri made his way through the crowd into the hallway. Again, he encountered Jamie, who had a grin on his face.

"What did I tell you, Zimri?" Jamie said. "Cut-and-dried."

"Apparently the jury thought so, too."

"Of course they did. They did their Christian duty." Jamie lit another cigar. "I kind of feel sorry for Luther, though. He's not really a violent nigger like some of them. But he's got to serve as an example to the others, else they'd be down on our necks like foxes on a hen house."

"It's not over yet, you know. Flewellen could get the verdict overturned on appeal."

Jamie laughed. "Not likely. I know Judge Bullins in Milledgeville. He gives short shrift to niggers who raise their hands against their masters. Remember, Luther was guilty on two counts: one on murdering a white man, and one on assaulting a white man 'with a weapon likely to produce death.' That second one is all it takes.

Like Mr. Bates said, it don't matter what Luther's intent was."

"I agree that the prospect looks grim for Luther. But we'll have to wait and see."

Jamie shook his head. "You are a piece of work, Zimri. Here you are pulling for the nigger that murdered your wife's father. You ought to be ashamed of yourself."

"I'm a newspaperman, Jamie. I'm bound by my profession to report the facts, and the fact is that Luther still has an appeal."

"Oh, yeah," Jamie said. "I forgot—you're supposed to be completely objective. Well, a little bird told me that you paid for Dr. Houghton to come down here from Milledgeville and testify on behalf of the defense."

"I didn't pay him to come down. I paid for his expenses because he wouldn't have made the trip at his age if I hadn't."

Jamie took a puff on his cigar and grinned. "I'm afraid the distinction is lost on me, Zimri. Like some of Dr. Houghton's 'expert' testimony. Seems to me you've got an ethical problem there."

"Ethical? I don't think so."

"Maybe. Maybe not. That's for you and your own conscience to wrestle with. But I can't stand here all day and parse the niceties of journalistic responsibility with you, Zimri. I've got a plantation to run. Give my love to Elizabeth."

"I surely will, Jamie."

"When's the baby due?"

"Next week. Possibly any day now."

"Doc Parcher will take care of her."

"I'm sure he will."

Jamie smiled and pulled on his cigar. "He knows his stuff, you know."

Zimri did not respond to this jab, thinking it better to allow Jamie to have the last word. As he watched him stride confidently out of the courthouse, he thought of what he had said about his paying Dr. Houghton's expenses. Had he overstepped the bounds of journalistic responsibility? Was it really the ethical dilemma that Jamie said it was?

He chuckled to himself. Jamie, the arbiter of ethical responsibility? That was like petitioning a wolf for an opinion on the justice of slaughtering sheep. He shook his head and walked out into the afternoon sunlight that was already beginning to cast long shadows in the street.

CHAPTER 27

Friday, 15 October

Attended the hanging of Luther Caldwell. It was a dreary, over-cast day, and unseasonably warm. Scaffolding was erected in the town square and all manner of people came out to watch, black and white, young and old.

Mayor Pritchard mingled among the crowd, shaking hands and canvassing votes for his re-election in November. Shopkeepers, apprentices, drovers, farmers bringing their produce to market, all interrupted their tasks for the sake of a little entertainment to start the day.

Sheriff Beasley himself followed Luther, his hands tied behind his back, up the stairs to the platform. Irwin Rutledge, a young Methodist clergyman, led the procession until they arrived at their prescribed places. Rutledge read the appropriate verse from the Bible in such circumstances:

Yea, though I walk in the valley of the Shadow of Death,
I will fear no evil...

Luther stared ahead expressionless. None of his relatives were present, as Jamie forbade any of them to attend. Nor did he attend himself.

Luther seemed resigned to his fate. When Sheriff Beasley asked if he had any last words, he simply said:

"Naw, suh. I'm in the hands of the Good Lord now."

The hangman then put a burlap bag over his head to spare the women and children the gruesome sight of his eyes and tongue bulging out, pulled a lever, and Luther's lithe body plunged below the platform.

Cheers went up from the young apprentices in the crowd, and hats were waved as if it were the Fourth of July.

"God rest his soul," said The Reverend Rutledge, and the two remaining members of the procession, along with the hangman, filed back down the stairway. Beasley and his deputy went beneath the platform to confirm that Luther was dead, whereupon a couple of grave diggers cut him down and lifted the body into a dog cart, and the crowd began to disperse, returning to their various modes of business.

Zimri returned to the office to write up the last of his reports on Luther's trial and final ordeal. He gave Jed the copy to set into type and went home for dinner. When he arrived, he discovered Dr. Parcher in the hearth room, drying his hands with a towel, wearing a big grin on his face.

"It's twins," he said. "Just as I thought. Two healthy little girls."

Zimri went into the bedroom and found Elizabeth sitting up and cradling two tiny red-faced creatures in her arms, smiling at him.

"Aren't they beautiful?" she said. "What will we call them?"

"Fortunate," he said. "Fortunate and Lucky."

"Oh, Zimri, be serious. We can't call them Fortunate and Lucky."

"Why not? That's just what they are."

Elizabeth looked at him doubtfully. "Well, Lucky might be all right for one. But what child can go through life being called 'Fortunate'?"

They compromised and decided that the younger one—by six minutes—would be called 'Fortunata.'

Zimri thanked Dr. Parcher and paid him for his services. When he had left, he returned to the bedroom and found Maybelle rocking the twins in her arms.

"Whooo-ee!" she said. "These little sweetpeas are the purtiest little things that I ever did see. Just like their mama."

Little Charlotte, standing up in her crib and hanging onto the railing, stared at her two little sisters with apparent approval. "Bab-by! Bab-by!"

"That's right, honey," Elizabeth said. "They're our brand new little baby girls. You'll have to help me look after them."

Zimri laughed. "Charlotte's hardly fourteen months. She's not going to be much help. And with Maybelle going back to Belle Oaks—"

"We'll need to hire both of those Carter girls," Elizabeth said. "I don't know how else I could manage."

"Don't you worry none," Maybelle said, still rocking the twins. "I'll stay on till you gets back on yo' feets."

"Thank you, Maybelle," Elizabeth said. "I don't know what we'll do when you're gone."

Maybelle gave the twins back to Elizabeth. "Don't you fret none. I tole you everything's gone be all right. Now I got to get back to the kitchen to fix some vittles for you and Mr. Zimri."

"Oh, I'm not hungry, Maybelle."

"You got to eat, Miz Lisbeth. And so do yo' babies. You feed them, and I'll feed the grown-ups and lil' Miss Charlotte."

After dinner Elizabeth sat up with the twins for a while cooing and tickling them until they fell asleep. Finally, she fell asleep herself, and Maybelle carefully picked up the twins and put them in the new cradle that Zimri had made for them. Then Maybelle went back to the kitchen and Zimri sat down at his desk to open his mail.

Most were bills, including one from R. Hoe & Sons in New York for the next installment on the new printing press. Another, postmarked Philadelphia, was from Omri Sparks thanking him again for his companionship on the trip from Norfolk, and informing him that his quest in Savannah to purchase the freedom of his niece had been successful.

Another letter was postmarked Savannah. There was no return address. Curious, he slit the envelope open with his letter knife and noted a hint of perfume.

Dearest Zimri—

He put the letter down with such violence that it stirred Elizabeth.

"Zimri?"

"Go back to sleep, darling. You need your rest."

"What? Oh..." She closed her eyes again and seemed fast asleep.

Zimri stared at the folded letter for several moments and then as if it were a poisonous snake, picked it up carefully by the edges and unfolded it again.

Dearest Zimri,

I must apologize for being so long in writing you, but I have been so busy that I have hardly had time to think of anything else— and yet I do think of you, if only for a few moments before I close my weary eyes each night.

I am happy to say my latest venture was a success. It was profitable for both me and my associates, many of whom do not expect pecuniary rewards.

But alas, as a single woman and struggling actress, I do not have the luxury of pursuing my goals without regard to financial compensation. Consequently, my new venture will be devoted solely to personal aggrandizement though I am willing for others to share in the profits according to the extent of their participation.

In short, I am proposing to build two new steamboats that will ply the waters of the Ocmulgee from Martinville to Savannah. They will carry cargo—principally cotton—to the markets there in half the time that it now takes by wagon or flatboat. I have spent the last two weeks in Savannah—where I have good connections—securing the financing. But alas, I have at this point only enough money pledged to build one of the boats. There must be two to make the venture economically successful, as while one vessel is sailing down river to deliver the cargo to market, the other will be returning to pick up the next load. And since the new company thus formed will primarily benefit the citizens of Martinville, it is only fitting that at least half of the investment should come from its business community. The terms will be most agreeable to all investors, I assure you.

Zimri, I ask for your help. I realize that you are but a small-town newspaperman, and have little capital to spare yourself, but from all reports you are a man of considerable influence and reputation in Martinville. All I need for you to do is to set up a meeting with prospective investors so that I may present my proposal.

Forgive me, dearest, for turning what should be a love letter into a cold business proposition. But I am not unmindful of the fact that this venture will bring me into your arms once again. Every fiber of my being cries out for the tenderness of your touch. I have considerable talents, as you know, but no woman can exist long without knowing that there is a man somewhere who is uniquely attuned to her deepest emotional and physical needs. And Zimri, for me at least, you are that man.

You see that there is no return address. This is for reasons of security, both personal and professionally. Therefore, I ask that your answer be delivered in care of General Delivery, the Post Master, Savannah, Georgia. The addressee shall be:

C. Rinaldi, esq.
Au revoir, mon cher
Cora
P.S. I will be in Martinville on the 29th.
P.P.S. I am looking forward to meeting Elizabeth.

Zimri stared at the second post-script almost in a state of stupefaction. The nerve of that woman! The effrontery! The shameless...honesty? She makes no pretence to wanting anything but the selfish gratification of her desires...no hint of jealousy in regard to Elizabeth—in fact she wants to meet her!

And this business proposal…it sounds like a scam. A con game to defraud and deceive the most prominent citizens of Martinville and then to leave him, Zimri, holding the bag. That is, the bag that will be all that's left of his reputation. It would ruin him!

Nevertheless, he read the letter over again, as he had the first in New York. He re-read carefully the main points of the business proposal. It actually sounded quite feasible, not like a hare-brained scheme. Martinville could use a local steamboat company. It could lead to exponential growth of the local economy. And her estimate of the time it would save in getting cotton to market in Savannah was actually too conservative. Half? Surely it would reduce delivery time by at least two-thirds.

He read over the last paragraph again. *Every fiber of my being cries out...a man uniquely attuned to her deepest emotional and physical needs...*

He folded the letter up and placed it in its envelope. Then he paced in front of the hearth for several minutes. Finally, he pulled the letter from the envelope and read it again. He thought of Elizabeth and the twins. He thought of Cora and that day in New Haven. He shook his head as if to shake out the image of Cora in her nakedness, in her voluptuous indecency. He thought of Elizabeth again and her enormous belly before the birth of the twins and the vague disgust he felt at making love to her while in that condition. He looked over his shoulder and caught a glimpse of Maybelle finishing up in the kitchen. He returned his eyes to the fire.

After a few moments, he knelt down and extended one corner of the letter into the fire. As it slowly blackened the edge of the paper and then burst into bright flame, he released it into the hearth. Then the envelope, with the same slow start, and the same sudden burst of flame.

He stood there staring into the fire until he heard the twins crying. Then he went into the bedroom, where he found them already quiet again, each nursing at one of Elizabeth's breasts, and Elizabeth herself looking up at him, smiling.

CHAPTER 28

By the end of the month, circulation of the *Mercury* had already grown by thirty percent as a result of the increased capacity of the new cylinder press, as well as Jed's assiduous efforts in selling new subscriptions. Advertising revenue had increased by forty percent.

Maybelle went back to Belle Oaks and Zimri hired both of the Carter girls, Louise and Tessie, at a salary of a dollar a week each. Louise was the oldest at nineteen, and had worked as a cook for two other families before coming down with pneumonia the previous winter. Tessie was only sixteen, but was an accomplished seamstress, and seemed particularly good with children. Zimri was impressed with Tessie's apparent high intelligence and curiosity as well as her domestic skills. The first day, after being instructed as to her duties, she stood before Zimri's growing library and perused the titles.

"I can read, Mister Zimri," she said.

"Can you, now?"

"Yes, sir. My daddy's master taught him to read when he was a slave, and he taught me and Louise, only Louise didn't take to books like I did."

"And what books have you read, Tessie?"

"Well, I done read six books already. Let's see, the first, not countin' the Bible of course, was *Aesop's Fables*, and then there was *Reynard the Fox*. Them books are for little kids, you know. But then I moved on to *The History of King Arthur*—I really liked that one, especially the part about Sir Lancelot and Guinevere— and *Pilgrim's Progress*. That one was a mite boring, but it was all right. After that I read *Gulliver's Travels*, and that was real excitin,' with Gulliver travelin' to foreign lands and all, and gettin' into a heap of trouble, but always gettin' out of it somehow. And what else? Oh, yeah—*Robinson Crusoe*, but I didn't like the way Robinson treated Friday like he was his slave or somethin.' Now I'm working on *The Adventures of Don Quixote*, about a crazy old man in Spain who goes around whuppin' up on windmills 'cause he thinks they be giants. I ain't so sure about that one, but it be kinda funny, though."

Zimri smiled and took down a volume from the top shelf of one of the bookcases. "Well, when you finish that one, you might be interested in reading this. As long as you've finished your chores and put the children to bed, of course." He handed her the volume.

"*The Tales From Shakespeare*," she said. "Who Shakespeare be?"

"He was a playwright in 16th Century England."

"Play-rite?"

"That means he wrote plays for the theatre. He was very popular in his time."

Tessie leafed through the heavily illustrated book. "It got nice pictures don't it?"

"It has nice pictures, doesn't it?"

She looked up from the book. "That's what I just said. Didn't you hear me?"

"I heard you all right." Zimri reached for another volume. "Here, you might want to look at this one, too."

"*The American Speller*, by Noah Webster. He a school teacher?"

"I believe he was for a while." He pointed to a two-volume set on his desk. "And when you're finished with that, you can consult his latest work, *The American Dictionary of the English Language*. I bought it while I was in New York recently."

"You been to New York?"

"Just got back."

"My gracious, Mister Zimri, you musta been everywhere and know everything."

Zimri laughed. "Hardly. The more you learn the more you realize how little you do know. But it's a worthy endeavor—and quite enjoyable, too."

Tessie looked down at the *Speller*. "I can read all right, but I ain't too good at writin.' This book teach me how to write?"

"It'll go a long way to doing that. Why don't you keep it?"

"Keep it? You mean for good?"

"I mean for good. I don't really need it anymore, though it was a good friend for many years."

"Oh, thank you, Mister Zimri! I'll memorize every last word of it."

"That may not be necessary, but it will be a good guide."

Tessie clutched the book to her breast as if it were bound in gold and hurried off to the kitchen to show Louise.

"What are you thinking, Zimri?" Elizabeth stood in the doorway to the bedroom. "You know it's against the law to teach them to read, much less give them a book."

Zimri looked at her curiously. Her figure was nearly restored, though her complexion was somewhat sallow, and the cheeks sunken. Still, her former beauty shone through the now shapeless maternity clothes. A shawl covered her shoulders. "It's a shameful law that is rarely enforced these days. Especially against white people."

"Still, what if Tessie advertises it to the world just as she is to her sister at this very moment?"

"I'll caution her to be discreet."

She crossed the room and embraced him. "I hope you will, darling. I'm beginning to get worried about our relations with the darkies, especially after what happened to Luther."

He put his arms around her and patted her shoulder. "It was a bad business. The jury had made up its mind before the trial even started."

"Maybelle said there was talk at Belle Oaks."

"What kind of talk?"

"I don't know exactly. She wouldn't say. But it's not hard to guess."

"You mean of an uprising?"

"That was the gist of it. I can remember when there was a slave revolt in Charleston. I was a girl then in boarding school. Everyone was terrified."

"The Vesey Rebellion."

"Yes, that was it. How do we know it won't happen here?"

"Charleston's a big city. Slaves aren't so close to their masters there as they are at a plantation like Belle Oaks. There'll be talk for a while, and then it will die down."

"How can you be so sure?"

Zimri loosened his embrace and looked into her eyes, which seemed red, as if she had been crying. "Because I know Carmichael and Leon and Old George and the others. They won't let it happen."

"I hope you're right."

"Have you been crying?"

Elizabeth turned away. "I've just been sad since the birth of the twins. I can't really explain it."

"You just need to get out of the house for a while. You've been cooped up too long. Why don't we go boating tomorrow?"

"Boating? Isn't it rather cool for that?"

"Nonsense! This is balmy weather by New England standards."

"Well, I'm not from New England—I'm not cold-blooded like

you."

Zimri laughed. "Now I'm cold-blooded! Do I look like a pirate?"

"As a matter of fact, you do resemble Blackbeard—only without the beard."

"You know, I grew one on the ship—I must have frightened all the passengers."

"Mmm. I'm sure you didn't frighten the ladies. They were whispering how handsome you were."

Zimri embraced her again in a bear hug and lifted her off her feet.

"Zimri! Put me down!"

"Oh, Mr. Zimri!" It was Louise at the door of the kitchen. "Miz Lisbeth's not so well yet."

"She's growing fatter by the minute, Louise." Zimri nevertheless put Elizabeth down. "Let's get some of your good cooking in her so she'll have plenty of energy tomorrow for the cruise."

"Cruise? Lawdy, you goin' on a cruise?"

"Just a couple of miles downriver."

"Oh, Zimri," Elizabeth said. "What will I wear?"

"Yachting clothes. What else?"

Elizabeth giggled. "I left my yachting clothes in Charleston."

"Then wear your new dress—Louise will prepare a basket."

"Oh, Lawdy yes," Louise said. "I know just the thing—Blueberry shortcake and peach cobbler!"

"I'll need my shawl," Elizabeth said. "And wool socks."

"And a parasol, for it will be sunny, I'm told."

Elizabeth smiled and kissed him. "You're hopeless, Zimri."

The next morning Zimri drove the gig to the new municipal wharf at the end of Second Street and rented a skiff equipped with oars as well as a sail. Elizabeth wore the dress that Zimri had bought her in New York, a somewhat frilly one with lots of bows and ribbons, but considered suitable for outdoor excursions. The parasol's red fabric contrasted with the blue of the dress and gave the ensemble a Japanese look.

"Zimri, I hope you know what you're doing," she said, stepping cautiously into the boat as he held the bow steady.

"Of course, I do." He climbed in after her, took his seat amidships, and pushed off with his oar. "I grew up on Long Island Sound." The small boat glided out into the calm waters of the river.

"You grew up on a farm."

"Yes, but only a few miles from the shore. Zeke and I built a boat once and hid it in the undergrowth near the beach."

"And what happened to it?"

"A storm came along and carried it out to sea."

She laughed. "So much for your nautical experience."

"But we learned to handle the boat in the meantime."

Now out in the channel, Zimri dropped the centerboard and raised the sail. There was a gentle breeze from the southeast. "Once Zeke and I sailed all the way to Plum Island and back."

"I haven't the foggiest idea of where Plum Island is."

Zimri hauled in the mainsheet and the boat began to pick up speed. "Neither did we. We landed there by accident."

"Oh, marvelous! I'm so reassured now. You're a born sailor."

"The point is, we got back safely. Amazing how quickly you learn when you're scared out of your wits."

Elizabeth leaned back onto a pile of cushions in the bow and turned her face up to the sun. "Well, at least this isn't Long Island Sound—no danger in being washed out to sea. The sun feels wonderful on my skin. Goodness! No wonder I've felt so listless lately, cooped up in a dark room all day."

"Just what the doctor ordered."

They sailed gently downriver past the hub of Martinville's commercial center, past the cemetery, to which Zimri contributed several trees and rose bushes, past the new iron works belching black smoke into the atmosphere, until they came to peach orchards, and finally, acres and acres of cotton. Many of the cotton plantations along here had their own docks for loading flatboats, which were poled downstream to Darien, unloaded there, and then loaded onto packets bound for Savannah. It was a lengthy, time-consuming process.

"What are you thinking, Zimri?"

"There's that question again. Same answer—nothing."

She opened her eyes and looked at him leaning carelessly on the tiller, waistcoat unbuttoned, beaver hat tipped at a rakish angle. "Liar!"

Zimri chuckled. "All right. I was thinking about these flatboats—how much cotton they can carry and how long it must take them to get to market."

"Must you always be thinking of business?"

"No—sometimes I think of how pleasant it is to be sailing along the river on a sunny day with my beautiful wife."

"That's more like it. If you had said that first, I might have taken more of an interest in your flatboats loaded down with cotton."

"Husbands are always learning."

She smiled and closed her eyes again. "Wake me when we get to Savannah."

Zimri felt the wind shift and tacked towards the opposite shore. As the boat grew closer he saw a number of Negroes, their trouser legs rolled up, digging in the mudflats for clams. He assumed they were free blacks, for it was still harvest time, and slaves would be occupied in the field. In fact, he thought, they must be all related, because there were less than thirty free blacks in the whole county.

As the boat came within fifty yards or so of the Negroes, he saw that the tallest was Boone Carter, the blacksmith. One of the girls was Tessie. He waved just as he came about, and they waved back. How extraordinary, he thought—Negroes enjoying a Sunday afternoon just like everyone else. The family all together—except for Louise, who was looking after the children—having a fine time digging for clams. No doubt they would take them home, steam them over a big pit fire, and drink a little corn liquor, while the younger children would play hide-and-seek and blind man's buff. Simple pleasures!

"Isn't that Tessie?" Elizabeth opened her eyes just as the skiff came about and headed upriver. She was facing the shore.

"Tessie and her father and the whole family, it seems. Except for Louise."

"What are they doing?"

"Digging for clams."

"How strange"

"Strange? How?"

"Their running about loose like that—without supervision."

Zimri glanced one last time over his shoulder at the Carters. "They're free, Elizabeth—just like you and me. They're not children."

Elizabeth seemed to consider this for a moment. "Still, it makes me a little nervous. There's no telling what they're up to."

Zimri smiled. "Like plotting a rebellion?"

"I can't imagine Louise or Tessie participating in anything like that—but their father might. Or if not a rebellion, then perhaps an escape."

"Escape? From what?"

"I don't mean them—the free blacks. I mean the slaves." Zimri kept his hand firmly on the tiller, as there was downstream pressure on the rudder. "Where would they go? A sheriff's posse—even the militia if necessary—would round them up before they could get thirty miles. Of course they could try the river, but most can't swim and fewer still could handle a boat."

Elizabeth closed her eyes again. "Maybe you're right. But I think there ought to be a law against free blacks just roaming around the countryside like that."

Zimri looked at her intently as she seemed to doze off. He wondered if she were so tainted by her upbringing that she could never see blacks—any blacks—as self-reliant human beings.

The wind had picked up and the river became a bit choppy. He let the boom out until they were in a good broad reach, the bow pointing directly towards the wharf.

CHAPTER 29

Zimri sat at his desk on a brisk autumn day reading galleys for the next issue. The paper had now expanded from four pages to six, and the number of new advertisers would soon require eight pages. Business was good.

He had been in the office since six, and Jed was out interviewing candidates for the upcoming mayoral election. He heard the bell attached to the front door ring.

"I'll be with you presently," he said. He hoped it would be a new advertiser. He set the galleys aside, buttoned his waistcoat, and stepped out from behind the partition that concealed his small office from the entry.

"Hello, Zimri."

It was Cora. For a moment he was speechless. He hadn't really expected her to come. But now she was there before him, in a fashionable white dress with matching bonnet and parasol. She was stunning.

"Cora. I had forgotten—the twenty-ninth, you said."

She approached him, using her parasol like a walking cane, tapping it loudly on the floor as if in admonishment. "You didn't return my letter."

"Cora—I didn't think you could be serious."

"I am quite serious. I have just been to the bank to see your Mr. Hamilton—he speaks highly of you, by the way—and deposited one thousand dollars. He was very appreciative." She stopped only a foot or so in front of him and planted the point of the parasol firmly on the floor. "You, on the other hand, seem less so. But I will give you another chance make it up to me." She closed her eyes, stood on her toes, and pursed her lips. "Kiss me."

Zimri looked nervously around the office, saw no one, and looked again to the window facing the street. "Cora—this is insane. I can't kiss you here."

"Why not?"

"You know why not. Because—"

"Not a big one—just a little one. A greeting kiss."

"Cora—" he glanced around once more. "All right." He kissed her gently but quickly. The effect of those soft, sensuous lips against his surprised him, as if they had been some exotic but forbidden fruit that he had somehow expected to be sour.

"Oh, how I've missed you." She suddenly flung her arms around him, one hand clutching the parasol tightly, and gave him a passionate, lingering kiss.

He briefly surrendered to her, feeling himself becoming aroused as she pressed her body against his, but then grasped her by the shoulders and pushed her away at arm's length. "Cora, this is madness. You must get back on the stage and return to Savannah or wherever you came from."

The tension suddenly went out of her shoulders and she seemed to pout like a little girl. "Oh, I don't want to go back to Savannah or New York. I want to be here with you, darling."

"It's impossible." Zimri released her shoulders and adjusted his waistcoat as if to restore order and decorum. "Now, please, Cora, get back on that stage before the rumors begin to fly."

Cora seemed to collect herself. She planted the point of the parasol once again at his feet and leaned against it. "There will be no rumors if we work together as a team. I am staying at the Central Hotel. They have a meeting room there. All you have to do is to extend an invitation to your most prominent citizens and entrepreneurs and I will do the rest. We need not meet on a social basis until my plan is accomplished."

"Your plan? Cora, I've been thinking about that—"

"Good. You think it is a sound one?"

"Well, yes, it seems quite feasible, but—"

"I'm glad you approve. It is quite feasible—in fact, it will be hugely successful, and will make your investors rich. Tomorrow morning at the hotel—at nine o'clock. Can I count on you, Zimri?"

"Tomorrow? But that's not enough time, Cora. Why can't it—"

"It has to be tomorrow because I've got to be in Milledgeville on Friday."

"Milledgeville? Why?"

"I have to see an old friend."

"Why can't your friend wait?"

"He's already waited—for too long. Can I count on you?"

Zimri sighed and nodded his head. "All right. Yes, you can count on me."

"Good. I knew I could." She smiled broadly and leaned forward to kiss him once more, this time lightly on the lips. "If you care to have supper with me tonight, I'll have something sent up to my room."

"Cora, you know I can't do that."

She turned the point of her parasol up from the floor and rested it on her shoulder like a soldier ready to march. "A lady hates to dine alone. I suppose I'll have to ask some traveling salesman at the hotel to join me."

"That might be best."

Her eyes grew big. "You wouldn't be jealous?"

"Not in the least."

"Liar. Sometimes I don't know whether I can really trust you, Zimri. I hope you prove me wrong."

Zimri said nothing.

"I'll see you and your friends tomorrow at nine. Au revoir."

"Yes. Au revoir."

Cora turned and went to the door, twirling her parasol as she went. Just as she reached for the knob, Jed appeared and opened it for her. "Why, thank you, sir." She glanced reproachfully at Zimri. "I'm glad to see that there are at least some gentlemen in this town."

She passed through the door pausing only for a moment to open her parasol and continued down the sidewalk at a leisurely rate as if window shopping.

Jed stood at the open door gaping. "My gracious, Mr. Rhodes, I do believe that is the handsomest woman I ever saw."

Zimri shoved his hands into the pockets of his waistcoat as if looking for something he'd lost. "You're not alone in that opinion, Jed. Just about every man who's—have you seen my watch?"

"Your watch? No, sir—you never take it out of your waistcoat except to tell the time."

"That's true, but—" Zimri gave up searching his pockets and looked towards the door. "Never mind, Jed—I think I know what happened to it."

Zimri spent most of the rest of the day calling on various members of the business community, including the mayor and nearly every member of the town council. These men, for the most part, were founders of Martinville like himself, and had prospered during the town's first ten years. Most were skeptical, but their trust in Zimri ensured that they would at least give this mysterious woman a hearing. And the rumors, of course, concerning her being an actress of some renown in New York—which Zimri did not deny—made the proposed meeting all but irresistible.

At the end of the day Zimri returned to his office and told Jed and Peter they could leave—he had some work to do and would be late.

At six-thirty, he closed up the office and walked down the street to the Central Hotel where he tried to look as if he were keeping a business appointment rather than an illicit tryst with a beautiful woman. He was acquainted with the desk clerk, a young man about Jed's age.

"Brendan, I understand a Miss Rinaldi checked in this morning. I have to speak to her about—"

"*Mrs*. Rinaldi." Brendan, a red-haired fellow whose freckles betrayed his Irish heritage as much as his name, took an envelope from a mail box and handed it to him.

"*Mrs*. Rinaldi?"

"Yes, sir. Her husband, Dr. Rinaldi, arrived on the afternoon stage."

"*Doctor* Rinaldi?"

"That's right. Mrs. Rinaldi said they would need to freshen up a bit, but that when you arrived to send you right up to their room. They're expecting you for supper."

"For supper...the two of them?"

"Yes, sir. I don't know whether there will be another party or not." Brendan looked around the lobby furtively and then leaned closer to Zimri. "Just between you and me, Mr. Rhodes, her husband is, well, getting pretty far along in years to be married to a woman like that."

"Is he? Well, I guess I'll just have to see for myself."

Brendan chuckled. "Rumor has it that she's an actress down on her luck and she married this old geezer for his money. I'll bet he's as rich as Croesus."

"I wouldn't be surprised, Brendan. Thanks for the information."

"Anytime, Mr. Rhodes. You going to do a story on her?"

"Depends. We'll see how our little interview turns out."

"Good luck, Mr. Rhodes. This ought to be a good one."

Zimri opened the envelope and extracted a short note as he approached the stairs:

> *My Dearest Zimri,*
>
> *I am so glad you decided to join myself and Dr. Rinaldi for supper. Of course I will return your watch to you—so silly of me to have jostled you so that it popped out of your waistcoat and into my parasol. A freak accident!*
>
> *Awaiting your arrival. We are in Room 301.*
>
> *Cora*

He put the note in his pocket and ascended the two flights of stairs to the third floor. Room 301 was at the end of a long hallway. He raised his hand to knock, hesitated, then rapped three times.

"Entrez."

He opened the door and saw Cora standing in the center of the large room, wearing a sort of caftan with a high waist and a red sash cinched tightly just beneath her breasts. The caftan was of white silk, embroidered with blue and gold thread in an intricate design of flowers and bees. Her black hair was pulled back in a chignon, with a few tresses falling over her shoulders.

Zimri took a cursory glance around the room. "Has Dr. Rinaldi stepped out?"

Cora laughed. "Yes. Permanently. He left by the rear stairs about a hour ago."

Zimri closed the door behind him and placed his hat on the clothes tree. "That was a rather short marriage, it seems."

"One of convenience, I'm afraid." She approached him and gave him a kiss. "Take off your coat, Zimri, and make yourself comfortable. Supper will be up in—oh, before I forget." She went to a writing desk, opened a drawer, and extracted Zimri's gold watch. "Your watch. I hope you'll forgive me for being so clumsy."

Zimri took the watch from her, checked the time, and put it in his waistcoat pocket. "On the contrary, that was as dexterous a piece of sleight of hand as I've ever witnessed."

Cora giggled. "Well, I must admit that my theatrical training comes in handy every now and then. But no harm done."

"No. No harm done."

She went to a window and pulled back the drapes. "How do you like my room?"

"Very nice. They seemed to have spared no expense."

"Come look, Zimri." She opened a pair of French doors that opened onto a balcony.

Zimri followed her out onto the balcony. The sun had gone down but there were rays of light illuminating the tops of the clouds so that they glowed like Chinese lanterns. The river glistened below, only a hundred yards away. "Beautiful. Our little town will soon be a tourist destination."

"Oh, I should say so. It's like a little Florence."

"Florence? You've been there?"

She turned to him and smiled. "I grew up not far from there.

Perhaps you will accompany me to the land of my birth someday."

Zimri shook his head. "Cora, you are impossible. As much as I'd like to, you know I could never do that."

She put her arms around him. "Never is a word I prefer not to use, darling. It's so self-defeating."

He gently disengaged himself and retreated into the room. "You are not a woman to be defeated, I can see that. And I'm sure the gentlemen that I've invited to listen to your proposal tomorrow will see it as well. The question is, can they trust you?"

She followed him into the room, closed the French doors behind her, and drew the drapes. "Sit down, Zimri—there, on the sofa."

Zimri stared at her for a moment, then complied.

Cora sat down on the sofa, but at a distance. "Do *you* trust me, Zimri?"

Zimri hesitated, looked up at the ceiling, then at a rather mediocre painting over the mantelpiece depicting a scene of classical ruins and scantily-clad young maidens gamboling in a pastoral paradise. "I don't know, Cora. I hardly know you."

"Hardly know me? Why, Zimri, I feel as if we've known each other for centuries. I anticipate your every gesture, your smiles, your frowns, your moods, your laughter, even your thoughts." She reached out and took his hand in hers. "And I feel...I feel that when I'm in a room with you that you anticipate my thoughts as well. Sometimes I feel as if we need not speak at all."

Zimri looked into her eyes as if to read some of those thoughts. "Yes, I've felt that, too. It frightens me sometimes."

"But why, darling? It is so rare—"

"You know why."

Cora smiled, then brought his hands to her lips and kissed them. "You see? I was right—you are reading my thoughts."

"I wish I weren't."

"Because of Elizabeth? Of course. But it's so unnecessary, darling. Elizabeth can come with us."

"To Florence? And the children, too, I suppose."

"Why not?"

Zimri laughed loudly, then surprised at his own outburst, checked himself. "You are an amazing woman, Cora. Conventional morality seems to have made no impression on you."

She lowered her eyes as if to study his hands. "Morality is a word that means many things to many people. Those who speak most of it seem to observe it least."

Zimri said nothing, but did not take his eyes off her.

She looked up at him. "As for your friends, I can understand why they would be skeptical. That's why I have planned a little demonstration of my good faith for tomorrow."

"Demonstration? What demonstration?"

"It will be a surprise. Of course, I want you to come, too."

"Come where? Where are we going?"

"Not far, darling. You'll see."

There was a knock on the door.

"Oh, it's our supper. I hope you like quail."

"Of course I do." He rose to open the door, but stopped before he was halfway there. "What about Dr. Rinaldi?"

"Let's say he just stepped out for a moment."

"A long moment. All right."

The waiter rolled a cart into the room with numerous covered dishes and a bottle of champagne in a bucket of ice. After making a rather awkward comment about the imminent return of Dr. Rinaldi, Zimri tipped the waiter and followed him to the door. Returning to the cart, he noted that there were three plates and three champagne glasses. "Ah, I hope Dr. Rinaldi doesn't eat too much."

"He has the appetite of a bird," she said. "But we'd better dirty his plate a bit."

"We'll use it as an hors d'oeuvres tray."

There were in fact hors d'oeuvres, some fish roe with cream cheese and crackers, that Cora set upon 'Dr. Rinaldi's' plate while Zimri uncorked the champagne.

Over dinner they discussed their time in New York together. Zimri told her of the storm off of Cape Hatteras and his subsequent encounter with Omri Sparks.

"Omri?" she said. "You met with Omri Sparks?"

"Yes—you know him?"

"Not personally. He's published several of our books."

"Books? What books?"

"Of the Anti-Slavery Society. Well, they're not exactly books, really. More like pamphlets. He's a very good printer."

"He didn't tell me about that. He was on his way to Savannah to purchase the freedom of his niece."

Cora seemed to take a great interest in this information. "And was he successful?"

"Yes. He wrote me recently to tell me so."

"So simple. If only there were enough money to buy *all* the slaves their freedom, it would save a great deal of trouble."

Zimri refilled their champagne glasses. "There's not enough money in the U.S. Treasury for it, I'm afraid. And even if there were, most slave owners would never sell."

Cora leaned back in her chair. "No, they wouldn't would they? So their precious property must be taken from them."

Zimri sipped from his glass. "By force?"

"By force. Or subterfuge."

Zimri chuckled. "These slave owners are not so easily fooled, Cora. What do you propose should be done? Wheel up a giant Trojan horse as an offering, herd all the slaves into it during the night, and have a mule train pull it all the way back to New York?"

Zimri expected her to laugh, but she didn't. Instead, she gazed at the painting over the mantelpiece.

"No. New York's no longer safe. It would have to be Canada. Or perhaps a ship to Africa."

Zimri looked at her curiously. He was beginning to feel the effects of the champagne. The tilt of her chin showed her long, lithe neck to its greatest advantage. The caftan gown had a split bodice, revealing a portion of the underside of her breasts. He had always thought of her as having a dark, olive complexion, but at least in this light, her skin seemed almost translucent, ivory. He hardly remembered her last words.

"Africa? Oh, yes—there's been talk of that in the legislature. I don't see that it would work, though."

She slowly turned her eyes towards his. "Why not?"

"Because black people have been here for nearly two hundred years now. There're acclimated to our culture. In short, they're Americans now. They would find Africa a strange place with strange ways."

She raised an eyebrow. "Stranger than slavery?"

"That's the one thing they wouldn't find strange. There's plenty enough of that in Africa."

She turned her eyes back to the painting and took a sip of her champagne. "I suppose you're right. Exotic lands always seem more seductive at a distance."

The mere passing of the word 'seductive' through her lips was enough to make Zimri forget about Africa altogether. He felt himself becoming aroused to the point that he was in a quandary as to whether to stand up. He should leave, shouldn't he? Elizabeth would be waiting up for him, assured that he was working late.

He put his glass down on the cart tray, buttoned his waistcoat and stood. "It's been a lovely evening, Cora. And a delicious meal. But Elizabeth's waiting for me and we've both got to get up early tomorrow for the meeting."

Cora stood. "Early? The meeting's not until nine o'clock. Stay a little, Zimri. A woman gets lonely in a hotel room by herself."

"Lonely? You must be used to it by now, for all the traveling you seem to do. There'll be plenty of time for—"

Cora reached for the top button of his waistcoat and began unbuttoning it.

"Cora—"

She kissed him softly at first, then with more passion, and he felt her hand beneath his shirt. He opened his eyes and grasped her wrists, intending to stop her and leave immediately, but as he gazed into her eyes he felt his resolve melting and relaxed his grip.

She loosened her chignon so that her long silken hair cascaded over her shoulders. "Stay a while, Zimri...stay."

CHAPTER 30

The next morning Zimri rose early and inspected his rose garden before breakfast. The perpetual roses were doing well, especially the tea roses, which Zimri was experimenting with by crossing them with wild roses. The result seemed to be a heartier, more frequently blooming plant.

When he returned from the garden, still in his nightshirt, he was met by Elizabeth at the front door, who had a shawl on over her dressing gown.

"Aren't you cold, Zimri?"

"Not at all. Lovely fall weather. Good morning, darling."

"Good morning."

He gave her a kiss and they both retreated inside where they could smell the bacon Louise was cooking. Zimri had already started a fire in the hearth before going out to the garden. "It will turn cold soon, though. I'm afraid the first frost will kill off my hybrids, but we'll see."

"Zimri…" she nestled against his shoulder as they stood before the fire.

"Yes, dear?"

"When you came in last night, I smelled perfume on your clothes. It wasn't my perfume—I haven't been wearing any lately."

Zimri stiffened his back. "That was probably Miss Rinaldi's."

"Miss Rinaldi? Who is she?"

"An entrepreneur from New York. She's presenting a proposal to a number of investors this morning at the hotel. I was interviewing her for a story."

"You must have gotten very close to her."

Zimri forced a laugh. "She got very close to me. She's very expressive and effusive—always touching the person she's talking to."

"And you say she's from New York?"

"Yes."

"Did you know her there?"

"I was introduced to her while I was there, yes. I had no idea that she would one day pop up in Martinville."

There was a long silence. "Tell me that you're not having an affair with her."

Zimri did not expect to be confronted with this question so directly. "She has no interest in me, Elizabeth, other than as a contact to promote her steamboat scheme."

"You didn't answer my question. Are you having an affair with this woman?"

Zimri started to confess, but his courage failed him. "No, dear. We are not having an affair. She's here strictly for business."

"But why would she come all the way to Martinville to invest in a —what did you call it?—a steamboat scheme? There must be plenty of opportunities for that sort of thing much closer to home."

"For one thing, she seems to have contacts in Savannah. For another, she's a shrewd businesswoman and recognizes the fact that Martinville is in the heart of Georgia's cotton country and lacks an efficient transportation system."

She stared intently into his eyes for what seemed to Zimri an eternity. "I believe you, Zimri. I don't know why I should, but I believe you."

"You should because I love you and you know I've never lied to you before."

"Breakfast's ready!" Louise came out of the kitchen with a huge plateful of scrambled eggs and bacon. "Glory be! Y'all ain't even dressed yet. Well, never mind. Jest set down and eat these vittles whiles they still hot."

After breakfast, Zimri dressed and drove into town, where he spent an hour in the office before heading for the hotel. The meeting was in the library, where the staff had lit a fire in the hearth and set chairs out to accommodate the investors. There were scrambled eggs and sausage and biscuits with smoked ham being served by uniformed waiters and a large punch bowl of champagne in the center of a massive oak table.

Zimri mingled with the guests as they awaited the appearance of Cora.

"What I want to know, Zimri, is what business does an actress have in getting mixed up in business—especially the steamboat business?" Mayor Pritchard snatched a biscuit stuffed with ham from a passing waiter and popped it into his mouth.

"She's an unusual woman, Tom," Zimri said. "You'll see."

"Who is she, anyway, Zimri?" Oliver Hamilton said. "She came into my bank yesterday, made a big deposit, and left before I could find out anymore about her. Since then I've been hearing she's an actress."

"That's true, Ollie," Zimri said. "She's been quite successful at it, too."

"Is that where she gets all this money, Zimri?" It was John Lewis, the milliner, who was taking full advantage of the free punch. "She came into my shop yesterday afternoon and bought two of my most expensive dresses, a caftan I imported from Constantinople, and two or three hats. Good gracious! If I had more customers like that I could retire."

"I heard she was in a play in New York where she played the part of a mulatto." Victor Steingart was a commodities broker who often bought planters' crops at rock bottom prices in bad years and resold them at an exorbitant profit as livestock feed to the federal government. He was widely thought to be a Jew, but Zimri knew him to be a Catholic who immigrated to America from Poland in the last century.

"That's true, Victor," Zimri said. "I saw the play in New York myself. She's a fine actress."

But what's she doin' playing the part of a spook?" Bob Cruikshank owned a saw mill near Martinville. "She got nigger blood in her?"

Zimri hardly thought this question worth responding to, but was saved from making the effort by the appearance of Cora at the entrance to the library. All conversation stopped. Even Zimri was taken aback. She was wearing a man's trousers and a velvet-trimmed cutaway jacket with a high collar and brocaded waistcoat. All that was missing was a top hat. She carried a tightly rolled tube of paper in her right hand and marched up to a reading table in front of the hearth.

"Gentlemen," she said. "Welcome to the future of Martinville."

There was some murmuring among the assembly. She continued:

"As Mr. Rhodes has no doubt informed you, I am Cora Rinaldi, Italian immigrant, Yankee actress, and one hundred per cent American entrepreneur."

There was muted laughter in the room.

She proceeded to explain her proposal to build two steamboats in the local boatyard and to create a company to be called Georgia Steamlines, Inc. The steamboats would ply the waters of the Ocmulgee between Martinville and Darien, where cargo, principally cotton, would be transferred to coastal packets delivering their loads to ports such as Savannah, Charleston, Philadelphia, and New York. There would be 5,000 shares of the company offered initially, with an option to issue another 5,000 within two years. Each share would have a par value of ten dollars. As chairman of the board, she would be the majority shareholder, retaining one thousand shares for herself.

"And what are you puttin' into the kitty, little lady," Mr. Cruikshank said. "Aside from your pretty little cat eyes?"

Cora smiled and waited for the laughter to die down. "Mr. Hamilton?"

Mr. Hamilton nodded. "She opened an account with us yesterday. In the name of Georgia Steamlines, Inc. The money's there."

"Thank you, Mr. Hamilton." She then unfurled the tube of paper she had laid on the reading table. "Gentlemen—see for yourself. These are the blueprints for the two steamboats—the *General Oglethorpe* and the *Miss Cora*."

There was sporadic, muted laughter.

"You'll forgive me for indulging in a bit of vanity, gentlemen," she said. "But it is, after all, my idea. Besides, I think General Oglethorpe would enjoy a little feminine company."

There was more spontaneous laughter as the potential investors all gathered around the table to inspect the blue prints.

"How do we know you won't take our money and just pull out of town?" Mr. Steingart said.

"I anticipated that question, sir," she said. "And as soon as you've finished with your ham and biscuits, I will ask you to accompany me to the municipal wharf for a demonstration of my good faith."

The investors exchanged glances.

"What do you have to lose, gentlemen?" she said. "A few minutes of your time? Besides, you've already had enough ham and biscuits that you could skip dinner today altogether."

There was more laughter, followed by some last-minute grabs for the biscuits and refills of punch, and gradually the assembled guests began to follow Cora out of the hotel and down to the wharf.

When the party arrived at the wharf, Cora led them to a warehouse with a padlocked door. She produced a key, unlocked the door, and stepped inside. Lamps were lit, and before them lay two large crates marked 'Georgia Steamlines, Inc., Martinville, Georgia.' She then handed a crowbar to Zimri.

"Will you do the honors, Zimri?"

Zimri did not answer, so curious was he as to what was contained in the crates. All the investors gathered round as he began prying the lid off of one of them.

"A steam engine!" Mr. Cruikshank said.

"That is correct, Mr. Cruikshank," Cora said. "Two steam engines to be precise. One for each vessel. If something were to happen to either, you would still have these engines, not to mention the money to go ahead with the project, as Mr. Hamilton will be keeping a careful eye on it."

"Who's going to build the boats?" someone said.

Cora waved her hand towards the door through which they had entered. A man in a plaid lumber jacket smoking a pipe stood there with his arms folded across his chest. "Gentlemen, I'm sure you all know Mr. Reed, owner of the Martinville Maritime Company. He'll be glad to answer any technical questions you may have about the construction of the two vessels."

The investors did indeed gather around Mr. Reed and began plying him with questions. As they did so, Zimri put down the crowbar. "You seem to have thought of everything, Cora."

"I try to be thoroughly prepared, whether for an acting role or for a business venture." She laughed. "It's amazing how much the two pursuits have in common. Did you sleep well last night?"

"Like a bear in winter."

"I'm so glad. You looked very tired when you left. Was Elizabeth waiting up for you?"

"Yes. And though she fell asleep quickly, she let me know this morning in no uncertain terms that she had smelled perfume on my clothes."

"Ah! An oversight on my part. You see, I am not always prepared for every eventuality. Next time—"

"Cora—there will be no next time. Our relationship from now on must be—"

"Don't be hasty, Zimri. I can see that you're still tired. Gentlemen!"

The investors stopped to listen.

"If Mr. Reed has answered all of your questions satisfactorily, we will proceed back to the hotel and you can sign up for the number of shares you wish to purchase. The minimum will be one hundred."

The investors then resumed talking among themselves, nodding their heads seemingly in affirmation and began filing out of the warehouse.

Cora and Zimri trailed behind as they walked the three blocks to the hotel.

"Cora, I've been thinking."

"You're always thinking, my dearest. But the question is, is it of me?"

"Yes, in a sense."

"In what sense?"

"Your steamboat company."

"Yes?"

"I'd like to purchase two hundred shares."

She laughed and put her hands in the crook of his arm. "Why, Zimri, you *are* so romantic."

CHAPTER 31

The subscription for the steamboat company was a huge success, and Zimri was congratulated by the investors for bringing such a brilliant and innovative entrepreneur to Martinville. The construction of the vessels, however, would take at least four months, and the voyage of the first boat was set for early spring. In the meantime Cora excused herself to pursue 'other projects,' as she put it, and was seldom seen during this period.

One bright, cold day in December she arrived on the morning stage and trudged through the snow-laden streets to Zimri's office.

Zimri happened to be at the front window posting the latest edition of the *Mercury* and saw her approaching. She was fashionably dressed, as always, this time in a fur cap that covered her ears but allowed her luxuriant black hair to peek out from beneath it. She also wore a fox coat with a matching muff and high-buttoned black leather boots. There were snow flurries that swirled around her head like a halo, and Zimri, though charmed at this scene, chuckled to himself that this was no angel. At least not of the conventional sort.

She smiled as they made eye contact through the window and Zimri responded in kind. He opened the door for her.

"Oh, Zimri, how I've missed you!" She threw her arms around him and kissed him on the mouth.

Zimri was not unaware that Jed was standing but ten feet away, holding a sheet of proofs to be corrected. He disengaged himself quickly. "Jed, why don't you make Miss Rinaldi some coffee? She must be frozen to the bone."

Cora seemed to notice Jed for the first time. She began to remove her gloves. "Yes, it is quite cold. The stage was like an icebox."

"Let me take your coat, Cora." Zimri removed her coat and brushed the snow off. "Sit down by the stove and warm yourself."

Cora removed her cap, brushed the snow off and handed it to him. "I haven't even been to my hotel room—I was so anxious to see you."

Zimri wanted to take her in his arms and tell her how he had missed her, but checked himself as Jed returned with the coffee. "I think I'll have a cup as well, Jed. Sit down, Cora, and tell me about your latest adventure."

Cora sat down in a desk chair opposite the pot-bellied stove and began rubbing her hands together. "My latest adventure—let me see...well, I have just returned from Ohio via New Orleans and Memphis. There seems to be a great demand for steamboats all along the Mississippi and into the Ohio."

"You've started other companies?"

"Yes, but more as a silent partner. You might say I'm a consultant."

Jed returned with a second cup for Zimri and went back to the press room.

Zimri warned his hands with the coffee cup. "You say you've just come from Ohio. I understand they're pouring all of their money into the building of canals."

"And a waste of money it is, too."

"Why?"

"Because the railroads are coming. They'll make even steam navigation obsolete."

Zimri sipped his coffee. "Then are we fools here in Martinville to be investing in steamboats?"

"Not at all. It will be quite some time before the railroads are built. And steamboats are relatively cheap. But Zimri, darling, I didn't come here to discuss business."

"Oh? Then what?"

She put her cup down. "You haven't answered my letters."

"I can't, Cora. You know I can't."

"Why not?"

"Talk. The postmaster knows everyone and everything. It's suspicious enough that I receive two or three letters a month from you, but at least I can pass those off as business communications."

"And why can't you return my 'business communications?'"

"Because it looks too much like intercourse—I mean social intercourse."

A broad smile came to Cora's lips. "Are you so afraid of the other kind?"

Zimri glanced toward the press room, the door of which was open, and lowered his voice to a whisper. "Cora, you know I want to be with you—but it's impossible."

"You're always using that word—'impossible.' You use it too much."

"Some things are, I'm afraid. Can't we just remain on a professional level—as well as one of friendship?"

"Friendship is for members of the same sex—you are definitely of a different sex."

Zimri shook his head in exasperation. "Cora, you've got to give the whole idea up. Elizabeth and I are happy together."

"Are you?"

Zimri avoided her piercing stare. "Yes." He stood up to put more wood in the stove, brushing against Cora's knee in the process. "Sorry."

She clasped his hand in hers. "Don't be."

Zimri stood motionless for a moment, not looking at her, but not removing his hand, either. "I'll prove it to you."

She caressed his hand and put it to her cheek. "Prove what, my darling?"

"Come to the house tonight. For supper. Seven o'clock. I'll introduce you."

She looked up at him. "Seven? You must tell me how to get there."

"Out Mulberry Street. It's only half a mile from here. Anyone can tell you where it is."

"I'm sure I can find it." She kissed his hand and stood up from her chair. "How should I dress?"

"I'm sure you're a better judge of that than I."

She gave him a kiss on the cheek and looked around for her coat and cap. "Yes—I'll think of something. In the meantime I have some business to attend to. Is Mr. Hamilton in town?"

Zimri moved to help her with her coat. "Yes—he's always in town. A permanent fixture at the bank."

Cora buttoned her coat up and put the cap on her head. "That's the sort of man I like to do business with—dependable, predictable." She leaned forward to kiss Zimri, but he pulled away, again glancing towards the press room. "But those aren't always the qualities a woman looks for in a man of more…intimate acquaintance."

Zimri turned back to her. "No, I don't suppose—"

She stood on her toes and kissed him firmly on the mouth.

Zimri, assured that Jed was occupied in the press room, responded with as much fervor, redoubled even, and briefly lifted her off her feet.

"Oh, my goodness," she said when her feet returned to the floor. "That was anything but predictable."

"That's because it was the last time, Cora. I'll see you at seven."

At dinner that afternoon, Zimri informed Elizabeth that Miss Rinaldi would be joining them for supper.

"That's wonderful," Elizabeth said. "I've been dying to meet her. But Zimri, dear, there's something I've been hearing lately about her."

"And that is?"

"That she's an actress. Is that true?"

Zimri ladled some gravy onto his mashed potatoes. "That's true. What of it?"

"You didn't tell me that before."

"I suppose I didn't think it was important at the time. She was here as a businesswoman."

Elizabeth spooned some applesauce into Charlotte's mouth. The child was sitting on a highchair that Zimri had made for her. "Did you see her perform in New York?"

"Yes, I did. She was quite good."

"That was the night you and the Frenchman went to the theatre?"

Zimri affected to search his memory. "Yes, I believe it was. Why?"

"And you had supper with her?"

"Yes, the three of us." Zimri put down his knife and fork. "Elizabeth, I see what you're driving at. To ease your mind, nothing happened that night. Do you think I'd invite her here to meet you if it had?"

Elizabeth looked at him for a moment, then resumed feeding Charlotte. "No, I don't suppose you would. Forgive me dear, for being so jealous. But you're such a fine-looking man, I suspect every woman of wanting to be held in your arms."

Zimri smiled and wiped his mouth with his napkin. "And I suspect every man of wanting to hold you in his. Have I told you how beautiful you look since you regained your figure?"

"As a matter of fact, you haven't. But I will accept the compliment, however belated."

"Belated? It's only been a few weeks since you gave birth."

"Ten weeks to be exact. You men never remember the important things with any precision. The twins have doubled their weight in that time."

Zimri smiled. "And you've halved yours."

Elizabeth laughed. "Not so much as that—twenty pounds or so. At least I will be able to fit into my taffeta dress tonight—the one you bought for me in New York."

"Yes. Wear that. It shows your figure off to best advantage. And it's the latest in fashion."

"So I will not be outdone by Miss Rinaldi?"

"Not in the least."

That evening a hackney cab pulled up in front of the house at precisely seven o'clock. The cabman helped Cora out and escorted her to the front porch, where she paid him his fare and dismissed him. She was wearing the same fur hat that she wore when she arrived in town that morning, but not the coat. Instead, she wore a long navy blue woolen cape over the shoulders. She stood on the porch for a moment surveying the house and property, and knocked on the door.

Zimri opened the door. "Miss Rinaldi—you've come."

"Mr. Rhodes—indeed I have. May I ask what those covered plants are in your garden?"

"Roses." Elizabeth suddenly appeared at the door, resplendent in her taffeta dress. "Zimri loves roses as if they were his own children."

"And you must be the mother of those children—the human ones, I mean."

Elizabeth laughed. "I am indeed. Won't you come in, Miss Rinaldi?"

"Please call me Cora."

"Cora then. Close the door, Zimri—it's freezing. And take Cora's coat."

Zimri complied and after the two women exchanged compliments on one another's dresses, Elizabeth escorted Cora to the bedroom where she was acquainted with the children.

"They're all so beautiful!" Cora said, returning to the hearth room. "And all girls. Zimri you must be aching for a boy next time."

"Strange to say," Elizabeth said, sitting before the fire, "he isn't. He wants no part of boys."

Cora sat on the sofa next to Elizabeth, while Zimri sat in his favorite armchair. "No boys? Why, Zimri, don't you want a son to carry on the family name?"

"Girls can do it as well, " Zimri said. "Only when they get married it becomes their middle name. I'll settle for that."

Louise arrived with cups of eggnog and the three toasted to first the health of all, especially the children, and second, to the success of the steamboat project.

This change of subject seemed to pique Elizabeth's interest. "How is it that an actress such as yourself becomes a businesswoman, Cora? It seems an unusual progression."

"Not so unusual as one might think, Elizabeth," Cora said. "Acting is a very precarious profession, and every actor that I know takes up some other means of earning a living at some point."

"Yes, of course. I never really thought of that. But tell me, how did you come to acting in the first place?"

Cora seemed non-plussed at this question, as if she had not considered it before. "I don't know, exactly. I simply fell into it somehow."

Elizabeth seemed skeptical. "But surely you must have engaged in theatricals as a child, or had parents in the theatre. I can't imagine that one day you would simply decide to go off to New York and embark upon an acting career."

Cora seemed uncomfortable with this line of questioning. "I was orphaned at an early age. It seemed to be my only opportunity."

"Oh," Elizabeth said, setting her cup down. "I'm so sorry. I didn't mean to pry. It must have been very difficult for you."

Cora managed a smile. "You know how children are—they accept their circumstances without question. And when things are difficult—they simply adapt."

"Yes. I suppose that's true."

"Elizabeth's most difficult adjustment in childhood was to boarding school in Charleston," Zimri said. "And having to speak only French."

"Boarding school?" Cora said with renewed interest. "In Charleston?"

"Mademoiselle Gaillard's Académie," Elizabeth said. "And Zimri's right—we could only speak French. I felt like a foreigner in my own country."

"I know the feeling," Cora said. "Avez vous regrets, Madame?"

"Mais non," Elizabeth said, brightening at the opportunity to speak her second language. "J'étais heureux là, Mademoiselle."

Though Cora's vocabulary in French was quickly exhausted, this exchange seemed to delight Elizabeth, and the conversation carried over into supper, where Zimri felt virtually excluded. He did not mind, however, as he was pleased to see the two women getting along so well.

After enjoying a strawberry confection at the end of the meal, during which time Zimri indulged in a glass of brandy, Cora stood to take her leave.

"But how will you get home, Cora?" Elizabeth said. "It's too far to walk, and besides, it's snowing."

"Oh, it's not so far," Cora said, as Zimri helped her with her coat. "And perhaps the cabman will come this way before retiring for the night."

"Nonsense!" Elizabeth said. "They're not at all reliable, I'm afraid, and they may have other fares. Zimri will take you to the hotel."

Zimri looked hesitant.

"Why, that would be very nice of him," Cora said.

"You won't mind a bit, will you, darling? The gig's in the barn and Jupiter needs the exercise. It will take half the time."

Zimri at first intended to object, but could think of no good excuse. He looked at a smiling and expectant Cora, then to Elizabeth. "All right. It's a bad night out for a woman to be walking alone. I'll get the gig."

He went to the barn and hitched Jupiter to the gig, all the time grumbling to himself that Cora must have planned it this way. Of course she did! She plans everything with meticulous and unerring foresight. But no matter—it was only a half a mile or so to the hotel, and there would be no question of his going up to the room of a single woman, especially since 'Dr. Rinaldi' was nowhere to be found.

He drove the gig through the snow, staring straight ahead towards the lights of the town, intent upon getting it over with.

"Zimri," Cora said. She had both her hands in the crook of his arm, snuggling close for warmth.

"Yes, Cora?"

"I had a lovely evening."

"I'm glad you did. I enjoyed myself as well."

"Elizabeth is a dear girl. She *is* very young, isn't she?"

"Still only eighteen." Zimri chuckled as he loosened his grip on the reins. "And with three children already."

"But very mature for her age, don't you think? And highly intelligent."

"Two reasons that I married her."

They rode on in silence for a few moments.

"Zimri—"

"Yes?"

"I'm leaving for New York tomorrow morning."

"That's an arduous journey this time of year. By sea, or overland?"

"By sea. A packet leaves Savannah on Saturday."

"Don't count on it. It may be Sunday or Monday if the tide isn't right."

She tightened her grip on his arm. "Zimri—"

"Yes, Cora?"

"Stop here."

Zimri brought the gig to a halt and looked around him. They were in town now, just opposite the *Mercury*'s office. "Here?"

"I left my muff in your office."

"Your muff? Are you sure? I didn't see any—"

"I'm sure I left it there, darling. It's very special to me. Please."

"Oh, well, all right. If you're sure."

"I'm sure."

Zimri pulled up to the office and left the reins on the seat, knowing that Jupiter wouldn't wander in the cold and the snow. Cora followed him to the front door and waited while he fished in his pocket for the key.

"I see a light," Cora said.

"It's just the stove—Jed leaves some coals burning so that it won't be so cold in the morning."

"Oh, good—I'm freezing."

Once inside, Zimri lit a lamp and began looking around the office for the muff. "I don't see it—do you remember putting it down?"

"Perhaps in your office—behind the partition."

They went behind the partition and Zimri lifted the lamp high in the air and surveyed the scene. "Don't see it. Maybe you left it in the hotel."

"I don't think so—Oh, it's much warmer in here. I think I'll take off my coat."

"Cora—"

"What a charming little day bed! I didn't notice that before."

"Cora, put your coat back on. This is a poor excuse—"

"And such pretty little pillows! Did Elizabeth make these?" She sat down on the day bed and picked up one of the pillows.

"She did. Now if you don't see the muff—"

"I can't imagine where it would be—perhaps beneath one of the pillows." She picked up another one. "Help me, darling."

"Cora—oh, all right. I'll show you that there's nothing under the pillows." He walked over to the bed and picked up the remaining two pillows, one in each hand. "See? No muff. Now let's go."

Cora stood and moved closer to him. "You would make a wonderful Santa Claus. All you need is a white beard and a couple of these pillows beneath your waistcoat—here, let me show you."

"Cora, this won't work—"

"Of course it will. Just stand still and I'll show you. But first the jacket has to come off."

"Cora—"

She slipped his jacket off and hung it on a coat rack. "The problem is, you're not built like Santa Claus. Santa has a big stomach and a small chest, while you have a big chest and a small stomach. So we need to reverse the process. Stand still."

Zimri found this attempt to make him into Santa Claus amusing, and made no resistance as she unbuttoned his waistcoat.

"Now," she said, "we'll try two pillows at first." She picked up two of the pillows from the daybed and stuffed them one at a time beneath either side of his waistcoat. "Oomph! You're fatter than I thought. Perhaps one will be enough."

Zimri began laughing.

"Don't laugh—that only makes it harder." The pillows fell to the floor. "Now see what you've done. I'll have to start over."

"Cora, I don't think I'm ready to—"

She kissed him and began unbuttoning his shirt. "No—you're the wrong shape, the wrong size, and you're too young and too handsome."

He was no longer laughing but staring intently into her eyes. "You are the most seductive woman I've ever met."

"A seduction cannot take place without mutual consent. I cannot seduce you if you are not willing." She unbuttoned the last button on his shirt and then began unbuttoning the front of her dress. He stood transfixed as the bodice fell away to either side, exposing her breasts. There was no corset.

"The light, Cora—the Sheriff might—"

"Lock the door and pull the shades. He'll think you were working late." She kissed him again. "I'll wait for you on the bed."

Zimri hesitated, unable to take his eyes off of her as she sat in a chair and began removing her boots.

"Hurry, darling, I shall be cold without you."

Zimri went to the front door, locked it, and pulled down the shades.

CHAPTER 32

Elizabeth felt that she was growing stronger with every passing day. She seemed full of energy, and was restless, though there was plenty to do now that Christmas was approaching. The entire family was invited by Jamie to spend Christmas Eve and the following day at Belle Oaks.

She was busily wrapping presents one afternoon when Louise came into the hearth room with a worried look on her face.

"Miz Rhodes, I think someone's hidin' out in the barn."

Elizabeth looked up from a package she was in the process of tying a red ribbon around. "Hiding out? In the barn? Who?"

"I dunno. I think it be a tramp. Tessie said she heard a noise, a clanking noise like maybe a rake or a shovel falling, when she was out in the yard with Charlotte. She didn't pay no attention to it, but then she heard it again."

Elizabeth tied the ribbon into a bow and rose from her chair. "Perhaps it's a fox. Zimri said there've been—"

"No, ma'am. It ain't no fox."

"How do you know?"

"'Cause I went out to see for myself and I seed footprints in the snow near the well leadin' back to the barn."

Elizabeth was now becoming alarmed. "Perhaps they belong to my husband, or—"

"No, ma'am. Mr. Rhodes ain't no small man, but ain't got feets the size of a grizzly, neither."

"A grizzly! My goodness—you think it could be a bear?"

"That's what I'm tryin' to tell you, Miz Rhodes. It ain't no animal. Them footprints belong to a man, a big man."

Elizabeth glanced at the rifle that Zimri kept over the fireplace. "Where are the children?"

"They in the bedroom with Tessie."

"Tell her to stay there and lock the door from the inside. And you may as well join them."

"No, ma'am."

"What?"

"Beggin' your pardon, Miz Rhodes, but I feel safer in the kitchen with a butcher knife. Maybe help you out, too."

Elizabeth stared at Louise for a moment and then went to the mantle and took down the rifle. "All right. You'll be the last line of defense if something happens to me. Now where does Zimri keep those cartridges?"

"In the drawer, there in his desk."

Elizabeth went to the desk and opened the drawer. After rummaging through some papers, she came up with the cartridges. The rifle was a single-shot percussion type, the kind used by both her father and Jamie for hunting. She rammed a cartridge down into the muzzle, cocked the hammer, and went out through the kitchen into the snow-covered backyard. Louise picked up a butcher knife and started to follow.

"I told you to stay in the kitchen, Louise. If he outflanks us, we'll both be dead and there'll be nobody to defend Tessie and the children."

"Yes, ma'am." Nevertheless, Louise continued to follow her, albeit at a distance of about ten paces.

Elizabeth approached the barn door with extreme caution, stepping gingerly into the snow drifts to avoid making a squeaking noise with her shoes. She slowly lifted the crossbar that secured the door with one hand, while keeping the rifle ready in the other. As the door swung open, she grasped the rifle in both hands and pointed it into the darkness.

"Whoever you are, come out slowly with your hands up high."

There was no answer.

"I know you're in there. Now, come out like I said or I'll start firing."

"Don't shoot, Miz Lizbeth." It was a familiar voice, but still no figure appeared.

"Who is it? Identify yourself."

"It's me, Miz Lizbeth. Solomon."

"Solomon?"

"Don't shoot—I'se comin' out wid my hands up high, jest like you said."

"Who's Solomon?" whispered Louise.

"Shhh!" Elizabeth motioned her back, and returned her finger to the trigger guard.

Slowly, a pair of legs appeared from the shadows clad in ragged trousers, followed by a massive torso clad in an equally ragged and torn shirt. At last a face appeared, weary, haggard and frightened.

"Solomon!"

"I wasn't lyin,' Miz Lizbeth. Just don't shoot me."

"I'm not going to shoot you, Solomon. But how did you get here?"

She lowered the rifle and carefully uncocked the hammer.

"It be a long story, Miz Lizbeth, and I'se powerful hongry."

"Well, of course you are. Come into the house and—"

"No, ma'am. If it's all the same to you, I'll jest stay in the barn and maybe yo' cook can bring me some scraps and such."

"Scraps? Nonsense—Louise will cook up a plate of ham and eggs and grits for you. You're thinner than I've ever seen you, Solomon."

"I've been runnin,' Miz Lizbeth. Runnin' and hidin,' runnin' and hidin,' all the way from Mississippi...and I ain't et in—"

At that point Solomon toppled to the straw floor like a felled tree. Elizabeth put down the rifle and rushed to assist him. Louise quickly followed.

"Get him some water, Louise! Out of the bucket there. The poor man!"

After reviving him with the water, Elizabeth and Louise managed to help him to his feet. They tried to coax him to the house but he insisted on staying in the barn, whereupon Elizabeth sent Louise to get some blankets. Solomon was shivering from the cold and Elizabeth examined his bare feet, fearing that he might have frostbite.

"Can you feel your toes, Solomon?"

"Don't rightly know, Miz Lizbeth—don't feel much a'tall right now but my stomach."

"Don't worry—we'll get some food in you. But we have to warm you up first. You've got to come into the house, Solomon. You could die out here."

"Yes, ma'am. I mean, no ma'am. I don't want to die, but I'd rather die of the cold than go back to Mississippi."

Elizabeth washed his face with water and dried it off with a towel hanging from a hook next to one of the horse stalls. "You must not have had a bath for weeks. Here, let me—Solomon! Your back— what did they do to you?"

"Whupped me, Miz Lizbeth. Whupped me nigh every day. Said they was gonna break me if it was the last thing they did on God's earth."

"I'll get Louise to bring a wash tub and fill it with hot water."

"Yes, ma'am. That's mighty kind of you."

When Zimri came home for dinner around two o'clock, Elizabeth informed him of what had happened.

"He can't stay in the barn," Zimri said. "It's too dangerous."

"That's what I told him," she said. "He could freeze to death."

"I don't mean that. He could probably stay warm enough with blankets and the small stove between the horse stalls. I mean it's dangerous for him to stay here. He's a runaway."

They were both standing in the kitchen, looking out through the window towards the barn. Louise busied herself with preparations for dinner, with Tessie assisting her.

"We can't send him back to Mississippi," Elizabeth said. "They'll kill him."

"That's a fact," Louise said. "I ain't never seen a man with his back so cut up. It's a wonder he's still breathin.'"

Zimri stared at the barn in silence for a few moments. "Louise, can you keep a secret?"

"Yes, sir, Mr. Rhodes, I sho' can."

"Tessie?"

"Depends on what kind of secret, Mr. Rhodes," Tessie said. "I couldn't keep one if it wasn't right to."

"Girl," Louise said, turning sharply to her sister, "what you talkin' 'bout? If Mr. Rhodes ask you to keep a secret, then you keep it."

"Do you believe it's right to keep a man caged like an animal," Zimri said, still staring at the barn, "and beaten worse than a dog, Tessie?"

"No, sir, Mr. Rhodes, no way."

"Then neither of you will tell anyone—including your father—that Solomon is hiding in our barn?"

Louise and Tessie exchanged glances.

"No, sir," Tessie said. "We won't tell anyone, not even Daddy."

"And not your brothers and sisters?"

"Not even them," Louise said. "It ain't their business."

Zimri turned and looked at them both with a piercing stare. "I have your word?"

Tessie seemed to tremble. "Yes, sir, Mr. Rhodes. Cross my heart and hope to die."

"Louise?"

"I don't know nothin' 'bout no man in no barn."

"Good," Zimri said. "Then when you take meals out there it will be as an offering to the gods."

"Sir?"

"That's like Zeus or Apollo," Tessie said. "The white man's gods."

Zimri chuckled. "That's right, Tessie. And they're a hard bunch to please."

Zimri said little at dinner and returned to the office without visiting Solomon in the barn. Elizabeth thought this was curious at first, but then decided that he didn't wish to call any more attention to the barn than might have already occurred. Besides, she could see that he was struggling with the dilemma of what to do with the escaped fugitive. If caught, the fine would be only a few dollars, but certainly Zimri's reputation as a law abiding citizen, not to mention a member of the town council, would be tarnished.

As she sat rocking the twins before the hearth, she thought of the terrible suffering that Solomon had endured. It incensed her that some slave owners treated their slaves so cruelly. Her father had always treated his fairly, or at least it seemed so to her. And it was only when Luther had somehow lost his senses and attacked her father that Jamie lost his senses and beat him so cruelly. But that was understandable under the circumstances. And she had heard of no further excesses on Jamie's part since.

She began to doze off before the fire with the twins sound asleep in her arms. But she was just beginning to fall into a reverie when she was jolted awake by the sound of Louise's voice.

"Miz Rhodes, you better come quick!"

"What? What is it?"

She opened her eyes to see Louise standing before her in her apron, wringing her hands.

"It's Solomon. He's done heaved up the vittles I brought him and now he's on the barn floor shiverin' and shakin' like he's havin' a fit."

"It's the falling sickness," she said. "He's had it since he was a child. Where's Tessie?"

"I'm here, ma'am."

Elizabeth stood up from the rocker. "Here, Tessie—put the twins in the crib. Louise, get me a clean towel and follow me to the barn. There's no time to lose."

"Yes, ma'am."

When they arrived at the barn, they found Solomon in an advanced state of seizure. Elizabeth instructed Louise to hold his arms as best she could, and placed the towel between his teeth. His eyes were wide open and he was fully conscious. After several minutes, the violent tremors ceased. He was sweating, in spite of the cold, and focused his eyes on Elizabeth's.

"I'm sorry, Miz Lizbeth."

"Don't be, Solomon," she said. "It's not your fault. It must be

the excitement of your escape. You've been through a great deal.
But you're home now."

"Yes, ma'am. I'se home."

CHAPTER 33

Christmas Eve fell on a Friday, and Zimri closed up the office at noon. Jed was sent home with a bonus, as was Peter, in addition to sweaters that Elizabeth had knitted for them. It had been a very good year, and Zimri was feeling prosperous.

He decided to walk home, as it was a beautiful, cloudless day with cobalt skies, and fresh snow on the ground from the night before. He tipped his hat to pedestrians he encountered on the sidewalk, which had been extended all the way to Seventh Street, as well as to the occupants of carriages adorned with ribbons and wreaths for the coming holiday.

The colorful carriages made him think of Solomon. Solomon had taken it upon himself to repair the old phaeton that had sat in disuse in the barn since Elizabeth had given birth to Charlotte. He had replaced the iron fittings that were nearly consumed with rust, fashioned new reins and harnesses from hides Zimri had purchased from the new tannery north of town, and polished the brass carriage lamps until they gleamed like mirrors.

Certainly Solomon was making himself useful. But the question was what to do with him? It almost seemed a fortuitous event that he had returned, an opportunity for redemption. That is, Zimri's redemption. He had regretted selling Solomon almost from the moment the auctioneer lowered his hammer. And when he discovered that the loathsome Mr. Herzen had purchased Betty and the children from the equally loathsome trader...now perhaps he could buy him back. But then what? He would once again be a slave owner, and the very idea of owning another human being was becoming intolerable to him. Of course, he could immediately free him. But what would it cost? He had received nine hundred dollars for him, and surely his new owner had paid nearly twice that. And if he repurchased Betty and the two children, assuming that Herzen would sell, the expense would run well over two thousand dollars. And with all of these Christmas gifts and bonuses for Jed and Peter...No, it was impossible! At least for now. Besides, Elizabeth, who had always reproached him for his extravagance, would be beside herself if he announced that he was going to spend two thousand dollars to free the slaves that were hers to begin with.

No, Elizabeth was not ready for that. She wouldn't understand at all. In the meantime, Solomon seemed to be quite content, even happy, to serve his former masters. Still, the word that he was living in their barn and a fugitive from justice would eventually get around.

Ah, well. It was Christmas! He would worry about Solomon later.

When he got home, he found Elizabeth, Tessie, and even little Charlotte gaily decorating the tree. Louise was in the kitchen preparing dinner. He picked up Charlotte, grasping her beneath the armpits, and raised her high in the air. But instead of the usual squeal of delight that small children emit when feeling themselves flying through the air, Charlotte started crying. Zimri, alarmed, quickly brought her back down into his arms "What's the matter, my little darling?"

"She couldn't see who it was," Elizabeth said.

"What do you mean?"

"She knows you now by your touch and voice. But she can't see more than four feet in front of her."

Zimri bounced Charlotte in his arms, now eliciting giggles from her. "Four feet? How do you know?"

"Just watching her around the house. She bumps into things. She can't distinguish between me and Tessie until one of us is practically on top of her."

"How long have you known this?"

Elizabeth kneeled down and hung a small angel on the tree. "Maybelle was the first to notice. But I didn't really think anything of it until the other day when she was walking on her own in the bedroom and I coaxed her towards the hearth room. She ran into the door frame."

Zimri stared into Charlotte's eyes and saw only bright blue irises. "We'll have to call Doctor Parcher."

"He was here this morning."

"And?"

"She'll need spectacles, that's all."

"I had specs till I was twelve," Tessie said. "Then I didn't need them anymore." She hung a cotton doll on one of the upper branches.

"Well," Zimri said, bouncing Charlotte gaily up and down, "perhaps Charlotte will outgrow the need for them as well."

"Doctor Parcher said it could go the other way just as easily," Elizabeth said. "She could go completely blind."

"Blind? Nonsense!" Zimri put Charlotte down on the floor and steadied her on her feet before letting her arms go. "Come to Papa, Charlotte."

"Zimri—be careful."

"I am being careful. That's just about four feet. Come to Papa, Charlotte, come to Papa."

Charlotte stared ahead at him, wobbled a bit as if she were about to fall over, and finally rushed into her father's arms.

Zimri laughed and picked her up again. "See? She came to me without any help. Didn't you, Charlotte?"

Charlotte giggled and threw her arms around her father's neck.

"She knew you were there, Zimri. Don't be overly optimistic."

"Now look who's being the pessimist of the family. I insist on retaining my position as Chief Cynic. Except where Charlotte is concerned."

"Dinner, y'all!" Louise was at the door of the kitchen carrying a large platter with a steaming turkey on it, its drumsticks adorned with red and green paper crowns.

"Louise," Elizabeth said, "can't you say 'dinner is served?' We need to preserve at least some decorum around here."

"Sho,' Miz Rhodes." Louise assumed an air of mock dignity as she put the platter down on the table. "Dinner is served. How's that?"

"Better," Elizabeth said. "Tessie, can you see about the twins?"

"Yes, ma'am."

At dinner, Zimri's cheery optimism seemed to slowly evaporate.

"What's the matter, darling?" Elizabeth said. "Are you worried about Charlotte after all?"

"What? Oh, no, she'll be fine. I was just thinking about...some problems at the office that need to be cleared up. But they can wait until after Christmas."

Later Zimri excused himself from decorating the tree and went to the barn where he found Solomon brushing down the horses. "Looks like we'll be pulling up to the front door at Belle Oaks in high style, Solomon."

Solomon chuckled as he continued brushing the horses. "Yes, suh. That old carriage sho' shines now, don't it?"

"It surely does. Fit for a king. Or at least a prince. You've done a fine job with it."

"Thank you, Massa Zimri. It be my pleasure."

Zimri examined some of the brass and iron fittings. "You ever done any smithy work?"

"Oh, yes, suh. Out at Belle Oaks they had a shop where ol' Titus done all the smithy work. I used to hang 'round there, and some times he would let me pull a piece o' iron out of the forge and bang on it some. I'd make things out of it."

"What things?"

"Oh, jest toys, I guess you'd call 'em. Things a boy would want to play with. Sometimes useful things for my mama like spatch'las and skillets. I once helped ol' Titus make an iron gate with all kinda fancy designs in it. It be there at the entry to what they call the English garden to this day."

Zimri lit a cigar. "You know you can't stay here forever."

Solomon's face fell. "Naw, suh. I knows that."

"This is the first place they'll come looking when they realize you're no longer in Mississippi."

"Yes, suh. I knows that, too."

Zimri took a few puffs on his cigar and patted Minerva, the horse that Solomon was brushing, on the rump.

"Suppose I bought you back from your master in Mississippi."

Solomon stopped brushing and looked up. "Suh?"

"Suppose I bought you back from—what's his name?"

"Massa 'Gustus."

"What?"

"Massa 'Gustus. His name is 'Gustus Seymour."

"Oh. Augustus. All right. Suppose I contact this Master Seymour and offer to buy you back. Would you like that?"

A big grin came to Solomon's face and he started brushing Minerva with increased vigor. "Oh, yes, suh. I like that jest fine."

"You'd have to pay me back, you know."

Solomon stopped brushing. "Suh? How I'm gonna do that?"

"You'd have to agree to work for me for a year."

Solomon looked puzzled. "A year? That's all?"

Zimri affected to examine the sheen of Minerva's coat. "I don't like owning slaves, Solomon. I'm like a bank that has to repossess somebody's farm. They don't want to be in the farming business. And I don't want to be in the slaving business."

Solomon still looked puzzled. "Then what you gonna do wid me after one year?"

"Send you over to Boone Carter."

"Boone Carter? The blacksmith?"

"That's right. I'll make an agreement with him to take you on as an apprentice."

Solomon frowned and resumed brushing Minerva. "I don't know 'bout bein' the slave of no black man, Massa Zimri."

"You don't understand, Solomon. You'd be his apprentice. And with your experience working for Titus out at Belle Oaks, you wouldn't need but a year with Boone. Two, at the outside."

Solomon stopped brushing again and looked up. "Then who I'se gonna belong to?"

Zimri exhaled a cloud of cigar smoke and shook his head. "That's what I'm trying to tell you, Solomon. You wouldn't belong to anyone. You'd belong to yourself and no one else."

Solomon seemed frozen like a statue. His eyes bulged out and he seemed unable to speak.

"Technically," Zimri said as if working out the details in his mind, "you'd be a free man the day I sign the papers for your emancipation. But then you'd have to agree in writing to be my indentured servant for that first year. And, of course, I'd have to pay Boone to take you on as an apprentice. He's not likely to train you to be a competitor without some kind of compensation."

Solomon stared at Zimri as if stupefied. "I don't understand half what you sayin,' Massa Zimri, but I know what two of them words mean: 'free,' and 'mancipation.' You tellin' me you gonna make me a free man?"

"That's the long and short of it, Solomon. Sorry I was so round about in getting there."

Solomon dropped the brush, fell to his knees, and clasped his huge hands together. "Oh, Lawd, Lawd, Lawd, Almighty! I'se gonna be free?"

"That's right, Solomon. But there's still a ways to go. In the meantime, you've got to be invisible."

Solomon rose quickly to his feet. "Oh, yes, suh. I be invisible as a ole haint. Ain't nobody gonna see me till you get them papers from Massa 'Gustus. Not even the hoot owls gone see me, 'cause I be black as night."

"Good." Zimri turned to leave, but stopped before reaching the barn door. "Oh, there's one more thing, Solomon."

"Yes, suh?"

"Don't breathe a word of this to my wife. At least not until I've made satisfactory arrangements with Mr. Seymour."

"Oh, no, suh. This be between you and me."

"Exactly. Have the carriage ready in half an hour. We want to get to Belle Oaks before sundown."

"Yes, suh! I jest wisht I could drive you."

Zimri winked at him. "You're invisible, remember?"

Solomon chuckled. "Yes, suh. Sho' is. Jest me and the hoot owls—and even they cain't see me."

"That's the spirit." Zimri closed the door behind him and looked toward the street, where he saw several carriages passing by on their way to family gatherings. As he made his way back to the house, he was suddenly startled by a loud 'whoop' from the barn.

He had his doubts about Solomon's talent for making himself invisible.

CHAPTER 34

Elizabeth cradled the twins in her arms as Charlotte sat between her and Zimri and the phaeton. A light snow was falling, but it didn't seem so cold as she could feel the warmth of the horses rolling off of their bodies. They seemed to thrive in this weather and to equally enjoy the exercise after being cooped up in the barn for much of the past month.

Zimri said little during the ten mile trip to Belle Oaks, and she wondered what he was thinking. She supposed it was about Solomon, as he had spent some time with him in the barn before they had left. He had not consulted her as to Solomon's fate, and she felt a mild resentment at this. Sometimes he treated her like a child in spite of the fact that she had demonstrated her abilities, especially in regard to saving the business. Well, perhaps she had not really 'saved' it, but she had at least helped to put it on a more sound financial footing. But no matter, it was Christmas, and she was looking forward to seeing all the family at Belle Oaks, not to mention a chance to show off the twins.

When they pulled up to the front door Jamie was waiting in a festive, Bavarian-style suit. Elizabeth giggled to herself, thinking that he looked almost like one of the liveried house slaves, one of whom rushed to take charge of the horses and another who came to help them out of the carriage.

"Merry Christmas!" Jamie took one of the twins, Fortunata, from her arms and kissed her.

"Merry Christmas, Jamie," Elizabeth said. "Don't drop her."

"I wouldn't think of it! Why, you can't tell them apart."

"Even I can't tell them apart. They're identical."

Jamie took Lucky, kissed her, and cradled both twins in his arms. "And this is Fortunata, and this is—Lucky. I can tell because she's ever so slightly heavier. You said Lucky was growing at a faster rate."

"Right you are," Elizabeth said as she descended from the carriage. "By exactly eight ounces. Even Zimri can't tell the difference by their weight."

"I can tell by their eyes." Zimri had stepped down from the carriage and was unloading presents. "Lucky has a slight flaw in her right eye."

"A flaw?" Elizabeth closely examined the eye in question and saw nothing unusual. "Where?"

"At ten o'clock," Zimri said. "A little brown speck in a field of blue."

"I still don't see it."

"He's pulling your leg, Elizabeth. How are you, Zimri?"

"Feeling prosperous, Jamie. But I'm not pulling your leg, darling—look carefully. I noticed the other night, before the fire."

Elizabeth took the child from Jamie and peered intently into her right eye. "What? That? Oh, that's nothing. She's absolutely perfect—like her sister."

Jamie laughed . "You should know by now, Zimri, not to accuse a mother's child of having flaws. Better to praise them for growing fat."

"She's neither fat nor flawed," Elizabeth, said, not at all amused by either man's criteria for identifying the twins. "Let's get inside, Zimri. Let Leon take the gifts. It's too cold to be out here."

They all moved inside where they were greeted by Carmichael, who took their coats.

"How are you, Carmichael?" she said.

"Jest fine, Miz Lizbeth. We've missed you here at Belle Oaks."

"I've missed the place, too, Carmichael. Goodness! Everything looks so beautiful! You seem to have assumed your new duties with ease."

Carmichael, looking smart in his steward's uniform, grinned. "It ain't always been that easy, Miz Lizbeth. But we all is coming together as a team now." He then ushered them into the drawing room where there was a roaring fire, and in the center of the room, a huge Christmas tree.

Patsy, who was hanging ornaments, rushed to greet them and asked to hold Fortunata.

"Be careful with her," Elizabeth said. "She's not used to all of these strange people."

Indeed, there were a number of people there that the twins, and even Charlotte had not seen before. Mrs. Blake sat in a chair near the fire and seemed not inclined to get up. Her mother, however, Mrs. Devereaux, a woman of about sixty, was on her feet and making as much fuss over the children as Patsy was. Fanny and her parents, the Cochrans, were there, as well as Elizabeth's aunt on her father's side, Lizzie, for whom she was named.

"Bring Mr. Rhodes a whiskey, Carmichael," Jamie said. "And one for me and Mr. Cochran as well. We'll be in the billiard room."

While the men repaired to the billiard room, Elizabeth wondered at Jamie's unprecedented cordiality towards Zimri. It was as if he were trying to make up for the rudeness that he had often shown him in the past, but for what possible reason she couldn't fathom. Perhaps he was simply maturing, slipping more easily into the role of the master of Belle Oaks, finding it unseemly to be always sowing dissension within the family. In this same spirit, she felt that she should make an effort to befriend Fanny, who after all, was soon to be a member of the family and mistress of Belle Oaks.

She went to her mother's side first and inquired of her health.

"Not so good," her mother said. "Dr. Parcher says I've got rheumatism and gout and I've got to stop eating so many sweets."

"He's right, Mother," she said, noting that she had gained weight since she last saw her. "You're too young and pretty to have either rheumatism or gout."

Mrs. Blake looked at her sidewise, and laughed. "Pretty? I hardly think so. Those days are gone—just like James."

"Mother, you've got to stop dwelling on Papa's passing. You're not only still young and pretty, but rich. There must be scads of eligible bachelors who would love to make your acquaintance. You should get out more."

"Rich? I'm not rich. It's Jamie who's rich now and he can do with his wealth as he pleases." She leaned over the arm of her chair and watched Fanny playing with Charlotte near the tree. "And he's going to squander it all on that woman."

Elizabeth turned briefly to see Fanny dangling a chocolate snowman above Charlotte's head. "Fanny's a very nice girl. I'm sure that she—"

"No, she's not nice. She orders the servants around as if they were mutinous sailors, and tells Maybelle how to cook. As if Maybelle weren't the best cook in the county."

"I'll speak to her about it."

"Please do. She doesn't listen to a word I say. Treats me like a piece of furniture. The other day she had the gall to tell me that I would have to move out of my bedroom to the third-floor guestroom after she and Jamie are married."

Elizabeth glanced again at Fanny, who was now lying on her back near the tree and holding Fortunata up in the air. "She didn't."

"She did. I told Jamie and Jamie gave her a scolding, I can tell you. Told her that I could stay in that bedroom as long as I live if I so choose, and that they could make do in the Savannah room until

I pass away. There was a row between them that could be heard by every servant in the house."

"Good for Jamie," Elizabeth said. "Maybe now that she knows who's boss, she'll be easier to get along with."

"I doubt it. She's common, that's the problem. I could tell it the first time Jamie brought her around. The house slaves have better manners than she does."

Elizabeth patted her mother on the arm. "Give her a chance, Mother. She's young."

"Same age as you."

"I know, but I had all the advantages, thanks to you and Papa. She'll learn."

"I certainly hope so."

Elizabeth left her mother to mingle with the other guests, though she avoided Fanny for the time being. She paid her respects, however, to Mrs. Cochran, who, if anything, was a good deal more coarse than Fanny. But unlike her daughter, she seemed awed by her surroundings and maintained a reserve out of an apparent fear of revealing too much of her origins.

She naturally gravitated to her grandmother, Mrs. Devereaux, who had always been her favorite. It was she who had insisted that Elizabeth attend Mademoiselle Gaillard's Academy in Charleston so that she could perfect her French, the language of her ancestors. And it was she who always came from her home in the former capital of Louisville every summer to stay with them and play with the children and teach them songs in French, and to play games with them and to give them books to read like the *Chanson de Roland*, *Gargantua and Pantagruel*, and later, the plays of Racine and Moliére, many of which they acted out.

"Bon soir, ma chérie." Mrs. Devereax said, kissing her on both cheeks.

"Bon soir, Grand-maman," Elizabeth said, returning her kisses.

They conversed in French for some minutes, drawing a stare of amazement from Mrs. Cochran, who seemed to regard them as beings from another planet. Elizabeth noticed this, and immediately reverted to English.

"But Grand-maman, you must move to Belle Oaks. It must be terribly lonely in Louisville since Grandpapa passed away."

"Not at all, ma chérie," Mrs. Devereaux said. She was a petite woman, not above five feet tall, but exuded energy and vitality in stark contrast to her daughter. "There are so many things to do. I have my garden, of course, in spring and summer, and I read in winter when it's too cold to go out. And Oh! Didn't I tell you? We've formed a little theatre group."

"Oh that's marvelous!"

"Oui, c'est trés merveilleux! We rehearse in a dilapidated old barn just outside of town at present, but in the spring we'll have a brand new theatre. We open with Racine's *Phédre*."

"How exciting! Will it be in French?"

Mrs. Devereaux frowned. "Of course not. Do you think anyone but you or I would understand a word of it? No, my dear child, it will be in the King's English. You must come!"

"I would love to! Who is playing the role of Phaedra?"

Mrs. Devereaux struck an exaggerated theatrical pose, showing her fine profile. "Qui? C'est *moi*, naturellement!"

Elizabeth laughed and clapped her hands together. "Oh, of course I will come! You will make a marvelous Phaedra!"

Mrs. Devereaux suddenly assumed an expression of gloomy despair. "Mais, ma chérie, do you think I'm too old to play the part?"

"Of course not. If anything, you may be a bit too young. Phaedra fell in love with her stepson, after all."

"Hmm, yes. But they did marry young in those days you know."

"You'll be absolutely wonderful."

After a light supper followed by each family member opening one present as a prelude to the big day, the men repaired once more to the billiard room. Jamie, however, tarried for a moment.

"I have something for you, Elizabeth." Jamie looked about the room as if to ascertain whether they were being overheard or not, and assured that they weren't, produced an envelope from his coat pocket. "It came yesterday in the noon mail."

Elizabeth stared at the envelope for a moment, having little doubt of the sender's identity.

"Take it," Jamie said. "You can read it later if you wish. Zimri need not know."

She reached out for the letter, saw the usual multiple postmarks, one of which appeared to be in Greek, turned it over, and saw Randolph's familiar wax seal on the back. "I wish you wouldn't encourage him, Jamie."

"Me? How could I? He's five thousand miles away. I'm simply his go-between."

"A go-between is someone who mediates for two unmarried lovers. I'm neither unmarried nor his lover."

Jamie smiled ironically. "He seems to think otherwise."

"Then he is deluded in thinking so."

"Again, I'm simply the messenger. It's up to you whether you want to read it or throw it in the trash. I'll be in the billiard room if you need me."

Elizabeth put the letter in her sleeve and joined the others by the tree. She engaged in a game of blind man's buff with the children, but she could not stop thinking about what must be in the letter. After a round or two, in which Patsy played the blind man groping after the smaller children, much to their delight, she excused herself to go to the powder room and locked herself in. Then she sat on a low stool in front of a large mirror, slit open the envelope with a pair of scissors, and began reading:

Missolonghi, 17 Oct.

My Dearest Elizabeth,

I came to this little port town to pay my respects to Byron, who breathed his last here in the struggle for Greek independence from the hated Turks.

The struggle is not over, however, in spite of the expulsion of the Egyptians (lackeys of the Turks) by the European powers and the London protocol earlier this year declaring Greece an independent state. The Greeks are not satisfied, as the current government is a monarchy with few democratic freedoms and, as a further insult to the people, a foreign prince has been named as their sovereign.

I am fed up with politics. Every revolution seems to produce its opposite intention, nearly always playing into the hands of autocrats of one kind or another. I am beginning to think that people get the kind of government they deserve.

I am turning my attentions more and more to the spiritual—that is, religion. You know I never was a believer, and you yourself have heard my irreverent mocking of the church, of whatever denomination. But I think that my natural skepticism was directed more towards the hypocrisy of the clergy—they are much worse in Europe than in America, by the way—than to religious belief itself. Certainly we all need to be assured that there is a higher power than ourselves, some deity who directs, however mysteriously, human events that seem absurd and pointless on their face, but lead to an ultimate purpose, of which, alas, we are ignorant.

I would not be so ignorant.

Therefore I am turning my eyes eastward, to the Orient. To-morrow I embark on a schooner bound for the Levant, where I intend to visit Jerusalem before continuing overland to Persia, and ultimately to India. I have already begun to study Sufism—which seems to me to be infinitely more sensible than Christianity. Don't be shocked, my dear, all religions are rather arbitrary outgrowths of particular cultures in a particular time and place. The trick is to separate the spurious and merely silly from the one true path to redemption and salvation.

I apologize for again digressing into politics, and now religion. My only defense is that these are things that are on my mind, and I have no other sympathetic soul to share them with. The more I travel, the more people seem like shadows to me, mere images that shimmer like mirages in a desert landscape.

And you, my darling Elizabeth, are the only person on earth whose features are as distinct to me in my dreams as if you were standing before me in all of your elegant beauty. I have met women here who are beautiful and who—as soon as they perceive that I have money—throw themselves shamelessly at me, declaring that I am the most desirable man on earth. But they are nothing to me, for I know how hollow their claims are, and how mercenary their motives.

You are the only woman I have ever known who cares nothing for my wealth, who is as resistant to my alleged charms as a cat is to limburger cheese. I can only hope to prove myself worthy of you someday, and I know that the only way to do that is to acquire the character that I lack and that you, quite rightly, demand. I left you as a boy, but I shall return to you as a man. And when I do, nothing, not even Zimri, will stand in my way.

Until then, my love, I think of you every minute of every hour of every day. And if you think of me only once in a fortnight, I shall be the happiest of men.

Au revoir,

  Randolph

Elizabeth nearly burst out laughing at this last paragraph, for she knew that Randolph would be thinking of his hunting dogs at Lynwood more often than he would be thinking of her.

But what was his purpose? Did he seriously think that these 'love' letters from Europe and the Orient would succeed in seducing her when he returned? Was it only a calculated risk on his part; i.e., the risk of being repudiated and humiliated on the one hand, against the potential reward of seducing her and wresting her away from Zimri on the other? Would he even care about wresting her away from Zimri once he had obtained his object?

She folded the letter and started to put it back in its envelope, when it occurred to her that she may have been too hasty in her judgment. She read the letter over again—skipping the first part about European politics and Sufism. Did he really dream about her? And would he really confront Zimri when he returned, risking injury and perhaps even death for her sake? And would—

Suddenly there was a knock on the door. "Elizabeth, are you in there? The children think you have abandoned them."

"All right, Grand-maman." She quickly folded up the letter and replaced it in its envelope. "Tell them I'm coming."

"I think they need to be put to bed."

"Mais oui, Grand-maman. Tell them a story until I get there. I seem to have torn my dress."

"Ah. I will tell them the story of Sinbad."

"Très bien, Grand-maman." Elizabeth pulled the letter from the envelope and re-read it from the beginning.

CHAPTER 35

Subscriptions to the *Mercury* continued to rise during the next
three months. Zimri kept his usual late hours at the office, though
Jed was taking over more and more of the marketing side of the
paper, leaving more time for Zimri to write editorials. He was even
considering hiring a second reporter to cover the courthouse and
crime beat, two areas that he found to be somewhat mundane and
repetitive.

It finally had to be admitted that Charlotte had very poor eyesight, and Zimri took her to Savannah to see a specialist. The doctor there saw very little hope for improvement, but arranged to have
a pair of spectacles made for her that enhanced her vision to the
point that she seemed to see Zimri clearly for the first time. She
must not have found his visage too alarming, for though she looked
at him in puzzlement for the first few seconds, a huge grin emerged
and she rushed into his arms for a hug.

An early, albeit false spring arrived in the first week of March,
and Zimri's roses began to bloom.

Elizabeth gained strength with every passing day, and restless,
joined Mrs. Lasky in fund-raising for the new library. Her solicita-
tions were so successful that the building schedule was moved up
to early summer.

Jamie's wedding was set for the end of April, and Fanny continued to assume the duties of running the domestic affairs of Belle
Oaks, much to the consternation of Mrs. Blake.

One day, while working on an editorial at his desk, Zimri was
handed a letter by Jed, who had just returned from the post office.

"I think it's from Miss Rinaldi in New York," Jed said. "I saw
Mr. Reed at the post office, and he said the steamboats are just
about finished."

Zimri took the letter and put it aside with the others as if it were
to be dealt with later. "No doubt she'll be coming down for the
inaugural voyage. We'll need to do a story on it."

Jed remained standing before his desk, "Aren't you going to open
it, Mr. Rhodes?"

"In good time, Jed. I've got to finish this editorial before the
deadline." Jed stood mute for several seconds, obviously disappointed that Zimri wasn't going to share the contents of the letter
with him. After starting to speak, he seemed to think better of it,

and returned to his desk near the front of the office to sort out the week's billings.

Zimri continued to work on his editorial until dinner time, and then climbed into the gig to return to the house. But he had only gone a block or two when he stopped at the corner of Fifth Street and pulled the letter from his jacket. There had been a light rain that morning and the hood of the gig was still up, while the muddy street glistened with a patchwork of small puddles.

He took his pen knife out of his pocket and slit open the envelope.

New York, 5 March

Dearest Zimri,

The winter has been very cruel and lonely in New York, though I have been busier than ever. As demanding as some of my enterprises have been, nevertheless they have occupied my mind as well as my hands, eyes, and ears. And thus, in some measure, I have been relieved of the pain of separation from you, my love.

Soon, however, we will be reunited, as I am coming to Martinville for the launching of the General Oglethorpe and the Miss Cora. Mr. Reed has informed me that the two vessels will be ready on or about the 28th. Enclosed is an announcement of the glorious event, along with a solicitation of merchants to ship their wares via Georgia Steamlines, Inc. As you can see, those who sign up for the maiden voyage will enjoy a considerable discount. Please include the advertisement in your next issue.

Again I apologize, my love, for being so neglectful in writing to you, and consequently having to combine the personal with business. And I have so many things to tell you!

Alas, they must wait. I am dashing off to a meeting this very moment. I shall arrive at the Central Hotel on or about the 25th, depending, of course, on the unpredictable tides and weather.

Adieu, mon chéri,

Cora

Zimri lingered over the letter for a few moments, folded it, and put it back in his jacket. As Jupiter splashed through the puddles at a leisurely pace, he wondered at Cora's intentions. What could she possibly hope to gain by this insistence that they were lovers? To be sure, they had been…intimate. But even by her own admission she neglects to write—not that he wanted her to, in any case—and then, after months of silence, suddenly sends a letter reaffirming her passionate devotion to him. Devotion? He laughed aloud, startling Jupiter. The woman doesn't know the meaning of the word. Except possibly in regard to her 'cause.' Increasingly, he was beginning to think her only 'cause' was to enhance her position in life, to use him or anyone else who might help to advance her enterprises, so that she could ultimately retire a wealthy dowager with estates in America and Europe.

No, there would be no more 'affair.' Once the vessels were on their way laden with cotton, and the receipts were pouring in from local merchants, their relationship would be exclusively a business one. Besides, she would no doubt leave again—thank goodness!- and not be seen nor heard from for another six months. What a strange woman! As the gig approached the house, he saw Elizabeth on the front porch playing with Charlotte and the twins. Even from where he was sitting, he could see the steel rims of Charlotte's spectacles reflecting the sunlight. At least the child could see where she was going now. But certainly the spectacles would detract from her appearance as she got older, and it would be difficult for her to attract a beau. Perhaps she would never marry, and he would have to always support her. Ah, well, so be it.

Elizabeth waved as he pulled up to the gate and encouraged the children to do likewise. He waved back and stepped down from his seat.

As he was tying the reins to the rail he gazed at the domestic scene before him. It occurred to him that he didn't even know whether Cora had any children or not. Surely such a beautiful and passionate woman must have had at least one child, in wedlock or out. She was perhaps ten years older than Elizabeth. She could have two or three children, perhaps all away at boarding school. That would certainly explain her voracious appetite for money. But why would she never mention them?

Dinner was a rather monotonous affair consisting of cabbage soup and three-day-old ham. And Louise's biscuits were never up to Maybelle's, or even to Betty's, standards.

"What's the matter, Zimri?" Elizabeth said. "You seem far away."

"Do I? Sorry, I suppose it's the deadline I have to meet this afternoon. An editorial."

"What's it about?"

"Fugitive slave laws. They're too harsh, I think."

Elizabeth smiled. "That's not surprising—especially since you're harboring a fugitive slave yourself."

"It won't be much longer."

"Oh? Why not? Do you intend to return him to his master?"

Zimri finished his soup and pushed it aside. "No, I intend to *be* his master—for a time, at any rate."

"You're going to buy Solomon back?"

"That's right. And then free him."

Louise, who was serving the ham, nearly dropped the plate, but managed to set it down on the table. "Lordy, Mr. Rhodes—you gonna free Solomon?"

"After one year. And then he'll go to work for your father."

"For Daddy? Does he know that?"

"He surely does, Louise. It's all worked out. All I need is the bill of sale from Mr. Seymour in Mississippi. We settled on a fair price, for which Solomon will have to reimburse me in the form of his year of labor."

Louise seemed beside herself with joy. "Oh, Mr. Rhodes—I could just hug you." She bent down, and stretched her arms out toward him, but receiving a startled look from Zimri, thought better of it. "Solomon's just the nicest, most thoughtful man I ever did see, and you're the most nicest white man to do what you is about to do."

Zimri laughed. "And you'll be the nicest cook I ever saw if you'll learn to bake these biscuits like Maybelle used to."

Louise suddenly turned indignant. "Like Maybelle? She use too much butter in the batter."

"Well, maybe that's what I like about her biscuits."

Louise put her hand on her hip. "Well, I'll be—why didn't you tell me? I can bake 'em anyway you like, Mr. Rhodes."

"Now you know."

"You just wait right here." Louise then disappeared into the kitchen.

Elizabeth pushed her soup aside. "Zimri—is that wise? I mean where's Solomon going to go when he's free?"

"Go? He probably won't go anywhere. He'll have a trade after Boone finishes with him, and he can set up his own smithy shop if he cares to."

"And what about Betty?"

"What about her?"

Elizabeth glanced furtively towards the kitchen and lowered her voice to a whisper. "I've overheard Louise and Tessie saying that Solomon's been sneaking out at night to go see her at Herzen's place."

"He told me."

"He *told* you?"

"I told him to stop it unless he wants this whole deal to blow up in our faces. It's hard for him, but he gave me his word."

"His word."

"Yes, his word."

They continued to eat in silence for some moments, until Elizabeth put her knife and fork down with a clatter. "Zimri, you're a smart man in so many ways, but you're absolutely naïve about the darkies."

"Naïve?"

"Do you seriously believe that Solomon can stay away from Betty for a whole year?"

"No. No, I don't."

"Then how can you—"

"I intend to buy Betty back, too."

Elizabeth's jaw dropped. For the first time since he had known her, she was absolutely bereft of speech.

"I've talked to Herzen. He's agreeable. Says he can't control her, anyway."

"Zimri, we can't afford to buy Betty, too!"

"Herzen's given me a very fair price. He thinks I'm doing him a favor, taking her off his hands."

Louise swept back into the room with a plate full of steaming biscuits. "You try these, Mr. Rhodes. Tell me the truth, now. If you don't like 'em—"

Zimri picked up a biscuit and bit into it. "That's hot! But delicious—just right, Louise."

"I done tole you I can cook 'em any way you want. You don't need Maybelle no more wid me around."

"You've proven your point, Louise. No more complaints."

Louise placed one hand on her hip. "Well, I should hope not!" Then she disappeared into the kitchen.

Zimri smiled at Elizabeth, who managed a smile back. "You see, Louise's grammar is improving. Why not Betty's? Why not Solomon's?"

"You're an eternal optimist, Zimri Rhodes." She picked up a biscuit from the plate. "Ouch! That *is* hot."

"She warned you."

She blew on the biscuit two or three times and took a bite. "Delicious. But darling, what are we to do with four servants?"

"Prosper," he said.

CHAPTER 36

On the morning of the 25th, a Friday, Zimri, accompanied by Mayor Pritchard, Mr. Hamilton, and some of the other investors, stepped out of the lobby of the Central Hotel to meet the noon stage. It was a cool, windy day, with cumulous clouds scudding across an otherwise clear blue sky.

The stage pulled up under the portico of the hotel and the driver jumped down to loosen the leather straps securing the boot. A brown hand reached through the curtained window from the inside and turned the door latch. The door open, a tall, broad-shouldered Negro dressed in a brown frock coat, tri-cornered hat, and ruffled shirt stepped down into the drive. At nearly the same time, a second Negro, of nearly equal stature and dress, came around from the other side of the coach and began to assist the driver in unloading the luggage. The first man seemed to regard the assembled notables before him with contempt and lifted his hand to the darkened portal of the coach. A white-gloved hand appeared, followed by a dainty foot shod in green patent leather shoes. Then a pleated parasol to match the emerald dress, and finally Cora herself emerged, radiantly beautiful, with a shock of black curls cascading over her silk collar.

"Gentlemen—what a surprise!"

The mayor rushed to assist her, though the valet had already succeeded in bringing her safely to the earth. "Miss Rinaldi—we are indeed honored by your presence." He took her hand, bowed a little to kiss it, but a censorious look on the face of the valet deterred him. "How long we have awaited your return to our fair city of Martinville. It has been much the poorer without you."

"Thank you, Mayor Pritchard. It is good to be back. How are you, Zimri?"

"Doing well, Cora. I see you are here to instruct us in the latest fashion as well as to anoint the new steamboats."

Cora laughed and extended her hand to him. "The voyage from New York was beastly cold, and nasty. I decided to treat myself to a hot bath and a new dress when we arrived in Savannah."

"It quite becomes you." Zimri took her hand and, daring to do what Tom Prichard had not, kissed it. "Welcome back to Martinville."

Seeing this ritual performed so smoothly by Zimri, the other men, including Mr. Hamilton, Mr. Cruikshank, and Mr. Lewis, followed suit.

The mayor, not to be outdone, waited patiently for the others to finish, bowed deeply at the waist, and lifted Cora's hand to his lips. "Won't you join us for dinner, Miss Rinaldi? We've reserved a private table for you."

"Why, that would be delightful. Pierre! Beauregard! Take my luggage to the room. And wait for me in the stable—I'll want to take a drive after dinner."

Pierre, the taller one who helped her out of the coach, bowed about half as deeply as Mayor Pritchard had. "Yes, Miss Cora. I'll have a carriage waiting."

"And Pierre—make sure you behave yourself while we're here. You won't want another whipping."

Pierre, expressionless, bowed again. "Yes, Miss Cora."

Zimri stood for a moment gaping at Cora as the two black men hurried to remove her luggage to the room.

"Pierre fancies himself a ladies' man," she said. "Hotel maids are his specialty—I had to administer a little discipline to him in Savannah."

Mayor Pritchard chuckled, as did Mr. Cruikshank and Mr. Lewis. Mr. Hamilton, like Zimri, seemed somewhat disturbed by this comment.

At dinner, Cora regaled the investors with a story of her meeting the great English actor Edmund Kean and playing Ophelia to his Hamlet. Her audience thus held spellbound, she shifted the conversation to the upcoming launch of the *General Oglethorpe* on the following Monday morning. The *Miss Cora*, she said, was not quite completed, and its maiden voyage would take place the following week

After dinner, she persuaded Zimri to accompany her on a drive along the river. They sat comfortably in the back of a landau, driven by Pierre.

"You see the current is very swift now," she said. "The *General Oglethorpe* should arrive in Darien in record time."

"Yes," Zimri said. "The melted snow from the mountains has swollen all of the rivers in these parts. Cora—"

"It's such a lovely spring day." She put her hand on his. "Do you suppose we could find a nice cave somewhere along the riverbank?"

"I'm afraid I don't know of any. Cora, you've changed."

"Changed? How do you mean?"

"For one thing, I don't believe your story about playing opposite Kean in *Hamlet*."

She laughed and squeezed his hand more tightly. "Oh, *that*. I'm afraid I can't fool you, darling. I did meet Mr. Kean in New York last winter while he was on tour. But we only exchanged a few lines from the play while members of the press looked on. I confess I exaggerated a bit to impress the others. How did you know?"

"Because you haven't had time if your stories concerning your business ventures are true."

"Well, of course they're true. And you're right darling, I've hardly had a minute for anything else."

"Which brings me to the second point. Pierre."

"Pierre?" Cora looked at the back of her driver, who was sitting on a seat far ahead of them, and who was not likely to hear their conversation over the noise of the horses' hooves and the wheels of the carriage crunching the gravel along the road. "What about him?"

"Him, and the other one—"

"Beauregard."

"Yes, Beauregard. You say they're slaves."

"Yes."

"I thought you were an ardent abolitionist. It was your 'cause,' you said."

Cora placed her other hand on his and looked out over the vista of the river as it meandered eastward through the hills. "I've grown up a good deal this past year. A young woman wants romance and knights in shining armor—knights who will set the world right. I'll be thirty soon."

Zimri laughed. "Thirty? You're still young. Do ideals evaporate at the age of thirty?"

"It seems so. The weight of practical matters accumulates at an alarming rate. I don't want to spend my remaining years in poverty."

"And your financial goals cannot be reached without owning slaves?"

She tugged on his arms and smiled. "Now who's the idealist? You told me in Connecticut that slavery would simply melt away eventually. Like the snow in the mountains."

"The snow in the mountains has the sun to hasten its melting. Slavery's demise will only be hastened by the owners voluntarily releasing the poor wretches from their bondage."

"My! You're beginning to sound like some of my former abolitionist friends. What has prompted this revolution in your soul, my dear?"

Zimri flushed with embarrassment. He did not like being cast as a do-gooder. "It's hardly a revolution in my soul, or anywhere else. I think I've been fairly consistent in my position on the issue of slavery. It's you, it seems to me, who have experienced a revolution."

"Phaugh! Simply because I purchased a couple of slaves in Savannah to assist me in my personal needs? I no longer have time to arrange for horses and carriages, and to look for a porter to carry my luggage, especially in sleepy little towns like Martinville. You saw that there was no one to help me when I arrived at the hotel."

"Why not hire free men?"

"Because good ones are hard to find and they do not wish to travel and be away from their families." She moved closer and nestled her chin against his shoulder. "Oh, Zimri, let's not talk of such things. We only have a little time together."

Pierre continued to follow the river road, past the new iron works, past the loading docks, past the fields that were being readied for the next cotton crop.

"I think we'd better turn around, Cora," Zimri said. "It'll be dark by the time we get back as it is."

"Let it get dark. Pierre has the vision of a night owl."

"That may be so, but—"

"Oh, look!" she said, pointing to a high promontory at a bend in the river. "Let's stop there. Pierre! Follow that trail to the bluff."

"Yes, Miss Cora." Pierre turned the carriage off the main road and cracked his whip. The bluff was a good fifty feet higher than the road elevation.

"It looks much like the mountain bluff at New Haven," she said. "I'm sure the view is spectacular."

"No doubt. But we'll only have a few minutes to enjoy it. Then we'll have to head back."

"A few minutes is better than nothing. Stop here, Pierre."

The carriage came to a halt about twenty feet from the edge of the bluff.

"You see?" she said.

Indeed, it was a spectacular view, facing westward in one direction, with the sun beginning to set behind low clouds of pink and orange. In the other direction, eastward, purple shadows fell across the river's waters beneath spreading oaks along the banks.

"Pierre," she said, after a moment of gazing at the scene, "see if you can find us some apples."

"Yes, Miss Cora." Pierre climbed down from his seat. "The horses are plumb tuckered out. They'll need something to carry them back to the hotel."

Pierre then quickly disappeared into a grove of trees.

"Cora," Zimri said, "we can't—"

She kissed him on the mouth and drew him closer. "I want you, Zimri. I want you deep inside me."

"Cora, this is crazy. Pierre could come back at any—"

"He knows not to find those apples too quickly. Come darling, unlace me."

Zimri hesitated, then reached for the bowstring that secured her bodice. He loosened the string as if he were unlacing a boot, methodically, perfunctorily, feeling suddenly as if he were as much a servant to Cora as Pierre.

In moments the dress was on the floor of the carriage and he felt Cora's hands at his trousers, her fingers loosening the buttons to his fly. Now it was no longer a chore, but an arousal that overwhelmed any second thoughts he might have had. He slipped his braces off and the trousers fell to his thighs.

The tufted leather seats of the carriage were soft and comfortable, and it was easy to slide into a nearly prone position. Cora wore two petticoats beneath the dress, but these were easily removed. She lay before him naked but for a sort of pantaloon that was nearly sheer, and which she pulled off herself.

"Why do you stare so, darling?" she said.

"What man wouldn't?"

"Do you like what you see?"

"You know I do. You know I can't resist you when you're like this."

"Then come inside me—don't torture me with that look of reproach."

"Reproach?"

"Yes, as if I'm some harlot that only cares for erotic pleasures."

"What else would you call this?"

She raised up at the waist and took his face in her hands and kissed him. "I would call it passion."

He looked into her eyes now and saw an almost desperate longing for something that seemed to have nothing to do with sex. "What is it you want, Cora?"

She seemed surprised. "Why, you, darling. All of you."

"And if you can only have a small part of me?"

She laughed and the desperation in her eyes vanished as quickly as it had appeared. "Then I'll take what I can get."

Disarmed and even more aroused by her laughter, Zimri kissed her with the passion that she demanded and that he was all but helpless to resist.

CHAPTER 37

The following night, Saturday, Cora gave a recital at the new Martinville Musicale, only three blocks from the hotel. This consisted of a dozen songs, about half from the classical repertoire, and half popular American tunes. Zimri and Elizabeth attended, as did nearly all of the investors in the steamboat enterprise. In addition, many planters in the area, including Jamie and his fiancée, Fanny, were in attendance as the event had been advertised in the *Mercury* for some weeks in advance.

The recital was a success. Cora received a standing ovation, and many encomiums were to follow.

Much to Zimri's relief, she declined an invitation extended by Elizabeth to drop by for a late supper, pleading exhaustion due to the arduous journey from New York in addition to the energy required for the recital. It did seem to Zimri that she was uncharacteristically fatigued, and there was a bit of hoarseness in her voice, as if she had not been much in practice of late.

On Sunday, Elizabeth persuaded Zimri to make one of his rare appearances in church, as it was Easter and she was anxious to show off her spring clothes.

Cora was not at the service.

That evening, when Zimri asked Solomon to put the gig in the barn, he received a curious response.

"Don't you worry about me, Massa Zimri," he said. "I'se here to stay."

"Were you thinking of leaving?"

"Naw, suh. I jest want you to know I'm a man of my word."

"I know that, Solomon. So why would I worry about your leaving?"

Solomon patted Jupiter on the shoulder and seemed to avoid looking directly at him. "I jest thought I'd set your mind at rest in case you heard any rumors."

"Rumors? What rumors?"

"Jest talk. You know how people talk. I better put ol' Jupiter in the barn now, Massa Zimri. He look mighty tired."

"I suppose he is. Mrs. Rhodes and I took a long drive after church. Make sure he doesn't drink too much water."

"Yes, suh. I take good care of him."

Zimri walked back to the house, wondering at Solomon's comments. Had he been sneaking out to see Betty again at Herzen's place? Perhaps he felt he couldn't wait a year for his freedom. Perhaps he wouldn't be able to stay away from Betty long enough for him to buy her back from Herzen. He was a little short on cash now, what with all the expense of Christmas and installments on the new cylinder press, not to mention the fact that he had bought more shares in the Georgia Steamlines Co.

Rumors. What 'rumors' was Solomon talking about? Perhaps he was thinking of running off with Louise. Or so the other servants might think. Louise did seem to be attracted to him, taking every opportunity to praise him. He chuckled at the thought of Boone, a free black, going after a runaway slave to preserve the honor of his daughter.

He stopped on the way to the house to examine his roses when he had another, rather alarming, thought. But he quickly dismissed it as preposterous, shrugged his shoulders, and went into the house.

On Monday morning at precisely eight o'clock Cora met with Mr. Reed of the Martinville Maritime Co. at the doors to the boat house that housed the two steamboats. These doors were on the street side of the building and double-padlocked so that it required two keys, one in the possession of Mr. Reed, the other of Cora, to gain access to the vessels. The investors, including Zimri, were also present, eagerly awaiting the great moment.

When the huge doors swung open, however, there was a collective gasp. One of the twin cradles supporting the two boats while they were being constructed was empty. The door on the river side of the building was wide open, and the ramp to the water disappeared beneath the surface as if the missing vessel had been swallowed up by a monster of the deep.

Cora, dressed in a ship captain's uniform with gold braid on the shoulders, ran frantically to the cradle, seemed to turn white, mounted one of the broad rails of the ramp, and made her way all the way down to the water's edge, where she first looked downriver, then up.

"Gone!" she cried. "Gone! Pierre! Beauregard!"

After a few moments, as the assembled crowd began to murmur ever more loudly, Pierre appeared. "Yes, Miss Cora?"

"Where's Beauregard? He was supposed to have guarded the building all night. He was locked in!"

"He's gone, Miss Cora."

"I can see that he's gone, you fool! How did he make off with a seventy foot steamboat?"

"Dunno, Miss Cora. He was asleep in the *General Oglethorpe* when I checked up on him 'round midnight."

"Asleep? And you didn't wake him?"

"I did wake him. Guess he just dozed off again."

"And I suppose you just dozed off, too. Damn your eyes!"

At this point, Cora began beating Pierre with a gaff hook that happened to be handy, and had to be restrained by two or three of the investors. One of these was Zimri.

"Cora!" he said. "Have you gone out of your senses? It's not Pierre's fault—besides, we'll get the *General Oglethorpe* back. It may be nothing more than a prank."

"Prank?" she said, nearly on the verge of tears. "It's theft, pure and simple! It represents everything I've worked for, everything I have!"

"Don't worry, Miss Rinaldi," Mayor Pritchard said. "We'll get the boat back. I'll send a posse out. It can't have gotten very far."

"Oh, no?" she said, shaking loose from Zimri's grip. "They've got at least eight hours head start. And the current downstream is running at eight to ten knots. You'll need a race horse to catch up."

"We'll alert the planters downriver," Pritchard said. "They'll have to stop for fuel and supplies at some point."

At this moment a rider came galloping up to the front of the building and dismounted. It was Sheriff Beasley. The crowd parted to let him through.

"There's been a slave break," Beasley said. "Sixty, seventy of 'em. From different plantations. And they're using your steamboat, Miss Rinaldi."

"You see!" screamed Cora. "It was all planned!" She turned to Zimri with a look of contempt such as he had never seen in her. "Not a prank, Mr. Rhodes. A plot. And these darkies are too stupid and incompetent to have planned it by themselves. I suspect their leader is a white man with some seafaring experience. Mr. Reed!"

"Yes, Miss Rinaldi?"

"I will question you later. And you had better come up with some good answers. Mr. Beasley!"

"Yes, ma'am."

"Assemble a posse as suggested by Mayor Pritchard, and reserve your fastest horse for myself. After all, I am the one most subject to ruin here. I also want you to post no less than two, no four, armed guards on the premises until further notice. Is that clear?"

"I don't know if I can spare—"

"Mr. Pritchard?"

"We can deputize as many as we need, Aaron," the mayor said. "And we'll pay them out of the city treasury. This affects the whole economy of Martinville."

"Pierre," Cora said, "get two horses from the stable. Do you think you can do that without losing one?"

Pierre hung his head. "Yes, ma'am."

"Then get going. Gentlemen—I apologize for any negligence on my part that has jeopardized your investment. But if we move quickly, and the fools have not smashed the *General Oglethorpe* up on a sandbar, than we will recover the vessel and reschedule the launching. Zimri!"

"Yes, Cora."

"I trust you will not write this incident up in your newspaper as a 'prank.'"

"No, Cora."

"Mr. Reed—"

"Yes, Miss—"

"I want this boat house locked up as tight as a drum. Two guards outside, two inside. Do you understand?"

"Yes, ma'am."

"Gentlemen, my man will be here at any moment with the horses. Those of you who wish to join in the pursuit, please do so. But be prepared to shoot to kill, or do not come at all."

And with that final decree, Cora strode out of the building and into the street, where Pierre was waiting with the horses.

Later that afternoon the *General Oglethorpe* was found run aground some thirty miles downstream. It was abandoned, and there was considerable damage to the paddle wheel, but otherwise intact. It was decided that it would be towed back to Martinville for repairs but with the river running so rapidly, it would be another week or so before this could be accomplished. In the meantime, the *Miss Cora* was still on schedule to be launched the following Monday.

Though the investors, including Zimri, were much relieved at the recovery of the *General Oglethorpe*, many planters in the area were distressed that they had lost, at least temporarily, anywhere from one to twenty slaves each. Belle Oaks had lost no less than twelve, perhaps fourteen, and Jamie was furious.

"Leon was apparently the ring leader," he said the next afternoon while sipping a whiskey in his sister's hearth room. "And to think I trusted him to come and go as he pleased! There will be some changes around Belle Oaks, I can tell you that."

"What about Carmichael?" Elizabeth said.

"Carmichael's still with us. But I can't believe he didn't know about it. He knows everything that the darkies do. And, of course, Maybelle's too old and too set in her ways to run off—especially without Carmichael."

"And Otis, and Old George?"

"The same. They're not going anywhere. But I lost some of my best field hands. The young ones, especially, seem to think that there's some kind of utopia north of the Mason-Dixon line. But they'll find that jobs are not so easy to get, especially non-farm jobs that require years of training. And nobody will be looking out for them the way we planters do—the Yankee bosses kick them out the door at sundown and don't care what happens to them after that."

"Why couldn't you just free them and hire them back at a wage? Couldn't you make up the difference by not having to support them, just like the Yankee bosses?"

Jamie looked up at her from his whiskey, incredulous. "Where did you get that ridiculous notion? Zimri, no doubt. Well, running a newspaper isn't like running a plantation. You'd have to fire them all every year there's a drought, or a drop in the price of cotton. And then where would they be? They'd turn to scavenging and roaming the countryside, thieving and killing. No, Elizabeth, Negroes were made for hard physical labor. And they can't conduct their own affairs in a civilized fashion, so we have to do it for them. It's a fair exchange, and it's worked for over two hundred years."

This seemed to be an irrefutable argument to Elizabeth, and she wondered if Zimri weren't being foolish in his plan to free Solomon and Betty. Betty had already been repurchased from Mr. Herzen and was working in the kitchen with Louise. She couldn't see that Louise was any better off than Betty, the only difference being that Betty retired to the old slave quarters at the end of the day, while Louise had to make her way home to her father's place, often in the dark and in foul weather, some three to four miles on the other side of town. And what would she do when they no longer needed her or could afford her? She couldn't live with her father forever. Marriage, perhaps, but she would still have to find another job to make ends meet.

"I have to be going." Jamie placed his empty glass down on the coffee table and rose from his chair. "Thanks for the drink, Elizabeth. It takes the edge off. Oh, I forgot to tell Zimri when I was in his office this afternoon—I want my ad to run on the front page, not in the back with all of the legal notices and home remedies."

"I'll tell him, but he usually doesn't run ads on the front page."

"Tell him to make an exception. I want my niggers back, and I want 'em soon. The planting season's upon us."

"I'll see what I can do."

After Jamie had left, Elizabeth brooded over their conversation. She felt more and more torn between her brother's way of life— her way of life, too, until two-and-a-half years ago—and her current life with Zimri. True, Zimri was prospering and it seemed that they now had sufficient help—both free and slave—to run the household in a more or less efficient and genteel manner. But their fortunes could change so quickly, as this latest incident with the steamboats illustrated so well. And what would they have to fall back on? Of course she would have a paying job when the library is finished, but for how long would that sustain her interest? And the salary was rather pitiful, even for a head librarian.

She returned to the bedroom to check on the children. All were napping after dinner. Tessie was in the kitchen with Louise and Betty, no doubt exchanging gossip about the slave 'betrayal,' as Jamie called it. Somewhat at a loss as to what to do, she went to her desk and idly ran her fingers through her letter box. Inevitably, they came to rest on Randolph's missive from Greece. Where could he be now? Persia? India?

She unfolded the letter and read it again.

Randolph boasts of his wealth, she thought. Is he really so rich? She had never been to Lynwood, his father's estate near Charleston, but Jamie described it as being even more magnificent than Belle Oaks.

She gazed at the twins, still sleeping in their crib, and Charlotte, asleep in the bed. Then she folded up the letter and put it back in the letter box. She smiled at the thought of her 'gentleman's agreement' with Zimri. Was she really so naïve?

Surely Zimri has read the letter.

CHAPTER 38

Cora seemed to be a whirlwind of activity throughout the remainder of the week. She left town on Tuesday and went to Hawkinsville, where she had arranged to have the *General Oglethorpe* towed for the repairs. It was closer than Martinville, and a few miles downstream from where the vessel had been abandoned. There was also a master wheelwright there who could make a new paddlewheel, as the old one was too heavily damaged to be salvaged.

She returned on Thursday, whereupon she inspected the *Miss Cora*, and determined that progress was too slow. She therefore ordered that four more journeyman carpenters be hired, and that work proceed around the clock until the project was finished.

She surprised Mr. Hamilton by appearing at the bank as it opened on Friday morning and depositing an additional $3,000 as surety against any further mishap to the two boats. This information quickly circulated throughout the town.

That afternoon she came into Zimri's office just before closing.

"Any news of the renegades?" she said.

Zimri had his feet up on his desk reading the Thursday edition. He hadn't heard her come in. "Cora! No, no news. The renegades seemed to have vanished into thin air."

"Seventy-four of them." Jed was standing at the door to Zimri's office, wearing a printer's apron and wiping his hands off with a rag. "Hello, Miss Rinaldi. Didn't mean to interrupt, but I thought you might like to know. Seventy-five with your man Beauregard."

"The rascal," Cora said. "I always thought there was something shifty about him when I bought him in Savannah. Always looking from side to side, never straight ahead when you were talking to him."

"Seems there were six or seven wagons waiting for them at Empire Point. The slaves probably hid in the wagon beds with a tarp over them, or maybe even covered with feed sacks."

"It's all right here, Cora." Zimri handed her the paper. "Jed's tramped over six counties to get the story."

Cora took the paper and perused the front page article. "My, you've been an industrious reporter, Jed. What else did you find out?"

Jed's desire to impress Cora was painfully obvious. He stepped inside the office, put his rag in the pocket of his apron and folded his arms as if the victor in a foot race. "I know where they went."

"And where is that?"

"Overland. Some to the Carolinas, some to Tennessee and Kentucky."

"How did you find out?"

"Well, Miss Rinaldi, it's not so hard if you know where to look."

Cora glanced at Zimri. "And where did you look, Jed?"

"In the smithy shops. Horses need to be reshod, especially when hauling a heavy load."

"Why, I never thought of that. How clever of you. But how do you know they didn't change direction after stopping to be reshod or to take on supplies?"

"That's just it. Surely they've changed directions three, four, five times. But they've eventually got to meet up and head north and that's bound to attract attention."

"But why do they have to head north? Why can't they go east and board a ship?"

"That's not likely, Miss Rinaldi."

"Why not?"

"Because they're slaves. You can't transport slaves in Atlantic waters. It's against the law. And the port authorities aren't going to believe that sixty or seventy Negroes boarding a ship bound for Philadelphia or New York are free men. They might as well walk into the local sheriff's office and surrender."

"But they can hide in boxes and crates, can't they?"

"They'd starve before they got to New York. And if you'll pardon the expression, how are they going to relieve themselves? Not two out of ten would survive the trip."

"You seem to have thought of everything, Jed. I hope you're right."

Jed affected a humble attitude. "I may be wrong, Miss Rinaldi. But if I am, then whoever planned this thing is a lot smarter than I am."

"Not likely," she said.

There was a moment of silence as Jed seemed to glory in his triumph of investigative reporting, but did not know what else to say. Zimri thought for a moment that he was preparing to ask Cora to dine with him.

"Why don't you lock up, Jed," Zimri said. "Miss Rinaldi and I have some business to discuss."

Jed looked somewhat disappointed as if he should be included.

But then he took his leave, removed his ink-spattered apron and disappeared into the press room.

"What a nice boy," Cora said, when he had gone. "And so clever, too."

"He is that," Zimri said. "And a hard worker, too."

"You're very lucky to have him."

There was another long silence, during which Cora seemed to be mocking him.

"What is it, Cora? What do you want?"

She smiled. "Oh, nothing. I'm content to just to sit here and watch you work."

"I'm not working."

"You're always working. Or perhaps I should say thinking. That is your work, isn't it?"

"I suppose you could say that."

"What are you thinking now?"

Zimri sighed. "You're beginning to sound like Elizabeth. She always wants to know what I'm thinking. Even when my mind is a complete blank."

Cora laughed. "What false humility! You know your mind is never a complete blank. Now tell me what you're thinking."

"Good night, Mr. Rhodes." Jed struck his head in the door. "Good night, Miss Rinaldi. By the way, I really enjoyed your recital last week."

"Oh, thank you, Jed. I'm afraid I was a little out of practice, though."

"If you were, I couldn't tell it. You sounded like an angel."

"How sweet of you to say that."

Jed lingered at the door for a moment, again uncertain of what he wanted to say.

"Good night, Jed," Zimri said.

"Oh...yes, good night. I'll leave by the front door, Mr. Rhodes. Peter's already left."

When he had gone at last, Zimri looked at Cora with an ironic smile. "Jed seems to have taken a liking to you."

"As I said, he's a sweet boy. Now, where were we? Oh, yes, you were about to tell me what you were thinking."

"Was I?"

"On the very precipice."

Zimri rubbed his chin and took on a more serious mien. He leaned forward in his chair. "All right. I was thinking about something."

"I knew it!"

"I was thinking that...Elizabeth is getting suspicious."

"How unfortunate. She's not the suspicious type."

"No, she's not. But she can hardly help it."

"Why do you say that?"

"Your perfume, Cora. You've got to stop wearing it. It's all over me when I get home."

"It must be evident on the clothes of other men I deal with when they get home, too. But it doesn't mean that I've been...how shall I say...intimate with them."

"No. No, it doesn't. And Elizabeth knows that you are very....effusive, shall we say. Always touching people."

"I can't help it. That's the way I am. But if she knows that, what's the problem?"

Zimri frowned and began fiddling with a printer's rule on his desk. "They're other things, too."

"Like what?"

"Stains. On my trousers."

Cora threw her head back and laughed. "Oh, darling, what can I say? You're excitable when you're around me. It's bound to produce certain...tell-tale signs. Can't you have Louise wash them when you get home?"

Zimri flushed. "I did just that the last time. But it raises suspicions when a man comes home for supper and the first thing he does is to remove his trousers and hand them to the laundress."

Cora fairly roared with laughter. "Oh, darling, you're too funny. That's one thing I like about you— you're comical when you're trying to be so very serious. It's most charming."

"Comical or not, it has to stop."

Cora collected herself and put her elbow on the desk and her chin on the heel of her hand. "Darling, you're always saying that. 'It has to stop,' you say. But you don't want it to stop, and you know it."

He stared at her for nearly a minute. "No. I don't."

She stood up from her chair and came around to where he was sitting. She had a short silk jacket on, a rose-colored one to match her dress, removed it, and sat on his lap. A white lace, nearly sheer, covered her décolletage all the way to her neck, where the collar was secured with a black velvet ribbon with a cameo at its center. She put her arms around his neck.

"Cora, let's not—"

She gave him a lingering kiss. "Does that excite you, mon chéri?"

"You know it does."

"Then what are we to do about your poor stained trousers?"

"Stop doing what we're doing right now."

"I have a better idea."

"Such as?"

"Remove your trousers first."

"Cora, the front door's unlocked."

"Then I will lock it and pull down the shades." She rose from his lap and stared for a moment at the bulge in his trousers. "When I get back I don't want to see a man standing there with stains on his trousers. I fully agree with Elizabeth. It is a most ridiculous sight."

She removed her earrings, placed them on the desk, and went to the front room to do as she had promised.

CHAPTER 39

It rained the entire weekend and Zimri stayed home to catch up on his correspondence, which seemed to be growing in volume. His brother Zeke in Boston seemed intent upon re-establishing their relationship, and wrote frequently of the news in Boston and New York.

He had received a letter from Alexis in Paris, accompanied by a manuscript entitled *Du Système pénetentiare aux Estats-Unis et de son application en France.* The letter, in English, apologized for the manuscript being entirely in French but recalled that Zimri had told him his wife spoke French, and if she would be so kind as to translate it for him, would he mind too awfully much to offer his opinion?

Zimri knew little of the penal system in America, though he had witnessed the hanging of poor Luther. However, he was flattered that Alexis sought his opinion, and he enlisted Elizabeth's expertise to read the manuscript aloud to him. Though the material was very dry, she seemed to enjoy the opportunity to serve as his translator.

On Monday morning, at eight o'clock, he met with Cora, Mr. Hamilton, Mayor Pritchard, and the other investors at the padlocked door of the Martinville Maritime Co. There was little talk or fanfare at this meeting, as there had been at precisely the same time the week before. Rather, there was an atmosphere of apprehension as first Cora, then Mr. Reed inserted their keys into the padlocks and the heavy iron hasps popped open. The locks were removed, and the large barn-like doors swung open.

This time there was no gasp, but rather a stunned silence.

Both cradles were empty.

"Impossible!" Cora exclaimed.

"Is this some kind of joke?" someone said.

Cora ran to the empty cradle of the *Miss Cora*, looked wildly around the shed, jumped up on the ramp leading to the river, and ventured all the way to the water's surface where she looked first upriver, then down.

"Mr. Reed!" She came back up the ramp, spied out Mr. Reed among the crowd, and put her hands on her hips. "There were four guards here—two outside the building, and two in. Where are they?"

"I have no idea, Miss Rinaldi." Mr. Reed was visibly shaken and looked nervously at the others. "They were all in their places at ten o'clock last night when I checked on them."

"Ten o'clock?" Cora said. "And not again at twelve? And at two? And at four? They were your responsibility, Mr. Reed."

"I have a family, Miss Rinaldi. I couldn't come all the way in town every—"

"You have let me down, Mr. Reed. And you have let my investors down. Where's Pierre?"

"Right here, Miss Cora." Pierre called from the back of the crowd, where he was pulling a man gagged and bound from a paint closet. "And looky what I found."

The investors all rushed to the paint closet where Pierre was pulling a second man from the closet, then a third, and finally a fourth.

Mr. Reed, Mr. Hamilton, and Zimri all assisted in removing their gags, then the ropes that bound their arms to their sides.

"White men!" the first guard said as soon as the gag was removed. "Two white men—one with an English accent—and two niggers. They were on us before we could raise our weapons."

"Must've hid here in the paint closet at the end of the work day on Friday," spluttered a second guard. He had a bloodied forehead, but otherwise seemed unhurt. "Hit me 'fore I knowed what happened."

"Two of the biggest niggers I ever saw," said the third man, rubbing his wrists, which had rope burns on them. "Make your man here look like a pygmy."

Cora wasted no time apologizing to the investors but called on Sheriff Beasley once again to organize a posse. She sent Pierre for the horses.

"They will not succeed this time, gentlemen," she said. "It's a case of coming once too often to the well."

"How do we know you're not one of 'em?" It was Bob Cruikshank. "Show 'em the newspaper, Victor."

Victor Steingart reached into his jacket and produced a folded-up newspaper. He unfolded it and held it aloft. "This is a copy of *The New York Intelligencer.* One of my customers sent it to me. I'll read you the headline, gents. It says, 'New York Actress Active in Abolitionist Movement.'"

There was a stir among the assembly.

Mr. Steingart began reading from the article. "'Miss Cora Rinaldi, renowned for her convincing portrayals of Ophelia in *Hamlet,* and

Desdemona in *Othello*, has been active in abolitionist circles, according to our sources in Boston. She is said to be one of the closest confidants of Mr. William Garrison, a radical abolitionist who advocates immediate emancipation of the slaves and recently launched a newspaper to promote that end called *The Liberator.*'"

This caused considerable tumult among the investors, with Mr. Cruikshank calling for Cora's arrest.

Cora rapped on one of the cradles with a mallet she picked up from a work bench. The crowd grew silent. "That is old news, Mr. Steingart. Everyone in New York knows that in my idealistic youth I was sympathetic to the abolitionist cause. And yes, I did become acquainted with Mr. Garrison, who, at that time, I admired very much. But increasingly, his radical and intransigent ways caused me to reject his brand of abolitionist sentiment and we parted company. If our friend in New York had sent you the latest edition of the *Intelligencer*, Mr. Steingart, you would find that I publicly denounced both Mr. Garrison and the *Liberator* as being engines of anarchy bent on the destruction of the Union. And since I have been acquainted with Mr. Rhodes here, my political views have matured and I have come to the same conclusion that he has; that is, the preservation of the Union and the Constitution must trump the issue of slavery."

There was much muttering among the investors as they attempted to digest this information.

"And besides, gentlemen," Cora said, "am I not a slave-owner myself?"

There was a palpable silence at this comment, followed by more conversation.

Pierre appeared at the street door holding the reins of the horses.

"Gentlemen, I have no more time to lose. If you choose to no longer participate as a shareholder in the Georgia Steamlines Co., apply to Mr. Hamilton and he will refund your investment at par value. But I must advise you that we already have six contracts to ship cotton to Darien, and two steamboats to ship them—one of the vessels undergoing minor repairs in Hawkinsville, and the other, if the thieves' modus operandi holds true, will be recovered by sunset today. Let's just hope they have a better pilot this time."

Amid sporadic laughter Cora then strode to the door, where she mounted one of the horses, and with Pierre close behind, sped away.

Zimri was detained for some time by the others, who wanted to know what he knew of Cora's background. He assured them that, as far as he knew, everything that Cora had just said was true. He had always known of her abolitionist sentiments, he said, but he had no reason to believe that she was engaged in conspiracies to emancipate slaves. Besides, he said, she had invested a considerable amount of her own money in the steamboat enterprise, more than any other investor, and she was a practical woman of business. He intended to keep his own shares, he said.

This seemed to placate most of the investors, though he saw Mr. Lewis and Mr. Cruikshank take Mr. Hamilton aside and express their concerns as to the safety of their money. Apparently, Mr. Hamilton reassured them on this point, as the crowd soon broke up and the participants went their own ways. None, however, seemed inclined to follow Cora and her man in pursuit of the brigands.

Zimri went back to his office wondering at what had just taken place. He said nothing at first to Jed, who was taking an ad from a customer.

He sat down at his desk and put his feet up. What in the world was going on? He had long suspected Cora of being more actively involved in the abolitionist movement than she owned up to. But she seemed to have changed lately. It was no stretch of the imagination to believe that she had parted company with Mr. Garrison. But what if it was all an elaborate plot? A phony press conference announcing her split with Garrison, the building of two steamboats to effect the escape of a couple of hundred slaves, an underground network of abolitionist sympathizers to spirit them safely out of the South and into the North, perhaps to Canada. He had heard stories of this underground network. But it seemed to be confined primarily to Northern states like Ohio and Pennsylvania, where the general population was of an anti-slavery sentiment, and state laws forbade the return of fugitive slaves.

The baffling thing, however, was that the first seventy-five slaves had vanished without a trace! Not a single one had been apprehended, not a single sighting of suspicious movement had been reported.

"How did the launching go?"

"What? Oh. Not well, I'm afraid. Sit down, Jed. Tell me more about what you've learned of the smuggling trade."

CHAPTER 40

The *Miss Cora* was discovered late that same afternoon just as Cora had predicted. It was found undamaged, and securely tied up at a private dock in Pulaski county just south of Hawkinsville. This convenience allowed the two vessels to be reunited at the Hawkinsville pier, where the *General Oglethorpe* was just undergoing its first test run with its new paddlewheel.

The next day, the two vessels sailed upriver to Martinville, where they were tied up at the wharf. The christening ceremony was set for Thursday and with both vessels already in the water and having proven their seaworthiness, there was no need for a second launching. This also seemed to provide for better security, for the craft were out in the open for all to see, and Cora herself, along with her man Pierre, decided to sleep in the vessels with one or the other waking every two hours to see that the guards were performing their duties. In the meantime, each steamboat was loaded with some seven to eight hundred bales of cotton to be transported to Darien, and then Savannah.

Everyone seemed to be happy except the planters, who had now lost a total of one hundred and sixty-three slaves.

Jamie was livid to the point of apoplexy as he stood on the wharf the following day, shouting at Cora, who stood on the deck of the *General Oglethorpe*.

"Thirty-four slaves, Miss Rinaldi!" He stood about six feet from her, jabbing his forefinger at her. "Thirty-four! Do you know how many bales of cotton I'll have to ship to pay for the loss of thirty-four niggers?"

Cora folded her arms across her chest. "At sixteen cents a pound and sixty pounds to the bale, minus shipping charges, you'd have a profit of about eight dollars per bale, Mr. Blake. Your average slave, I would say, is worth about four hundred dollars. Multiply that by thirty-four and you'd have…let's see…$13,600...Eight into $13,600...that's about 1,700 bales of cotton, Mr. Blake. Two steamboat loads."

Jamie stood spluttering for a moment as he vainly attempted to verify Cora's calculations in his own head. Failing that, he lashed out at her again.

"That may be so, Miss Rinaldi, but it's no small expense. And from what I hear, you might be one of the thievin' nigger lovers yourself!"

"I'm a businesswoman, Mr. Blake, and I want my business to prosper. Why should I jeopardize my business by stealing the property of the very customers that I wish to serve?"

Jamie stood perplexed for a moment. "I don't know, Miss Rinaldi. This whole thing is crazy. Niggers escaping downriver in brand new steamboats that they couldn't possibly know how to operate, then these very same steamboats tied up at the wharf here loading the cotton they just picked to ship to Darien. It makes no sense."

"I must confess that it perplexes me in the extreme as well, Mr. Blake. But the vessels are here, for all to see, and ready to perform the task for which they were designed. We sail for Darien tomorrow. If you wish to cancel your contract, I will gladly do so at no charge, and my men will unload your cotton. Five hundred bales, if I'm not mistaken."

Jamie seemed to consider this for a moment. "Have you got room for another three hundred?"

"I'll see what I can do, Mr. Blake. It shouldn't be a problem."

"Just add it to the bill and give Zimri here the receipt. I've got to get back to Belle Oaks before the whole bloomin' labor force runs off to Canada." Jamie climbed back into his carriage and signaled his driver to get the horses moving.

Zimri stood at the wharf and watched as the carriage rode off, raising a cloud of choking dust in the process.

"Come aboard, Zimri," Cora said. "I'll show you around the *General Oglethorpe*."

Zimri turned to see her standing at the gangplank, her captain's uniform crisp and colorful, with its blue serge jacket, gold buttons and shoulder braid. All that was missing was an admiral's bicorn. He stepped aside to make way for two or three Negroes carrying bales of cotton on their shoulders, and then mounted the gangplank.

"I regret that my boatswain is not available to pipe you aboard, Zimri," Cora said, "but he's preoccupied at the moment."

Zimri stepped on the deck. "I can see that you are losing no time."

"On the contrary, we've lost an entire week. We have to make up for it."

Cora gave him a tour of the vessel which included a close examination of the steam engine below decks, as well as the cargo hold. There was a wheelhouse set into the center of the deck, slightly elevated so as to give a clear view of the way ahead.

"Where does the crew sleep?" Zimri asked.

"In the cargo hold. They'll put up hammocks at night. The captain and the first mate have a couple of bunks at the rear of the wheelhouse with a small galley. We've made it simple to keep costs down."

"Spartan, I would say." Zimri peered through a door in the wheelhouse, where he could see the stacked bunks, which looked like the kind built for children, and the galley, which looked like a closet equipped with a charcoal brazier set into a wash bowl. "Aren't you afraid of setting the whole thing on fire?"

"There's a vent to carry the smoke away. Just like a Franklin stove. And of course a fire bucket underneath in case things get out of hand."

Zimri looked at her skeptically. "I suppose there's a greater chance of the steam engine exploding in any case."

Cora laughed. "You worry too much, Zimri. This is the latest technology. Come along with me to the stern and Ill show you the new paddle wheel."

Cora led the way, stepping around coiled ropes and bales of cotton stacked on the deck. When they arrived at the stern, she pointed to the paddle wheel with obvious pride. "A wheelwright and six carpenters built this in three days. Iron rivets secure the spokes to the wheel, and the wheel itself is laminated oak. The paddles, on the other hand, are built to break away if they hit anything larger than a particularly ornery catfish. The vessel can then sail on until it can put in for repairs."

"You seem to have thought of everything, Cora."

Cora turned to him. "I don't like surprises in business. Love is another matter."

Zimri looked around to be sure they weren't being overheard. Most of the men were up at the bow, stacking bales of cotton on the deck. Pierre was shouting commands at them. "This is an odd time to talk of love, Cora."

"It seems that anytime is the wrong time for you to speak of love, Zimri. You've neglected me lately."

"Neglected you? You've been thoroughly immersed in this steamboat enterprise ever since you arrived. You've even been sleeping on the boat."

"But I asked you to come see me at the hotel the day I got back from Hawkinsville. I waited for you...and waited."

Zimri shook his head and rested his forearms on the railing of the *General Oglethorpe*. "I wanted to, Cora, but I couldn't. I simply couldn't."

"Why not? If you wanted to..."

"I can't live like you do, Cora. Like a gypsy. Always moving from one place to another, never putting down roots, never committing yourself to a community. I helped found this town, Cora. I've helped to build it. And it's prospering. I can't throw it all away on a lark."

"A lark? You think of me as a lark? As a plaything to be thrown away when you're tired of the novelty of it?"

Zimri looked at her and saw tears in her eyes. "Cora, you've never said anything about love until thirty seconds ago."

The tears began to flow freely now, streaming down her cheeks. "But I do love you, Zimri. I was afraid you would laugh at me."

"Laugh? No, never. You're too smart, too dynamic, too beautiful. I could never laugh at you, Cora."

"You say that, but I can feel that you are laughing at me now. You conceal your feelings so well."

"Conceal? Who is the master of concealment here? I still don't even know where you came from Cora."

"I thought I told you. Sorrento."

"Sorrento? Italy? It may as well be Sorrento, Georgia, for all I know. Who are your parents? Your friends? You never mention them. It's as if you suddenly stepped out of a cloud. Like an apparition." He turned back to stare at the paddle wheel and the river beyond. "A beautiful, alluring, anonymous apparition."

Cora withdrew her hand from his arm and brushed away her tears. "Anonymous. Then I am nothing to you. A dream."

"Yes, Cora, a dream. A wonderful, intoxicating dream. But I have to return to reality. To my wife and children. To my newspaper. Could you seriously expect me to simply walk away from them? To go with you to ...where? New York? I gave up New York ten years ago to find a place I could feel a part of, where I would be judged by my contribution to the community, not by my clothes, or my social standing, or the number of carriages in my carriage house."

Cora put both hands on his arm. "Don't you see, darling? That's why I love you so much. Precisely because you don't care about the things that everyone else does. Why, I believe you could live in...in a slave's cabin and be happy."

Zimri chuckled. "Slave's cabin? No, I don't think so. I still have a need for creature comforts. And I certainly cherish my freedoms under the Constitution."

"Yes...*your* freedoms. That's what it's all about, isn't it? *Your* freedoms."

He looked at her. "What do you mean by that, Cora?"

"I mean that freedom can be a commodity like anything else. Like this cotton. People want it for their own reasons. But it must be bought and paid for, nevertheless."

He looked out over the river. "That's a pretty cynical view of it. But I suppose you're right."

They said nothing to each other for several moments.

"The boats will return without me," she said. "I may be gone for quite a while."

"Where will you go?"

"New York. Then Boston."

"Tell me one thing, Cora," Zimri said.

"Yes, my love?"

"How did you do it?"

She looked at him with surprise. "Do what?"

"Get all of the slaves out. One hundred and sixty-three of them. Not a single one has been recovered."

She smiled. "I *am* clever, Zimri. But not that clever. It's as much a mystery to me as it is to you."

"Still, it's hard for me to believe that you didn't have something to do with it."

"Why? Just as I told your brother-in-law, I—"

"I know the rationale, Cora. And it sounds convincing. But it's too much of a coincidence. I mean the steamboats being built just in time for the escape, your mysterious comings and goings, your association with the abolitionists—"

"I told you, and the others. That was in the past, along with my acting career. I am now an entrepreneur."

"And a slave owner."

"Yes."

Zimri leaned over and kissed her on the cheek. "Goodbye, Cora."

She returned the kiss, but on the lips.

"Cora! There are people staring."

"Let them stare," she said. "Let them gossip. I don't care."

"Of course you don't. You don't live here. I do."

She slapped him.

"What was that for?"

"To save your precious reputation. Now get off my boat."

"All right. Goodbye."

Zimri went to the gangplank, took one last look at Cora standing with tears running down her cheeks, and walked quickly down the gangplank to the wharf.

As he walked up Second Street to his office, he wondered if that little scene would get back to Elizabeth. Well, what of it? Cora was impulsive, volatile—everyone knew that.

As he approached the office, though, his heart sank. Would he ever see her again? Surely she would return to look after her investment in the Georgia Steamlines Co. from time to time. But when?

"News from Savannah, Mr. Rhodes!"

It was Jed, holding up the front page of a Savannah newspaper. Zimri stepped inside the office and closed the door behind him. "What news, Jed?"

"Over one hundred Negroes were reported to have boarded the *HMS Arundel* off of Tybee island."

"A British ship?"

"Yes, sir. A man o' war. That's how they got around customs. Avoided the municipal wharf altogether. And nobody was about to stop a British warship to inspect the cargo."

Zimri took the paper from Jed and quickly scanned the article. "So Cora was telling the truth."

"Sir?"

"This thing is bigger than any individual or band of radical abolitionists. The British government seems to have been involved."

"Looks that way."

"And we're at the heart of it. Roll up your sleeves, Jed. We've got ourselves a story."

CHAPTER 41

The *General Oglethorpe* returned from Darien ten days later with seventy tons of freight, beating the flatbottom pole boats by a margin of six days. Three days later, after the *Oglethorpe* was once again steaming downriver with a new load of cotton, the *Miss Cora* arrived carrying eighty tons of freight, mostly machinery, but also the latest fashions in clothing from New York, London, and Paris.

The Georgia Steamship Co. was a success. Additional subscribers were readily found and the price of the stock rapidly appreciated. There was talk of adding a third boat, and a fourth.

Again, the only disgruntled citizens of the county were the planters who had lost some portion of their property in the slave escape.

Zimri sent Jed to Savannah to find out more details of the conspiracy, stopping along the way to question planters, merchants, smithies, and county sheriffs. It seemed that some ten to twelve wagons had been waiting for the renegades at the first steamboat landings on the Ocmulgee, where they were concealed in false bottoms with air holes cut into them, covered with sacks of feed or cotton, and driven all night to the Oconee River some thirty miles north. From there, the trail became murkier, but Jed surmised that the slaves were then concealed in barges until they arrived at one of the small islands in the Ogeechee just north of Savannah, where they waited for the right moment to be transferred to the *HMS Arundel*.

A complaint was lodged against the British Consulate in Savannah, but it was met with a blunt denial. It was not the business of Her Majesty's Navy, the Consul General said, to assist in the escape of fugitive slaves. The *Arundel* happened to be anchored near Savannah after routine military maneuvers in the British West Indies. It was en route to England, and did, in fact, contain a number of free blacks in the crew. That, the Consul General said, may have caused a casual observer to falsely conclude that the *Arundel* was taking on fugitive slaves. The black sailors, he further explained, wary of being apprehended by Southern authorities, often spent their leave visiting the more remote coastal islands of Georgia and South Carolina, returning to the ship at sunrise.

This explanation convinced neither the planters nor the denizens of Martinville and a letter-writing campaign was launched directed at no less a personage than Andrew Jackson, President of the United

States. There were numerous letters also addressed to the *Mercury*, and a lively debate over the incident ensued, with the net result that the *Mercury* increased its subscriptions by sixty percent.

President Jackson issued a brief statement in Washington some weeks later saying that he had been satisfied by the British Ambassador that Her Majesty's Government had nothing to do with the unfortunate incident, and declined to pursue the matter any further.

This statement by the President was reprinted on the front page of the *Mercury* and all of the newsstand issues were sold out by noon that day.

Zimri considered it a dead issue, but one he had much profited by. He turned his attention to more private matters, though not necessarily ones of his own choosing.

"Jamie's getting married next month," Elizabeth said one evening at supper. "We should do something for Fanny."

"Like what?"

"Like...have a party for her. Here. We could serve canapés on the front porch. The roses are beautiful this time of year."

Zimri cut into a slice of beef. "I don't know that I want people tramping through my rose garden."

They won't be 'tramping.' They'll just be looking."

"Well, all right. As long as you keep an eye on them."

"You'll be here, too."

"Me? I thought it was for the ladies."

"Zimri, you know nothing about etiquette. This isn't a baby christening, it's a sort of coming-out party for the bride. To introduce her to everyone."

"Why can't she be introduced at the wedding?"

"Because it will be too late then. All you need to do is to show up. Betty and Louise will prepare the food and drinks, and I'll send out the invitations."

"All right."

They ate in silence for several minutes.

"Zimri..."

"Yes?"

"You've been...distant lately."

"Have I?"

"Yes."

"I've been busy with the paper."

"You're *always* busy with the paper. I don't mean that."

"What then?"

Elizabeth put down her knife and fork and put her hands in her lap. She sat up straight in her chair. "I mean emotionally. You seem to look right through me these days."

Zimri looked up from his plate. He saw a very pretty young woman, blue eyes, blond hair cascading over her shoulders, wearing a lively spring dress with a bold pattern of blue and pink chrysanthemums. "Look through you? I couldn't do that even if I wanted to. I enjoy the view too much."

"A very husbandly thing to say. But you know what I'm talking about. You're preoccupied. And not with the paper and all this business about the escaped slaves. You've never had a problem with leaving your work at the office."

"What then?"

She looked down at her plate. "A woman."

Zimri finished chewing on a piece of beef, and washed it down with some cider. "What woman?"

"I don't know. You tell me."

"You heard about Cora throwing her arms around me and kissing me on the boat."

"Yes."

"You know how she is. She kisses everybody."

"I haven't heard that."

"Well, she does. Especially when she gets excited, or feels optimistic about the future, or simply because it's a beautiful day. Besides, that was weeks ago. She's gone now."

"And you miss her."

Zimri affected to struggle with the carving knife. "Miss her? Well, I suppose I do. She seems to liven things up around here."

"Do you love her?"

He put the carving knife down. "I can't deny...that I care for her."

Elizabeth sighed and looked towards the ceiling. She seemed to be steeling herself for the next question. "Have you...have you been to bed with her?"

"Elizabeth, if you persist in—"

"Please answer the question."

Zimri looked down at his plate. "Yes."

Elizabeth seemed to bite her lip, and continued to stare at the ceiling. Tears began to trickle down her cheeks. "I've always trusted you, Zimri."

"I know you have."

"Then how could you betray that trust?"

"I have no satisfactory answer for that."

Elizabeth wiped the tears from her face. "I don't suppose I can expect you to stay away from her."

"On the contrary, she seems to be staying away from me. She's a gypsy, Elizabeth. I don't know that she'll ever be back."

"She has business interests here."

Zimri put his napkin down and pushed his chair away from the table. "She does. But she seems little interested in the steamboat company now that it's succeeded. She'll likely move on to other projects."

"But she will return at some point."

Zimri sighed. "I suppose so."

"And when she checks into the Central Hotel you will go to see her."

"In the lobby, yes. But I promise that—"

Elizabeth threw her napkin onto the table and stood up. "You don't understand, Zimri! It's not that you have slept with her in the past and promise never to do it again—it's that you still *want* to!"

"I can't help that, Elizabeth. All I can do is to refrain from being on intimate terms with her."

"Intimate?" She burst into tears. "That's just it. I don't care what you do with your body—or her body. If she were a prostitute I wouldn't care so much. But it's the fact, by your own admission, that you are on *intimate* terms with her. That's just what I miss, Zimri—intimacy with you. It's no longer there, no matter how often we make love. Oh, what a comical cliché. 'Make love.' All we've been doing for the past month is to make horrid sounds that wake the children!"

She ran into the bedroom and slammed the door.

Zimri sat in his chair for several minutes staring at nothing in particular.

After a while Betty came into the room. She evidently had heard everything. "You finished, Massa Rhodes?" She reached tentatively for his plate.

"Yes, Betty. We're both finished."

Betty gathered up the plates and started for the kitchen. "Massa Zimri..."

"Yes, Betty?"

"I wants to thank you for what you done for me and Solomon."

"What? Oh. Well, it's not done yet, Betty. You both have another eight months of service before you earn your freedom."

"I knows that, Massa Zimri. But that ain't nothin.' We've waited all our lives and didn't think the day would ever come."

"Well, it'll be here soon enough. And after another year or so with Boone, you'll be completely on your own."

"That's what I wanted to talk to you about."

"What? What do you mean?"

"I mean that with Solomon being a 'prentice and all with Mr. Carter we ain't gonna have 'nuff money for a place to live."

"Can't you stay at Boone's?"

"He says he ain't got no room, not with two daughters at home, and one of them 'bout to get married and her husband movin' in with 'em."

"Married? Louise is getting married?"

"Naw, suh. It be Tessie."

"Tessie? Well, what do you know…Elizabeth's right—I have been out of touch. You and Solomon can continue to live here if you like. But it's a long way for Solomon to go every morning. And there's not much room in these cabins out back for children."

"Solomon say he can join them two cabins together if you let him. Then it be like two bedrooms—one for me and Solomon and one for Sally and Aaron."

Zimri considered this. "All right. I don't see why not. But you'll have to keep the children from knocking down my rose bushes."

Betty smiled. "They knows better than that, Massa Zimri. They knows them rose bushes are like your own chillun."

"That they are, Betty. That they are." This thought plunged Zimri into a deeper gloom. What if Elizabeth ran off with that Benson fellow and took the children with her?

Betty started again for the kitchen and again stopped. "Massa Zimri…"

"Yes, Betty?"

"I was wrong what I said at the slave auction last year."

"At the auction? What was that?"

"I said you wasn't a good man like I thought you was. I was wrong, Massa Zimri. You a good man."

Zimri looked up and stared at her for a moment. "Thank you, Betty. Thank you."

CHAPTER 42

Fanny's party was a qualified success, with Fanny managing to insult several of the guests without realizing it, and making Louise and Betty thankful that they didn't work at Belle Oaks. Fanny made no distinction between slaves and free blacks, convinced as she was that all Negroes were born to serve white people without reservation or limit to their patience.

"Who do she think she is?" Louise said to Betty upon returning to the kitchen with an empty tray. "I can't be running to no carriage to get no shawl 'cause she feel a sudden draft. I ain't her slave—nor Miz Rhodes' neither."

"She poor white trash," Betty said. "She got to prove that she better than us."

Elizabeth exhaled a sigh of relief when the party was over and all the guests, including Jamie and Fanny, had left. She did not allow herself to relax for long, however, as she began to digest a bit of news that Jamie had whispered to her as he went out the door: Randolph was returning from Europe and the Orient in time for the wedding.

This bit of intelligence, which she dismissed as nothing more than an updating of the guest list at first, soon cast a pall over her. What were Randolph's intentions? Would he insist that she run away with him? Would he physically challenge Zimri—perhaps even to a duel?

She laughed at the notion, startling Zimri, who was standing by the hearth with a cup of punch in his hand. He had had a bit too much to drink at the party, it seemed. As Zimri simply turned away and went to his desk, she continued her musings in regard to Randolph. It was absurd, of course, for her to imagine that Randolph was coming to rescue her from her bourgeois marriage to Zimri, much less to shoot him down in a duel.

What she wanted was to have Zimri back. Hadn't he suffered enough over the past week? After all, he had freely confessed to his affair with Cora. But her pride would not let her forgive him. At least not yet.

She adopted an attitude of cool civility to Zimri over the next week as the wedding approached. They said little to each other over the dinner table, but no harsh words were exchanged, no reproaches made or implied. No terms of endearment passed their lips except when directed towards the children.

On the day of the wedding, a Saturday, Zimri put on his morning suit, the one he had worn to John Davies' wedding in Connecticut. Elizabeth put on a tulle-over-satin dress that Zimri had recently bought for her at John Lewis' shop as a kind of sacrificial offering to atone for his sins. She accepted it without comment, though she thought it even more beautiful than the dress he had bought her in New York the previous summer. As she adjusted her hair in the mirror over the dresser and Zimri went out to the barn, she wondered whether he still loved her. His quiet sulkiness at the beginning of the week had turned to an aloofness, a disinterested nonchalance that she couldn't decide whether was studied or genuine. She was sure that she wasn't fooling *him*. He must know that it was agony for her to pretend that she didn't care for him, that her superficial indifference was all an act. She yearned for him to at least touch her, to show some involuntary reflex of affection when they awoke in the morning like a kiss on the cheek before either of them were fully awake.

But this did not happen.

She sat before the mirror, having finished her toilette, staring blankly at herself without seeing, wondering whether she shouldn't give in and run to Zimri and forgive him and declare her love for him to be eternal and unconditional, just as she had the day of their own wedding.

Instead, she rose from her dresser, collected her purse and her parasol, and went to the front porch where she sat on the swing, waiting for Solomon to bring the carriage around to the front.

"My, my, you look as purty as a picture."

She turned to see Betty standing in the doorway, wiping her hands on her apron.

"Thank you, Betty. You would think I was the one getting married."

"You don't look a day older than then. I remember when you came down the grand staircase at Belle Oaks wid yo' arm on yo' Daddy's and Massa Zimri waitin' fo' you in the grand hall 'bout to bust his buttons he was so proud."

"That's very kind of you to say that, Betty, but I think Fanny's quite pretty."

"She may be pretty, but she don't carry herself the way you do. And she ain't got the polish, neither."

"That's enough, Betty. I won't hear any more about Fanny's lack of polish. She hasn't had the advantages I've had. But she'll learn soon enough."

"Lawd, I hope so. Well, looky here—Massa Zimri done duded himself up like he done that day, too."

Zimri was walking on a path through the rose garden, his gray top hat bobbing above the plants like the smoke stack of a river steamer. He stopped to examine one of the hybrids he was experimenting with, oblivious to the fact that he was being watched.

Elizabeth smiled. "He does cut a fine figure, doesn't he?"

"He sho' does. And looky there—Solomon look like he gonna be the best man."

Solomon was driving the phaeton around from the barn, wearing a black suit with a fancy frock shirt and a red cravat. A black top hat sat at a jaunty angle on his head and he sat rigidly on the driver's seat, holding the reins and the whip high in the air as if he were taming a lion rather than driving horses.

"Whoo-ee!" Betty grinned from ear to ear. "That's my man! And looky—he got a rose from Massa Zimri's garden in his lapel to match his tie! He gonna charm the feathers right off them pea hens at Belle Oaks. The cocks are gonna be so ashamed of they selves, they gonna tuck they own tail feathers between they legs and run all the way back to China."

Elizabeth found this colorful description of Solomon's sartorial splendor to be amusing, and envied Betty for her pride in, and devotion to, her husband. It wasn't that she wasn't proud of Zimri—any woman would be—but she was no longer sure of her devotion to him, or his to her. There was a rift in their relationship, and she did not know whether it could be repaired.

They traveled the ten miles or so to Belle Oaks in silent expectation that the other might broach the subject of their relationship and offer some olive branch, but neither did. She grew increasingly angry that Zimri would not, or could not, apologize in a more expansive way than he did at dinner the day he had confessed to his infidelity. Actually, he never did apologize, did he? He only promised not to do it again, and it was merely an *implied* promise at that. He would only meet Cora in the lobby of her hotel, he said. How magnanimous of him! Presumably, he would no longer go up to her room to satisfy his carnal appetite for her. Cora did have a rather spectacular figure, didn't she? Very tempting for any man. Elizabeth's own body was shapely and respectable enough, but she felt that her breasts were too small and her derrière a bit on the flat side. Cora looked as if she had stuffed a pillow in her back-side, and it sat up as if buoyant, as did her more than ample bosom. Is that all that men cared about? Breasts and buttocks and bestial intercourse?

She grew more angry as she imagined Zimri and Cora in various compromising positions. Then she slid into a deep gloom precipitated by a sense of inadequacy. Was she simply too boring in bed? Was that it? It occurred to her that she knew very little about sex, really. Her mother had never broached the subject except to explain, awkwardly and with a palpable sense of disgust, the menstrual cycle and how a woman was to deal with it—which was to conceal it, especially from men. And there were no books about it, only silly romance novels that alluded to sexual intercourse in the most oblique and maddeningly obscure ways. Even Jane Austen's novels, more intelligent and honest than most, offered no hint of what happened between a man and a woman once they found themselves alone behind closed doors. Suddenly, she burst out laughing, startling Zimri.

"What is it, Elizabeth? You must share your amusement with me."

She shook her head. "Oh, it's nothing. A silly thought occurred to me, that's all."

The silly thought was that the only thing that happened between a man and a woman behind closed doors in an Austen novel was...talk. They talked. And talked.

"Well, we're here," Zimri said. "My lord, look at the carriages!"

Solomon pulled in line with the others as they came in from the drive and formed a semi-circle to the right of the fountain, which was spouting water from the mouths of its stone dolphins. It took nearly a half-hour before the carriage pulled up to the front door, where the liveried servants assisted the guests from their carriages and each was greeted by Jamie, dressed in his morning coat, white tie, and white carnation He threw his arms around his sister.

"Elizabeth, you look stunning! How are you, Zimri?" Jamie pumped Zimri's hand and immediately looked past him to the next guest.

"Quite well, Jamie, I—"

A servant quickly ushered them into the house where they were presented with a festooned staircase, vases filled with flowers of every description, and a large buffet table overflowing with roasted turkeys, chicken, smoked ham and every conceivable delicacy.

Waiters circulated with trays laden with glasses of champagne, whiskey sours and mint juleps.

"I'm afraid Jamie has his hands full at the moment," Elizabeth said. "Oh, there's Mother. I'd better speak to her."

She left Zimri standing rather awkwardly by himself in the center of the foyer, while she went to the settee beneath the staircase where her mother was sitting, looking forlorn and confused. "Mother, you should be greeting the guests at the door with Jamie. Don't you feel well?"

"Not so well."

"Well, then, what is it?"

"Fannyitis."

"Oh, Mother, you've simply got to learn to get along with Fanny. Where is she?"

"Upstairs, terrorizing the servants."

Elizabeth found this amusing, and even credited her mother with recovering her sense of humor. "She can't be as bad as all that. What's she doing?"

"Her wedding dress was too long, she said. Three of the maids are trying to hem it now. And the train is too short. She sent Mazy out to find more silk and lace. We may be here for a while."

"Well, we've plenty of time. Where's her father? Is he about?"

"In a manner of speaking. He's been drinking since ten o'clock this morning. Drunk as a loon."

Elizabeth laughed. Her spirits were buoyed. All seemed normal for a wedding at Belle Oaks.

"Hello, Elizabeth."

She didn't recognize the voice at first and turned around to see who it was. "Randolph!"

"It is so good to see you. You're as beautiful as ever."

"Why, thank you, Randolph. But I've had two more children since we last saw each other, and it's added ten years to my figure."

"Not at all. You're as lithesome and vivacious as I remember you. If anything, you're a bit thinner."

"She eats like a bird," her mother said. "Always did."

"And how are you, Mrs. Blake?" Randolph kissed her hand.

"Not so well," she said.

"I'm sorry to hear that. Is there anything I can get for you?"

"I think a mint julep would help."

"I'll have one here for you in—ah! Waiter!" Randolph waylaid a passing waiter and plucked a mint julep from his tray. "Elizabeth?"

"Champagne, please."

"My preference as well."

Randolph distributed the drinks and raised his glass to Elizabeth's. "To beauty in all of its manifestations—especially in the form of the two charming ladies before me."

They all tipped their glasses and drank.

"I feel better already," Mrs. Blake said.

"So, Randolph," Elizabeth said, "you must tell us all about your adventures in Europe and Asia."

Randolph looked cautiously at Mrs. Blake, then at Elizabeth. "You received my letters?"

"Yes. I did."

"Then you already know the gist of it. There's not much more to tell."

"I can hardly believe that, Randolph." She glanced at her mother, who seemed to be taking a greater interest in the conversation than before. "Your letters were few and brief. I imagine you must have had adventures far beyond those little summaries you provided."

"Well, yes, there were some difficulties in Asia—"

"Adventures? Did I hear something about adventures?" It was Zimri.

To Elizabeth, it was as if a bull had suddenly crashed in from the street, threatening all of the crockery. Zimri had never seemed so graceless as he did now. "Yes, dear. You remember Randolph?"

Zimri's face fell as the name and the face registered. He extended his hand. "How do you do, Mr.—"

"Benson. Randolph Benson."

"Of course. You were at our wedding a couple of years ago."

"Two and a half years ago, to be exact," Randolph said curtly. "In this very house."

"Yes," Zimri said. "I remember you as a friend of Jamie's."

"Quite so," Randolph said.

An awkward silence ensued, during which everyone looked at Zimri as if he must be leaving at any moment.

"I feel that I've intruded," Zimri said. "Forgive me. I did not intend to eavesdrop."

He then wandered off, looking very ill at ease until he succeeded in flagging down a waiter.

"You are much thinner yourself, Randolph," Elizabeth said. "I must say it becomes you."

Randolph laughed. "It was an enforced diet. I wouldn't recommend it."

"Enforced? What do you mean?"

"Bandits."

"Bandits!" Mrs. Blake said.

"I'm afraid so, Mrs. Blake. I rather stupidly traversed a part of Afghanistan without paying the expected tribute to the local warlord. Before I knew it, my guide and I were attacked by brigands, trussed up like heifers and thrown into the darkest pit in Asia."

"My Goodness!" Mrs. Blake said. "How horrible."

"What did you do?" Elizabeth said, fascinated. "What *could* you do?"

"Fortunately, I had deposited a sum of money with a merchant banker in Kandahar, an Englishman, for safe-keeping. My guide, who spoke Pashto, negotiated with our captors and we agreed on a price."

"A ransom!" Elizabeth said.

"Exactly. My English friend in Kandahar was contacted, we were led—blindfolded—to a remote mountain pass, the ransom was paid, and we were released."

"How utterly awful!" Mrs. Blake said. "And were the bandits apprehended and punished?"

Randolph laughed. "I'm afraid not, Mrs. Blake. It's a rather lawless part of the world. I felt lucky to escape with my life."

This tale had nearly the same effect on Elizabeth as Othello's account of his adventures in Africa had on Desdemona. She was mesmerized by Randolph's exploits in such far away, exotic places, and it seemed to her indeed, as he had suggested in his letter, that he had left America as a boy and returned as a man. There was none of the foppishness about him that she had remembered from last summer at the picnic, none of the preoccupation with romantic poetry, however fine, none of the self-absorbed sentimentality. He seemed to make light of his obvious sufferings—for though he was rich, he had exposed himself to the most frightful dangers—and to have emerged a man of courage, character and mature judgment. In short, he was a man of the world.

She wondered, however, if she weren't jumping to conclusions. "Tell me, Randolph, did you find what you were looking for in the Orient?"

Randolph looked into his glass and seemed to study the contents. Then he held the glass up to the light. "You see these tiny bubbles, Elizabeth?"

"Yes, of course."

"How many would you say are in the glass?"

"Oh, I don't know. Hundreds, I suppose. Thousands. Why?"

Randolph swirled the champagne around in the glass and examined the contents from a slightly different angle.

"Imagine that each of these bubbles represents an entire universe."

"An entire universe in each one?" Mrs. Blake said.

"Yes, Mrs. Blake. In each one. And imagine furthermore that the glass is a universe unto itself, and that each glass of champagne in this room is but a fraction of the whole."

"My goodness!" Mrs. Blake said. "My head already hurts just thinking about it."

Randolph laughed. "Mine, too. That's why I gave up looking for eternal truths. There are too many of them. And some are so simple that they defy reduction and analysis."

"Well, I must say," Mrs. Blake said. "This conversation has gone over my head. Do you suppose you could get the attention of that waiter over there? They never seem to be around when you need them."

Randolph cheerfully obliged and signaled the waiter. While their drinks were being refreshed, Elizabeth found that she could not keep her eyes off of him. He seemed far more handsome than when he left for Europe. Still in his twenties, he seemed to be a much older man, yet still younger than Zimri. And unlike Zimri, whose ideas were limited to the practical matters of business and politics, Randolph seemed to have, in her eyes, achieved a kind of Olympian wisdom.

Suddenly the orchestra struck up a wedding march and Fanny appeared at the top of the stairs. She did look striking, with her flaming red hair in stark contrast to her white lace gown. The three maids, who had been sewing up to the last minute, each held a portion of the train in their hands and slowly followed Fanny down the staircase. She was nearly to the bottom before the maids had taken their first steps at the top.

Her father awaited at the foot of the stairs, and was obviously inebriated, but nevertheless grinning from ear to ear and holding his arm out for his daughter to grasp. Jamie stood near the middle of the room, beaming with pride, his hands folded in front of him, standing at the edge of a red carpet that led from the drawing room to the small chapel beyond. As there were not enough pews for all to sit in the chapel, most of the guests remained in the drawing room or grand entrance hall until the brief ceremony was over.

When the newly bound couple emerged from the chapel, the orchestra broke into a Virginia reel, and the party really began in earnest.

While Fanny took the first dance with her father, who repeatedly stumbled and had to be assisted to his feet by others, Randolph asked Elizabeth to dance. She was flattered and suddenly realized that she hadn't danced since her own wedding. (Zimri had danced with her that day, and quite well, too, but never since.)

After two more dances, the last one a waltz, Randolph suggested that they get some air on the terrace. She hesitated, looked around for Zimri, did not see him, and consented.

They sat on a stone bench that overlooked the south lawn, which ran for nearly a hundred yards to the edge of the woods, and contained a series of geometrically shaped gardens, all linked by walking paths. Elizabeth remembered playing along these paths with Jamie and her friends as a child, and how they would often hide from each other among the shrubs until their mother called them to dinner.

"The flowers are all in bloom," she said. "It's lovely, isn't it?"

"Yes," Randolph said, breathing heavily. "Jamie has done a magnificent job of keeping the old place up. I haven't seen it look this good since...well, in a couple of years."

They sat for some moments enjoying the fresh air and the beauty of the setting. She felt the warmth of his body even though they were no longer touching. There was an odor of musk—was it cologne?—about him that seemed to be drawing her to him. She reproached herself for even thinking such a thing and moved slightly to her left, as if to adjust the petticoats of her dress.

"What will you do now, Randolph?"

Randolph put both palms down on the stone bench, his left hand touching her dress, and seemed to consider this. "My father is not well."

"I'm sorry to hear that."

"That's one reason I came home early. The other was to see you."

"Randolph—"

"No, don't reproach me. It's true. I can't do anything about the way I feel about you. It's as strong as it ever was. Stronger, actually."

She said nothing.

"But you asked what I planned to do. In the short run, I plan to run the day-to-day affairs of Lynwood. Long term, I don't know. I may sell off some land—"

"Oh, don't do that!"

Randolph looked at her with surprise. "Why not?"

"I—I just think that it's—from what Jamie tells me—a magnificent estate. It would be a shame to diminish it in any way."

Randolph studied her face intently. "Would you like to see it?"

"Why, yes, I would. Very much. Perhaps Zimri and I—"

"I mean without Zimri."

She looked around the terrace, where more and more couples were enjoying the fresh air. She did not see Zimri. "I think that would be impossible, Randolph. Zimri would never allow—"

"Then bring him."

"What?"

"Bring him. He's nothing to me. It's only you I'm interested in."

This boldness on Randolph's part frightened her. She forced a rather feeble laugh. "I suppose you plan to shoot him down in a duel, as you proposed in your letter."

"I was joking. No one fights duels anymore. Bring him. I'll put you both up in the grand suite my father reserves for visiting dignitaries. Lafayette stayed there just last year."

"And under what pretext would I induce Zimri to travel all the way to Lynwood to stay with his once arch rival?"

"Does he hunt?"

"Not that I know of. His only recreation is his roses. He's not fond of—"

"Is this a private party?"

It was Zimri. He had stepped out from one of the tall French doors leading from the ballroom and was standing just behind them.

Randolph rose to his feet and extended his hand towards him. "Not at all, old man. Please join us. I was just telling your wife how lucky she is to have grown up here at Belle Oaks."

Zimri looked skeptical. "Yes, she is lucky, isn't she? Born with a silver spoon in her mouth."

Elizabeth took this as a veiled insult. "Randolph was just telling me about his own estate near Charleston, darling. Lynwood. Jamie says it's even grander than Belle Oaks."

"Then it must be quite a spread," Zimri said without irony.

Randolph chuckled. "I would characterize it as something more than a 'spread.' It's quite charming, really. And plenty to do— lakes for swimming and boating, miles of riding trails, and…hunting. You do hunt, old man, don't you?"

"I did as a boy growing up in Connecticut. It's been years, though."

"Then you know how to handle a musket."

"Yes."

"You see, Elizabeth, your husband is not so much a bookish recluse as you led me to believe. You must do me the honor of a visit to Lynwood. I insist."

"That's very kind of you, Randolph," Zimri said. "But I don't think that we really have the time to travel to—"

"Nonsense! It's only five days journey. Less, if you take one of the steamboats that Elizabeth tells me you've invested in. Stay a week, two weeks, as long as you like."

"Oh, Zimri," Elizabeth said. "It does sound like fun. I haven't been anywhere since we've been married. Besides, you've had your trip to New York, while I—"

"We'll think about it, Randolph," Zimri said. "May I have a word with you, Elizabeth?"

"Well—"

"Of course," Randolph said. "Forgive me for monopolizing your wife's time, Zimri." He heartily shook Zimri's hand. "But do seriously consider my offer. You'll be just in time for the finest quail hunting in the world."

Once Randolph had gone back into the house, Zimri sat down on the stone bench next to Elizabeth.

"Elizabeth, it's one thing to be sociable and take a few turns on the dance floor with another man, but—"

"I do believe you are jealous, Zimri."

"Jealous? All right, I'm jealous. But aside from that, it's highly improper to—"

"Look who's talking about what's proper and what's not."

Zimri sighed. "All right, Elizabeth. You're right—I can't cast stones. But all the same, I wish you'd—"

"He's that 'boy,' remember? Even more spoiled than I or Jamie. And he does have some fascinating tales to tell of his travels in Europe and Asia. If you give him a chance, I think you might come to like him."

"Possibly. I don't know the man that well."

"All the more reason to get better acquainted. I'm sure that he'll invite Jamie and Fanny, too. It would be like a house party."

"I get the distinct feeling that your whole purpose in accepting is to torment me."

Elizabeth laughed and put her hand on his knee. "Poor Zimri. I had no idea you were so sensitive. No, darling, my purpose in accepting is to escape Martinville for a while. I feel that I'm suffocating there. I need some fresh air, a change of scenery."

"Three to four weeks away from the office is a long time. I'll have to—"

"You were gone two and a half months to New York and Connecticut."

"All right, Elizabeth. I'll think about it. Can I get you a glass of champagne?"

Elizabeth sensed that Zimri was nearly at his threshold of tolerance for wifely dissent, and accepted his offer. While he went in search of a waiter, she gazed out over the lawn and mused over their relationship. Zimri was a good man, but he was a plodder. He believed in the old Puritan work ethic despite his renunciation of its religion and its narrow provincialism. Even his constant pruning and trimming of his roses seemed somehow middle-class, pedestrian.

Randolph, on the other hand, was born an aristocrat. Regardless of his flirtations with republican democracy in Europe, he would never shake off that sense of superiority, of noblesse oblige. And noblesse oblige wasn't such a bad thing, was it? When one had wealth it was only proper and fitting for one to take responsibility for one's dependents, slave or otherwise. She wondered how many slaves Randolph had. Four hundred? Five?

"Here you are my dear—your champagne."

She looked up at Zimri. For a moment, she had hoped it was Randolph.

CHAPTER 43

Zimri avoided the topic of Randolph's invitation whenever Elizabeth brought it up, which was often.

Summer was approaching, and she continually complained about the rain, the mud, and the heat.

"Heat?" Zimri said. "We're at four hundred feet. Benson's place must be near sea level."

"But it's on a river."

"We're on a river."

She sat on the swing on the front porch reading while Zimri tended to his roses only a few feet away. "It's not the same. They get breezes from the ocean."

"According to Jamie, Lynwood is a good thirty miles from the ocean."

"That's about a hundred and fifty miles closer than we are."

Zimri clipped one of his hybrids from its stem. "We'll be much cooler here. Speaking of breezes, I feel one coming up now."

"I will go mad if we stay here another month."

"And I will go mad if I hear another word about Lynwood."

She started to speak, but instead stuck her tongue out at him and went back to reading her book.

Zimri sat at his desk the next morning working on an editorial when Jed returned from the post office with the mail. While skimming through the letters, he recognized the careful, script handwriting of one postmarked Beaufort, South Carolina.

Cora.

After making a show of opening a couple of letters to the editor, and seeing that Jed had disappeared into the press room, he carefully slit open the envelope that had caught his attention.

Beaufort, 17 May

My Dearest Zimri,

How I have regretted my abominable behavior that last day in Martinville, on the General Oglethorpe. It was childish and thoughtless of me, and I deeply regret any discomfort or embarrassment it may have caused you.

But I am inclined to impetuosity whenever I am in your pres-

ence, my darling. *The hazel tint of your eyes, the fine profile, the arch of your brow when confronted with cant or sham, the long tapered fingers that would be the envy of a concert pianist; all these things combine to excite me whenever I am near you.*

I work furiously, and often with little sleep, to fill the void of your absence. Sleep? I often dream of you, but when I awake to discover that you are not there beside me, I cry until the sun comes up and dry my tears before the mirror (concealing them with powder so that I may not appear as a weak, hysterical woman at my first business encounter of the day).

Speaking of business, I am here at the Beaufort Inn (a very fine establishment, I must say) arranging for a steamboat enterprise similar to the one that has been so successful in Martinville. The planters here have not so far to go to sell their crops in the markets of Savannah and Charleston, but the superior speed of the steamboats to that of either flatboats or horse-drawn wagons will save them two to three days of transit time, especially since these vessels will be fitted for the open sea.

I seem to have become a shipping magnate! But enough of business, my darling. I long to see you, to touch your face, to kiss your lips, to feel your powerful arms around my shoulders, and your long, supple fingers probing into my secret spaces where only you are allowed to go. I thrill to the very thought of it.

I will be in Beaufort for nearly a month. You must come to me, my darling, you must. I know not what excuse you can think of to give Elizabeth, but I am confident that your fertile mind will come up with something. Elizabeth, the poor dear, must be preoccupied with her children. The twins are precious! I caught a glimpse of them while...no matter the occasion, only that they are beautiful and do great justice to their father.

Meet me in the dining room of the Beaufort Inn on Wednesday, June 1st at four pm. I promise you that the meeting will be discreet—in fact, you will not recognize me as I will be utterly transformed in appearance. And I will have a gift for you that will, I hope, make up for my boorish behavior on the boat.

Au revoir, mon chéri,
Cora

Zimri carefully folded the letter up and resolved to throw it into the trash—he must rid himself of this woman!

"How's Miss Rinaldi?"

He looked up and saw Jed standing in the doorway. "Miss Rinaldi?"

"I recognized her handwriting. Did she say anything about the escape?"

"No. No, she didn't. Apparently, it was of little concern to her. All she cared about was getting her steamboats back and turning a profit."

"It's a pity. I mean that she doesn't have some intelligence as to what became of the slaves. I'm at a dead end with it."

"Let it alone, Jed. We'll probably never know the full story."

"I guess not. Still..."

"Don't you have a jury trial to cover?"

"Jury trial? Oh, yes, sir."

Jed pulled his watch from his waistcoat. "They're at recess now. The judge said the court will reconvene at two o'clock."

"Maybe you'd better get back early to make sure you don't miss anything."

"Oh, I've got plenty of—well, I guess you're right. It's pretty boring, though, Mr. Rhodes. Horse stealing again."

"Seems to be a regular epidemic these days."

"Yes, sir."

After Jed had left for the courthouse, Zimri unfolded Cora's letter and re-read it. Beaufort was no more than a few miles from Lynwood, according to Jamie.

Things were running smoothly at the *Mercury*. Jed could certainly handle things for the first few weeks of the summer, when many merchants and planters would be leaving for their houses on the coastal islands of Georgia. And Elizabeth would never stop singing the praises of Lynwood until he took her there.

But what of its proprietor, this snake-in-the-grass Randolph? Elizabeth was obviously attracted to him. And they had had some relationship in the past, though he knew for a fact that Elizabeth was a virgin when he married her.

What a comical scene that had been! Elizabeth undressing behind a screen and then emerging in her undergarments, with pantaloons to her knees and a corset as tightly buttoned as a chastity belt. The room suddenly plunged into pitch-black darkness. He stubbed his toe on the bedpost, crying out in pain, and she lit a candle to examine the injury. It was bleeding. She would get him a bandage, she said. He didn't object, and sat on the bed in his nightshirt waiting as she brought a wash basin to clean the wound, and then wrapped a bandage around the big toe so many times that it seemed to be twice its normal size. The candle again extinguished, she lay rigidly on her side of the bed and suggested that they consummate their marriage after the swelling of his big toe went down. No, he said. It was no longer painful. You could open the wound again, she said, and get an infection. Infection from what? I don't know, she said. She had heard of men getting infections and passing it on to their wives and then to their children, who were born blind or crippled. That's another kind of infection altogether, he said.

What a night!

He folded the letter up again, put it in a drawer, and locked it. Elizabeth would not stumble across this one. And how delighted she would be when he told her that they were going to Lynwood after all! But he must not be too precipitous. He must make it appear that she has finally worn down his resistance. That he would really enjoy quail hunting with Randolph.

Randolph. The man has no conscience where women are concerned. Vastly rich. A globe-trotting playboy. No telling how many women he bedded down in Europe and Asia...speaking of infections!

His imagination was getting the better of his reason now...No, Elizabeth was not likely to go to bed with this man. Not while they slept under the same roof, at least. He would be able to keep an eye on her, except when he was out hunting, and of course then he would be keeping an eye on Randolph. The only other opportunity they would have to be together would be while he was visiting Cora in Beaufort. And that would be only for...a day? Yes, he could leave Lynwood early that morning and return by nightfall. He would make it clear to Cora that this must be absolutely the last time they would see each other. He doubted whether she would even return to Martinville on business. There was no need for her to.

He stood up from his desk and looked at his watch. Dinner time. He would have a leisurely meal with Elizabeth and casually, magnanimously, consent to the journey to Lynwood. Louise and Tessie would take care of the children.

He reached for his jacket, locked the front door and left through the press room.

CHAPTER 44

In the last week of May, Elizabeth and Zimri set out for Lynwood in a stagecoach bound for Savannah.

She had been surprised when Zimri suddenly announced that the trip would do them both good, that they had never really had a honeymoon, and that young couples should have changes of scenery at least once a year. They were prospering, he said, and could afford it.

She was even more surprised when they stopped at the inn at Dublin to find that Zimri's ardor for her had been miraculously rekindled, and hers for him. They lingered in bed for so long the next morning that they had to skip breakfast in order to be on time for the stage's departure.

Perhaps he was right—they only needed a change of scenery, a change of routine. Even as they approached Lynwood several days later, after a shopping spree in Savannah, she felt that her earlier censure of Zimri had been too harsh. A husband would stray occasionally—that was a fact of life. Her own father had had numerous liaisons during his lifetime, some even with his own slaves. Her mother, after one or two fits of jealousy, had stoically accepted this state of affairs, and seemed relatively happy right up until her father's death. She simply didn't think about it anymore, she once told her, and as long as her husband was discreet, she would not take him to task for it.

The stage stopped at a little town called Yemassee, where they were met by an elegant landau driven by a liveried and top-hatted Negro who introduced himself as Pliny the Elder—though he allowed that most called him simply Pliny, except when his son Pliny the Younger was present. This amused Zimri to a great extent, and he seemed to relax expansively in the back of the landau with his arm around her as they embarked on a long, straight road shaded by a canopy of moss-laden oaks.

"I've spotted a dozen species of wild roses since we left the main road," Zimri said. "This is truly a fertile country."

"Jamie tells me that Lynwood is the largest plantation in the state," she said. "Actually three plantations assembled by Randolph's father and grandfather. They have over six hundred slaves."

"Six hundred thirty-two," Pliny the Elder said from his driver's perch. "They was two born this morning—that we know of, that is."

The bay horses pulling the landau trotted briskly down the well-traveled road and crossed a bridge over what Pliny said was the Combahee River. Here, they began to see vast fields tended by hundreds of slaves as far as the eye could see.

"Them bolls be rotten pretty soon," Pliny said. "Right now they mostly weedin' and thinnin.' Give them bolls plenty of room to bust open."

They drove on for a few more miles before seeing any buildings other than an occasional barn or silo.

"What's that round structure in the distance?" Zimri said. "It looks like a castle keep."

"That be the old mill. Ain't been used for grindin' corn for years now. They gots a machine to do the grindin' these days—kinda like a cotton gin."

"It's very picturesque," Elizabeth said. "Like something out of a medieval romance."

Pliny spat to one side. "Ain't good for nothin' now. 'Cept lockin' up slaves."

"You mean it's a prison?" Zimri said.

"Somethin' like that." Pliny spat again. "Marster William never used it as such."

"Who's Master William?"

"That be Marster Randolph's daddy. Marster William say he don't need to lock no slaves up, nor whip'em neither. But he be feelin' poorly lately, and Marster Randolph...well, he have a different way of doin' things."

This information unsettled Elizabeth and she avoided Zimri's gaze for the next half a mile or so.

Pliny turned onto another road and the landau soon approached two immense stone pillars joined by an elaborately filigreed wrought iron gate with a coat of arms and the name 'Lynwood' worked into it. Adjacent to one of the pillars was a guard house from which a uniformed servant stepped out, acknowledged Pliny, and swung open the huge gates.

"I don't see anything but more fields," Zimri said. "How far is the house, Pliny?"

"'Bout a mile," Pliny said.

The landau passed more rows of crops tended by scores of Negroes who paid no attention to them. Finally, they came to a large orchard.

"Peaches?" Zimri said.

"Freestones," Pliny said. "They 'bout ripe now. Sweet as your Georgia peaches, from what I hear tell."

"We'll have to see about that," Zimri said.

Once through the orchard, they came upon a broad avenue flanked by live oaks. The oaks soon gave way to poplars, and the poplars to the façade of the main house.

"Jamie did not exaggerate," Elizabeth said. "It is truly magnificent!"

The house was of a Greek Revival style with towering Doric columns stretching from one corner to the other, creating a broad veranda that apparently encircled the entire dwelling. This was a 'low country' house, with the main floor elevated above the ground floor, and a double curved staircase leading from the drive to the entry. A rose garden with a delicate, less pretentious fountain than that of Belle Oaks nestled between the two wings of the staircase.

"There must be fifty rooms," Zimri said, as the carriage pulled up to the house.

"Fifty-six," Pliny said, alighting from the driver's seat. "Marster William was up at the state house in Columbia for more years than I can count, and sometimes he invited the whole bloomin' Senate to Lynwood for shootin' and dancin' and galavantin.' Lawd, they kept us runnin' and fetchin' all day long and into the wee hours. Them days are gone, though."

Pliny helped Elizabeth down from the carriage while Zimri lingered to examine the roses.

"Welcome to Lynwood!" Randolph stood at the top of the stairs wearing a Panama hat, linen trousers, and an open-collared shirt.

Two servants scampered down the staircase to take their luggage.

"It's beautiful, Randolph!" Elizabeth said. "How could you ever leave?"

"Sometimes I wonder why I did. Come on up. You're just in time for tea. Or something stronger, if you've a mind."

Elizabeth started up the stairs but stopped when she realized that Zimri wasn't keeping up. "Zimri! There's plenty of time for that later."

Randolph laughed heartily. "Let him linger over the flowers to his heart's content. My gardener will give him a tour before supper."

"Perpetual hybrids," Zimri muttered to himself below. "Albas, damasks, gallicas, polyanthas, tea roses...suppose you crossed the tea roses with—"

"Zimri!"

Zimri looked up distractedly, as if rudely awakened from a dream. "Coming, Elizabeth. Hello, Randolph. Your man here has—"

"Take Master Zimri around to meet Winston, Pliny. I'm sure they'll have more to talk about than plantation gossip over tea."

Zimri seemed about to object, but Pliny made a little bow and indicated a path that led to the greenhouse.

Elizabeth, meanwhile, continued up the stairs where Randolph met her with open arms. She felt that his embrace was a bit too enthusiastic, politely disengaged herself, and asked to be allowed to freshen up before tea. Randolph readily complied, and summoned a maid to lead her to her room while two valets followed with the luggage.

By the time she was escorted to her room on the second floor, which was cavernous compared to their bedroom in Martinville, she was very tired from the day's journey and stretched out on the canopied bed for a few moments rest. The next thing she knew, Zimri was calling her name.

"Zimri?"

"You must have been exhausted. I'm afraid we've missed tea."

She sat up. "Missed it? What time is it?"

"Five-thirty. I expect they'll be serving supper about seven."

She rubbed her eyes. It was still light outside, but there were long shadows cast over the lawn and drive. Their room was on the front side of the house, the east side. "I must have fallen asleep. I hope they don't think we're being rude."

"I spoke to Randolph. He said that you can make up for it at supper. He wants to introduce us to his family."

Zimri sat on the edge of the bed, his cravat loosened, his hand on hers.

"How was the garden tour?" she said.

"Quite interesting. Their man Winston was sent to England by Randolph's father years ago to learn all he could about gardening. He's practically a walking encyclopedia of horticulture. And I've only seen a fraction of the whole."

"Then you'll have your day cut out for you tomorrow."

"Actually, I've got to go to Beaufort."

"Beaufort? What for?"

"To see the editor of the *Gazette* there. He's an old friend—used to edit the *Journal* in Milledgeville."

"Can't you wait until next week? It's rather rude to leave your host immediately after arriving."

"He's leaving for Savannah on Friday. I don't know when else I'll be able to see him. Besides, it'll only be for one day."

Elizabeth smiled. "Aren't you worried that Randolph will seduce me in your absence?"

"Not in the least." Zimri reclined on the bed and fluffed up a pillow. "Now that you've had your nap, it's time for mine. Wake me a half-hour before supper."

CHAPTER 45

Zimri arose early the next morning, before Elizabeth, and set out for Beaufort, which was only some fifteen to twenty miles away. Randolph presented him with a magnificent roan stallion that he said was familiar with the way to Beaufort.

"Cassio could find it blindfolded," Randolph said. "Just let go of the reins any time you feel that you're lost."

"I should be back by dinner tomorrow." Zimri swung his leg over the horse's rump and settled comfortably in the saddle.

"Take your time," Randolph said. "Stay another day or two if you like. I'll make sure that Elizabeth has plenty to occupy herself with while you're gone."

Zimri stared at Randolph for a moment before urging the horse into motion. "I'm sure you will, Randolph. But she still tires easily. Nothing too strenuous."

"I wouldn't think of over-exerting her, old man. She'll be safe with me."

Zimri gave Randolph another dubious look, clicked his tongue, and was off. As he cantered down the drive towards the gate, he wondered if he weren't being foolish to leave Elizabeth in the hands of this playboy scion of one of the richest families of South Carolina. At least the house was full of people—the father, the mother, two sisters and their guests, two brothers and their friends from the College of Charleston, at least three cousins, and about twenty-five house servants coming and going at all hours. It would be hard to find any privacy outside of a spare bedroom, and Elizabeth was not likely to allow herself to be lured into one of these without the presence of a family member or friend…or was she?

As he passed through the gate, he increased Cassio's gait to a more comfortable gallop and ruminated over his impressions from the previous evening. The father, William, was apparently an invalid and did not feel up to being introduced. But from all appearances of the house, the furnishings, the six thousand volume library—he was a very cultivated man. Half the servants and many of the animals—like Cassio here—had names from either Shakespeare or the Roman poets. His gardener was trained in England. There were numerous works of art throughout the house, even a gallery devoted exclusively to portraits. He looked forward to meeting the old man upon his return.

He came to a bend in the Combahee where there was a ferry to carry him across to the main road into Beaufort. As he stood on the deck he enjoyed the light breeze coming up the river and the faint odor of talc coming off of Cassio's mane. Cassio was an uncommonly well-behaved horse, especially with a complete stranger on his back.

His thoughts turned to Cora.

What would he say to her? What did she want from him? If she was preoccupied with growing rich as she claimed to be, why didn't she find a rich man—like Randolph? Now that would be a pair. Aggressive, acquisitive, over-sexed. They had a lot in common, didn't they?

It suddenly occurred to him that he had never really questioned Cora's interest in him. Why, there were scores of men wealthier and—despite Cora's assertion to the contrary—more handsome than he. She was uncommonly beautiful, brilliant, an actress of considerable talent...why him?

He re-mounted Cassio on the opposite bank and continued along the road that Randolph had indicated on the map, noting landmarks along the way. There was a serenity about this low country, as they called it, that surpassed even that of the high river bluffs of the Ocmulgee. Perhaps it was the sea island breezes that snaked their way up the sounds and river channels, perhaps the gently swaying saw grass, or the occasional majestic oak that erupted from the grassy hammocks. Every now and then he would allow Cassio to stop and drink from one of the tidal pools and note that the water was teeming with life—minnows, tadpoles, mullet, tiny shrimp; mud flats bubbling with clams and oysters. This was where fertile land met fertile sea, and it was no wonder that the inhabitants— white ones, at least—were fat and prosperous.

He entered Beaufort from the north, which Randolph described as the least attractive approach, composed of sawmills, quarries, brick works, and tanneries. The odors were not so pleasant in this neighborhood, but soon he arrived at the high street, or Bay Street, as they called it. Here were the grand houses of the gentry, with mossy oaks clinging to high bluffs overlooking the Beaufort River.

Cassio seemed to need no guidance at all at this point, and Zimri wondered where they would end up if he simply let go of the reins. He did so, and Cassio moved at a walk, easily weaving in and out of carriage traffic, seemingly nodding to other horses as if they were old friends. At last he came to a stop in front of a large, three-story hostelry with a veranda facing the river and a miniature version of the staircase at Lynwood. The neat, hand-lettered sign on the lawn read:

The Beaufort Inn
Est. 1790

A smile came to Zimri's face. *Randolph has been here before. With whom? Ah, well, he was a bachelor, wasn't he? He certainly had more legitimate business here than he, Zimri, did.*

It suddenly occurred to him that the proprietors would surely know Randolph's horse. *Perhaps he should tie Cassio to a hitching rail down the street, closer to town...now he was acting like a criminal. What did he have to hide? He was a guest of Randolph's and was in town simply to see an associate. As a matter of fact, Sam Chapman, the editor of the* Gazette, *was probably in his office at that very moment and it wouldn't hurt to go by and see him.*

He checked his watch. *Noon. He had plenty of time...yes, that was an excellent idea. Besides, if he went by to see Sam, no one could say he lied about his reasons for coming to Beaufort. A good alibi...here he was thinking like a criminal again!*

Sam Chapman was a short, stocky, balding man of about thirty-five, who relished the gossip that came his way concerning the wealthier denizens of Beaufort County. They dined in a waterfront tavern across the street from the the *Gazette*'s offices, with a fine view of the river and the docks, with shrimp boats, cutters, and sloops being loaded and unloaded.

"It's a prosperous town," Sam said, prying open an oyster with his knife. "A playground for rich Yankees in the winter, and a thriving fishing community in the summer. We ship a lot of the planter's cotton and rice out of here, too."

"What do you know of the Bensons?"

"William Benson, the old man, was one of the most influential men in the legislature until he fell ill about five years ago. Some kind of palsy, I think. His hands shake, and he can't walk."

"And Randolph?"

"The black sheep of the family. Got kicked out of the College of Charleston for having young ladies up to his room. One of them said she was raped. But the old man paid off the family and no more was heard from her."

"Rape? Do you think she was?"

"Don't know. But that wasn't the only time. I heard one story about Randolph that would curl your hair."

"Well, let's hear it."

Sam swallowed his oyster and washed it down with some Madeira. Then he looked around the busy dining room and leaned forward in his chair. "Now I got no proof of this one, you understand, but I heard it from a reliable source."

"And?"

"And my source says that when Randolph was about sixteen or so, he and some of his pals got drunk on the old man's vintage wine and gang-raped a slave girl."

"What happened to the girl?"

Sam lowered his voice and leaned closer. "Here's the scary part. My source says that in order to prevent the old man from finding out—for she was one of his favorites—they tortured the girl."

"Tortured? How?"

"With a poker. Seems that Randolph got especially angry because she resisted him more than the others, and rammed the poker up her—well, you know."

"Your source is sure of that?"

"Like I said—he's a reliable source."

They ate in silence for a few moments.

"Then what happened?" Zimri said.

"Nothing. That is, nothing happened to Randolph. But the girl disappeared. As far as the old man was concerned, she simply ran off. But my source thinks she died and Randolph and his pals buried her somewhere on Lynwood, maybe down by the river."

Zimri pushed his plate away and finished his glass of Madeira. "That's quite a story."

Sam shrugged his shoulders. "Just rumor. Can't prove it, can't print it."

Zimri spent the next hour or so exploring the streets and shops of Beaufort and, discovering a fine book shop, lingered for some time there. After purchasing a copy of *Farquhar's Low Country Architecture*, which included a complete set of drawings for Lynwood, he checked his watch: three forty-five. He stopped by a feed store to purchase a bucket of oats for Cassio and found him where he had left him, tied to a hitching rail in front of a flower shop. He was tempted to go into the flower shop, but thought of the time, and paused only long enough to see that Cassio received some nourishment.

He arrived at the Beaufort Inn at precisely four o'clock, tied Cassio to the rail, adjusted his cravat, and ascended the staircase.

Upon being directed to the dining salon, which was now serving tea, he found himself in a well-furnished room overlooking the front lawn and the river. There were only a few people sitting at the widely scattered tables: a young couple with a child, a middle-aged couple, a minister by himself, and an elderly woman by the window...no sign of Cora.

He checked his watch again, thinking he might be too early. A waitress approached him.

"Mr. Rhodes?"

"Yes?" He was surprised that the waitress knew his name.

Your mother is waiting for you at table four—by the window."

"My...mother?"

"This way, please."

Zimri followed the waitress over to the table by the window, and suddenly alert to the ruse, resolved to play his part.

"Zimri, my son." the elderly woman said with a maternal smile, "You're such a bad boy, pretending you don't recognize your own mother. Sit down."

The waitress took their order for tea and retreated to the kitchen.

Zimri took his seat. "Sorry, Mother. I've been preoccupied with business matters." He was astonished at Cora's disguise. She looked to be in her sixties, dressed in black as if she were in mourning for her recently deceased husband.

She reached across the table and placed her hand on his. "I'm so glad you came. You don't know how lonely a mother can be in her old age."

Zimri smiled. "You're not so old, Mother. I'd say no more than thirty."

"Shh!" Cora put her forefinger to her lips. "My dear Zimri, you're such a wit. Now do tell me what you've been up to lately."

"I've just been visiting one of my colleagues at the *Gazette*—Mr. Chapman. He is a wealth of information about Beaufort."

"Is he now? And what does he have to say about it?"

Zimri looked around the salon. The minister was reading his paper, the young mother was tying her son's bootlace, and the middle-aged couple seemed mesmerized by the passing carriages and pedestrians. "He says that Beaufort is very prosperous."

"How very observant of him."

"And that Lynwood is the most prosperous of all the plantations."

"Lynwood? I'm not surprised."

The waitress returned with their tea, along with some cakes. When she had gone, Cora meticulously measured out two teaspoons of sugar into her cup.

Zimri followed her lead. "Milk?"

"No, thank you."

"Nor I."

Cora stirred her tea. "There are many prosperous plantations in Beaufort County. But in point of fact, Lynwood is mostly in Colleton County. Why did Mr. Chapman single out Lynwood?"

"I suppose because it is the largest in the area."

"I see."

"And possibly because he knows that I'm staying there."

Cora's eyebrows, dusted with gray, arched high above her lids. "You're staying at Lynwood?"

"Yes."

"How fortunate for you. May I ask how that came about?"

"Randolph Benson is a friend of my wife's."

Cora lowered her eyes and took a sip of her tea. "I see."

A silence of several minutes followed. The young couple with the child, who was crying about something, got up and left. The middle-aged couple seemed frozen into their respective positions, like statues. The minister folded up his paper and paid his bill, making a little bow to the remaining patrons before leaving.

"Mother—"

"Yes, my son?"

"Perhaps you'd like to take a stroll along the waterfront after we finish our tea."

"Yes. Yes, I think I'd like that."

They finished their tea and Zimri paid the bill. He then took her by the arm as if she were in need of assistance, and they strolled down the sidewalk, crossing the street at an intersection near town, and found a park bench overlooking the river.

After pondering Cora's sudden taciturnity at the inn, Zimri told her the story that Sam Chapman had told him.

"You seem upset, Cora."

"Do I? Well, who wouldn't be? It's a rather sad story."

"And you seem to know a great deal about Lynwood."

"Everyone around here knows about Lynwood—and the Benson family."

"But how would *you* know, Cora?"

She smiled. "You are too clever for me, Zimri. I was born...not far from here."

"You're no more Italian than I am."

"No."

"But why the disguise? Wouldn't it be an advantage in raising the money—"

"The powers that be here are very old-fashioned. They don't trust women in business unless they have the appearance of age and inherited wealth. They think I'm the widow of a shipping magnate from New York."

"Ah...a useful deception."

"It has proven so."

Zimri scarcely knew what to think of Cora at this point. Who was she? Could he believe anything, anything at all that she said? He decided to test her. "Cora—"

"Yes, my darling?"

"When you were a girl here in Beaufort..."

"Yes?"

"You would have heard many stories like the one I just told you."

"Yes. There were many such stories." Her eyes seemed to focus on a sloop not a hundred yards away from them, close-hauled, cutting through the white caps stirred up by the breeze.

"The girl would have been about your age."

"Yes."

"You knew her?"

"Yes."

"What happened to her?"

"She ran away."

"She wasn't murdered by Randolph and his pals like Sam said?"

"No."

"How do you know?"

She turned her face towards his. "Because I am that girl."

Zimri was so stunned that he could think of nothing more to say. He simply gaped at her for several moments and turned his eyes once again to the river. The sloop, its sails now wildly fluttering in the wind as the vessel came about, seemed about to capsize.

"What did you do after the...incident?"

"What could I do? No one would believe me...except—"

"Except who?"

"My father."

"Your father? A slave?"

Cora smiled. "No. My father is William Benson."

Zimri could hardly absorb all of this at once. Every answer to his questions provoked more questions. It was as if he had opened a long-locked closet and everything was tumbling out at once. "Randolph is your brother?"

"Half brother. After Father's first wife died, he was so grief-stricken, he went to my mother for solace."

"And she was—"

"A cook. She was always preparing treats, delicacies—he had sent her to France, where she studied under a great chef. She loved to please him with her 'creations,' as she called them."

"And is she still at Lynwood?"

Cora's voice, for the first time, faltered. "Yes. In the cemetery."

Zimri put his arm around her. "I'm sorry, Cora. I had no idea—"

She placed her head on his shoulder. "Don't feel sorry for me, Zimri—in a way, Randolph and his friends liberated me."

"Liberated you?"

"Yes. When I told my father what happened, he gave me five thousand dollars and told me to go as far away from Lynwood as possible. At first I went to Rome because I loved the art and architecture I had read so much about in Lynwood's library. But after six months I found my funds depleted, and I could not make a living there. So I sailed for New York."

"Is that when you changed your name to Rinaldi?"

"Yes. After Antonio Rinaldi, my favorite architect."

After watching the river for some time in silence, they strolled back to the inn at a leisurely pace, enjoying the last rays of the setting sun and the cool evening air. When they arrived at the desk, Cora suddenly gave him a maternal kiss on the cheek. "Why don't you go up to your room to freshen up, Zimmy, dear?" she said. "You must be hot and dusty from your journey."

"My room? Cora—"

Cora glanced at the proprietor, who stood behind the desk with the register open before her. "Just sign in—it's all arranged. Your room is adjacent to mine with a connecting door in case you need me in the middle of the night. You always were susceptible to bad dreams, weren't you?"

Zimri glanced cautiously at the proprietor, a matronly woman of about fifty. "Mother, I think I'd better get back to—"

"Nonsense, my son. It's getting dark already. You don't want to be stumbling around in the dark in a strange country. Besides, you'll be fresh in the morning."

Zimri was bemused for a moment and looked to the proprietor as if for advice. But instead of advice he was greeted with a smile and the keys to his room dangling from the woman's outstretched hand.

CHAPTER 46

Elizabeth sat on the veranda of Lynwood in a rocking chair, sipping on a lemonade. The sun was almost directly overhead now, and she adjusted her sun hat so as to shade her eyes and protect her skin. It was a delightful morning, with blue skies and only a few cumulous clouds drifting to the southwest.

She put down her book for a moment and noticed a rider coming up the drive. It was unmistakably Zimri. She could tell by the way he sat his horse, and the way his elbows stuck out when he was cantering. Why did he seem to be in such a hurry?

He slowed to a trot when he saw her, and waved. She waved back. It had only been a day, but she had missed him. Especially last night when she was partnered with Randolph's mother for whist. My, she was a blockhead! Randolph and his sister Jane had trounced them.

Zimri handed the reins to a waiting servant and bounded up the stairs. "Elizabeth! Are you all right?"

She looked at him, puzzled. "Of course I'm all right. Why shouldn't I be?"

"Oh—I don't know. It's just that I was worried that you might go riding or something and—"

She stood up from her rocker and kissed him lightly on the lips. "It's sweet of you to worry, darling. As a matter of fact, Randolph and I did go riding yesterday, but there were no mishaps. You can't imagine how immense Lynwood is! Why, we covered barely a tenth of it."

"Elizabeth—I think we should return to Martinville."

"Return? We just got here! Why—"

"What's this I hear about returning?" Randolph emerged from the front door, dressed in his riding clothes. "You can't be talking of leaving, Zimri. We're having a party tonight—in your honor."

"I've business to attend to—more than I had anticipated. There's a town council meeting coming up at the end of the week—"

"And I'm sure they can carry on without you just this once," Randolph said. "Though if you insist, you can go and I'll send Elizabeth along after you later."

Zimri balked. "No—no, I think it would be better if she comes with me."

"Why, old man? Does she have a vote on the council?"

"No, but she can help get circulars out to drum up support for the new bridge over the Ocmulgee. We'll have to petition the legislature and—"

"And the bridge will be built. Trust me, it's the easiest kind of money to raise. You're too much of a worrier, Zimri."

Zimri glanced at Elizabeth. "Perhaps you're right."

"Of course I'm right!" Randolph laughed heartily and slapped Zimri on the back. "Come inside—I want you to meet my father. He's feeling much better today."

Elizabeth watched as the two men disappeared into the house. She had never seen Zimri act so peculiarly. He seemed agitated, nervous. And what was this nonsense about sending out circulars to drum up support for the new bridge? Everybody knew the measure would pass.

She sat back down in her rocker and picked up her book again. *Emma.* She didn't know why she kept reading these Jane Austen novels. They had so little to do with her. There must be some American fiction out there *somewhere*.

After dinner, a dozen guests went riding along the Combahee, where Randolph pointed out various projects under way, including the draining of a swamp and the building of dikes. Lynwood, he said, would in this way be able to increase its rice production five-fold and thus surpass all other rice planters in the state. He seemed genuinely enthused about the projects, and Elizabeth noted that she had heard no more about Byron and Keats and republican revolutions since they arrived.

Zimri, on the other hand, still seemed anxious, troubled. He brought his horse alongside hers while Randolph was explaining to the group the importance of irrigation for rice production.

"My editor friend in Beaufort," he said, "related some rather unsavory stories about our host."

"Oh?" she said. "Unsavory? In what way?"

Zimri lowered his voice to a whisper. "Rape."

Elizabeth stared at him in disbelief. "And how did your friend come about this intelligence?"

"He's been the editor here for several years. He's heard it all."

"And he's sure that every word of it's true?"

"Perhaps not every word. But he's capable of separating fact from fiction."

"Of course. He's a newspaperman."

"Don't be flippant, Elizabeth. He's a reliable...source. I'm not here to spread gossip—I simply want to warn you to be on your guard."

"Then be advised I am so warned." She spurred her horse forward, leaving Zimri trailing behind. As she pulled up alongside Randolph, who seemed to brighten at her presence, she wondered if what Zimri's friend had said was true. Certainly Randolph was widely regarded as a ladies' man when she was in school in Charleston and he was at the College. And he had made some rather aggressive overtures towards her, both before and after she was married. But rape? She hardly thought so.

"I hope I'm not boring you with all of this talk about irrigation and rice paddies, Elizabeth."

"Not at all, Randolph. I find the subject fascinating. And I think it's wonderful that you're finally settling into your true vocation."

"Vocation? I hadn't thought of it that way. But I suppose it is my vocation. I was born to it...and I'm beginning to find that it suits me."

"I've always admired a man who knows who he is and where he is going."

"Do you? Well, yes—I suppose all women do." He glanced back at Zimri. "And Zimri—does he know who he is and where he's going?"

"Yes...in his own small way."

Randolph seemed to like this answer—a bit too much, she thought. Now she regretted that she had said it. But Zimri so infuriated her at times. He carries on an affair—almost openly—with another woman and then has the gall to suggest that an old friend like Randolph is on the verge of raping her. Yes, he has pursued her— also rather openly. But he has always been a gentleman and however much he once praised the adulterous behavior of libertines like Byron, has never given her cause to fear for her safety. And now—now! He seems ever so much more mature, so much more manly in the best sense of the word. The Grand Tour has apparently had its intended effect. His father knew what he was doing.

After the excursion along the Combahee, the group returned to the main house where Randolph announced that the evening's festivities would begin at six-thirty for drinks on the riverside terrace, followed by supper and dancing. Elizabeth and Zimri retired to their room to rest.

"I think we should leave tomorrow." Zimri sat on the edge of the bed and removed his boots. Elizabeth reclined on a chaise near the window, reading.

"Go right ahead," she said. "If you think the town council can't possibly conduct its business without you."

"Of course they can. I was simply grasping at some plausible excuse to give to Randolph. But aren't you the least bit worried about the children?"

"The children are perfectly safe with Louise and Betty and Tessie. Lord! One servant for each child! We didn't have such luxury at Belle Oaks when I was growing up."

Zimri put his boots on the floor, swung his legs onto the bed and stared at the lining of the canopy above his head. "I've known Sam Chapman for a long time, Elizabeth, and—"

She closed her book with a loud clap. "I don't know anything about Sam Chapman. But I do know that you're jealous of the attention that Randolph is paying me."

"Shouldn't I be?"

"No. He's been a perfect gentleman ever since we got here. Do you know that he sent Jane to sit up with me last night in case you came in late?"

"No. I didn't know that."

"If he were so intent on seducing me, why didn't he offer to sit up with me himself?"

"Perhaps he didn't want to get caught in the act in case I did show up."

"Oh!" She opened her book again and pretended to be immediately absorbed in reading, though the words on the page appeared as a blur.

Zimri stretched his legs out on the bed, and folded his hands behind his head. "We'll stay through the weekend. That should be sufficient time to fulfill our social obligation. Assuming, that is, that Randolph behaves himself." He closed his eyes and yawned.

Elizabeth said nothing but was furious. So that was the last word! As if she could have no objection whatever. Five days of travel to get here and Zimri wants to pull out after only three days in residence. Why, they've hardly had time to unpack!

She sat fuming while Zimri apparently slept. She opened the book again, closed it when she found she couldn't concentrate, and exhaled as if she had been swimming under water.

Why did she marry this man? Oh, he was handsome enough, perhaps even more handsome than Randolph on his best day. And she had looked up to him as a mature, refined man who had seen the world—but at sixteen, the world for her extended no farther than New York. Now she knew better. There was a vast world out there beyond the shores of America. And what a difference the year—or nearly a year—abroad had made in Randolph! And surely he would return to Europe from time to time, perhaps once a year, perhaps to live for one, two, three years. And he would take his wife—should he marry—with him to London, Rome, Paris. Paris! The home of her ancestors, the pinnacle of civilized society, the citadel of fashion!

She gazed at Zimri on the bed, who was now snoring.

How disgusting! Those animal, barnyard sounds emitting from his nostrils. Zimri was really no more than a farm boy who grew to hate farm work. Of course he would. Who wouldn't? Heavy labor was for Negroes. They were conditioned to it, born to it, just as Randolph was born to lead. She wondered for a moment if Randolph would ever run for the legislature like his father. No doubt he would. It was certainly in the interests of a large planter to do so.

She placed the open book across her chest and closed her eyes. Yes, Zimri works hard. He was prospering. Someday, his newspaper might even be the largest in the state. Well, no, Martinville would never be so large as Savannah, and it would require a large city to support a large paper. Then he would always be a small-town editor, and she the small-town wife of that small-town editor.

This thought distressed her, and she took some time in falling asleep.

CHAPTER 47

Zimri stood rather woodenly at the edge of the dance floor of the ballroom with a glass of brandy in his hand. It was particularly good brandy, he noted, perhaps the best he'd ever had.

He had never been much of a dancer. Though his parents were not Puritans, much of the community in which he grew up were, and dancing was generally frowned upon. And many of these contradanses, or reels, as they were often called in America, were quite intricate and required years of practice. Of course, both Elizabeth and Randolph had been instructed in these dances from an early age, and he had to admit that they moved beautifully together.

Still, he didn't like their dancing together, and he felt foolish standing at the edge of the dance floor like a wallflower, merely watching.

"They make a handsome couple, don't they?" Mrs. Benson said, who was sitting in a chair not far from him. She was speaking to her eldest daughter, Emma.

"Shh!" Emma said, apparently spying Zimri out of the corner of her eye. "Yes, Mama, they dance quite well together. But I'm sure that Mr. Rhodes cuts as fine a figure on the dance floor as anyone here."

"Oh, no doubt," Mrs. Benson said, taking the hint.

Zimri contemplated breaking in on Randolph, but then was restrained by the thought that he would certainly make a fool of himself, especially in light of the comment he just heard.

"Say, Zimri, old boy."

It was Harry, Randolph's youngest brother. He had a mint julep in his hand and was obviously a little drunk.

"Oh, hello, Harry," Zimri said. "I'm surprised to see you standing here among the old folks. Where's your sweetheart?"

"Oh, Nan? She's not really my sweetheart. In fact, she's my cousin—second or third or once-removed. Something like that."

"A very pretty girl, nevertheless."

"Yes, she is, isn't she?" Harry teetered a bit as he sipped on his mint julep. "I expect we'll get married someday. Keep it all in the family, you know." He forced a little laugh. "But say, Zimri, I've been meaning to talk to you about something."

"And what is that?"

"The darkies have been talking lately."

"The darkies? What darkies?"

"Our darkies." Harry grinned from ear to ear. "You might say I've been a bit closer to them than Randolph."

Zimri looked at Harry for the first time during the conversation. He was a slight young man, quite pleasant in appearance, but unremarkable except for an astigmatism that caused him to look at one slightly askance. "What have you heard, Harry?"

"Nothing terribly interesting, really. Just that they seem to be fascinated lately with that mysterious escape of slaves in Martinville a couple of months ago. It was in all the Charleston and Savannah papers, and of course it eventually trickles down to them. Gives them ideas, you know."

Zimri found this to be a curious topic for Harry to bring up as house slaves milled about all around them. "Do you think they're on the point of a revolt?"

"Oh, no, no, no. Nothing like that. Our darkies are too complacent, you know. They're well-fed and well-treated and they know it. But I just wondered that, as a newspaperman, whether you knew something more about it than we do. I mean, how did so many slaves escape without a trace? And is it true that the British government set the whole thing up? I mean, it's an act of war, if you ask me."

"Well, I suppose it could be if the British were really behind the whole thing. But why would they risk another war with America for the liberation of a handful of slaves?"

Harry screwed up his face as if stymied. "I hadn't thought of it quite like that. I suppose it would be rather stupid of them, wouldn't it? But what about the reports of that man o' war—"

"Perhaps it was a fortuitous accident—that is for the slaves. Or perhaps the captain of the *Arundel* was telling the truth when he— excuse me, Harry. I need to speak to my wife about something."

"What? Oh, sorry—but I don't see her, old boy. Maybe she stepped out for—"

Zimri was nearly half way across the dance floor before Harry could finish his sentence. Elizabeth had indeed stepped out onto the terrace with Randolph, though Zimri had not seen either of them do so. He didn't mind so much Elizabeth dancing with the man— well, all right, he *did* mind—but it was something else to monopolize her time off the dance floor as well as on.

When he emerged on the terrace, he saw several couples enjoying the fresh air, but neither Elizabeth nor Randolph were anywhere to be found. Where did they go?

"Mr. Rhodes?"

Zimri turned around to see Mrs. Benson emerging from the ballroom with a young woman in tow. "Yes, Mrs. Benson?"

"I want you to meet my niece, Samantha Knight. Samantha, this is Mr. Zimri Rhodes, the newspaper editor I was telling you about."

"How do you do, Miss Knight. Forgive me, but—"

"Samantha wants to be a journalist, don't you Samantha?"

Samantha, tall, pale and thin, blushed. "It's just a thought, Aunt Polly."

"Just a thought?" Mrs. Benson said. "Why, that's all you've been talking about since you got here. Now you just tell Mr. Rhodes all about yourself, especially about all those poems you're been writing. I'm sure he'd like to read some of them."

"Mrs. Benson, I—"

But Mrs. Benson disappeared almost as quickly as she had appeared, leaving Samantha looking like an abandoned scarecrow. Zimri felt he could not simply walk away from her.

"Tell me, Miss Knight—"

"Samantha."

"Samantha. Tell me how you came to be interested in journalism."

Samantha, who had been as shy as an orphaned calf up until this point, suddenly became very animated and loquacious.

Zimri listened patiently for what seemed like an hour until one of Harry's friends from the college came up and asked her to dance. This unexpected request surprised and delighted Samantha to the point that she profusely apologized for breaking off the interview, but said that she hoped to continue the conversation with him at a later date.

Once she and her suitor were gone, he crossed to the other side of the terrace and looked out across the moonlit lawn for some sign of Elizabeth. Seeing none, he took the steps down to a gravel path that meandered through the garden to the river. He had noted earlier, when they were out riding, that there was a dock at the edge of the river with a sloop tied up at the end of it. As he approached the river's edge, torches illuminated either side of the dock, leading all the way out to the end.

He hesitated at the first step onto the dock, feeling that he was almost a parody of the jealous husband. Hogarth's prints came to mind. Was he about to make a fool of himself? He considered turning back and rejoining the party but his curiosity, if not his jealousy, got the better of him.

He stepped forward, deciding that it was perfectly natural as a guest to explore the grounds and particularly to be lured out onto the dock on a moonlit night. What else were the torches for?

Still, he walked quietly.

When he got near the end of the dock he heard voices and stopped.

"Elizabeth—I'm not the same man."

"I can see that, Randolph. But then, I'm not the same woman, either."

"What do you mean?"

"I mean that I have responsibilities now. Children. A husband. Ties to the community. I've been selected to head up the new library."

Randolph laughed, then checked himself. "Forgive me for laughing, my dear, but we have a library here that contains more volumes than your little library in Martinville is likely to accumulate in twenty years. And some of them are quite rare. You could peruse them to your heart's delight."

Zimri could make out two figures sitting in the stern of the sloop. Dark clouds were passing slowly overhead, eclipsing the moon and obscuring both the observer and the observed.

"If you are proposing once again that I divorce Zimri and—"

"I'm not proposing that at all."

"Then you haven't changed, Randolph. I won't be your mistress."

There was a moment's silence in their conversation, and Zimri stepped back into the shadows, away from the torches.

"Are you suggesting that if something were to happen to Zimri, that you would—"

"I'm not suggesting anything, Randolph. Oh, I'm so confused, I don't know what I'm suggesting."

"Elizabeth—"

Zimri could see that Randolph had placed his forefinger under Elizabeth's chin and was lifting it up.

"I've waited for three years, and traveled half way around the world, thinking of nothing but this moment. This moment, Elizabeth. I care about nothing else. I would give all that I own, the deed to Lynwood, anything and everything, for one kiss from you."

"Oh, Randolph—"

"One freely given kiss, Elizabeth. I will not force myself on you.

Can you not spare but one kiss?"

Zimri watched with growing fury as he saw Elizabeth's head move towards Randolph's. Their lips met. Zimri's heart sank. He felt that Elizabeth had been lost to him forever. He hoped for a moment that the kiss would be brief—perhaps she was just humoring him. His request for a kiss seemed pathetic. But the kiss continued. She was giving freely of herself.

His immediate impulse was to leap into the boat, box Randolph's ears and toss him overboard. He could do it, too. He was much stronger than Randolph.

But then what would that accomplish? He would have attacked his host—one of the cardinal sins of Southern culture. And what recourse would Randolph have but to challenge him to a duel? He was old-fashioned enough and enough of the Romantic that he would certainly do it. And what if he, Zimri, killed his man? He would be doubly condemned in the eyes of society. Attacked his host, and then killed him in a duel—on the man's own property.

And if Randolph killed him? Well...then Elizabeth would get her wish. Lynwood. The height of luxury and prestige. She would be the American aristocrat she was born and bred to be.

These thoughts caromed through his mind in a split second. He condemned himself for being too much the thinker, a Hamlet. But he was not Hamlet. He knew all too well he was capable of hotheaded violence. A violence that would destroy everything that he had worked for over the last ten years.

Slowly, silently, he withdrew.

CHAPTER 48

Zimri said nothing to Elizabeth about the incident on the dock the night of the party. When they retired to their room, he noticed a coolness towards him on her part, but made a point to be cheerier than usual, and even asked about what she was reading.

The next morning he awoke early, before daylight, to join Randolph for quail hunting. As he sat on the chaise pulling on his trousers, trying not to wake Elizabeth, he wondered if he weren't stepping into a trap. Would Randolph try to shoot him and be rid of him for once and for all? It seemed unlikely. For one thing, there would be many others in the hunt, including his younger brothers. The next eldest, Edward, would no doubt be delighted to see Randolph taken away in shackles so that he could inherit the estate. There seemed to be much bad blood between them, especially since Randolph returned from abroad and took over management of the plantation.

He met Randolph and the others for breakfast in the parlor overlooking the east lawn. The first rays of the sun were faintly visible and a light mist obscured much of the wooded area in the distance. The air was cool but humid.

"An excellent day for quail hunting," Randolph said. He stabbed a slice of ham with his fork. "The dogs love this kind of weather—not too cool, not too hot. You're sure you can handle a bird gun, Zimri?"

"It's been some time, Randolph, but I'm sure that it'll all come back to me."

"Perhaps we'd better let you shoot off a few rounds before we start—just so you'll be comfortable and not be at a loss when the dogs flush a covey."

"We don't want to warn the birds that we're coming, do we?"

Randolph laughed heartily. "Right you are, Zimri. I can see you're already thinking like a hunter. Edward! Are the dogs ready?"

"Since four this morning, Randolph. Haven't you heard them howling?"

"I must admit I slept late. My bedroom's like a tomb." Randolph shoved his plate aside and stood. "All right, everyone, let's get moving!"

Randolph led the procession out to the kennels where his dog trainer, Tucker, a slave of about fifty or so, awaited with about fifteen or twenty hounds tethered together. Randolph called each by name, tossing out scraps of ham and bacon to them from the breakfast table.

The bird guns were handed out from the back of a wagon that also contained supplies and refreshments. Zimri found that his gun was similar to the one he kept at home over the mantelpiece but had never fired. A percussion type, converted from a flint striker. Much simpler and safer to operate than the one he had as a boy.

The hunting party climbed into the wagon and Tucker drove them to the edge of the pine forest about a half a mile away. They stopped, got out, and the dogs ran eagerly ahead through the tall grass. Tucker whistled and the dogs stopped.

"Keep the stock to your shoulder, Zimri," Randolph said. "When the dogs flush them, you won't have time to get set."

Zimri dutifully took this advice, and resolved to follow Randolph's instructions to the letter.

They had hardly gone twenty yards before the dogs flushed a covey. Randolph fired so suddenly that it startled Zimri. By the time he had lifted his gun and taken aim, four of the birds were down and two were out of range.

"Not quick enough, Zimri." Randolph said "Stay alert."

As the party moved on through the woods, several more coveys were flushed, and each time Zimri was too late to get a bird into his sights. He reproached himself for his ineptitude, noting that Randolph had already bagged some eight or ten birds.

They moved into a more densely wooded area and the party spread out. Zimri lost sight of the others, except for Randolph, Edward, and Harry. Even Harry seemed adept at this kind of hunting, having nearly matched Randolph's kills.

Zimri heard the muffled shots of the hunters on his right. It seemed that everyone was easily bagging game except him. He determined to fire at the first sound of rustling brush rather than waiting for a visual sighting of the birds.

A dog ran ahead of him, stopped, and pointed. He could not see exactly what the dog was pointing at. The brush was thick here, nearly shoulder high. He raised his gun and aimed at the clump of tall grass where the dog was pointing. Nothing happened. No sound. He looked around but did not see Randolph. The party had moved off farther to his right it seemed. The sound of gunfire was becoming more faint.

Suddenly he heard a rustling in the grass where the dog was still pointing. He saw what looked like a mass of speckled plumage and fired. A covey of quail erupted from the grass. The dog plunged ahead after them.

"My God. I've been shot! Help! Help!"

When Zimri arrived at the clump of tall grass, he found Randolph sitting on the ground with his back against a pine tree, clutching his left shoulder.

"You fool!" he said. "You were to stay close to me—not let me out of your sight."

"I'm sorry, Randolph. I was anxious to—"

"Don't touch me! You've done enough damage. Tucker! Where's Tucker?"

Tucker came running as did Edward and two of the other hunters.

When Tucker arrived, he took out a penknife and cut open Randolph's shirt. "It ain't nothin,' Marster Randolph. You jest got peppered with some bird shot, that's all."

"Well, it feels like it went clear through the bone."

"Naw, suh. It ain't but skin-deep. Lucky y'all wasn't huntin' bear."

Tucker went to fetch some liniment and bandages from the wagon while the others stood around Randolph and offered their opinions as to his chances of survival.

"I'd say about fifty-fifty," one of Randolph's college friends said. "You could bleed to death between here and the house."

"Very funny, McGrath. I'll remember that the next time your horse throws you and you break your neck."

"Tucker's right, Randolph," Edward said. "It's just a flesh wound—but you'd best have a doctor look at it."

"I could be laid up for a month. Damn you, Zimri!"

"It's not his fault, Randolph," Edward said, "He's an amateur. You should have kept an eye on him."

"I couldn't watch him every minute! And how do I know that he didn't—" Randolph looked at the others, then Zimri. "Oh, forget it. Sorry, Zimri. I'm a little upset."

"I don't blame you, Randolph. If there's anything I can do—"

"No, there's nothing you can do. Here comes Tucker with the bandages. He knows more about gunshot wounds than most doctors."

Tucker applied the liniment and bandages to Randolph's shoulder, and formed a sort of human stretcher with the other men to carry him to the wagon, which lay at the edge of the tree line.

Randolph encouraged the others to go on with the hunt, but Zimri and Edward elected to return to the house to assist Randolph in any way that they could. It seemed to Zimri that Edward was taking charge, and that Randolph resented it.

A doctor was sent for, and Randolph was carried on a litter from the wagon to the house. Many of the guests saw the wagon coming and rushed out into the yard.

Elizabeth was among these guests.

"Oh, my God! What happened?" she said.

"I shot him," Zimri said.

"You what?"

"It was an accident. I...I somehow got confused as to his position and fired at what I thought was a covey about to emerge from the brush."

"Zimri! You didn't! You couldn't!"

"He did," Randolph said with a grimace. The four slaves who were carrying him on the litter stopped for a moment on the veranda. "But it was my fault—I let him out of my sight."

"Oh, Randolph! Is it serious?"

"According to Tucker, it's just a flesh wound. But I'm sure the doctor will have to pick out the shot to keep it from getting infected. It will no doubt be painful."

Elizabeth turned to Zimri, who stood by looking rather helpless. "Why didn't you follow instructions? Oh! I should never have let you go—you're no sportsman!"

"Elizabeth, I—"

"Never mind," she said. "It's done. Just stay out of the way, Zimri. Has anyone sent for a doctor?"

"Yes, ma'am," Edward said. "But he'll have to come all the way from Beaufort. Might not be here until nightfall."

"Well, take him to his room. I'll see that some broth is brought up. The bandages should be changed every two hours to prevent the wound from getting infected."

"You heard the lady, boys," Edward said. "Take Master Randolph to his room."

The procession continued on into the house where it was again stopped by the appearance of Mrs. Benson, who seemed on the verge of hysterics. Edward, however, calmed her down, assured her that the wound was not serious, and the slaves proceeded to Randolph's bedroom.

Zimri remained standing on the veranda, at a loss as to what to do next. Should he simply quit the place and return to Martinville? It would look too much like he was running from the consequences of his own poor judgment. Besides, he couldn't leave without Elizabeth, and she would no doubt want to stay and nurse Randolph at least for a few days whether he needed it or not. Strange how she suddenly assumes control in what she sees as a crisis. Randolph would be perfectly all right. He was milking this little scrape for all the sympathy he could get, especially from Elizabeth.

He exhaled some cigar smoke and looked to the woods. He heard faint sounds of gunfire. Apparently, the others didn't take this little accident seriously. Especially Randolph's friend McGrath. Even Harry declined to return to the house. And Tucker had already rejoined them with the wagon.

Still, he had made a mess of things. Better if he'd thrown Randolph off of the boat last night and accepted his challenge to a duel. On the other hand, if he were no better a shot with a pistol than he was with a shotgun, he'd be a dead man. He chuckled quietly to himself. Poor shot? He had hit what he was aiming at, hadn't he?

"Mr. Rhodes?"

He turned around to see Samantha Knight standing behind him, wearing a colorful summer dress and a straw sun hat. "Oh, hello, Samantha. I suppose you've heard what all the excitement was about."

"Yes. But it seems that it's nothing serious. Randolph's always been something of a complainer. And he loves to upset my aunt."

Zimri laughed. "I'm glad that someone has this whole affair in perspective. But I must confess that I feel rather like a fool, having accidentally shot my host."

"He'll be fine. And no one could ever regard you as a fool, Mr. Rhodes. Mr. Chapman tells me that you're the best editorial writer in the state of Georgia."

"Sam said that? You know him?"

"I worked in the office of the *Gazette* last summer while home from school. He thinks very highly of you."

Zimri puffed on his cigar. "Well, I'm glad someone does. I'm afraid I'll be a persona non grata around here for a while. Especially with my wife."

"I'm sure she'll get over it, just as Randolph will. But if you're going to stay at Lynwood for a while, Mr. Rhodes, I was wondering whether you might take the time to read a story I'm working on."

"Well, I don't know if—"

"It's not very long, really. At least not yet."

Zimri felt that he should humor the girl. "What's the story about?"

"Cora Rinaldi."

Zimri's cigar nearly fell from his mouth. "Cora Rinaldi? What do you know about her?"

"Quite a lot. She comes to Beaufort every so often. In fact, she's there now, disguised as an old woman trying to raise money for a steamship company."

Zimri looked around the veranda. There were a number of guests sitting in the rocking chairs or milling about chatting some distance away. "How do you know this, Samantha?"

"Because I go to school in New York and I've seen her in plays. Even in disguise, one can see the mannerisms, the fine features, the figure. I'm a great fan of hers."

Zimri didn't know what to make of this. "Why do you think she's trying to disguise herself?"

"I don't know. But I've heard rumors about her—that she's really a mulatto who once was a slave on a plantation near here, and that she ran away to New York and became an actress because she could so easily pass for white."

"Suppose that's true. Then why would she return and risk being exposed and returned to her master?"

"I don't know. That's what's so intriguing to me. I want to find out."

"Perhaps the woman you saw is not Miss Rinaldi at all, but a legitimate businesswoman interested in investing in a prosperous town like Beaufort."

"She may be a legitimate businesswoman, but she *is* Cora Rinaldi. Of that I have no doubt."

Zimri suddenly wondered if this girl were attempting to blackmail him. What did she want? "What can I do for you, Samantha? You seem to know a great deal about this—"

"I just wondered whether you might like to see what I've written so far. I'm sort of stuck."

Zimri looked into Samantha's eyes and saw nothing more than the innocence and ambition of youth. "All right, Samantha—I'd be glad to take a look at it."

"You would?" Samantha clapped her hands together. "Oh, thank you, Mr. Rhodes—I'll run up to my room right now and get it."

Zimri waited for no more than a few minutes. Samantha came

running up to him nearly out of breath, extending a brown envelope secured with a red string. She stood looking at him in silence
for a moment as if expecting him to open up the envelope and read
it on the spot.

"I'll read it later in my room, Samantha. I've got a lot on my
mind at the moment."

"Oh—of course. Well...thank you, Mr. Rhodes. Thank you ever
so much."

"My pleasure, Samantha. I'll give you my critique tomorrow after dinner."

"Wonderful. That'll be perfect. Thank you, Mr. Rhodes."

Samantha turned and, in spite of her height, fairly skipped like a
little girl back into the house.

Zimri saw that his cigar was almost burned down to a stub and
tossed it into a nearby spittoon. Nasty things. He should stop smoking altogether.

He looked at the envelope. 'Mr. Zimri Rhodes—Confidential,' it
said. He loosened the string and extracted a five or six page manuscript. The title page read:

Cora Rinaldi: Actress or British Spy?

CHAPTER 49

Elizabeth did not appear at dinner and Zimri, after taking some ribbing from McGrath and the others for having shot his host ("The food isn't all that bad, is it Zimri, old boy?"), he retired to the bedroom and extracted Samantha's article from its envelope.

He heard a scream, followed by another. Unmistakably Randolph's voice. The doctor had arrived.

He skimmed through the article at first, looking for names and dates that might be significant. One item caught his eye:

The HMS Arundel was indeed on its way home to Britain laden with rum and spices from the West Indies. But according to crew members of the steamship packet Savannah, which was passing near the Arundel that morning, over one hundred Negroes were taken aboard the warship. The Arundel has a crew of one hundred eighty-four. Could it be that the vast majority of this British man'o war's crew were Negroes? Not likely.

Zimri put down the article for a moment. This girl was very thorough. What else did she find out? He picked it up again.

Is it not a strange coincidence that over one hundred escaped slaves were thought to be in the area at the same time? The British Consul in Savannah claims that it was simply that: a coincidence. No less a personage than the President of the United States says that he agrees with him. But there are other, stranger coincidences surrounding this event. Miss Cora Rinaldi, an actress/entrepreneur from New York City, had only a short time before launched two steamboats on the Ocmulgee River in Martinville, Georgia. This otherwise unremarkable event was made somewhat remarkable by the fact that not one—but two—steamboats were absconded with on nearly the same day that one hundred and sixty-three slaves disappeared from plantations in the Martinville area.

Zimri paused to reflect on the events of that week and then read on:

It is not so remarkable that Miss Rinaldi, like most actresses, enjoys only periodic employment and therefore must supplement her income from time to time by other means. What is remarkable, however, is that Miss Rinaldi seems to appear in precisely those places where slave breaks occur, while promoting her various enterprises. In Natchez, Mississippi, for example, she was soliciting investors for a company that purported to ship cotton via riverboats upriver to Memphis and Cincinnati. The cotton arrived as promised. So did over two hundred slaves that disappeared into the free states of Ohio and Illinois. Coincidence?

Apparently, Miss Rinaldi has made no attempt in any of these entrepreneurial adventures to conceal the fact that she is a fairly well-known actress in New York. Indeed, she seems to exploit this fact to her advantage. Investors are eager to associate themselves with her celebrity. And from all accounts, not one investor has lost money.

But who is Cora Rinaldi? Is that her real name? Where did she come from?

It is no secret that the British Government is less than sympathetic with the institution of slavery. Parliament is embroiled at this very moment with debate over whether it should be abolished entirely in its West Indian possessions. But how is it to disrupt the lucrative slave trade between the West Indies and the Southern United States? Clearly, Great Britain needs an ally within the heart of American slave country.

Is that ally Miss Cora Rinaldi?

Zimri put the article down and chuckled. 'Clearly,' Samantha was jumping to conclusions here. 'Clearly,' she had no proof— only circumstantial evidence. On the other hand, she could make considerable trouble for Cora. She had seen through her disguise. She says nothing about that in her article. Perhaps she is simply waiting for the right moment.

He put the article back into its envelope and into a drawer next to his side of the bed. He then lay on the bed and closed his eyes.

Cora could no longer conceal her activities as a liberator of slaves. Samantha was right about that part, at any rate. If she chose to expose her as a runaway slave, then Cora would certainly be arrested on the spot, and any plans for an escape in the Beaufort area would be aborted. But then she legally belonged to Randolph's father. Perhaps Randolph would claim that she belongs to the estate, regardless of his father's wishes, and pitch her back into slavery.

He must put this Knight girl off somehow and warn Cora. Perhaps he could make some excuse to return to Beaufort Sunday afternoon or Monday morning. Cora...Elizabeth... the two women he loved—yes, he now knew that he loved them both—were in the grip of this monster. How to extricate them?

He awoke to the sound of Elizabeth closing the door to their room. When he opened his eyes, he saw her glare at him for a moment, then go to the wash basin beneath the window and wash her hands. "How is he?"

"He'll survive. No thanks to you."

"Elizabeth, I—"

"There's nothing more to be said, Zimri. The poor man! It was excruciating having to watch the doctor cut out the pellets one by one. So much blood!"

"Didn't the doctor administer morphine?"

"He did. It didn't seem to have much effect." She sat before the mirror and began to remove pins from her hair.

"Elizabeth, I think we'd better leave on Monday."

"Leave? I can't leave while Randolph's in this condition. He needs me."

"Needs you? The wound is superficial, Elizabeth. There are plenty of—"

Her eyes went to his image in the mirror. "Superficial? How would you know? You didn't even have the decency to come to his room while the doctor was here."

"What could I have done? You said yourself that I'd only be in the way."

"I was angry. You should have been there—to show that you were concerned, if nothing else."

"If I'd come, you would only have told me to leave."

Elizabeth stood and pulled her dress over her head. There was a flounce of petticoats, and she laid the dress over a chair. "Let's not talk about it—I'm exhausted. You've had your nap, now let me have mine."

"I'll wake you for supper."

"Don't bother. I'm not hungry." She lay on the bed, stretched out on her back and yawned.

Zimri sat up and swung his feet from the bed to the floor. He looked at her over his shoulder. Her eyes were closed and she was feigning sleep.

He looked at his watch. Five o'clock. He pulled on his trousers and his boots and decided to go and look for Samantha.

CHAPTER 50

"He's running a high fever," Elizabeth said of Randolph the next afternoon. "I've sent for the doctor again."

Zimri sat in a chair next to the window as Elizabeth washed her hands in the basin. She looked lovely, with a lock of blond hair hanging down over her forehead, her long white neck exposed to the collar bone, and the laces to her bodice loosened so that she could wash her breasts as well.

"I've got to get back to Martinville, Elizabeth. Jed can only do so much in my absence."

"Then go. I'll follow you when Randolph has fully recovered."

Zimri was expecting this answer, but he still didn't like it. "And when will that be?"

"How should I know? Once the fever breaks he'll need close attention for several days. His mother is practically useless, and his sisters seem preoccupied with their beaux. I suppose it'll be at least another week."

Zimri sighed. "The children must miss you terribly."

She dried her hands and arms with a towel and looked at him with contempt. "And I miss them terribly. But I must fulfill my responsibilities here first. Don't try to make me feel guilty for your own purposes."

"My only purpose is to restore my wife to her family and her home."

Elizabeth pressed the towel against her bare breasts and sat in a chair facing Zimri's. "Let's hear no more about it. I will see you—and my little darlings—in ten days' time."

Zimri could think of no more to say. He could only hope that Elizabeth would be as good as her word and that she would eventually see through Randolph's façade of culture and gallantry. In the meantime, he had his own responsibilities to fulfill, the first of which was to warn Cora about Samantha.

The following morning, he visited Randolph in his bedroom to once again offer his apologies and to take his leave.

"Don't give it another thought, old man," Randolph said. "It was as much my fault as yours—as McGrath said, I should have never let you out of my sight."

Elizabeth sat in a chair next to the patient, looking at Zimri as if to say, "You got off lightly, you fool. Now go."

After paying his respects to Mrs. Benson and to Randolph's sisters, Zimri climbed into the carriage that was to take him to the stage depot at Yemassee.

"Marster sho' done walked into that one," Pliny the Elder said as he cracked his whip over the horses' heads.

"What do you mean, Pliny?"

"I means that he got ahead of hisself, and you too, that day ya'll was huntin,' so's he could shoot all them birds hisself and leave you wid none."

Zimri tried to reconstruct the scene in his mind. "You mean he rushed ahead of me just to make me look bad?"

"That's about the size of it," Pliny said. "I seen it before wid other guests. Marster don't like nobody to beat him at nothin.'"

Zimri leaned back in the landau's plush seat and reflected. Well, maybe it wasn't so much his fault after all.

At the Yemassee depot, he gave Pliny a large tip and went into the tavern to purchase a ticket for Beaufort. After waiting for an hour for the next stage, he arrived in Beaufort around noon. He first paid a visit to Sam Chapman.

"What do you know about this Knight girl, Sam?"

"Samantha?" Sam leaned back in his chair and took off his spectacles. "She's a smart girl. Comes from one of the best families in Beaufort County. Why?"

"She works for you?"

"Sometimes. Summers, mostly, when she's home from school. Occasionally sends me a piece about fashions or the theatre when she's in New York."

"Have you read this article of hers about Cora Rinaldi?"

"Cora Rinaldi? The actress?"

"The same."

Sam sat up in his chair and replaced his spectacles. "She's done a couple of pieces on Miss Rinaldi. Theatrical reviews. Seems particularly smitten with the woman. Other than that—"

"She showed me a piece she's working on now while I was at Lynwood."

"And?"

"The basic premise of the story is that Miss Rinaldi is a British spy."

Sam laughed. "And has she got some evidence to support this premise?"

"None. It's pure speculation."

Sam seemed bemused. "Like I said, she's a smart girl. She usually backs up what she says—or writes. What's your concern in this?"

"I just don't want to see you or your paper embarrassed. Much less sued for libel."

Sam regarded him with alarm. "Libel? No, no. We don't want that. You've talked to the girl?"

"Yes. She understands that she's treading on thin ice. Says she'll have to do some more legwork."

"Legwork? I don't think so. This paper is just beginning to show a profit. We couldn't survive a major judgment against us. And this Miss Rinaldi is likely to have the resources to drive us out of the county."

Zimri smiled. "I wouldn't be surprised. You know these New York lawyers—like a pack of hounds cornering a hare."

Sam brooded over this for a few moments and then stood up from his desk. "Thanks for the warning, Zimri. I'll have a talk with the girl. How long are you going to be in town?"

"I'm leaving for Martinville early tomorrow morning."

"So soon? Why don't we step next door and have a drink? It's almost dinner time."

After dinner with Sam, Zimri went to the Beaufort Inn to find Cora. When he approached the reception desk, the proprietress greeted him in her usual cordial manner.

"Mr. Rhodes? Your mother checked out this morning." She handed him an envelope. "She left this for you."

Zimri took the envelope and asked to be seated in the parlor for a cup of coffee. He took a chair by the window facing the river and looked out. It was a gray day and getting grayer. He slit open the envelope with his pen knife and extracted a one-page letter:

6 June, Beaufort

Dearest Zimri:

I regret that I could not remain long enough to enjoy your manly charms as I did that magical evening we shared last week. But duty calls. I have finished my work here and must return to New York for consultation with my business partners. They are a parsimonious lot, and insist upon a strict accounting of my expenditures. Don't they realize that nothing succeeds without money?

I hope that you and Elizabeth have enjoyed your stay at

Lynwood. I have so many memories of that place, both good and bad, that I confess that my feelings about it are such a jumbled confusion that I scarcely know what to make of them. On the one hand, my father, master of more than six hundred slaves, was always very kind to me, and took especial care that I become educated to the highest degree possible. I was an eager and capable student, and I think if we were to meet again today, he would not be disappointed in me.

On the other hand, he, like so many other Southerners of good intention, is caught up in the pestilence that is slavery. Men like my father have grown so dependent upon this odious institution economically as well as psychologically—even their self-esteem is dependent upon it—that they would as soon cut off their right arm as do without it. Therefore, I see little hope for the 'fading away' of this abhorrent practice that you have so often spoken of.

As for Elizabeth: she, too, is caught up in this evil system, though I think she scarcely thinks of it at all. Temperamentally, I think she could as well do without it as with it. She seems, from my brief observation of her behavior and manner, to have little need of the trappings of wealth and privilege that most Southern women do. I could be wrong, but I believe that she could be quite happy living with you in your little log cabin in Martinville for the rest of her days.

As for me, I do not think I could ever live in the South again, whether in a mansion or a shack. Even if slavery were to be abolished tomorrow, I could not live with the whites, who consider me to be black because I exceed the 'one drop' rule, nor could I live with the blacks, who consider me to be 'high yaller,' and therefore not to be trusted. Surely, there is much racial prejudice in the North. But it has never been institutionalized as it has in the South, and there is a greater premium placed on merit than on lineage, especially in New York.

So, darling, what are we to do? You will not leave Martinville, and I cannot leave New York except to pursue my various entrepreneurial projects. And you seem uncomfortable with the idea of dividing your private life into two parts: one for Elizabeth, and one for me. Why must you choose? Most men would find it an ideal situation: a loving and maternal wife to care for hearth and home; and a stylish but discreet mistress who is never jealous, nor demands that you divorce the 'old cow.'

If you must choose, I will understand. But know that whatever

you decide, I will always love you, always need you, always dream
of you awake or asleep.

   So come to me, Zimri. Come to me in New York, or Savannah,
or Martinville. But come to me.

              Au revoir, mon chéri,

                    Cora

   Zimri put the letter into his coat pocket and finished what was left of his coffee. He took a room, had his luggage sent up, and went for a walk along the waterfront. Shrimp boats were returning from the open sea and he sat on the same park bench that he and Cora had sat upon less than a week earlier and watched them for a while. Smoke stacks. Steam engines. Cora was right—steam was the future.

   But the future, however bright, was far away. His current situation was more problematic. Elizabeth seemed on the verge of divorcing him. Cora was a runaway slave, a quadroon (twenty-five times the requirement of the 'one-percent rule'), and was the legal property of the very man who had ensnared his wife as well! Perhaps he could return to New York and marry Cora. What was so wonderful about Martinville, anyway? A sleepy little frontier town. He could sell the newspaper for a princely sum, settle half the proceeds on Elizabeth (as if she would need it!), and remove to New York, where he could use the money to start or purchase another paper. He could live with Cora openly there, married or not.

   But how could he give up little Charlotte, with her blond curls and poor eyesight, and boundless affection for her father? Everyone said she looked more like him than Elizabeth. And Lucky and Fortunata— they would be great beauties like their mother. How could he not be there to witness their unfolding, miraculously, like roses from tiny buds?

   This was a dilemma with which he had never been faced. Of course, there were still many unanswered questions, many possibilities to be played out. There was no solution to be found at the moment.

   He decided to go find Sam and get drunk.

CHAPTER 51

Elizabeth stopped by the kitchen at Lynwood that evening to pick up some broth for Randolph, a practice that had almost become a ritual since the hunting accident. She preferred to take it to him herself because first of all, she felt the cook had a tendency to put too much salt into it and she wanted to test it first; and second, she enjoyed spoon-feeding Randolph as if he were a child. This was not necessary, of course, as Randolph was not so seriously injured that he couldn't feed himself, but it gave her a sense of being needed. Besides, Randolph made the most curious and humorous faces as she did it, as if they were playing a delightful children's game.

As she walked down the long hallway to Randolph's room, she encountered the doctor, who was just leaving.

"How is he, doctor?" she said.

Doctor Fischer, an elderly man with unkempt white hair sticking out in all directions, responded with his usual sarcasm. "How is he? Not well, I'm afraid. The room is too warm, the dancing in the ballroom keeps him awake at all hours, and the oysters sent from the kitchen this morning were not fresh. Nor was the champagne. Past its prime, you know."

"But what about the fever?"

"Fever? Bah! There's no fever. He just needed to open a window, that's all. What's that you're bringing him?"

"The chicken broth that I—"

"Won't hurt him, but he needs something more substantial than that to regain his strength. Bring him some beef and potatoes. Better yet, some of that venison that he had hung up in the smokehouse last week."

"Beef? Venison? Don't you think—"

"If you really want to play nursemaid, Miss—"

"Rhodes. Elizabeth Rhodes."

"If you really want to do some good with that broth you've got there, Miss Rhodes, take it to the old man."

"You mean Mr. Benson?"

"Who else? He needs it far more than his son does, I'm afraid."

"Why? What's the matter with him?"

"Pleurisy. Not to mention pneumonia, palsy, a weak heart, and gout. It's remarkable that he's lasted this long. And with all that, he doesn't whine or complain like his son does."

Elizabeth stood nonplused at the doctor's summation of the two men's condition and temperament. Was Randolph really such a chronic whiner, while his father was the one truly in need of care? She felt foolish standing there in the middle of the hallway holding the tray with broth and sandwiches.

"I'll go wherever I'm most needed, Doctor."

Doctor Fischer looked at her patronizingly. Then he patted her on the shoulder. "You might as well take it to Randolph. The old man is hardly able to lift his head up. Besides, I left him sleeping, which is a major accomplishment in his case. But don't be surprised if you find Randolph a bit distant."

"Distant? What do you mean?"

"It seems that he has brought more than just a few souvenirs from the Orient home with him. Good night, Miss Rhodes."

Elizabeth watched as the doctor walked briskly down the hall, swinging his medical bag like a basket laden with freshly picked apples. What an odd man!

She approached Randolph's door and knocked lightly. She heard a low murmur and slowly opened the door. There was Randolph's immense bed with pictures of hunting scenes on either side, a musket propped in the corner, and vases of flowers on tables and bureaus. The damask curtains were pulled tightly so that only a few rays of the evening sun streamed through, casting patches of light on the oriental rugs.

Sitting upright in the bed, pillows between his back and the headboard, was Randolph. His head was covered with a sort of fez, she thought it was called, with a single tassel hanging down at one side. He was wearing a silk smoking jacket with a beautiful oriental design of flowers, birds, and fire-breathing dragons. A long clay pipe extended from his mouth, and he was sucking on it rhythmically with his eyes closed.

"Randolph?" He made no sign of recognition at first, save for a fluttering of the eyelids, which closed again.

"Randolph, I've brought you your broth and some finger sandwiches."

Randolph made no sign or sound.

She gently closed the door behind her and approached the bed. He lay perfectly still except for short, shallow breaths as he inhaled the smoke, which escaped through his nostrils when it escaped at all.

She placed the tray down on the night table next to his bed.

"Randolph, Doctor Fischer says that—"

Randolph's eye lids half-opened and his eyes vaguely focused on her. "Fischer...is an idiot."

"Oh, Randolph, I don't think so. He seems to know—"

"The Orient is far ahead of us in so many ways, Elizabeth." He patted a spot on the bed next to him. "Come sit beside me...here."

"Well...all right. If it'll make you feel better."

"Yes...it will."

She approached his side of the bed cautiously, as if he were a wounded animal in the forest.

He put down his pipe on the nightstand next to a plate of white crystalline powder surrounded by spent matches.

"Randolph, are you sure it's good for you to be smoking? Dr. Fischer says—"

Randolph exhaled slowly, and suddenly clutched his side.

"Oh, I'm sorry. It must hurt." She sat down on the bed and adjusted a pillow that supported his head. He closed his eyes for a moment, apparently in some pain, and then opened them again. At closer quarters, they appeared to be bloodshot, the pupils contracted to the size of pinholes.

"Did Dr. Fischer give you some morphine? You seem to be drowsy. Perhaps—"

Randolph put his arm around her waist. "'In Xanadu did Kubla Khan a stately pleasure dome decree...'"

"You've been reading poetry again. What is that from?"

"'Where Alph the sacred river ran'...Come lie beside me, Elizabeth."

She hesitated. "What if someone should come in and—"

"No one enters my room without knocking...I want you here, beside me."

"Well...all right." She cautiously lay down beside him, his arm now around her shoulders.

"'A damsel with a dulcimer in a vision once I saw...'"

"What is that from, Randolph? It's beautiful."

"'It was an Abyssinian maid, and on her dulcimer played...' The pain is gone. You see, Elizabeth, your mere presence has alleviated my pain."

She smiled. "I'm so glad, Randolph. I wanted to be of comfort to you."

He rose up from his pillow. "Yes. Yes, you are a great comfort to me." He kissed her full on the mouth. Surprised, she pulled away, but he seized her arm, and pulled her to him.

"Randolph! You're hurting me. You mustn't—"

"You are my Abyssinian maid, Elizabeth. I've waited for you...and waited...and now that you've sent Zimri away there's nothing to—"

She wrenched her arm loose. "I didn't send him away! I merely told him I would stay here as long as I was needed. But it seems that you are making a miraculous recovery." She tried to get off the bed, but Randolph pulled her back.

"You will not deny me, Elizabeth! No, not this time. Now you belong to me."

"Belong to you? Let me go, Randolph!"

Randolph's grip tightened around her arm and he flung her down onto her back and rolled on top of her. She tried to push him off, but he was too strong for her. As he raised up slightly and slipped his hand beneath her dress, she hit his injured shoulder as hard as she could with her fist. He cried out in pain and rolled off of her.

She leaped off the bed and ran for the door.

"Elizabeth! I command you to come here—"

She jerked at the handle of the door but the door did not move.

"Elizabeth...don't go. I need you..."

She jerked the lever in the opposite direction and the door opened. It was heavy, heavier than she ever remembered it being, but finally it swung open and she ran down the corridor to the stairs, where she almost collided with a servant carrying a tray of cordials.

Once inside her own room, Elizabeth slammed the door shut and locked it. Then she threw herself on the bed and cried.

After a half-hour she turned onto her back and wiped the tears from her eyes. She stared for sometime at the blue liner on the underside of the canopy. What had she done? She *had* sent Zimri away, as if he were no more than an awkward suitor whose company she had tired of. Her lawful husband! And the kindest man in the world. Now he was gone and could no longer protect her from this...this monster. Yes. Zimri was right, Randolph was a kind of monster—a rapist, he said—who lived only for pleasure. How could she have been so deaf, so stupid, so naïve? And that white powder...what was it? Of course—opium.

Poor Zimri! How she had misused him. How much wiser he was than she! That was one reason she had married him—-he was older, more experienced, wise to the base, even the depraved, instincts of men. For that was what Randolph was—depraved.

She sat up in the bed and looked around the room. Her clothes were strewn about—upon Zimri's departure, she had immediately become more careless, even sloppy. The trunk sat in a corner with its lid open. She could leave tomorrow morning—no, tonight. She wouldn't be able to sleep a wink in any case. Perhaps Pliny would drive her into Beaufort where she could get a room and then set out for Martinville first thing in the morning. She went to her trunk and began throwing dresses and petticoats into it without regard to whether they would wrinkle or be crushed.

In minutes she was packed. She looked in the mirror, brushed her hair and put on a bonnet that she cinched beneath her chin. And, oh, yes, a shawl. It was warm out, but the breezes coming off the water could be quite cool.

She rang for a servant and then sat down on the lid of her trunk and waited...and waited.

She looked at the clock on the mantelpiece. Six-forty-five. She had been waiting now for ten minutes. It had never taken more than five for a servant to answer her ring since she had arrived. The house slaves were wonderfully efficient at Lynwood. Strange. She got up and pulled the bell cord again and went to the window. The sun had gone behind the house and there was still enough light to see the carriages parked in the driveway, but they were all askew, the horses apparently wandering in search of fodder without servants to attend them.

What was happening?

She opened the huge mahogany door and ventured out into the hallway, where she saw Jane looking first one way, then another. Other guests began stepping out into the hall as well.

"Jane?" she said.

"In all of my days at Lynwood," Jane said, wringing her hands, "this has never happened. Please forgive me, all of you. I'll go downstairs and see what could have become of the servants."

Jane then hurried to the staircase and soon disappeared from sight.

Elizabeth and two or three of the other guests remained standing in the hallway, unsure of what to do.

"Could they all have gotten sick at the same time?" one woman said, a cousin of Randolph's from Charleston.

It suddenly dawned on Elizabeth what had happened. But she decided to keep it to herself so as not to alarm the others. "Perhaps they all went to a revival meeting or something of that sort. There must have been some misunderstanding about—"

"Revival meeting? On Monday night? Oh, dear! It's a slave revolt! We'll all be murdered in our beds! Harold! Harold!" And the cousin ran into her room and slammed the door shut.

Elizabeth heard a loud clink as the bolt locked into place. Others in the hallway looked equally alarmed, and followed suit. She found herself alone in the hall, but her curiosity got the better of her fear. She walked cautiously to the end of the hall where there was an alcove with a small window within it overlooking the west lawn. She looked out.

The rays of the setting sun cast enough light on the lawn that she could see all the way down to the river bank. There were several white men on the dock, accompanied by a few black men—one of whom she recognized by his tall stature and white hair—Pliny. The white men, it appeared, were Randolph's brothers, Edward and Harry. Edward seemed to be pointing downriver towards Beaufort. Then he strode towards the house, with the others following.

Not a revolt, but an escape! Just like the one at Belle Oaks. At least they were not attacking their masters. She made her way quickly back to her room and locked herself in.

CHAPTER 52

Zimri awoke the next morning with a throbbing headache, but was nevertheless obliged to meet the stage in front of the Beaufort Inn at dawn. Breakfast consisted of more ham and eggs than he felt like eating, and several cups of coffee.

He was not a drinker. And this warm summer morning with dark clouds already threatening with distant thunder reminded him of why. It simply wasn't worth it. Sam was much more accustomed to it. He seemed to put away several whiskeys before dinner each day without it affecting his work.

And he had accomplished nothing. The same dilemma was there when he awoke as when he went to bed the night before. What would he do about Elizabeth? That is, assuming that he could do anything. If she refused to return to Martinville except to collect the children and her meager belongings, there wasn't much he could do.

He felt better by the time the stage arrived in Savannah, though the thunderstorms washed out the road and prevented them entering the city by the usual route. A good meal at the hotel revived his spirits and he spent the remainder of the evening reading *Farquhar's Low Country Architecture* and turned in early.

It wasn't until he got to Dublin, after three and a half days on the road, that he overheard a passenger speaking of a slave escape near Beaufort.

"Two hundred and fifty of 'em—but they killed six or seven and captured another dozen or so."

Zimri was sitting alone at a nearby table reading a two-day-old copy of the *Georgia Journal*.

"Either these niggers are gettin' smarter," the man's companion said, "or somebody's helping them. You say two hundred of them got clean away?"

"More like two-thirty, I'd say."

"How'd they do it?"

"Most of 'em by steamboat. Sailed down the Combahee River to St. Helena Sound, picking up plantation niggers along the way at pre-determined points. Highly organized."

Zimri scanned the *Journal* for any mention of this, and found none.

"That's what I'm talking about," the second man said. "Niggers ain't smart enough to do that. Some white man had to help 'em."

"White woman, you mean."

"Woman?"

"One of the ones captured was a white woman dressed up like a little old lady. They say she was the ringleader."

Zimri's ears pricked up.

"You don't say," the second man said. "I knew it! Who is she? Where did she come from?"

"Yankee. That's all I heard. Probably one of those nigger-lovin' abolitionists from Boston."

"A woman, though—imagine that! How did the rest of 'em get away?"

"A cutter waitin' for 'em off Lady's Island. Gone before anyone could call the militia out."

"I'm telling you," the second man said, "it ain't right. These Yankees coming down here and stealing our property."

"It's gonna lead to war if you ask me. North and South are like night and day. They don't understand the niggers like we do. They're like children."

"Ornery children if you ask me. Innkeeper! Two more whiskeys."

Zimri was more perplexed than ever. Cora captured! Was she hurt? Where did they take her? Should he turn around and head back to Beaufort? If he did so, what could he accomplish?

He folded up his newspaper, finished his coffee and went to his room, where he tried to distract himself by reading his book on architecture. But he found he couldn't concentrate. And when he came across a paragraph about Antonio Rinaldi, he lay the book face down on the nightstand next to his bed, put his hands behind his head, and stared at the by now familiar picture on the wall depicting a dozen or more black slaves picking cotton on a plantation.

He had to do something. But what? Well, he was almost to Martinville now—he would be home tomorrow afternoon. He would need more information about the escape—and Cora's capture, particularly, before he could take any action. Besides, the children were no doubt wondering if their father would ever come home. He pictured Charlotte running up the front walk with open arms to greet him. Yes, he must see about the children first.

The next morning the stage got off a little late due to a thunderstorm, but soon he was on his way home. Several of the passengers had apparently heard the news of the events in Beaufort and seemed to be able to talk of nothing else.

"I think it's disgraceful," one woman said. Zimri recognized her as the wife of a dry goods merchant, but did not know her name. "There should be stricter laws about Negroes moving about."

"What do you propose, Mrs. Sinclair?" one gentleman said. "That they should be chained to posts, or caged like animals?"

"I'm proposing nothing of the kind, Mr., ah—"

"Barley. Edwin Barley."

"Mr. Barley. I should think that curfews and passes would be enough."

"We have that now," Mr. Barley said. "It seems to have little deterrent value—at least to organized rebellions or escapes such as we have just heard about."

"Well, then," Mrs. Sinclair said, "perhaps we should issue passports to Yankees. They seem to be the ones instigating these outrages."

"Passports?" Mr. Barley said. "Now there's an interesting idea. Every American required to carry a passport in order to cross state lines? The Jacobins adopted a similar measure during the French Revolution—the ultimate destination of most travelers seemed to be the guillotine."

"Bah!" Mrs. Sinclair said. "You're just being contrary, Mr. Bailey. What would you suggest?"

Mr. Barley, a well-dressed gentleman of about fifty with well-manicured nails and a silver-headed cane that he seemed to use as a theatrical prop rather than as a necessary support, remained silent for a few moments. "I would suggest that the Federal government compensate the slave owners—after all, there are relatively few of them—and send the Negroes back to Africa where they belong."

Mrs. Sinclair laughed. "That's hardly original, Mr. Barley. It has been suggested innumerable times and each time it has been dismissed as unworkable, not to mention exorbitantly expensive. And of course it would utterly ruin the Southern economy. Why, you sound like an abolitionist yourself!"

"That I am, Mrs. Sinclair."

"I thought so! So you see, you should be required to carry a passport yourself—or perhaps denied one at the Mason-Dixon Line. Where are you from, may I ask?"

"Thomasville."

"And what do you do there?"

"Farm."

"I don't suppose you own slaves."

"Actually, I do. About three hundred."

Mrs. Sinclair seemed taken aback. "And what would you do without them?"

"Farm."

Mrs. Sinclair looked as if she had been insulted and turned away to stare out the window. "You are a strange man, Mr. Barley."

"So I've been told."

Zimri found this conversation to be amusing, but chose not to join in. Instead, he followed Mrs. Sinclair's lead and turned to stare out the window. The skies were clearing, the road was improving, and he could see the spire of the new church steeple at the top of Mulberry Street sparkling in the sunlight.

CHAPTER 53

The stage pulled up in front of the Central Hotel about four o'clock in the afternoon and Zimri opened the door and stepped into the muddy, rutted street almost before it stopped. He gave a quarter to the doorman and asked him to set his trunk aside to be picked up later. Then he crossed Mulberry Street, avoiding the puddles as best he could and made his way to the office.

Jed was out in the field working on a story, according to Peter, who had lately been promoted to office manager. A third employee, Jason, was now doing Peter's former job in the pressroom.

"Everything all right, Peter?"

"With the *Mercury*, you mean?"

Zimri thought this was a curious answer. "Yes, I mean the news-paper."

"Oh, yes, sir. Everything's just fine. Ten new subscriptions this week."

"Good. Very good. I think I'll take the gig and go see my children, then come back and catch up with things."

"Your children? Oh…all right."

Zimri stared at Peter for a moment. He seemed to be nervous, evasive. "The children are all right, aren't they?"

"As far as I know, Mr. Rhodes. Well, actually, I heard Jed say something about little Lucky being sick…I think."

Zimri chose not to question Peter any further, but left by the back door and got into the gig. After picking up his trunk at the hotel he headed for home.

He was greeted by Solomon who seemed troubled as he took the reins of the gig.

"What's the matter, Solomon? Is something wrong with Lucky?"

Solomon cast his eyes to the ground. "Don't know how to tell you this, Massa Zimri. But Lucky, she's—"

Zimri didn't wait for Solomon to finish his sentence, but hurried up the walk to the front porch where Betty stood with tears in her eyes, wiping them away with her apron.

"Don't know how it happened, Massa Zimri," Betty said. "Tried to wake her along with Fortunata and—"

Zimri pushed past her and into the hearth room. There was Char-lotte, playing with a toy he had made for her. She looked up, smiled broadly, and rose unsteadily to her feet. He picked her up and kissed her, and then carried her into the bedroom. Betty, Louise, and Tessie all followed.

He saw Fortunata on her back in the crib, apparently just waking up from a nap. But he did not see Lucky.

"Where is she?" he said.

"There, Mr. Rhodes," Louise said. "There in the little pine box."

He gave Charlotte to Louise, and went to the corner of the room where Elizabeth kept her desk. There, to the far side of it, was the pine box that Louise described, with a black muslin curtain draped about it like a tent. He pulled back the curtain and looked inside the box.

Lucky was lying face-up, her eyes closed, her skin gray. She was already beginning to emit an unpleasant odor. Zimri closed the curtain carefully and looked at the three women standing before him

"When?" he said.

"Yesterday, Massa Zimri," Betty said. "Louise came in to see about 'em early in the mawnin' and Lucky jest warn't breathin' none. We done tried everything we knows how to do, but—"

"Did anyone go for a doctor?"

"Yes, suh," Betty said. "Solomon went tearin' into town and found Doc Parcher tendin' somebody with a broke leg and he come in twenty minutes. But it be too late."

"Did he say how it happened?"

All three women shook their heads.

"He must have some idea. Some theory—"

The women simply looked down at the floor until Tessie put Charlotte down, raised her head and spoke. "Doc Parcher says she might have rolled onto her stomach and put her face in the pillow. But she's not as strong as Fortunata, he says, and she might not have been able to roll onto her back again when her breathing stopped."

Zimri stared at Tessie for a moment, then at the other two women, who avoided his gaze. "Three of you. All three of you were here, and no one checked to see if the twins were safe and well?"

The three women simply shrugged and continued staring at the floor.

"Doc Parcher say it ain't no one's fault," Betty said. "We done tried, Massa Rhodes—"

But Zimri didn't allow Betty to finish her sentence and stormed out of the room, pushing her roughly aside. Then he went out onto the front porch, sat down on the swing, and cried.

After a few minutes he looked up to see Charlotte standing in front of him, her arms around his knees. "Don't cry, Daddy. Lucky's gone to Heaven."

This made him start crying again, but he wiped his tears away and picked Charlotte up and set her down in his lap. "That's right, Charlotte. Your little sister's gone to Heaven."

"Betty says she'll be happy there."

"I'm sure she will." He hugged Charlotte tightly and looked out at his rose garden. The flowers were in full bloom, his hybrids displaying a rainbow of colors.

The child looked up at him imploringly. "Where's Mommy?"

"She's coming along soon. She had some business to tend to in South Carolina." He looked over his shoulder and saw Betty standing in the doorway, tears in her eyes. "Betty, you'd better take Charlotte and give her some supper. I've got to go back to town."

"Yes, suh."

He kissed Charlotte on the cheek, placed her on her feet, and stood. "I'll arrange for the funeral tomorrow afternoon. We'll have it right here."

"Yes, suh. We'll all be here wid you."

"Sorry for my outburst—I know it wasn't your fault."

"No, suh. Twarn't nobody's fault. God done chose to take her now, 'stead of later. He got his reasons."

"I suppose he does. But it's hard for me just now to imagine what those reasons are."

"Yes, suh. I knows how you feel. I lost two babies my ownself. Don't seem like they's no sense in it. But I still got them two."

Zimri noticed for the first time that Betty's children, Aaron and Sally, were standing at the edge of the veranda staring at him with enormous brown eyes. He smiled at them and they smiled back. "And I have two remaining as well."

Betty smiled. "Yes, suh. And fine chillun they are, too. Come here, little Charlotte—yo' Daddy's got business to tend to. I'll make you a nice pot pie for supper."

Zimri took the gig back to town, but took the long way, along the river. He drove slowly, and Jupiter seemed content with the pace. The river was no longer swollen and rushing downstream as it was in the spring, in spite of the recent rains. The air was cool near the riverbank, and he stopped just south of the wharf. There were four steamboats plying the river now, with one loading and another headed downriver. The one at the wharf was the *General*

Oglethorpe. The other was too far away to read the name. What would happen to Cora's steamboat empire? The company had pretty much run itself in her absence, and he supposed it would keep on going. There was a board of directors, after all.

Oh, what a mess it had all come to! Cora captured and languishing in some jail—or perhaps sent back to Lynwood. Lynwood—the name was becoming synonymous in his mind with Hades. He should have shot Randolph in earnest. The thought of him putting his hands on Cora...Elizabeth. What's become of Elizabeth? Her child dead. She knows nothing about it yet. Is this what it would take for her to come to her senses? Is this 'God's reason,' as Betty suggested?

He snapped the reins and Jupiter started moving again. He didn't really believe in God, now did he? At least not in the conventional sense. Perhaps he was a Deist, like Washington and Jefferson. God, or some supernatural force, created the universe and then moved on. Indifferent to our fate, to human suffering.

He stopped by the undertaker's and made arrangements for the funeral. Then he went to the office, where he found Jed just back from his self-imposed assignment.

"Sorry about Lucky, Mr. Rhodes," Jed said. Peter was standing beside him, his head hanging.

"Couldn't be helped, Jed. Or at least so it seems."

"I'm sorry, too, Mr. Rhodes," Peter said. "I just didn't know how to tell you when you walked in the door."

"I understand, Peter. It's not an easy thing to do. Tell me what you've been up to, Jed. I'm about two weeks behind on things."

"I just got back from Milledgeville, Mr. Rhodes."

"And?"

"The state legislature just passed a whole passel of laws clamping down on blacks."

"Slave or free?"

"Both."

"They've heard about the escape in South Carolina?"

"Yes, sir. That and others. And about Miss Rinaldi."

"Miss Rinaldi? They think she's the one who directed these adventures?"

"Yes, sir. But not 'think.' They know."

"And how do they know?"

"Seems one of the posse members pulled off her wig and recognized her as Cora Benson—an escaped slave."

Zimri sighed. He knew what the next revelation would be and he hoped it would be the last of the day. "And?"

"They sent her back to where she came from—a plantation called Lynwood."

Zimri pulled out the chair to his desk and sat down. "You've done your homework, Jed. Got your notes with you?"

"Yes, sir. Right there on your desk."

Zimri surveyed the stack of papers on his desk. He picked one up and scanned it. "All right. Let's get to work."

CHAPTER 54

Elizabeth was not fond of traveling alone. There were so many dangers, so many men who regarded a lone woman as fair game, married or not. She tried to display her wedding ring at every opportunity and made a point of introducing herself as 'Mrs.' Elizabeth Rhodes, but some of the men she encountered, both on the stage and in the inns, seemed either not to notice or not to care.

She was relieved when the stage arrived in Dublin and the proprietor of the tavern recognized the name on the register.

"Oh, Mrs. Rhodes," he said. "Your husband was just here day before yesterday."

"I'm glad to hear it," she said. "He left a day or two ahead of me because I had...some business to attend to. He looked well?"

"Oh, yes ma'am. Kept to himself, though. Seems to be a great reader."

Elizabeth smiled. "Yes, he is, isn't he? He's a newspaperman." The proprietor chuckled. "I should have known. Read every newspaper in the place. Even the ones a week old. Would you like to have his room?"

She hesitated a moment. "Yes. Yes, I would."

The proprietor handed a key to an earnest-looking young man who picked up her bags and escorted her to the room. She gave him a tip and when he had left, she removed her bonnet, sat in a chair and removed her boots, which were muddy from the rains.

She loosened her corset, exhaled, and leaned back in the chair. She was exhausted from the day's journey, what with the intermittent rain, the fording of two rivers, the incessant bumping of the stage whenever it wasn't stuck in mud, and the unwelcome advances of a corpulent and particularly unattractive man who said he was a riverboat gambler and kept drinking from a flask all the way to Dublin. She hoped she wouldn't encounter him at supper.

She opened her eyes after a few minutes, surprised that she hadn't fallen asleep—or had she?—and found herself looking at a painting of slaves picking cotton in a field. It made her think of Lynwood.

What a nightmare! The eerie scene of Randolph smoking opium in his bedroom pushed its way into her consciousness, followed by images of a dozen slaves shackled together and being herded like animals into a hog pen. She couldn't get the downcast expressions, the matted and mud-caked hair, the lacerated and bleeding backs, out of her mind. What miserable creatures they were! Nothing like the happy, contented, and smiling faces in the picture.

And Randolph, sobered by this time from his narcotic stupor—for it was the next morning—snatching a whip from one of his overseers and brutally whipping one of the recaptured slaves, who turned out to be one of Pliny's sons—Pliny the Younger. Poor Pliny—he wept and pleaded with Randolph until finally Randolph grew tired of swinging the heavy bull whip. She almost felt guilty about asking him to drive her to the Yemassee station to catch the stage to Savannah.

How wrong she had been about Randolph! Fortunately, he was so angry about the slave escape—Pliny said more than fifty from Lynwood alone had eluded the posse—that he hardly paid any attention to her when she said she must leave.

"Go on," he said. "Join your cowardly husband. Things will be right again here at Lynwood soon enough. And then you can choose."

She had said that she had already made her choice, but Randolph only laughed and strode back to the house to finish his breakfast.

She decided to skip supper so as to avoid the riverboat gambler. Besides, she really wasn't very hungry. She got up and locked the door and proceeded to undress down to her underclothes. She sat on the bed and looked around for something to read. She wished she had purchased a book in Savannah but hadn't because she was still reading yet another Jane Austen novel and finished that one by the time they had arrived at Jenk's Bridge, twenty miles from the city.

She looked in the drawer of the bedside table and discovered a thick volume, prettily bound, entitled *Farquhar's Low Country Architecture*. She opened the cover and, on the frontispiece, there was a familiar signature: Zimri Rhodes.

It was just like Zimri—he was becoming more and more absent-minded, it seemed. He needed looking after. She turned the pages slowly and imagined that she could feel the warmth of his hands on each leaf. She hardly looked at the beautiful engravings depicting the great mansions of South Carolina, including Lynwood. It was the knowledge that Zimri had cradled this book lovingly—for he did love books almost as much as his roses—only hours before that calmed and soothed her until she at last fell asleep.

The next morning she awoke refreshed and eager to get home. It was only fifty miles, and the dark clouds of the day before gave way to bright sunshine and blue skies. The riverboat gambler's drinking seemed to have finally caught up with him and he slept like a baby all the way to Martinville.

Babies! She couldn't wait to see her own. Charlotte, who was nearsighted but quite bright for her age; Lucky, frail but with an already precocious and charming personality; and Fortunata, the boisterous and most energetic of the three. How different they all were in personality and temperament! She considered herself to be lucky to be only nineteen and already the mother of three beautiful, healthy children. Perhaps she would have more, but not too many. Three or four were enough. She didn't intend to become a baby factory, as delightful as the little darlings were. There were things to be done in Martinville, a city to be built! The library foundation, the new college that was being talked about—certainly she would want to get involved in that—the Horticultural Society that Zimri was forming that would include the building of parks and public gardens; the possibilities were endless! And how much more exciting and stimulating than being the mistress of a plantation, with servants waiting on one hand and foot so that one didn't have to lift a finger except to remove a canapé from a silver tray. No wonder Mrs. Benson was such a dullard—there was nothing for her to do.

She looked out the window of the stage as it rounded a bend and the town of Martinville, with its prominent new church steeple, came into sight. This was a real homecoming; she had defected, in a way, allowed herself to go astray and be seduced by the false promise of a glamorous life in another world she knew little about. If only Zimri would forgive her and take her back. Oh, she had been so obtuse! So absolutely rude and insensitive to her loving and caring husband!...yes, he had gone astray, too. That was a fact. But he had freely admitted it and asked for her forgiveness and she had coldly refused. What a ninny she was!

The stage pulled up to the Central Hotel and the porters took down her bags and her trunk. She tipped them and asked the doorman to summon a hackney, of which there were only two in Martinville. The sleepy driver finally pulled up in front of the hotel and with the help of one of the porters, loaded everything into his cab.

"You're Mrs. Rhodes, ain't you?" The driver said as they turned around and headed for the house.

"Yes, I am," she said proudly.

"My condolences, ma'am. I know it must be hard."

She looked at the driver as if he must have mixed her up with another Mrs. Rhodes—or Rose, or Roach. "Condolences? Why, you must be mistaken—I've had no misfortune to—"

"No? Oh, well, then. I beg your pardon, ma'am. Best keep my big yap shut."

The driver did not say another word as they traveled the last few blocks to the house. Her high spirits were suddenly deflated as she wondered what on earth could have prompted him to offer his 'condolences.' Was he simply illiterate and didn't know the meaning of the word?

As the cab pulled up in front of the house, it suddenly occurred to her that something might have happened to Zimri. Did he have an accident between Dublin and Martinville?

The man, who was not young, struggled with the luggage until Solomon appeared and picked the trunk up and balanced it on one hand like a waiter carrying a tray.

"Welcome home, Miz Lizbeth." He said this without his usual broad smile and good cheer.

"Is there something wrong, Solomon?"

"Wrong?" Solomon looked at the driver, who was waiting for his tip. "Not exactly, Miz Lizbeth. I mean some things ain't right—I'd better let Massa Zimri explain it to you."

She looked at him with a puzzled expression and tipped the driver, who drove off. So Zimri is all right...

Solomon led the way up the path to the house and suddenly Charlotte appeared at the door. Elizabeth stooped and extended her arms as Charlotte ran towards her.

"Mommy! Mommy's here!"

"Hello, Precious! Did you miss me?" She picked up Charlotte in her arms and kissed her. "Is Daddy home?"

"Hello, Elizabeth." Zimri stood in the doorway in shirtsleeves and his tie loosened. He held a tumbler of whiskey in his hand.

"Zimri? Is something wrong? I know you weren't expecting me so soon—"

"No. But I'm glad you're here. Come in and sit down. You must be tired from the journey. Solomon, take Mrs. Rhodes' things to the bedroom."

"Yes, suh."

Solomon walked quickly through the open doorway with the trunk, leaving Zimri and Elizabeth standing on the porch looking at each other.

"I've missed you, Zimri."

"I've missed you, too."

"Can you forgive me for being so foolish?"

"I can. But you'd better come inside...I've got something to tell you that will come as a shock."

She stood staring at him for a moment. "The twins?"

Zimri nodded. "Lucky."

She put her palms to her face. "She's ...dead?"

"I'm afraid so. In her sleep. Two days ago."

She went numb. She could feel the blood drain from her face. "Where is she?"

"Buried next to the barn. The funeral was yesterday. We couldn't wait any longer."

She allowed her hands to fall from her face. Her shoulders drooped. And that was the last thing she remembered.

CHAPTER 55

Elizabeth awoke to find herself lying in her bed looking up at the exposed timbers of the house. It was quite a change from looking at the high smooth ceilings at Lynwood first thing in the morning. And of course there was no canopy on the bed here, and few pictures on the walls.

"Elizabeth?"

She turned her head and saw Zimri's face, his eyes fixed on hers, his large hands covering hers like two enormous mittens. The revelations upon her arrival now rushed back into her consciousness.

"Where is Fortunata?" she said.

"Here. In her crib."

"Hand her to me."

Betty was standing nearby and picked up the baby and handed her to Zimri, who then carefully set her beside Elizabeth.

She began to cry.

"Shh!" Elizabeth said. She pulled Fortunata close to her and immediately the child stopped crying. "She's grown fatter."

"Yessum," Betty said with a smile. "She's been eatin' solid foods since you left for South Carolina."

"If only I had never left."

Betty's smile evaporated and the entire company, including Tessie and Louise, fell silent for some moments.

"Speaking of food," Zimri said, "you should eat something."

"I'm not at all hungry, Zimri. Could I see the grave?"

She handed Fortunata to Betty, who put her down on her back in the crib. The child seemed to be fast asleep.

Tessie took Charlotte, who had been watching wide-eyed all this time, by the hand. "Come on, Charlotte—let's play hide-and-seek."

At the grave site, which consisted of a plain wooden cross with Lucky's name on it and the dates of her birth and death, Elizabeth bent down and placed a single rose on the freshly turned earth. "Goodbye, darling."

For the first time since she heard the news, she began to cry. Zimri put his arm around her shoulder and escorted her back to the house.

"Can't we get a stone marker of some kind?" she said.

"I've already ordered one from Jim Grimes. It'll be ready in a day or two."

"That's good."

They went to the front porch and sat on the swing until the sun went down. Neither spoke until Betty called them to supper.

Elizabeth still didn't feel much like eating, but Zimri persuaded her to make the attempt. She had lost several pounds on the trip home.

After supper, they returned to the porch and sat again on the swing. It was a cloudless, moonlit night, and the stars seemed to burst out at them like fireworks.

"It's a beautiful night," Zimri said.

"Yes," she said. "Isn't it? How strange that such beauty can follow such...sadness."

"There will always be the two—happiness and pain. There's no separating them for any length of time."

They remained in silence for several minutes, gazing at the stars.

"Zimri?"

"Yes, Elizabeth."

"You were right about Randolph."

"Doesn't surprise me."

"I was just angry at you, I think."

"With good reason."

They fell silent again for some moments.

"You've heard about the slave escape?" she said.

"Yes."

"I saw him whip Pliny's son."

"Oh?"

"There was no need for it. The son was in chains, exhausted from running through the swamp all night. Randolph seemed to enjoy it."

"That doesn't surprise me, either." Zimri pulled a cigar out of his shirt pocket. "Do you mind if I smoke?"

"No, of course not."

Zimri lit the cigar and took a few puffs. "They're nasty things, but they seem to relax me lately."

"I don't mind. The ones you smoke smell like cherry. What do you call them?"

"Cheroots." He laughed. "Not really a proper cigar."

She took his hand and placed it in hers. "I'm glad—I can't stand the proper ones."

They sat enjoying the moonlight for another quarter of an hour without speaking.

"Zimri?"

"Yes, my darling?"

"Do you want to have more children?"

Zimri did not respond at first, taking several puffs on his cigar. "Do you?"

"I don't know."

"Plenty of time to decide."

"Yes...that's what we need now—time." She laid her head against his shoulder and closed her eyes. It seemed to her that the nearness of his body had never been so comforting as it was now. This man, this good man, who had given her children seemed to be the only person on earth who truly cared for her, who understood her crazy swings of mood, who could forgive her for almost anything.

Suddenly she opened her eyes and raised her head. She looked into his eyes.

"What is it, Elizabeth?"

"I didn't sleep with Randolph."

Zimri stared at her for a moment in apparent wonder, then smiled. "It didn't occur to me that you had."

"Not even for a moment?"

He puffed on his cigar. "Well, perhaps for a moment. You're a very attractive woman. And considering all that Randolph has to offer, the temptation must have been great."

She laid her head again on his shoulder. "Not so great. Mere baubles and bombast."

Zimri laughed. "Baubles and bombast. You may have the makings of a poet in you, Elizabeth."

Later, while they were preparing for bed, Elizabeth remembered that she had recovered Zimri's book on architecture. She reached into her valise and extracted it while Zimri was putting on his nightshirt.

"Did you forget something at Yopp's Tavern, Zimri?"

"Forget something? No, I don't think so."

"Are you sure?"

Zimri pulled the nightshirt over his head and looked at the book in her hand. "Farquhar's book on architecture. Where did you find it?"

"In the drawer beside the bed. They put me in the same room."

Zimri took the book and opened it. "At least I remembered to put my name in it."

"It's a beautiful book."

"Yes, it is. I bought it for the engravings, really."

She sat before the mirror and unpinned her hair. "Perhaps it will give you some ideas. We could expand this house someday. Or perhaps build a new one."

"Yes. I was thinking of that."

Elizabeth imagined a large house with tall columns and a grand staircase, with a library for Zimri and a nursery for...her eyes caught the reflection of the crib, which was built for two, but only Fortunata lay on one side sleeping. She stared at the empty side for a moment and burst into tears.

Zimri came to her side and seemed to immediately understand what had happened. He sat on the bench next to her and put his arms around her. "Go ahead and cry, Elizabeth. A loss like this won't be gotten over in a single evening, or month, or year, try as we might."

She returned his embrace with all her strength, as if she would slip into oblivion otherwise. "Oh, Zimri don't ever leave me—I couldn't bear life for a minute without you."

"Nor could I without you."

CHAPTER 56

Zimri sat at his desk at the *Mercury* working on an editorial for the next issue. It was a clear, warm day and he would much have preferred to be home cultivating his roses, but this particular editorial seemed urgent. It was his way of dealing with the events of the past week or so, but it was larger than that, larger than his own experience, and he wasn't so sure that he wasn't pushing this thing too far. He would have to have Jed read it over for his opinion.

As he leaned back in his chair to read over the piece, there was a sudden banging of the front door. The way his office was partitioned off now he couldn't see who had just come in. He would have to see about putting a window into the partition.

"Zimri!"

He looked up to see Elizabeth standing in front of his desk with a rolled up newspaper in her hand. She slapped it down on his desk, whereupon it flopped open to the front page. It was the latest issue of his rival's paper, the *Patriot*. The banner headline read:

MISS RINALDI A RUNAWAY SLAVE!

"Did you know about this?" Elizabeth said.

Zimri picked up the newspaper and scanned the article. "Yes. Yes, I did. Jed told me when I returned to town."

"Then why didn't you tell me? And why isn't it on the front page of the *Mercury*?"

"I didn't think it concerned you. Besides, the news about Lucky..."

Elizabeth took off her sun hat and hung it on the coat rack next to the door. She sat down in the chair opposite his desk. "Of course I was upset about Lucky, but you should have told me. This is something that *does* concern me."

"In what way?"

"In what way? Why, Zimri, you're being as inscrutable as a sphinx. You know in what way."

"I'm not sure I do. Cora has turned out to be something other than what she purported to be. A mulatto. A slave. A runaway. And it seems that she ran away from Lynwood—many years ago."

Elizabeth stared at him with a look of incredulity. "Zimri—she's made half the town of Martinville rich. She's made you rich."

Zimri chuckled. "Hardly. I've only got a few shares in the company."

"Well, nevertheless, she's made you richer. And now she's in the clutches of that fiend Randolph. We have to *do* something for the poor woman."

"What would you suggest?"

Elizabeth cast her eyes about the room as if the answer to this question were lying atop a book or a newspaper. "I don't know...but *something*. Can't you write to the Governor?"

"Of South Carolina?"

"Yes, of course."

"What would I say to him? That he should emancipate a runaway slave who has stage-managed the escape of hundreds of others? I don't think he would be moved."

She stared at him for a moment. "Don't you feel the slightest responsibility to do something for her?"

Zimri stared back for a moment and then placed the draft of his editorial on the desk. "This is all I know to do."

Elizabeth looked at the draft in Zimri's hand, which was in his clear, fine script, and began reading:

Slavery: An Abomination Not Worthy of a Civilized Society

The recent capture of Miss Cora Rinaldi, New York actress and entrepreneur, in the state of South Carolina has once again exposed the absurd notion that Negroes are fit only to serve whites as domestic chattel and can in no way be elevated to the status of an educated, self-reliant people.

Some will say that Miss Rinaldi, who has heretofore passed for white, is an exception. She is in fact, the daughter of a white father and a mulatto mother. But this condition is far from rare in our Southern culture—it is actually quite common, though Southern men, especially, are loathe to admit it. In any case, the exact admixture of black and white blood in any given individual seems to have little to do with ability, intelligence, or moral integrity.

Miss Rinaldi, for example, came to this town less than one year ago with little to recommend her as a woman of business, much less of vision...

Elizabeth put the draft down on the desk. "This will be the end of the *Mercury* if you print this, Zimri. And they'll run you out of town."

Zimri smiled. "It will not be the end of the *Mercury* and no one will run me out of town. This is *my* town, and there are those who helped me to build it that will come to my aid if I am attacked."

"Are you sure?"

"Quite sure."

"Oh, Zimri, I don't know. It's at once not enough to help Cora, and too much for a small Southern newspaper to take upon itself. The *Mercury* an abolitionist paper? They'll burn it to the ground."

Zimri picked up the draft and re-read the first few sentences. "It's a risk I'll have to take. Jed!"

Jed, who had lately taken to wearing tailored suits, appeared at the doorway. "Yes, Mr. Rhodes? Oh, hello, Mrs. Rhodes."

"Hello, Jed. You look very nice today."

"Thank you, Mrs.—"

"Now that we've established your fashion credentials, Jed, how about taking a look at this editorial and giving me your opinion. I'd like to see it in the next issue."

Jed scanned the leader and looked dubious. "Yes, sir. I'll see what I can do."

Elizabeth waited until Jed had gone. "Even Jed is shocked. And he has his finger on the pulse of this community. Why can't you be a little more...discreet, and think of some way to help Cora on a personal level?"

"Like what?"

"Like...helping Cora to escape from Lynwood."

"That's against the law, Elizabeth. Are you advocating that I break the law?"

Elizabeth set her jaw firmly. "Yes."

Zimri smiled. "What would Jamie think of such a notion?"

"I don't care what Jamie would think. For all of Cora's—and your—transgressions, I do not want to see her raped and tortured. This editorial, Zimri, in spite of its fiery rhetoric, is nothing but a piece of paper—mere words. Can't you take some kind of *action* for a change?"

This comment wounded Zimri as no other charge against his character could. He was a man of ideas, it was true, but every man of ideas, at some point, feels the inadequacy of 'mere words,' as Elizabeth put it, in a moment of crisis. And she was right—Cora's capture and imprisonment at Lynwood was a crisis. He could not simply fire off an editorial condemning the institution of slavery, and wash his hands of his responsibility. "I've got work to do, Elizabeth. Don't you have something to occupy you here in town to-day?"

She sighed. "Yes. A meeting of the Library Foundation. We've got to decide on what books to buy."

Zimri rose from his chair. "Mere words, eh?"

"Touché," she said, though without enthusiasm.

He kissed her on the cheek. "We'll talk more about it at supper tonight. I have a feeling that the hearth room would serve better as a den for conspirators."

She kissed him back. "Until supper then."'

Zimri watched as Elizabeth left the office and disappeared into the bustle of the street. When he went back to his desk, Jed appeared, editorial in hand.

"You've read it?"

"Yes, sir."

"Well, what do you think?"

"I think it'll cause trouble."

"I knew that. I mean what do you think of the content, the style?"

"It's very well written, of course."

"But?"

"But nothing. I can find no fault with your argument. Slavery has never been morally defensible."

"I still sense a 'but' lurking somewhere in the back of your mind."

"Well, the problem is—is it worth losing half of our subscribers?"

"Half?"

"Maybe more. The *Patriot* will pounce on this and we'll see a lot of defections."

Zimri took the editorial in his hands and re-read portions of it. "You think it's incendiary?"

"To some people, yes. But it's calm and closely reasoned. Only a few hotheads will see it as incendiary."

"And those are the people we have to worry about."

"Yes, sir. I suggest you post a guard inside the front door for the first few nights after publication."

"Know any volunteers?"

"Yes, sir. Me, for one."

Zimri smiled. "Jed, if the building is left standing after the first week, remind me to give you a raise."

"I'll hold you to it, sir."

"Be sure that you do." Zimri then sat down at his desk and took out his red pencil, marking the copy up like his schoolmaster used to do back in North Bradford.

CHAPTER 57

The editorial caused more of a stir than even Jed had predicted. The word 'storm' would be more appropriate. The *Patriot*, also as Jed had predicted, pounced:

The editor of the Mercury, Mr. Zimri Rhodes, though a respected member of the community as well as a co-founder of the city of Martinville, has often been taken to task for his liberal and outspoken opinions. But this time he has gone too far: he has attacked the very institution that has made the South the most prosperous, the most envied agricultural economy on earth. And it is the height of hypocrisy for Mr. Rhodes to call for the abolition of slavery when he himself owns several slaves.

"You can cancel my subscription!"

Zimri put the *Patriot* down to see who the latest defector was. He had had the window installed in his office so that he could see everything that was going on. This time it was John Lewis, the alcoholic milliner. He saw Zimri through the window, scowled, and left. On the way out, he almost bumped into Bill Portman. Portman nodded to Jed, took up the pen to sign the cancellation form, and saw Zimri. He put down the pen and came to Zimri's door.

"You got a minute, Zimri?"

"Of course, Bill. What can I do for you today?" Portman stepped uneasily into the office.

"Sit down," Zimri said. "Coffee?"

"No, thanks, Zimri. Just thought I'd let you know face-to-face that I'm canceling my subscription."

"I'm sorry to hear that, Bill. Any particular reason?"

"Same reason as everybody else."

Zimri sighed. "I suppose there's no point in pretending that I didn't know. I'll be sorry to lose you, though."

Portman cast his eyes to the floor. He seemed troubled. "I can't say as I disagree with your editorial. You're right—slavery is an abomination. I got niggers that can outsmart six John Lewis' any day of the week. But I can't do business without 'em."

"Couldn't you free them and hire them back?"

"With what? I'm a small planter, Zimri, and I don't have the cash to pay farm hands through the winter months, not to mention during a drought. I'd go belly up without the ten slaves I got."

"What about sharecropping?"

"What?"

"You know—tenant farming. Let your tenants cultivate a portion of your land and turn over a share of the crop to you. That way you don't have to pay them anything, and when the crop is bountiful, you both win."

Portman seemed to consider this, and then shook his head. "And when the crop is bad, I'm even worse off than before. Less crop, less share."

Zimri sighed. "I'm not a farmer, Bill. You know your business better than I do. But it seems that there must be some alternative to this system of bondage. Other parts of the country seem to get along pretty well without it."

"But they ain't farmers like we are. Up north they got factories. Come six o'clock, everybody closes up and goes home. Farms don't never close. 'Cept when there's a drought, or a flood, or a late frost. And then we starve."

"I grew up on a farm in New England. No slaves, and we never starved."

A big smile gradually came to Portman's face. "You'd argue the pin feathers off a duck, Zimri. Guess that's why you're a newspaperman." He stood up. "Well, I ain't got time to argue with you anymore. I got a sick mule at home that ain't doin' me any good layin' around the barn when I got cotton ready to be picked. So long, Zimri."

"So long, Bill. Just sign the cancellation form on the way out."

"Cancellation form? I ain't signing no cancellation form. If I don't get my paper, how am I going to know what's going on around here? Besides, you got a sense of humor. Those crackers over at the *Patriot* take themselves too seriously."

Zimri smiled. "I'll have to remember to hire a cartoonist."

"You get a good one and I'll subscribe for life."

Zimri's colloquy with Bill Portman was the highlight of the day. The rest was an endless stream of disgruntled customers, some of whom made little effort to conceal their disgust with his editorial. A few muttered 'nigger lover' under their breath as they left the office.

About five minutes to six, Jed put the cancellation forms into a drawer and pulled a musket out of a closet.

"Do you really think that's necessary, Jed?"

"Don't know Mr. Rhodes. Maybe nothing will come of it, but—"

"Come of what?"

Jed pushed a cartridge into the muzzle of the musket. "Those layabouts that hang around Murphy's Saloon across the street. They're sitting on the front porch right now, getting liquored up and scowling at us."

"Are they armed?"

"Not that I can see. But they may just be waiting for us to leave so they can come over here and toss a brick through the window. Or worse."

Zimri went to the front window and looked out. "The same louts that attended the auction last year."

"The auction?"

"Never mind. Any more muskets?"

"Yes, sir. I brought two, just in case."

"Good. Where's Peter?"

"He went home."

"Well, it looks like you and me, Jed. I've got an extra cot in my office."

"Oh, I don't think I'll be sleeping tonight, Mr. Rhodes. You're welcome to it."

Zimri sat up with Jed until midnight, a musket in his lap and his eyes glued to Murphy's Saloon. The young men who had been drinking there all afternoon seemed to have gone home without incident. The lights of the saloon gradually went out, one by one.

"I don't think we're going to have any company tonight, Jed. Why don't you go on home?"

Jed looked at him with no sign of fatigue in his eyes. "It's when everything's quiet and peaceful that you've got to really be on your guard, Mr. Rhodes. I know those boys—they never pass up an opportunity to cause trouble when they know they can get away with it."

Zimri looked across the street as Brendan Murphy, the proprietor, locked the front door of his establishment and walked towards Cherry Street. "Looks like a tomb over there."

"Yes, sir. But that's not where they'll come from. I'd better cover the back door."

"I checked it ten minutes ago. Locked tighter than a drum."

"There's a window, though—I'll see about it."

Jed stood up from his chair and walked past Zimri's office towards the pressroom. Just as he arrived at the door of the pressroom, Zimri, who was still watching the saloon across the street, heard the crash of breaking glass. He leaped to his feet with his musket at the ready, but it was too late. An explosion rocked the office and knocked both of them off their feet.

Zimri, dazed and disoriented for only a few seconds, picked himself off the floor, retrieved his musket and ran to the press room. He heard Jupiter's unmistakable neighing, and the sound of other horse's hooves slamming into the hard clay behind the building. He kneeled down to examine Jed, whose face was covered with soot and grease but no blood.

He put down his musket and dragged Jed out of the doorway to the pressroom. By this time Jed seemed to have regained his senses, and Zimri sat him in a chair. Then he went back to the pressroom and found a water bucket. The fire had already spread from the floor to the trays containing back issues of the *Mercury*. Zimri doused the trays, but the water had little effect. He looked up and saw the exposed timbers of the roof burning.

"I'll ring the fire bell, Mr. Rhodes!"

While Jed ran out into the street to sound the alarm, Zimri went to the well pump in the alley and filled the bucket, threw water against the walls and up into the timbers, returned to the well and repeated the process until volunteers began to arrive. Fortunately, most of the firemen lived within a few blocks of the building.

In thirty minutes the fire was out.

"At least the new press is relatively undamaged," Zimri said, standing in the blackened pressroom. "It could have been worse."

"It'll get worse before it gets better, Zimri."

Zimri turned to see Tom Pritchard, the mayor, standing behind him. "Hello, Tom. What makes you think that?"

"Those boys—or whoever did it—will be back. Or if not them, someone else."

Zimri knew Pritchard had little sympathy for his political views, but he was bound to uphold the law. "I don't suppose you think the Sheriff will have any luck tracking the perpetrators down."

"How can he? There's no evidence and half the town thinks you ought to be run out on a rail."

"And the other half?"

Pritchard shrugged his shoulders. "The other half doesn't care. Oh, they might secretly agree with your position on slavery—it sounds high and mighty on paper—but they won't be coming to your aid if something like this happens again. And it will happen again. I just hope you and your employees don't get hurt."

"Hope?"

Pritchard sighed. "All right. I'll have Aaron post a deputy here so you and Jed can go home and get some sleep. We're here to protect you, just like we do every citizen. Don't get your back up, Zimri. I'm just trying to tell you what you're in for as long as you take unpopular stances like this."

"I knew what I was in for when I wrote the editorial, Tom. And there'll be more." Zimri stepped over some charred debris and walked past Pritchard and into the alley.

"I hate to say this," Pritchard said, "but it's your funeral."

"Thanks for the advice, Tom."

Pritchard pulled out his watch and looked at it in the dim light of the oil lamps left by the firemen. "Three o'clock. Where's Aaron? We need a deputy here!"

CHAPTER 58

Cora lay on an iron bed bolted to the floor of the abandoned mill that Randolph used to incarcerate his most intractable slaves. Her left wrist was manacled, as was her right leg, and the chains secured to the tabby walls. She fixed her eyes on the small window about twenty feet above her head, the only source of light in the room. She could hear rats scurrying across the floor, making little squeaking sounds as they foraged for what little food they could find.

Her dress was torn and muddy, and she had not had a bath in three days. She had been disappointed, though not surprised, to find herself alone in the mill. She did not know where the others were. The surprise on the old-timers' faces, when she appeared at the kitchen door brandishing her pistol! Especially Lillian, who took over as her father's chief cook after her mother died.

Poor father! He seemed to be in a coma, apparently not even aware of what was going on. Not that she had been allowed to see him but the other slaves had informed her of as much. Randolph was the master of Lynwood now.

Randolph—that scoundrel. He neither commanded the love nor the respect of the slaves. He had always been lazy, moody, arrogant when feeling insecure, which was often, and given to tantrums when denied what he desired.

Oddly, he had desired her—at least for a time. And when he couldn't have her, he turned to cruelty.

As if summoned by her thoughts, the heavy deadbolt on the door to the room slid back with a thud, and Randolph himself appeared. She languorously turned her head in the direction of the door without bothering to sit up. There was no need to show this man respect or fear.

"Cora."

She watched as he stood at the door. Apparently, no one was with him. He looked somewhat disheveled, as if he had just risen from a deep sleep. His expensive French shirt, open at the collar, was stained red with wine. He carried a riding crop in his right hand.

"Cora, I'm speaking to you."

"I can hear you."

"Are you sick? Sit up."

"I'm rather tired, Randolph. And hungry. I can't eat that slop you give to the other slaves. The rats seem to like it, though."

Randolph's eyes went to the corners of the room. "I'll see that you get better food. That porridge is for the malcontents, the troublemakers."

Cora laughed and turned her eyes up to the ceiling. "And I'm not a troublemaker? I almost feel insulted, Randolph. I've liberated at least forty of your slaves."

"We'll track them down. You're a clever woman, Cora, but the odds are against you."

"They always have been. But one can overcome the most formidable of odds if one is persistent."

Randolph cast about for something to sit on, and spying a chair with a broken back, pulled it up next to the bed. He sat down and stared at her for several moments. "If anything, you're more beautiful than when you were a girl."

She laughed again, though this was quickly followed by a cough. "You're such a flatterer, Randolph, no wonder the ladies could never resist you. And your timing is impeccable. Here I am your prisoner, chained to the wall and starving. What better time to make a proposition?"

Randolph flushed with anger and brandished his riding crop. "Don't laugh at me, Cora. I swear, you'll regret it."

Cora coughed. "I wouldn't think of laughing at you, Randolph. I was hoping we could laugh together. About old times."

Instead of growing more angry, Randolph suddenly seemed contemplative. He took out a silver flask from his waist pocket, unscrewed the cap, and drank from it. "Yes, old times. We did have some good times together didn't we?"

"Yes—until you discovered you had a penis."

Randolph smiled. "That did change things between us, didn't it? We were inseparable as children—have some brandy, Cora. It'll be good for your cough."

"A warm bath would be good for my cough. And some clean clothes."

"I'll see that you get both. In the meantime, have some brandy. It's the same label as Napoleon's."

"Another flatterer with a penis problem. But whereas you have only six hundred slaves or so, Napoleon enslaved half of Europe. Don't you feel you have some catching up to do?"

"Damn you, Cora!" Randolph suddenly stood up and struck her

across the face with his riding crop.

She didn't cry out, but only felt her cheek to see if it was bleeding. It wasn't, but a welt was emerging.

"I'm trying to help you, Cora." Randolph shook with anger. "But all I get in return is sarcasm and ingratitude. Don't you know that I can have you hanged?"

Cora remained silent for several moments. "What do you want from me, Randolph?"

Randolph seemed to cast about, as if stymied by this question. Then he said:

"I want you to care for me—as you did when we were children."

She turned her head and looked at him. "I do care for you, Randolph. But it's mixed with pity—pity and wonder."

"Wonder?"

"Yes. I wonder how such a pretty, loving boy could grow into such a selfish, sadistic, self-doubting man."

"Self-doubting? If I'm self-doubting, it's no thanks to you. You've got a wicked tongue, Cora. You've always had a wicked tongue, and father always let you get away with it. He enjoyed watching you make fun of me, and he took all the more pleasure in it because you were a slave!"

Cora smiled. "He did indulge me, didn't he? I never understood why."

Randolph took another swig from his flask. "Because you were Galatea to his Pygmalion, Cora. He was fascinated with the idea of raising the lowliest of humans—a slave girl—to the highest level of sophistication. And if it hadn't been for that unfortunate incident with my college friends, I think he would've encouraged us to marry!"

"That was unfortunate. The so-called 'party' in the wine cellar, I mean."

"I was drunk. The others were egging me on."

"Yes, I guess boys will do that. What's a little rape among friends?"

Randolph took another swig from the flask. "You're getting sarcastic again. Maybe when you get cleaned up and get some food in you, you'll feel more sociable. I'll send a maid over with whatever you need."

"It's beginning to feel like the Palace Hotel."

Randolph shook his forefinger at her. "It is the Palace Hotel compared to where you'd be if I hadn't insisted on the sheriff turning you over to me. There're a lot of planters out there that would like to see you strung up from a lamp post and dragged through the streets as an example to every nigger in the county."

"I suppose I should feel fortunate only to be shackled to the wall of a medieval torture chamber."

Randolph shook his head. "I'll be back tomorrow. In the meantime, Cora, *think* a little. Think about the position you're in."

"I am thinking about it."

"Good. Sleep well."

After Randolph had gone, Cora pulled on the chains to test their strength. Assured that the iron bolts driven into the wall would not budge, she again turned her eyes to the window high above the floor. The amber light from the setting sun was growing more faint.

She wondered whether anyone had ever escaped from this room.

CHAPTER 59

Two weeks passed without further attacks on the *Mercury*. This, in spite of subsequent editorials by Zimri that alternately ridiculed the Southern mentality that perpetuated slavery and condemned those who would threaten the Union with secession. The reason, according to Jed, was that Aaron Beasley, the sheriff, marched over to Murphy's Saloon the day after the bombing and announced that any further violence against the *Mercury* or to his good friend Zimri Rhodes would be met with swift justice. He didn't specify what form this justice would take, but apparently it made an impression on those to whom the threat was directed.

In the meantime Zimri had written to his old friend Omri Sparks in Philadelphia about the possibilities of enlisting the aid of abolitionists in freeing Cora from her captivity in South Carolina. He received a prompt reply:

7 July, Thursday

Dear Zimri,

It was wonderful to hear from you. Thank you for asking about my niece. Yes, she is doing quite well here in Philadelphia. At the moment she is living with me and my wife while working in my book bindery. In the meantime, she is attending classes at the Academy for People of Color in order to improve her reading and writing skills.

As for Cora Rinaldi, she is the talk of New York and Boston as well as Philadelphia. The abolitionist societies seem to be combining their resources to devise some sort of plan to either purchase her freedom or to facilitate her escape. From what I hear, however, neither option seems likely to be successful, I am sad to say. Her owner, Mr. Randolph Benson, has already been approached and offered a considerable amount of money, but he refused to sell. An escape, on the other hand, is fraught with danger in no small part due to her notoriety and celebrity. I'm afraid that I can offer no solution of my own.

I will continue, however, to keep you abreast of developments in this part of the country as I hear of them. In the meantime perhaps some sort of compromise with Mr. Benson may be worked out.

Sincerely yours, Omri

Zimri laid the letter aside and put his feet up on the desk. What could he do alone when so many influential members of the abolitionist societies could do nothing? His escape plan, which was rather vague and amateurish, would stand little chance of success. Actually, he did have a few advantages over the abolitionists. One, he was familiar with Lynwood, having recently spent the better part of a week there. Two, he was closer; perhaps four days journey. And three, he was pretty sure of the precise location of Cora's imprisonment.

Of course, he could end up getting Cora hanged, and perhaps Solomon and himself as well...

Another thought: what if other slaves wanted to come along? The whole plan could become unmanageable, doomed from the start. Randolph and the authorities in Beaufort would be on high alert for a second mass attempt.

No, it would have to be Cora alone.

"Mr. Rhodes?" Jed stood at the door of his office.

"Yes, Jed. Come in and have a seat. What's on your mind?"

Jed stepped inside, but remained standing. He looked troubled. "I don't exactly know how to tell you this, Mr. Rhodes—you've been very good to me."

"I've tried to be, Jed. And I appreciate your efforts—often beyond the call of duty. You're not thinking of leaving me, are you?"

"Well...yes, sir."

"Why, may I ask? Is it those ruffians across the street?"

"Oh, no sir—I'm not afraid of them. Besides, Sheriff Beasley has put the fear of God in them. I don't think they'll give you any more trouble."

"Then what is it, Jed?"

"Mr. Anderson at the *Patriot* saw me walking by his office the other day and asked me to step inside for a chat."

"And?"

"He said the *Patriot* is going to go from a weekly to a daily."

"I see."

"And he says he'll be needing more help. Wants me to be in charge of subscriptions and advertising."

"How much is he offering you?"

"Ten dollars a week."

"You know I can't pay you that much. Not with the decline in our own subscriptions."

"Yes, sir. I know that."

"I hate to lose you, Jed. You're not only a good ad man, but as loyal an employee as I could hope to have. I can pay you eight dollars, but even that would be a strain on our current finances."

"That's very generous of you, Mr. Rhodes, but I'm getting married next month."

"Oh? Well, congratulations. Who's the lucky girl?"

"Lucy Cutler."

"Fine girl. I'm sure you'll be happy together."

Jed cast his eyes to the floor and seemed determined not to look at Zimri for the remainder of the interview. "I'm going to need every penny I can get, Mr. Rhodes."

"I understand, Jed. I'm a married man myself. You'll soon have little ones on the way."

"I expect so."

There was an awkward silence during which Zimri thought Jed might not be able to move without assistance. "I'll need some notice, Jed."

"Friday all right?"

"That's only two days from now."

"Mr. Anderson wants me to start Monday."

"Then I guess it'll have to be Friday."

Jed avoided Zimri's gaze. "I'm sorry, Mr. Rhodes. I've liked it here. You've taught me everything I know."

"I appreciate that, Jed. But a man has to look out for his family."

"Yes, sir."

Jed stood frozen to the spot for several more seconds, still staring at the floor.

"Is there anything else, Jed?"

Jed finally looked up and his eyes met Zimri's. "Yes, sir."

"What's that?"

"Will you come to my wedding?"

Zimri smiled. "I'd be honored to, Jed. Just let me know the date."

Jed smiled broadly. "I'll have Lucy send you an invitation."

"That would be fine, Jed."

Jed turned to go but lingered for a moment. "On second thought, I'll deliver it to you myself."

"That would be even better."

With Jed gone, Zimri considered his situation. He had had to let Jason go the previous week. Now he was down to one employee and a steadily declining circulation. Peter was learning rapidly, but he couldn't hold a candle to Jed for intelligence and initiative. If things got any worse, he'd have to let him go, too.

He had hoped that the *Mercury* would be able to go to a daily format itself by this time. If it hadn't been for the editorials, the shoe would be on the other foot. The *Patriot* would be struggling to survive, and the *Mercury* would be...Oh, what was the use? What's done is done. He couldn't just suddenly change his tune about slavery and the Union, could he? On the other hand, he needn't have been so rash. He might have moderated his views so that his readers over time would come to see the inherent moral contradiction of a Christian society that condones slavery.

He stood up from his desk and looked at his watch. Four o'clock. Not much happening here, anyway. He put on his jacket, straightened his cravat, and donned his hat. He felt he needed to go somewhere but he didn't know where. Perhaps it was just to get out of the office. Perhaps it was to avoid Peter, who might also submit his resignation.

He slipped out into the alley and climbed into the gig. It was a good day for a drive along the river.

The days were long now with the sun not setting until eight o'clock or later. When Zimri got home it was still light and after putting the gig in the barn, he lingered in the rose garden to examine his hybrids. They were growing like weeds, but were much prettier. He had even succeeded in developing one of a bright red color, a true red, which was quite unheard of. Most roses were white or pink, with varying shades in between. He clipped one of the red ones from its stem and brought it into the house.

"Oh, Zimri—that's lovely. How did you do it?" Elizabeth smelled the flower and looked for a vase to put it in.

"I'm not sure," he said. "I crossed a hybrid with a tea rose, neither of which was red, and this was what I got."

"Can you do it again?"

"I think so."

She put her nose to the flower, which was now in a crystal vase. "It smells lovely, too. I'd like to have a dozen."

"I'll see what I can do."

"Betty, Louise, come look!"

At supper, with Betty in the kitchen, and Louise gone for the day, Zimri broached the subject of Cora's captivity.

"I don't know if I can do anything for her," he said.

"You promised that you would."

Zimri held the two ends of a corn cob in his hands and was about to bite into it. "Yes, I did. But Lynwood is like an armed camp now. They seem to be digging in as if expecting to be attacked by an army."

"How do you know?"

"Sources. Friends in Philadelphia, New York."

"How do they know what's going on in Beaufort, South Carolina?"

"News moves fast these days. Especially when it concerns someone like Cora. She's the darling of the abolitionists." Zimri bit into his corn with a loud crunch.

"Can't you do that more quietly?"

Zimri chewed and swallowed. "How can one eat corn on the cob quietly?"

"One can cut the kernels off with a knife—like this."

Zimri watched as Elizabeth carefully shaved several rows of corn off her cob. "Since when have you become so fastidious with corn on the cob? It's *supposed* to be eaten with one's hands."

"Well, have it your way. But this is more refined—and a lot less annoying to one's dinner companions."

Zimri looked around the hearth room until his eyes rested upon the bookcases in the corner. "You've been reading those English novels again. The English can't eat anything without a knife and fork."

"That may be true but—what were you saying about Cora?"

Zimri cautiously took another bite of his corn. "How was that?"

"Quieter. But we were talking about Cora."

"Yes. Well, any kind of escape attempt is going to be very difficult. And very dangerous."

"Couldn't you hire somebody to do it for you? Seeing as how you have no military experience."

"I beg your pardon. I served in the Connecticut Militia before I came to Georgia."

"Really? You never told me that. What rank?"

"Corporal. I was only sixteen."

Elizabeth shook her head. "I'm afraid that won't be much help, Zimri. You need someone who has experience leading men into battle."

Zimri put his corn cob down on his plate, wiped his mouth with his napkin, and stared at her. "Who would you suggest?"

"I'm afraid I don't know of anyone who would satisfy that requirement. But you must know of someone among the men you deal with in the course of your business. Clearly, it would be an enterprise beyond your abilities."

Zimri shoved his plate aside. "Elizabeth—are you trying to make me angry?"

"Why, no. Why should I want to make you angry? Please darling, don't take it personally. I just don't want you to get hurt—or arrested. They could send you to prison, you know."

Zimri drank some cider. "The more people who know about something like this, the more likely the scheme will be exposed. I'm quite capable of conducting an operation of this kind, Elizabeth. Just leave the details to me."

"Do you mind if I offer a suggestion?"

"Not at all."

"Let Solomon do the dangerous part."

Zimri smiled. "Solomon's much stronger than I am. I fully intend to put his muscles to good use."

"And one more thing."

"Yes, my pretty co-conspirator?"

"How are you going to get Cora to the North once you've freed her?"

"Ah—you've put your finger on it. That's what's been troubling me the most about the whole affair. Every port will be manned with constables on the lookout for her."

"It's simple—have her dress as a man."

Zimri's eyes grew large. "Yes—that may work."

"And don't take her to Charleston or Savannah. As you said, they'll be expecting her there. Take her to Grand-maman's."

"Grand-maman's?"

"Grand-maman Devereaux. In Louisville. It's only two days' ride from Lynwood and no one will be expecting her to go inland."

"Yes, but what about Grand-maman Devereaux herself? She owns over a hundred slaves."

Elizabeth reached for the cider jug and poured herself a glass. "Grand-maman cares more for adventure than for the fugitive slave laws. Besides, she wrote me a letter the other day saying how much she admired Cora and what a scoundrel Randolph is for not giving her her freedom."

"Grand-maman said that?"

Elizabeth raised her glass to his. "Mais oui, Monsieur. À l'aventure noble!"

Zimri clicked his glass against hers. "À l'aventure noble!"

She laughed. "Très bien, mon chéri. Your accent is improving!"

CHAPTER 60

Elizabeth came home from a meeting of the Library Foundation one afternoon to find Jamie's horse tied up at the hitching rail in front of the house. She had not seen him since the funeral service for Lucky that was held at the new church a few days after she returned from Lynwood.

She had walked home, feeling that the exercise would do her good. Tessie was on the front porch entertaining Charlotte.

"Is Mr. Blake here?"

"Yes, ma'am. He's in the hearth room waiting for you."

Elizabeth picked Charlotte up, kissed her, put her down again and went inside. "Hello, Jamie. What brings you to town?"

Jamie was sitting in a chair opposite the hearth, with his hat on his lap. "Where's Zimri?"

"I suppose he's in Savannah by now."

"What's he doing in Savannah?"

She removed her bonnet and sat in a chair next to the coffee table. "I don't know, exactly. Business, he said."

"Well, whatever business he has there, you can tell him when he gets back that he's no longer welcome at Belle Oaks."

"Oh, Jamie, you can't mean that."

"I do mean that. I always knew he was an abolitionist, but now he's come out publicly with it. And I won't have any damn abolitionist setting foot in my house. You're still welcome, of course."

"Well, thank you for that at least. But how can I visit Belle Oaks without my husband? If he's not welcome, then I'm not welcome."

Jamie rose from his chair and slapped the brim of his hat against his thigh. "Suit yourself. I'll make an exception at Christmas. Otherwise, the servants have instructions to bar him at the door."

"Jamie, you're not being reasonable."

"Reasonable? I'd say you're the one not being reasonable. You never should have married a damn Yankee. They don't understand our ways down here. The niggers are happy except when some Yankee comes down here and starts putting ideas into their heads. Besides, I always thought he was in cahoots with that Rinaldi woman. Turns out I was right."

"He knew nothing about her activities at the time of the escape in Martinville. He was as surprised as anyone."

"I seriously doubt that. Seems that he's hoodwinked you as well as everyone else around here."

"He's been perfectly honest with me."

"Hah! He hasn't been honest with you since the day he proposed to you. I didn't want to say it then, Elizabeth, but I'll say it now—he married you for your money."

She rose to her feet. "My money! What money? You inherited everything!"

Jamie placed his hat on his head and adjusted the brim. "Daddy was still alive then. Zimri must have naturally assumed that you would receive a large portion of the estate someday."

"He assumed no such thing. Besides, Daddy never tried to hide the fact that he wanted you to be his successor—his only son. I admit, though, I was a bit disappointed when it turned out that he had left me nothing at all. Zimri, on the other hand, didn't seem to care."

Jamie looked hesitant. "There's something I never told you about Daddy's will, Elizabeth. I didn't think the time was right."

"What? What about the will?"

"I was waiting to see whether you'd come to your senses about Zimri, to see what kind of man he was, and to possibly...break it off."

"Break it off? Divorce him, you mean."

"Yes. But it seems that you're too stubborn, or too pious, or too blind to do that. So I'll tell you, anyway."

Elizabeth said nothing but looked at him expectantly.

"Daddy set aside a considerable amount of money for you. But he was suspicious of Zimri's motives just like I was."

"A considerable amount? How much?"

"Thirty thousand dollars."

Elizabeth put her hand to her mouth. "Oh, my goodness."

"But you can't touch it until you're twenty-one. In the meantime, I'm the trustee."

A range of possibilities as to what she could do with the money ran through her mind. "And if I should still be married to Zimri on my twenty-first birthday?"

"Unfortunately, there will be nothing I can do about it. I could only withhold the money if you either become incompetent or commit a crime of moral turpitude."

"Moral turpitude?"

"You'd have to murder someone or open up a whore house. As far as I'm concerned, being married to an abolitionist falls into the same category, but that's not what the law says."

"Someday you'll see, Jamie."

"And someday you'll see. In the meantime, I guess we'll just have to see differently."

She kissed him on the cheek. "You're a good man, Jamie. And so is Zimri. You just come from different worlds, that's all."

"I come from the same world as you do. That's what's so frustrating and hard to understand."

"I'm not sure I understand, either."

Jamie made his way to the door, but hesitated before leaving. "You can bring him out to Belle Oaks on New Year's, too. I'll be so drunk I won't care if he's an abolitionist or the devil himself."

She smiled. "Goodbye, Jamie."

"Goodbye, little sister."

After Jamie had left, she heard Fortunata crying and went into the bedroom to see about her. Elizabeth picked her up, patted her on the back, and took her out onto the veranda.

"Mr. Jamie was hoppin' mad before you came up, Miz Rhodes." Tessie was sitting on the steps and bouncing Charlotte on her knee. "You sure calmed him down good."

"He's not the ogre he seems at times, Tessie. Just a bit stubborn." She sat down on the swing with Fortunata's head against her breast.

"Fortunata's growing fat," Tessie said. "I'll bet she's gained two pounds since you got home from South Carolina."

"Now that you mention it, she does seem heavier."

They sat in silence for a few moments, with Elizabeth swinging slowly back and forth, and Tessie jiggling Charlotte on her knee.

"Miz Rhodes?"

"Yes, Tessie?"

"What are you going to do with all that money?"

Elizabeth stopped swinging. "Tessie! You've been eavesdropping!"

"Couldn't help it, Miz Rhodes. The doors and windows were all open."

Elizabeth resumed her swinging. "I don't suppose it was the quietist of conversations in any case...I don't know what I'll do with the money, Tessie. I'll have to talk it over with Mr. Rhodes when he gets back."

"Yes, ma'am." Tessie picked up a bright red ball and threw it into the yard. Charlotte scampered after it. "Miz Rhodes?"

"Yes, Tessie?"

"I was thinking about what you could do with the money. Part of it, anyway."

"What would you suggest, Tessie?"

"Well, we colored folks sure could use a good school. There ain't one for a hundred miles around here. I don't think it would cost too much for just one little schoolhouse. My daddy would be willing to make the iron things you'd need for nothin'—like a bell for instance."

"Why that's quite a nice idea, Tessie. But don't you know it's against the law for white people to teach colored people to read and write?"

"But it ain't against the law for colored people to teach other colored people to read and write. Colored people like me, for instance."

Elizabeth considered this. "I'm not a lawyer, Tessie, but I don't think it's legal for anyone to teach colored people to read. I'll have to ask my husband when he gets home."

"Yes, ma'am."

Later, after supper, with Tessie gone home and Betty retired to her cabin, Elizabeth sat up reading for a while but found it hard to concentrate. Where was Zimri now? He and Solomon must be approaching Lynwood. Or perhaps they're staying in Beaufort while they plan the escape in more detail. Oh, why did she ever encourage Zimri to embark upon such a foolish venture? And all for the sake of his lover! What was she thinking?

Of course she was angry with Randolph. She wanted to hurt him somehow. But this was not the way to do it. Barring him from her door, just as Jamie had barred Zimri from Belle Oaks, would have been enough. And now Zimri, as a result of her prodding and needling, even suggesting he was being cowardly for not making the attempt, was now in extreme danger! Yes, extreme danger. For if he and Solomon were caught, Zimri would go to jail and Solomon, just on the verge of emancipation, would probably be sold back into slavery.

What had she done?

She leapt up from her chair by the hearth and began pacing around the room. What could she do now that the die was cast? She had written Grand-maman and told her of the whole plan. What if she did not find it so amusing and adventurous as expected? What if she alerted the authorities?

She went into the bedroom to check on Charlotte and Fortunata. Sound asleep. The darlings. She could never leave home again without them. Oh, no! Never, never, never!

But then she could not simply sit in Martinville and do nothing. She wandered out into the hearth room, paced for a few more moments, and then went onto the veranda and sat on the swing. The stars were out.

Somehow, this was the most peaceful and tranquil part of the house. She felt calmer now.

But what should she do?

It dawned on her that she must be in Louisville when Zimri and Solomon—presumably with Cora—arrived. Grand-maman would be overwhelmed with the three of them, and though a brave, self-confident sort of woman, she would need help in concealing them for a week or possibly longer. Her slaves would no doubt spread the word through their grapevine and as Zimri said, the more people that knew of the plot, the more likely its exposure.

It was clear to her now what she must do. She would take the children with her to Louisville. Betty could drive them. She would be delighted to be near Solomon in any case—no doubt she was sitting in her cabin right now just as anxious about her husband as she—Elizabeth—was about Zimri. And Louise and Tessie could stay and look after Aaron and Sally.

She went back into the house, put a shawl around her shoulders, and went out the back door to the slave's cabin.

"Betty!"

"Miz Lisbeth?" Betty had just put Aaron and Sally to bed. It was a small cabin, even after Solomon had joined two together, and the children stared out from beneath their covers at the unusual sight of a white woman at their door.

"We've got to go to Louisville."

"Louisville? That's a good two day's drive, Miz Lizbeth. Why you want to—"

"That's where Solomon and Zimri will meet us. You want to help Solomon, don't you?"

"Oh, yes, ma'am! I'se been worried sick 'bout this cockamamie plan of theirs—beggin' yo' pardon, Miz Lizbeth, but it never made much sense from what Solomon tole me."

"No, it doesn't, does it? And I'm afraid it was my idea from the start."

"Yo' idea?"

"Yes, but never mind. We'll leave first thing in the morning."

"Yes, ma'am, I'll be ready. But what about—" She indicated the children with a gesture of her hand.

"Louise and Tessie will look after them. We're taking Charlotte and Fortunata with us."

"Oh—yes, ma'am."

"Louise will be here at six-thirty. We'll leave directly after breakfast."

"Yes, ma'am."

"Come help me pack."

Betty turned to the children and wagged her finger at them. "You chillun get to sleep now. When I get back I don't want to see no goose feathers flyin' round where you done busted them pillows upside one another's head."

And she ran out into the darkness, only steps behind Elizabeth.

CHAPTER 61

Zimri stared into his glass at the bar of the Yemassee Tavern. "What's this—the local brew?"

The bartender laughed, dried off a glass, and put it on a shelf. "I don't think you'd care much for the local brew. That there is made in Kentucky. The best we got."

Zimri took a sip. "I see what you mean. Smooth and sweet. Better than what I got in Savannah. How is it that a little tavern out in the middle of nowhere like yours carries the best Kentucky bourbon?"

The bartender, who was also the proprietor, dried off another glass. "Mr. Benson used to stop in here from time to time. Insisted on the best. This is the last barrel, though. The old boy died last week."

"Mr. Benson died?"

"Afraid so. It's a shame. He was the finest gentleman I ever met. When you came in, I could see that you were of some...refinement yourself. No sense wastin' it on the rednecks."

Zimri took another sip. "What do you think will happen now to Lynwood?"

"Word is that it's already going to seed. Randolph, Mr. Benson's eldest son, ain't got the sense God gave a jackass. Oh, he's got lots of book learnin,' no doubt about that. But he's got no common sense—spouts off poetry to his field hands one day and goes on a whipping spree the next. They don't know what to expect."

"What about the younger sons?"

"Edward and Harry? Well, Edward's got some sense, but there's not much he can do. The old man left everything to Randolph except for some thoroughbreds and the like. And Harry's a sort of namby-pamby—pretty useless."

Zimri finished his whiskey and put a quarter on the bar. "How much for the room?"

The bartender picked up the quarter and put it in a drawer. "Six bits. And a quarter for your man in the barn."

"A quarter? He's sleeping with the horses."

"Well—all right. Ten cents."

"Okay if he brings my things up to the room?"

"Sure. But make sure he don't get too comfortable there. The sheriff's deputies are doin' spot checks for runaway slaves at all hours of the night. He got his papers?"

"He does."

"Should be no problem then. That big escape last month's got everybody jumpy."

"I'm not surprised. We'll be moving on tomorrow morning—early."

"In that case, I'll need the six bits for the room plus ten cents—in advance."

Zimri paid him the eighty-five cents and went out to the stable to find Solomon.

It was still light outside when Solomon arrived at Zimri's room with his portmanteau and set it down on a luggage rack. Zimri loosened the straps and extracted *Farquhar's Low Country Architecture* from a side pocket. He placed the book on the table in the center of the room and opened it to the section that dealt with Lynwood.

"Lock the door."

Solomon complied and returned to the table.

"Have a seat, Solomon. I want you to memorize this map and the drawing of the mill."

"Yes, suh. But I cain't read nothin.'"

"Not necessary. Just get a clear picture of it in your mind."

"Yes, suh." Solomon sat down in one of the chairs and Zimri struck a match and lit a candle.

"You see this? This is the main house."

"Yes, suh."

"And this round building upriver to the west is the mill."

"I sees that."

Zimri ran his finger westward along the river from the mill to a spot about a mile upstream. He marked it with an 'X.' "This is where we hid the boat earlier today."

"Yes, suh. Nobody's gone see it under all them branches."

"Let's hope not." He traced his finger back along the river to the mill. "Getting downstream to the mill will be easy. It's rowing back upstream that will be the hard part."

"Ain't no problem for me, Massa Zimri."

Zimri smiled. "That's where your strong back comes in." He moved his finger to a cross-section of the mill. "See this window? It's on the river side—about twenty feet up."

"How big is it, Massa Zimri?"

"Big enough for you to squeeze through. But the problem is,

there's an iron grating there—with four bars at the corners holding it in place. That's what the hacksaw is for. How long do you think it'll take you to cut through the bars?"

"That saw we got's plenty sharp. Maybe ten minutes each bar."

"Forty minutes. Meanwhile, Cora will be wondering who the hell you are."

Solomon laughed. "I'll jest tell her Massa Zimri sent me."

"The next problem is getting Cora up to the window and back down to the boat. She might be pretty weak, or even sick."

"No problem. I can carry her up to the winder over my shoulder, and when I get there, tie the rope round her waist and lower her down real gentle like."

"You're not going to have much room to sit in that window."

Solomon examined the drawing of the window more closely. "I can leave a couple of inches on one of them bars I cut and wrap the rope round it. Then I can lower her down like on a winch. I don't have to sit in the winder that way. I could even do that standin' on the flo.'"

"Good. Once she's in the boat, you'll lower yourself down and we'll be on our way."

Solomon stared at the map for a moment. "One thing bothers me, though, Massa Zimri."

"What's that?"

"What if she ain't alone?"

Zimri sighed. "That's a chance we'll have to take. But it'll be about four o'clock in the morning at that point. If anybody's with her, it'll be another slave or two."

"But we cain't take them, too."

"No, we can't. You'll just have to try to make them understand that. Cora can pass for white. They can't. And we don't have any papers for them."

"Yes, suh. They'll jest have to wait till next time."

Zimri closed the book and put it back into his portmanteau. "Assuming there is a next time. We may find ourselves right back in that fortress along with them."

"Yes, suh. Jest a chance we have to take."

Zimri looked intently at Solomon. "You don't have to go through with this, you know. I've already signed your emancipation papers and left them with Mrs. Rhodes. You could leave now and arrive in Martinville a free man."

Solomon seemed to consider this for a moment. "But I wouldn't

WINDS OF THE SOUTH

be able to sleep at night, Massa Zimri, knowin' you was back here in the county jail."

"I could pay a fine and get out soon enough, Solomon. But they would whip you—maybe worse than your old master in Louisiana did."

Solomon reached with one hand to the small of his back—apparently an involuntary reflex. Then he brought the hand around again. "Ain't no whuppin' gonna keep me from my freedom, Massa Zimri. If you signed the papers, then I'se already a free man. Even if they put me in jail, I'll be a free man in jail—jest like you."

Zimri smiled. "If you ever change your mind about being a blacksmith, Solomon, you might consider becoming a lawyer."

CHAPTER 62

Zimri rose at three a.m. and stumbled about in the darkness for a minute or so before finding a match to light a candle. He pulled on his trousers and boots, slipped on a russet flannel shirt that he hoped would blend in with leaves, brush and earth, and checked to see that the percussion cap of his pistol was properly seated, hoping all the while that he wouldn't have to use it. Then he went looking for Solomon.

Solomon was already up and hitching the horses to the wagon. "Mawnin,' Massa Zimri."

"Morning, Solomon. A little cool this early."

"Yes, suh, but it'll warm up all right. You won't need that jacket come daybreak."

"Reckon not. I'll meet you out front."

"Yes, suh,"

Zimri then went around to the front of the tavern where he had deposited his portmanteau and waited. He lit one of his cheroots and sat in the darkness on the front porch. By the time Solomon had brought the wagon around, the proprietor and his family had begun to stir. Solomon heaved the portmanteau into the back of the wagon and Zimri climbed onto the seat and took the reins in his hands.

"We got everything?"

"Yes, suh. Even got some ham and biscuit's the cook done give me last night. She seem to take a shine to me."

Zimri smiled and urged the horses on. "Why wouldn't she?"

About thirty minutes later they arrived at the spot on the Combahee where they had hidden the boat the day before. They pulled back the branches, roused a family of squirrels that had set in for the night, and transferred the rope, saw, and oil lamp to the boat. Solomon tied the horses to an enormous old live oak and they pushed off downstream.

"New moon," Zimri said. "Right on schedule."

Solomon rowed the boat with help from the current, which was not as swift as the day before. All the elements seemed to be cooperating.

As they rounded the last bend of the river the looming image of the mill came into view. It was partially illuminated by a few lights in the main house some three hundred yards further downstream, as well as the torches that lined the dock.

"I sees the winder, Massa Zimri," Solomon said, looking over his shoulder. "T'ain't no problem for me."

"Good. But it's the iron grating I'm concerned about."

Solomon grinned. "Ain't no need to worry. Boone done showed me some tricks wid cuttin' iron. Won't take me mo' than thirty minutes."

Zimri checked his watch. "We'll see."

They rowed up to the base of the mill and Solomon tied the bow to the iron frame of the dilapidated water wheel. Now they were whispering.

"Too bad this water wheel is in such sorry shape," Zimri said. "You could use it as a ladder."

Solomon reached for one of the paddles, grabbed it, and easily tore off a piece, which crumbled in his hand. "Ain't even good for firewood. I'm gonna have to throw this plumb bob through the winder like we planned."

Zimri looked at the iron weight attached to the end of the rope with some concern. "It's going to make a hell of a racket if you don't put it through the first time."

Solomon grinned as he coiled the rope and looked up at the window. "I'll put it through, Massa Zimri. It'll make a racket, all right. On the *inside*. Enough to wake Miz Cora up, but nobody in the big house."

"I hope you're right."

Solomon then stood up in the stern of the boat, steadied himself, and began swinging the iron bob in one hand while holding the coiled rope in the other. When the rope was extended in an arc about three feet from his fist, he let go and Zimri saw the bob, trailing the rope, sail up to the window and pass between the iron bars and into the mill. There was a muffled clank of metal against stone.

"You did it!" Zimri said.

"Who's there?"

"Cora! It's me."

"Zimri?"

"None other. Cora—are you all right?"

"I'm hungry. The bastard has put me on bread and water until I agree to be his concubine."

"Don't worry, Miz Cora. We brung you some ham and biscuits."

"Who's that?"

"Solomon," Zimri said. "Just stay calm and light a candle."

They heard Cora's distinctive laugh. "Candle? What candle? Do you think Randolph would—"

"Solomon will bring you one. Just sit tight. He's got to saw through the iron bars."

"Oh, Lord."

"Secure the end of the rope to something, Cora. A piece of machinery, a post, a—"

"How about an iron ring on the wall?"

"Perfect!"

"Unfortunately, I'm chained to it myself."

"Don't worry, Solomon will make short work of the chain."

"With what? His teeth?"

"A saw."

"We don't have time. The sun will be up in—"

"Solomon works fast. You'll see."

Indeed, Solomon scaled the wall in a matter of seconds once Cora had secured the end of the rope. Zimri watched as he wedged himself in the window, with one hand on an iron bar for support and the other furiously sawing away at the base of another. In five minutes he had cut through the first bar and started on the second.

Fifteen minutes into this process, the cocks began to crow and the first rays of light appeared over the horizon.

"Zimri?"

"Yes. Cora?"

"Sometimes the cook sends me some grits or scraps of bacon in the morning."

"When?"

"I don't know exactly. Maybe five-thirty."

Zimri looked at his watch. "It's ten after five. Plenty of time."

Solomon cut through the last bar and carefully lowered the grating down to the boat. Zimri untied the rope and Solomon pulled it back up again. Then he tied the end onto the short section of the remaining bar and lowered himself down into the chamber.

Zimri listened.

"You skinny as a rail, Miz Cora."

"I've been on a diet."

"You didn't tell us you was hooked up to two chains."

"I forgot—they're like jewelry. After a while you don't notice the weight."

Zimri was alarmed at this information. "Solomon! We don't

have time to saw through two chains. Can't you smash them with something?"

There was a pause.

"Ain't nothin' to do it wid, Massa Zimri. Nothin' but a rickety table, couple of chairs. Some old gears—"

"Gears? From the water wheel? Can't you pull one off and use it as a hammer?"

"I could try."

Zimri then heard Solomon straining and groaning for a few moments.

"Ain't no use, Massa Zimri. They's locked up with rust."

"How are the chains attached to the wall?"

"Just iron rings. Maybe I can yank'em out."

"Try."

Again Zimri heard straining and groaning. Finally, there was a loud clattering against stone.

"Marvelous!" Cora said. "You're as strong as Samson!"

"Good work, Solomon. Now try the other one."

More straining and groaning, with the same result.

Zimri heard Cora clapping as if she had just witnessed a circus performance. "You must be the strongest man who ever lived! But what are we going to do with the chains?"

"You'll have to carry them, Cora."

"Oh, my—I don't know if I can."

"You'll have to—Solomon's going to be carrying you."

"She's skinny, Massa Zimri, but she ain't weak. Here, Miz Cora—gather them chains up in yo' arms like they was a baby."

"Umph! Like a baby what—hippopotamus?"

"You can do it, Cora." Zimri waited in tense silence for the next two minutes as the sun began to appear on the horizon. There was a thick mist hanging over the river.

He looked up and saw Cora's head emerge through the window, her black hair longer than before and matted in places. Her face was pale and thin. She cradled the chains in her arms and struggled to hang on to them.

"Drop the chains, Cora. Solomon will lower you into the boat."

Cora complied and the chains dropped about halfway down the wall. She exhaled a sigh of relief.

Suddenly, there was a loud knocking on the door on the landward side. "Miz Cora! I brung you some vittles."

Cora froze in the window for a moment. Zimri could now see

Solomon's head as well, and his huge hands gripping the one remaining stub of an iron bar.

"Thank you, Annie Mae, but I'm not hungry this morning."

"Not hungry? You ain't et nothin' but bread fo' two days!"

"Just the same, I've got no appetite. Just leave it by the door."

"By the do'? Then how you gonna get it? I got to return this here key befo' Marster Randolph know it missin.'"

"Then just take it back. I'm sorry, Annie Mae—I just can't eat anything."

"You sound—you sound like you far away. Where you at?"

"It's my voice. I'm losing it. I just need rest."

There was a long silence.

"I'll get the doctor."

"No, no. I just need rest, that's all. Master Randolph will be upset if you call a doctor."

"Well...all right then. But I'll come check on you 'bout noon."

"That would be wonderful, Annie. I'm sure I'll feel better by then."

"You jest rest up till then, you hear?"

"Yes, yes. I will."

"You got plenty o' water?"

"Oh, yes. I'll drink some now."

"Good. I'll be back."

"Thank you, Annie Mae."

The three of them waited in silence until they heard Annie Mae's footsteps fade away.

Solomon tied the rope around Cora's waist and lowered her down into the boat. Chains still dangling from her wrist and ankle, she embraced Zimri and held him tight.

"Oh, Zimri—I knew you'd come."

"Solomon's right—you're as thin as a bird." He put his hand to her forehead. "And you seem to have a fever. Here—eat something while I help Solomon into the boat."

Cora took the basket of food from him and sat down with it in the forward seat. As Solomon lowered himself to the boat, she greedily devoured two or three biscuits stuffed with ham.

"That's it, Solomon—easy. Don't upset the boat."

"Naw, suh."

Once in the boat, Solomon snapped the rope a couple of times like a whip until it popped loose from the iron bar and fell into the boat.

"Now let's get out of here." Zimri untied the boat from the decrepit water wheel, Solomon sat amidships and put the oars into the water, and they were off again upstream, rowing against the current.

"Maybe I'd better take the oars, Solomon. You must be exhausted."

"Ain't tired a t'all, Massa Zimri. This here is like a Sunday picnic."

Zimri looked at Cora, who was still pushing biscuits into her mouth. "Go easy on the biscuits, Cora—you don't want them to–"

There was a sudden shift of weight in the boat, followed by the port gunwale dipping low into the water. Zimri turned to the sound of the noise and saw Solomon lying prone on the bottom of the boat, shaking violently.

"What's wrong with him?" Cora said.

"The falling sickness," Zimri said. "Grab that oar!"

Cora reached for the starboard oar, which Solomon had let go of and was pitched high into the air, though still in its lock. Zimri grabbed Solomon beneath the armpits and managed to shift his weight to the center of the boat in time to prevent its capsizing. The boat soon stabilized itself, though it had taken on a good three or four inches of water. Solomon continued to shake.

"Hand me a towel!" Zimri said.

"Towel? Where—"

"The basket!"

Cora managed to locate the towel in the bottom of the basket and handed it to him. Zimri twisted it tightly, rope-like, and forced it between Solomon's teeth.

After another minute or so, Solomon's eyes opened and the shaking began to subside.

Zimri removed the towel from his mouth.

"I'se sorry, Massa Zimri," Solomon said. "I guess the 'citement caught up wid me."

"It's all right, Solomon. We've taken on a little water, but we'll soon be on our way. Put your head in Cora's lap and stay calm. I'll man the oars."

Solomon lay his massive head in Cora's lap. She gently stroked his brow and, assured that he was comfortable, picked up a large tin cup that had been rolling about in the bottom of the boat and began bailing.

Zimri pulled on the oars.

Solomon lifted his head. "I'se all right, now, Massa Zimri."

"Just relax, Solomon. Everything's under control."

As they rounded the first bend in the river, they saw a group of slaves working in the rice fields. One of them looked up and saw the boat with its three occupants. One by one the others looked up, too, until they all stood transfixed at the scene they were witnessing.

"What a shame we can't free them all," Cora said. "There's Libby, who helped raise me, and Hector, who taught me to ride." She suddenly stood up and waved at them. The boat rocked, took on more water and Zimri pulled her back down into her seat.

"Cora!"

The slaves looked puzzled for a moment, then waved back, uncertain of who they were waving to.

"I'm sorry," Cora said. "That was stupid of me."

"The overseer looked our way for a moment," Zimri said, "but now he's turned away again."

"I'll be back," Cora said in a whisper.

Zimri pulled on the oars as the sun emerged from the steaming mist rising from the river.

CHAPTER 63

It was a sultry summer afternoon when Elizabeth, Betty, and the children approached the small town of Louisville. There was no breeze, and though the sun was low in the hills to the west, the heat was oppressive.

"Thank goodness, we're here," Elizabeth said. "I don't think I could stand much more of this heat."

"It sho' is hotter than Martinville," Betty said. "Guess they don't get no breeze from the mountains like we do."

"Mama, I'm thirsty," Charlotte said from the back of the wagon.

"We'll be at Grand-maman's house soon, darling," Elizabeth said. "I'm sure she'll have some cool lemonade for all of us."

They crossed a rickety bridge over a narrow stretch of the Ogeechee river and turned onto the main road through town.

"Straight through the middle of town, Betty," Elizabeth said. "Past the courthouse."

"Yessum."

They continued along the dusty road at a slow pace until they reached the first buildings, which consisted of a tavern, a boarding house or two, a feed store, and a blacksmith's shop.

"Mebbe we ought to stop and get some water for the horses, Miz Lizbeth. They seem mighty tired."

"Oh, all right. There's a public trough at the courthouse. We'll just—oh, my goodness!"

Betty let the reins go slack and the horses gradually came to a halt. "Lawd o' Mercy! Charlotte, keep yo' head down in the back there. This ain't a sight fo' you to see."

"Mama, I want to—"

"Do like Betty says," Elizabeth said, clutching Fortunata closer to her breast.

Betty pulled the reins tight again, clicked her tongue, and the horses started moving.

"Just keep moving, Betty. Grand-maman's house is only a couple of miles north of town."

As the wagon lumbered ahead, kicking up more dust, the scene that had so shocked them came into clearer view. There, in front of the courthouse were four Negro men hanging from a scaffolding by their necks, heads lolling to one side. Young boys with sticks were poking at them, causing the bodies to slowly twist one way, then the other. One picked up a clod of earth and threw it at one of the bodies.

"That's what you get, nigger!" the boy yelled. "Hangin's too good for you!"

Then the other boys, seeing this sport as infinitely preferable to merely poking sticks at the victims, put them down and joined their comrade in throwing clods of earth or rocks or whatever they could find to serve as missiles.

"Get on out of here!" A man emerged from the front door of the courthouse, dressed in a uniform of sorts. "Shoo, I said! Shoo!"

The boys scampered off and though Elizabeth stared straight ahead while Betty urged the horses on, the man removed his hat, put it against his breast and addressed her. "Afternoon, Miss—ain't you kin to Mrs. Devereaux?"

Elizabeth recognized the man as one of her grandfather's former employees, though he had grown gray and somewhat stooped since she last saw him. "Stop a moment, Betty."

Betty pulled back on the reins and the wagon came to a halt. Charlotte raised her head to see what was going on and Betty pushed her down again.

"Yes," Elizabeth said. "Mrs. Devereaux is my grandmother. I'm Elizabeth Rhodes."

"Ah, yes, Miz Rhodes! I thought I recognized you. I used to drive niggers for your grandpa."

"Mr. Pearson."

"Yes, ma'am. That's me. Why, I remember—"

"What's happened here, Mr. Pearson? Why were those unfortunate men hanged? And why are they being left here to shock the world?"

Mr. Pearson glanced at the four bodies, still clutching his hat to his breast. "Rebels, Miz Elizabeth. Murderers. They tried to start a slave uprisin' at your grandmother's place and butchered an overseer in cold blood. Nearly took his head off with a machete."

"My grandmother's? Clos de Rive?"

"Yes, ma'am."

"My God! Is she all right?"

"Oh, yes ma'am. These renegades stormed the house and tried to get to her, but two of the house slaves stood in their way to protect her. One of 'em, Louis, got cut up pretty bad before the other ran the four of 'em off with a musket. They lit out for the swamps along the river but got lost and we caught up with 'em early the next morning."

"My goodness. Was anyone else hurt?"

"No, ma'am. Oh, just some scratches and bruises when we was pullin'em out of the swamp. They was pretty much chewed up by the time the dogs got through with 'em."

"Why doesn't somebody cut them down and give them a proper burial?"

"Judge says to serve as a warning to the others." Mr. Pearson put his hat back on his head and spat a dark stream of tobacco juice to the ground. "There was a big escape in South Carolina not long ago. That mulatto actress from New York City was behind it, they say. Judge says the niggers need to know we ain't gonna put up with that kind of foolishness 'round here."

"I don't see any Negroes in town, Mr. Pearson. It can't be much of a deterrent."

Mr. Pearson smiled broadly. "Oh, they all know about it, all right. Word spreads fast."

"Still, I don't see the point. Only these horrid little boys seem to...never mind. Let's get moving, Betty. Grand-maman is expecting us."

Betty pulled on the reins and the horses started moving again.

"She'll be glad to see you, Miz Rhodes." Mr. Pearson stepped out into the street as the wagon pulled off. "She surely will."

As they pulled out of town and turned onto the Augusta Road to Clos de Rive, they saw several men on horseback approaching, brandishing muskets. They came to an abrupt halt in front of the wagon, forcing them to stop. One man, apparently the leader, came alongside Betty and raised his musket, pointing it directly at her.

"Where you going with this nigger?"

"This Negro belongs to me, sir," Elizabeth said. "And who, may I ask, are you?"

"I'll do the asking here, ma'am. And I'll do it only once more. Who are you and where do you think you're going with this nigger?"

"My name is Elizabeth Rhodes, not that it's any of your business. And I'm going to visit my grandmother, Estelle Devereaux."

"Miz Devereaux?" He lowered his weapon. "I beg your pardon, Miz Rhodes. I didn't know you by sight. But we've had trouble with rampagin' niggers lately and—this here your maid?"

"And governess. She takes care of my children when I travel."

"I reckon a lady like you needs a body servant. Again, my apologies, Miz Rhodes. But we've got reports of an escaped mulatto woman who may be traveling in disguise."

"If my Betty is traveling in disguise, it's a very good one, don't you think? She's as black as coal."

The man smiled. "That she is, Miz Rhodes. That she is. Okay, boys, let'em on through."

Betty pulled back on the reins and clicked her tongue. They were moving again and soon they came within sight of the ornate wrought-iron gates of Clos De Rive. An elderly black man dressed in Clos de Rive's distinctive livery—burgundy and gold—stepped out from a guard house.

"Ain't no deliveries till—Oh, it's you, Miz Rhodes."

"Hello, Ephraim. I've heard all about the uprising. Is my grand-mother well?"

Ephraim swung open the gates. "She's done had the fright of her life, Miz Rhodes. Won't move out the house if you set it afire and barbecued chickens in the parlor. 'Fact, she ain't et nothin' since she saw Mr. Sims wid his head nearly lopped off."

"And where is Mr. Sims now?"

"Six feet under. In the old cemetery back o' the church."

"Well, at least he got a proper burial."

"Yessum. It were fit and proper, which is more than a body can say about Leroy, Thaddeus, Sam, and Jacques."

"Jacques? Jacques was one of the rebels?"

"Yessum. Don't know what got into him."

"Grand-maman's most trusted servant!"

"Yessum. She trained him up from when he was jest a gleam in his daddy's eye. Gave him his name and taught him French."

"No wonder she's so frightened! If she couldn't trust Jacques—drive on, Betty, it's getting dark."

"Yessum. Betty shook the reins and the horses pulled the wagon along the cypress-lined drive to the main house.

CHAPTER 64

The ferryman at the Savannah River crossing into Georgia studied the papers as if they were the last will and testament of a rich uncle. "This here says the nigger is a free man."

"That's correct," Zimri said. He lit a cheroot and tossed the spent match aside. "As of the twenty-sixth."

"Then what's he doing driving your wagon?"

"No place to go. He likes working for me."

The ferryman shook his head, folded the papers back up and handed them to Zimri. "I don't see the point. What's the use of freeing a slave if he ain't goin' nowhere?"

"Ask him yourself."

The ferryman looked at Solomon, who sat with slumped shoulders and a floppy straw hat on the back of his head. "I jest like knowin' I'm free."

The ferryman leaned to one side and spat. "Looks to me like you were better off before—now Mr. Rhodes ain't got to feed you or put a roof over your head."

Solomon grinned. "I'm building me a cabin in the woods not far from Massa—Mister Rhodes. Come fall, we'll have sweet potatoes, collard greens, tomatoes, and black-eyed peas—we ain't gonna starve."

The ferryman looked at Cora, who sat between Solomon and Zimri, dressed in kaki trousers, one of Zimri's flannel shirts, and a broad-brimmed hat pulled low over her eyes. "What do you think, boy? Think niggers are better off free or slave?"

Cora cleared her throat and avoided the man's gaze. "Don't know, sir. I guess a man likes to think he's free even if he ain't."

The ferryman laughed. "You put your finger on it, boy. It's all in a man's head, ain't it? Some's free that don't know it, and some's slave that thinks they free. All right, Mr. Free Nigger, just pull your wagon up on that plank there and park it in the stern. We got plenty more that wants to cross."

Once across the river, Solomon turned the horses onto the Waynesboro road towards Louisville.

Zimri exhaled a sigh of relief. "I think we can breathe easier now. They won't think of looking for you this far west."

Cora put her arm in Zimri's. "And I think you handled it beautifully. The ferryman didn't suspect a thing."

Zimri extracted his arm from hers. "Still, we're not out of the woods yet. There's no telling who may be watching us this very minute."

Cora sighed. "You're right. I'll have to stay in character. But I want to congratulate both of you for pulling my escape off so smoothly. I wish you'd consider joining the Underground."

Zimri shook his head. "My nerves couldn't stand it, Cora. I may have seemed calm back there, but inside I was shaking like a leaf."

"And Solomon," she said. "You're a free man now. Your new cabin in the woods would be a perfect place for a way station for fugitive slaves."

Solomon shook his head and kept his eyes on the road. "I don't think so, Miz Cora. Now that I'm free, I don't want to risk going to jail. I'se jest like Mister Zimri. I was so nervous back at the ferry, I like to go runnin' into the river to get acrost it—and I cain't even swim."

Cora laughed. "Well, you both could have fooled me—and did. Still, I hope you'll help us someday—in your own way."

"Yes, ma'am, Solomon said. "Anyway I can—'cept bein' what you call a stationmaster. I ain't ready for that."

"We'll see," Cora said.

They drove on for a few more miles before any of the three said anything. It was nearing mid-day, and the sun was high in the sky, with few trees to block its intense rays.

"Sho' could use some rain," Solomon said. "Things look parched ever' where you look."

"We'll stop in Waynesboro and water the horses," Zimri said. "It'll be dinner time, but we'd better eat in the wagon to be safe."

They continued for several more miles, passing through a grove of shade trees, which gave them some relief from the heat. They stopped beneath one of the trees for a few minutes and Solomon poured each of them some water from a jug. They all sat sipping the water and gazed out across a field that ran to the river's edge. They could see dozens of slaves working in the hot sun.

"Rice," Zimri said. "The climate seems suited for it around here."

"That be hard work," Solomon said. "I'll take bendin' over a smithy any day."

They continued to watch the black figures going about their business for a few minutes.

"Cora," Zimri said. "I've always wondered about that British man o' war off of Tybee Island last spring. You said you knew nothing about it, but—"

Cora laughed. "I lied. Sorry, but it was necessary at the time. It would have been quite an embarrassment for Lord Northington if the truth had gotten out."

"Lord Northington?"

"Head of the British Admiralty. He's an ardent abolitionist and has introduced legislation into Parliament to abolish slavery in the West Indies entirely. The *Arundel* happened to be anchored off the Georgia coast at the time and he offered its services. A great stroke of luck, actually."

"And President Jackson?"

"He suspected like everyone else, but had no direct knowledge, as I understand it. He didn't want to know."

"I can see why. What happened to the escaped slaves?"

"Some went to Canada, some to England. A few even went back to Africa."

Zimri sighed. "Where will it all end?"

"If the planters don't agree to a compromise of some kind—compensation, banning the extension of slavery in the new territories—there'll be war."

"War...and that means the destruction of the Union."

"Perhaps...but who knows? Perhaps after a half a million dead, they'll come to their senses."

"A half a million dead? You're too cynical, Cora. Surely it won't come to that."

"I hope I'm wrong."

After stopping briefly in Waynesboro without incident, they continued westwards towards Louisville and arrived at the outskirts of town shortly before sunset. Driving slowly through town—it was a Sunday—they saw few people on the sidewalks and drew little attention.

Then the courthouse, with its grisly display, came into view. Cora stared but said nothing.

"Keep moving, Solomon," Zimri said. "It's another mile or two to the house."

Solomon didn't respond immediately, but continued to stare at the bodies hanging from the gibbets, crows pecking at their decaying flesh. "I don't know if I can stay here, Mister Zimri. If this is what they do to black people—"

"We'll shoot our way out of here if it becomes necessary, Solomon. But whatever's happened here, it looks like the worst part is over. Now pick it up!"

Solomon looked at Zimri angrily, as if he did not intend to comply. But then he shook the reins. "Giddy up there, you hosses.
You been loafin' till now—giddy up!"

CHAPTER 65

Zimri knocked on the huge cypress doors of Clos de Rive with one of its heavy iron knockers in the shape of a stag's head. He had only been to Clos de Rive once, shortly after he and Elizabeth were married, and now he remembered the distinctive knockers. But he wasn't prepared for what happened next. A white woman, about thirty, dressed in the Devereaux household uniform, opened the door.

"Yes?"

"I'm Zimri Rhodes. Is Mrs. Devereaux home?"

The woman, rather plump with red hair pulled back into a bun, eyed him curiously, looked over his shoulder at Solomon and Cora sitting in the wagon, and slowly opened the door wider. "Mr. Rhodes. Yes, Mrs. Devereaux's expecting you. And your wife's here, too."

"My wife?"

"Yes. She and her maid arrived just—"

Suddenly Elizabeth appeared. "Zimri!" She flung her arms around him.

"Elizabeth! What are you doing here? I thought—"

"I was so worried about you, Zimri. I had to come—I hope you're not angry with me."

"No, of course not. But it's dangerous to be—"

"Daddy, Daddy!" It was Charlotte, who instantly clamped her arms around his leg, like a barnacle adhering to a pier. "Daddy's here!"

Zimri picked Charlotte up, cradled her in his arms and kissed her. "And Fortunata?"

"Asleep in the nursery," Elizabeth said. "I'll go wake her."

"No, no. There's time for that later. We'll need to unpack. Where's Grand-maman?"

"In her bedroom. She rarely leaves it now."

"What's happened? We saw the spectacle in town—"

"There was a revolt—right here at Clos de Rive. An overseer was killed."

"And Grand-maman?"

"She's safe. I'll tell you all about it after you've—who's that man in the wagon with Solomon?"

Zimri put his finger to her lips and shushed her. "That's my nephew—from Connecticut."

"Nephew? Oh, of course. Young..."

"Philip."

"Yes, Philip. Well, he will want to wash up after that hot, dusty journey. Mary—ask one of the houseboys to help Mr. Rhodes and his nephew with their luggage."

"Yes, ma'am."

Mary went off to find the houseboy, and Zimri stepped inside. "What happened to the colored servants?"

"Grand-maman banished them from the house and hired some whites from town. Oh, Zimri, she's terrified. Her favorite house slave was one of the instigators. She feels she can't trust any of them."

"She knows about...Philip?"

"Yes. Well, not Philip, exactly. But yes, she's expecting you to bring a guest."

Zimri looked back at the occupants of the wagon. "Will Philip be welcome here?"

"I don't know. She's very upset. This insurrection has changed her."

He handed Charlotte to her. "I'll see that Philip stays out of the way as much as possible. Is there a backstairs?"

"Yes."

"I'll have Solomon bring the wagon around." He kissed her and walked quickly down the staircase to the drive, where he climbed back into the wagon.

"They're all right?" Cora said.

"Yes, thank God. The old lady, too. Solomon, take us around to the rear of the house. Philip—you're going to have a room of your own."

"Philip?"

"My one and only nephew. Remember—stay in character. The servants are all white now."

"Certainly, Uncle Zimri. Perhaps we can go hunting tomorrow."

Zimri smiled as Solomon shook the reins and turned the wagon around. "My, you are a trusting soul, aren't you?"

Once settled in their rooms on the second floor—Zimri in Elizabeth's room next to the nursery—the three guests received written invitations to aperitifs in the library to be followed by supper in the dining room.

Cora appeared at Zimri and Elizabeth's room dressed in a blue suit, white silk stockings and a ruffled shirt with French cuffs. Her hair was cropped short, like a young man's.

"Cora?" Elizabeth stood in the open doorway astonished at the illusion before her.

"Don't you recognize me, Auntie Elizabeth? Your nephew Philip, at your service." She bowed deeply and kissed Elizabeth's hand.

Zimri, who was still tying his cravat, came up behind Elizabeth. "Where in the world did you get that suit?"

Cora stepped into the room and closed the door behind her. "Mrs. Devereaux must have a grandson. There's a whole wardrobe of boy's clothes in my room."

"Her brother's nephew," Elizabeth said. "In fact, I believe he's called Philippe—Philippe de Roulhac. He comes to visit from time to time, and she loves to dress him up—much to his mortification."

"Then perhaps I'd better change my name to something else."

"No, no," Zimri said. "I've already told Mary your name is Philip. Besides, it's only for the benefit of the new servants after all. Mrs. Devereaux knows who you are."

Cora put her hand to her mouth. "Oh, dear. You didn't tell me that. Then she knows that I'm a runaway?"

"Yes."

Elizabeth grasped Cora's hand and gave her a kiss on the cheek. "I wrote to her, Cora, and told her about the whole scheme."

"That was rather risky, wasn't it?"

"Yes, but it's better this way. We don't have to dissemble."

Cora laughed. "But Elizabeth, dear—my whole raison d'être is to dissemble." Suddenly her gay expression turned somber. "And now with this...uprising. I'm afraid she's not going to be very sympathetic."

Elizabeth looked at Zimri, then to Cora. "I'm afraid we have no other choice. We'll simply have to throw ourselves on the mercy of the court—the court of Clos de Rive."

"I infinitely prefer that to the sort of justice we saw in town."

This comment cast a pall over the conversation.

"We'd better go downstairs," Zimri said. "She's waiting for us."

"Uncle Philip!"

The three of them turned and saw little Charlotte standing in the open doorway between the bedroom and the nursery.

Cora suddenly brightened and spread her arms wide. "Charlotte! My dear little niece! How did you know it was me?"

"She heard us talking about Zimri's nephew," Elizabeth said. "She thinks that—"

"Ma petite niece!" Cora said in a husky voice. She picked Charlotte up in her arms. "My, how you've grown since I last saw you! You were a mere bébé then."

Charlotte seemed to enjoy this encounter immensely and her parents made no attempt to disillusion her.

"And where's your little sister, dear Charlotte? You must introduce me!"

"Nada's asleep," Charlotte said. "She's always sleepy."

At that point Fortunata began to cry.

"Oops!" Cora said. "Not any longer. Let's go in and see her."

"Well, all right," Charlotte said. "But she's cranky."

Cora laughed and carried Charlotte into the nursery. "Oh, not so cranky—she just wants to join the party. We mustn't let her feel left out!"

As Charlotte introduced Fortunata to Cora, Elizabeth exchanged amused glances with Zimri and followed them into the nursery.

Zimri listened for a few minutes while the two women cooed over Fortunata, and Elizabeth explained how she was always the stronger of the twins.

"Twins?"

"Oh..." Elizabeth said. "You didn't know. How could you? I lost little Lucky."

Cora seemed to make an effort to hold back tears. "I'm sorry, Elizabeth. Forgive me for being so clumsy."

"Lucky's in Heaven!" Charlotte said.

"I'm sure she is," Cora said. "Now perhaps you had better look after your little sister while Mama and Papa go downstairs to see Grand-maman."

"Yes—she'll wonder what's happened to us," Elizabeth said. She knocked on a door to the nursery and after a moment or two a young white woman appeared. "See that they're in bed by nine, Aggie. We shouldn't be much later than that."

"Yes, Mrs. Rhodes. Mary's bringing up some soup and crackers for their dinner."

"Make sure it's not too hot—cool enough to put your finger in."

"Yes, ma'am."

They all three descended the grand staircase and when they arrived at the foot of the stairs, a butler was there to greet them and direct them to the library.

Zimri noted that while Clos de Rive was not as large as Belle Oaks, it was more tastefully furnished and nearly every wall was filled with paintings.

"I haven't seen such artwork since I was in Florence," Cora said. "Your grandmother certainly has a fine eye."

"Most of it belonged to my grandfather," Elizabeth said. "He brought crates of it from his ancestral home in Bordeaux before the Revolution."

"Bordeaux? Then that explains the name of the estate. Did he plant grapes?"

"Yes. There's still a vineyard that produces some five thousand bottles of wine a year. But I'm afraid it's not up to the standards of the great vineyards of Bordeaux. They sell most of it to hotels and taverns that wouldn't know a fine wine from hard cider."

Zimri chuckled. "Or sour mash whiskey."

The butler, who seemed uncomfortable in his costume, stopped before a pair of tall paneled doors and opened one. "Mrs. Devereaux is over yonder—by the fireplace."

"Thank you," Elizabeth said. "It's Alphonse, isn't it?"

The butler blushed. "Actually, it's Alfred. But Mrs. Devereaux likes her people to have French names, you know."

"Well, Alfred. I think you're doing a fine job on such short notice."

"Thank you, ma'am. There's a waiter by the sideboard. He'll pour your drinks. We got some fine Scuppernong wine from the cellar this evening."

"That sounds delightful. Thank you."

"Elizabeth? Is that you?"

"Oui, Grand-maman."

"Entrez."

As they entered the library, Mrs. Devereaux stood from her chair to receive them. She was dressed in a blue chiffon dress with white lace sleeves. She let fall a Japanese fan which was suspended from a cord tied round her wrist. "And this must be Philip."

"How do you do, Mrs. Devereaux," Cora said. "I've heard so much about you."

"Dear boy, au contraire! I have heard so much about you. And how are you, Zimri? No worse the wear for your adventures, I trust."

"I'm fine, Mrs. Devereaux. We've been very lucky thus far."

Mrs. Devereaux looked at the waiter standing next to the sideboard. "Charles, pour Mr. Rhodes a whiskey. Elizabeth, what would you like?"

"A glass of wine, Grand-maman. The Scuppernong."

"Scuppernong? Nonsense. That's for the locals. We have some fine Sauterne. And what would young Master Philip like?"

"Whiskey," Cora said.

Mrs. Devereaux seemed slightly taken aback. "Whiskey? Why, you seem rather young to be drinking whiskey, Philip, but I suppose all the young men these days prefer stronger drink than they did when I was making my debut. Charles, you might add a dash of water to Master Philip's drink just to be on the safe side."

"Yes, ma'am."

Once the drinks were served and a brief toast to the families was made, Mrs. Devereauz banished Charles from the room and invited her guests to sit down. "We are quite alone now. Miss Rinaldi, I must say that I am astonished by your resemblance to my own nephew, Philippe. How do you do it?"

Cora laughed. "It's more a matter of mannerisms and bearing than appearance, Mrs. Devereaux. Men, of course, move differently than women. They pick up things differently; they cock their heads at a different angle when listening to someone speak. They even look at their nails differently."

"Their nails? How so?"

Cora spread the fingers of one hand palm down. "A woman." Then she turned the palm up and bent the fingers towards her. "A man. You see?"

Mrs. Devereaux laughed. "Of course! I saw my Gregoire do that a thousand times. But I never really thought about it."

They all sipped on their drinks and an awkward silence ensued.

"Miss Rinaldi—"

"Cora."

"Cora," Mrs. Devereaux said. "I must say that though I have never seen you on the stage, I admire you immensely."

"Thank you, Mrs. Devereaux. I cannot say that I've done any acting in the last year or so, however."

"You've been engaged in business matters."

"Yes. You might say that."

Mrs. Devereaux took another sip of her wine. "That is what I wish to speak to you about. We need not go into the details of your business at present. You are aware of recent events at Clos de Rive?"

"Yes, Mrs. Devereaux. I am sorry to say that I am. A most regrettable affair."

"Then you disapprove?"

"Of course. Your men had no plan. They were simply hell-bent for revenge. The result is not surprising."

Mrs. Devereaux betrayed the hint of a smile. "Then you do not condone killing for the sake of gaining one's freedom?"

Cora looked thoughtfully at a portrait of the Marquis de Lafayette that hung over the mantelpiece. "Only if it's absolutely unavoidable. Again, there must be a plan. And if the plan is good and it is well-executed, there will be little or no bloodshed."

Mrs. Devereaux seemed to study Cora intently. "Have you found it necessary to—"

"To kill? No, Mrs. Devereaux, I have not. And in sixteen escape attempts, only one has ended in failure."

"The most recent one."

"Yes. Three men were injured by dogs, and a fourth was knocked unconscious by the butt of a musket. All four were whipped so savagely that they were unable to rise from their beds for a fortnight."

"And you?"

"I was merely imprisoned." Cora smiled at Zimri. "Until yesterday."

Mrs. Devereaux looked at Zimri. "Yes—Zimri has proven himself to be quite resourceful. And you are a brave woman, Cora. And a remarkable one in every way. But I'm afraid that in my current position I cannot condone or contribute to your obviously passionate commitment to free every slave below the Mason-Dixon Line. You can understand that, can't you?"

"Perfectly," Cora said.

"I can have you arrested and sent back to Lynwood—in fact, the law demands that I do."

"I am aware of that, too, Mrs. Devereaux."

"Then you must also be aware that I have only one other choice as to how to deal with the current situation."

"And that is?"

"To turn a blind eye when you depart from Clos de Rive tomorrow morning."

Cora sat pensively for a moment. "I will be forever grateful to you, Mrs. Devereaux."

"I only regret that I will never live to see you performing at the

Park Theatre. I understand your Desdemona is sublime!"

Cora laughed. "It requires a great leap of the imagination for me, and not a little face powder. I hope you *will* see me in the role while I'm still young enough to play it."

Mrs. Devereaux stood. "Shall we go into supper?"

CHAPTER 66

The rain began before dawn and continued without letup as the carriage made its way through the rutted streets to the stage depot, which was nothing more than the front porch of a local tavern. They sat on a bench together with the rain dripping through the cracks in the porch roof, which hadn't been repaired in years.

Zimri felt the warmth of Cora's body close to his and was tempted to put his arm around her but dared not. There were two other passengers on the porch, a middle-aged dry goods merchant and his teenaged daughter, both of whom stared at Cora with a guarded curiosity. Her fever had returned, and she was trembling.

"Are you all right, Philip?" Zimri said.

"Yes, Uncle," she said. "I seem to have caught a touch of the ague."

"Sit closer to me then."

"All right, Uncle." She moved closer to him and closed her eyes.

Zimri spread the poncho he had brought with him over both their shoulders and pulled it above their heads so that it formed a sort of tent, with rivulets of rain running off it in all directions.

"No sense in staying out here," the merchant said. He stood up, as did his daughter. "The Waynesboro road is probably washed out. Stage won't be here for another hour, if then. Won't you and your nephew join us in the tavern, Mister? A spot of whiskey will warm him up."

Zimri raised his head. "Thank you, sir, but we'll wait out here. Don't want to get too comfortable inside or we'll chance missing the stage altogether."

"Where you headed?"

"Ohio."

"Ohio? That's a long ways, Mister. Especially with the boy in that condition. Sure you won't join us?"

"We're sure. Thank you all the same."

They proceeded inside, where the man escorted his daughter to a table and then went to the bar and ordered a whiskey.

Cora leaned her head against Zimri's shoulder and seemed to fall asleep under the relentless patter of raindrops against the roof.

Tennessee, Kentucky, and Ohio lay ahead. They all passed before Zimri's eyes as one vast country, with rocky promontories, deep gorges and endless forests. As a boy, he was enamored of the stories of George Washington and his adventures as a surveyor and Indian fighter. Zimri fancied himself then as the young Washington, slashing through the underbrush, clearing the land, and smoking the pipe of peace with the Indians after, of course, defeating them in a fair fight. But by the time he got to the western frontier of Georgia, the Indians had signed a treaty with the United States and most had moved on...

"Zimri—who are those men?"

It was a woman's voice, a familiar one, but distant.

He looked out of the coach window and saw a group of heavily armed men on horses, leveling their muskets at him.

"Get out of the coach," their leader said. "And keep your hands high."

"Is this a robbery?" Zimri said.

"Federal marshal," the leader said. "Do as I say."

Zimri glanced at Cora, who was shivering beneath a blanket, her eyes half open. She seemed to be unaware of what was happening. He tucked the blanket under her legs and cautiously opened the door to the coach. "May I ask what this is all about?"

"Contraband," the marshal said. He kept his musket trained on Zimri's forehead. "We understand there's a mulatto woman traveling in disguise in these parts. A runaway."

"There's no woman in here," Zimri said. He stepped down from the coach and indicated the open door. "Only my nephew, who's got the ague. See for yourself."

The marshal leaned forward and peered into the coach. "Take a look-see, Caleb. And pull that blanket off the boy there so's you can tell whether he's fish or fowl."

The man called Caleb got down from his horse and approached the open door of the coach. The marshal leaned farther forward to get a better view and as he did so, lowered the muzzle of his musket.

Zimri, caught between them, was unsure of what to do. If Caleb pulled the blanket off of Cora, surely the next step would be to order her outside of the coach to examine her more closely. While he was thus pondering his options, Caleb put his boot on the first rung of the steps and reached inside for the blanket.

A shot rang out and Caleb was thrown backwards. Zimri grabbed the muzzle of the musket, which was only inches from his head, and pulled the marshal off his horse. He turned the musket on a third man, whose horse reared at the sound of the shot. Zimri fired the musket at his chest and the man went flying. The fourth man raised his musket, fired wildly, and struck the side of the coach. Zimri produced a pistol from his jacket and aimed it at the man's head, but the man turned and spurred his horse away as fast as he was able. Zimri lowered the pistol.

He briefly examined the two men lying in pools of blood on the ground. Both dead. "Are you all right, Cora?"

"I am. Where's the driver?"

Zimri looked up and saw the driver some one hundred yards away, running towards a copse of trees, with the marshal close on his heels. "Halfway to Knoxville."

"You'll have to drive us."

He stuck his head inside the coach and saw Cora, still shivering, the smoking pistol in her hand. "You won't need that now. Best to keep that blanket over you."

"The blanket's got a hole in it."

Zimri smiled. "That's a pity. But it will still keep you warm." He tucked the blanket around her, gave her a kiss, and closed the door of the coach. "There's a fork in the road. Which way?"

"Is there a sign?"

"Yes."

"What does it say?"

"Kingsport, one hundred miles; Cumberland Gap, eighty."

"Cumberland Gap."

Zimri climbed up onto the driver's seat, seized the reins and clicked his tongue. The horses slowly began to move.

Elizabeth lay in the darkness listening to the rain and thinking of Zimri. She worried that he might escort Cora all the way to New York and never return. His love-making the night before had seemed perfunctory, un-enthusiastic. She sensed that he was in fact thinking of Cora, but she dared not accuse him. What good would it have done anyway? If he was in love with Cora there was nothing she could do about it.

What would she do if Zimri abandoned her? Perhaps she could take the money Papa left her and go to France. But France no longer had the appeal to her it once had when she so eagerly devoured Randolph's letters. Randolph! That seemed so long ago now—when she was merely a girl living in a make-believe world, like Patsy. No, France was out of the question...perhaps she could move to Charleston. There was a lively social scene there, of course, and she would have suitors…no, it was too close to Lynwood. It would be better to stay in Martinville, where suitors would be few, but where she was already established and she could put at least part of her inheritance back into the community. Tessie's idea about the new school was an excellent one, but it was impossible under the current law. Better to put her money and her efforts into the new library.

Well then, that wouldn't be so horrible, would it? Interesting work and growing children who loved her and a comfortable life not far from Belle Oaks. The only thing missing would be…Zimri. She burst into tears.

After a few minutes she wiped the tears away and fell asleep again. She dreamed she was feeding the twins, one at each breast, while gently swaying on the swing at home. She was watching Zimri in his garden, inspecting his roses with the greatest of care, and occasionally snipping one off with his shears. Finally, he had assembled a bouquet of his new hybrids, all deeply red in color, and approached the veranda. But when he extended the roses towards her, they suddenly dissolved into blood and ran onto her dress until the dress was soaked and the blood spread slowly upwards. Soon she and the twins were covered with it, and even Zimri, still standing before her extending his hand and smiling tenderly, became obscured by this blood that seemed to know no boundaries, no barriers to the mediums of air, earth, or water. And what was even more strange, this phenomenon did not seem to alarm her.

"Elizabeth?"

She opened her eyes. It was Zimri leaning over her, his hand brushing her hair back from her forehead.

"Is she gone?"

"Yes. On the stage for Tennessee and Ohio. A route that she calls the Underground Road."

She studied his expression for a moment, which seemed grave.

"Do you still love her, Zimri?"

"I don't know if that's the proper way to describe my feelings for her. She bewitched me for a time. But I'm here, Elizabeth, with you. I've made my choice, just as you made yours."

She sat up and put her arms around him. "Then I'm simply the lesser of two evils?"

Zimri chuckled. "Rather you're the greater of two goods."

EPILOGUE

Zimri heard a loud whistle.

He went to the window and carefully pulled back the curtain. There they were, blue-uniformed soldiers, some riding, most marching on foot, horses straining against the weight of supplies and heavy ordnance. And there was Georgia, waving at them, as if they were suitors calling on a Sunday afternoon.

He stepped out onto the veranda and grabbed Georgia by the arm.

"Get inside, Georgia."

She resisted. "But Papa, you always said that they were right. Besides—"

"They're still soldiers, Georgia. And they might do anything."

"That's sure a pretty granddaughter you got there, Pops," one of the men called out. "Where's her daddy? He a Johnny Reb who high-tailed it and left you holding the bag?"

This comment elicited laughter from the other troops.

"Inside," Zimri said.

Georgia seemed to suddenly be aware that she might be in danger and slipped in through the open door.

The procession continued and Zimri stood silently watching, hoping against hope that they would see nothing of value for them to take or destroy. Perhaps it was even a stroke of luck that they thought Georgia was his granddaughter and that there were no young men of military age in the house.

He looked down Mulberry Street towards town and could see nothing but more troops, more cannon, more wagons laden with booty from the plantations. This was a first-rate army, well-fed, nothing like the Confederates who had been reduced to a rag-tag guerilla force over the last two years, without proper uniforms, or even shoes. Belt buckles were polished, boots shined, caps set a smart angle.

"Zimri, come inside," he heard Elizabeth say. "They might shoot you."

Zimri suddenly felt foolish standing there, and careful not to make any sudden movements, followed Georgia inside. "I thought Ned or Zeke's boys might be among them."

"Even if they are," Elizabeth said, "we don't want them to stop."

Georgia went to the window and peeked out through the curtain. "They look hungry, Papa."

"Zimri!" Elizabeth said. "Did you lock the barn?"

"There's no point in it," Zimri said. "If they want the little we have, they'll take it."

"Hey!" A soldier shouted from the street. "Look at them roses. Purty, ain't they? I think I'll get one for my sweetheart."

"What sweetheart?" another soldier said. "That fat whore in Atlanta you diddled in her daddy's barn?"

There was uproarious laughter among the troops.

"She weren't no whore—she was a real Southern belle, she was!"

"Yeah, the kind that has her bell around her neck."

More laughter. Zimri went to the window and peered through the curtains. He saw a somewhat corpulent soldier with a ruddy complexion turn his horse off the road and plunge into the rose garden, trampling several bushes in the process. He leaned over and tried to pluck one of the hybrids from its stem but only got a thorn in his thumb for his efforts.

"Ouch! Damn thorns!"

"Come on, Stumpy, get your fat arse back in line. Uncle Billy didn't say nothin' about propriatin' no roses for no tarts."

"I told you, Francine ain't no tart. She's gonna meet me in Savannah."

"How she gonna get there? On a broom?"

There was more uproarious laughter, to which the stout soldier made no answer. Instead, he reached down again for one of the roses, plucked it from its stem and galloped back to the road, jumping a fence with surprising grace in the process.

Zimri closed the curtains and returned to the hearth, where he put some more wood on the fire. It was the end of November, and the weather had turned cooler of late.

"Do you want some soup?" Elizabeth said.

Zimri brushed off his hands and looked at Elizabeth standing in the kitchen door, her hands kneading her apron the way that Betty used to. Her hair was streaked with gray now, and her mouth framed by deep creases, but she was still beautiful. "That all we got?"

"Unless you want some beef jerky and collards."

"Soup will do."

"Georgia?"

"I'm not hungry, Mama."

"You need to eat, Georgia," Zimri said. "Give her some soup, Elizabeth. And some of those peach preserves for dessert." He picked up the poker and pushed a log farther back into the hearth as Elizabeth disappeared into the kitchen and Georgia went back to her sewing.

Satisfied that the fire was going well, Zimri went into his study, which he had added to the house before the war, and sat down at his desk. He remained perfectly still for a moment, listening to the sound of horses and wagon wheels that slowly diminished as the column of troops passed by.

Relieved, he picked up a letter from the blotter. It was from Charlotte, postmarked some four months earlier.

14 July, 1864
Paris

Dear Papa,

It is Bastille Day here and a carnival atmosphere with all sorts of costumes, enormous papier mâché heads, Punch and Judy shows, and of course, endless rounds of parties.

It is great fun, and Edwin and I have enjoyed ourselves immensely, visiting with all of the new friends we have made since coming to France three years ago. I find it a curious irony, though, that the French should so celebrate the anniversary of the bloodiest upheaval in their history, which started with cries of 'Liberté, Égalité, Fraternité,' and ended once again in tyranny. The Emperor, though respectful of the citizens' basic rights, nevertheless does not tolerate dissent. He is even now rattling his saber at Germany.

Sacre bleu! I almost forgot to mention that Fortunata has just delivered another child! You are now a proud Grandpapa for the fourth time! His name is Emile, and Fortunata says he looks just like you, but I rather think he favors Mama—she's the one with the French blood, you know.

I hope you both are doing well in spite of this nasty war between the states. Since Edwin decided to move his textile business here, it has thrived and we are even better off financially than we were in New York. Please accept the enclosed bank draft—but be sure to exchange it for U.S. dollars rather than Confederate notes, which Edwin says will soon be worthless.

Give my love to Mama.

Your most obedient daughter,
Charlotte

P.S. Has Georgia found a beau yet?

Zimri folded the letter and replaced it in its envelope. The bank draft was welcome, of course, but he had no idea of where to cash it. For the moment, at least, it was worthless.

There was a knock on the front door. Zimri got up and went to the window and peered out through the curtains. It was a soldier, apparently an officer. He considered whether to ignore him or open the door. Finally, he decided that it would be safer to answer—the officer knew someone was home due to the smoke rising from the chimney.

He passed into the hearth room and saw the others, particularly Georgia, looking at the door expectantly. "Keep to your sewing, Georgia—I'll get rid of him." He opened the door to discover a handsome young man, clean-shaven, about thirty years old. He stared at Zimri as if he were a specimen under a microscope.

"Mr. Rhodes?"

"Yes?"

"May I have a word with you?"

"You're having it."

"I'd prefer to speak with you privately."

"I don't suppose I can refuse." Zimri opened the door wider, the officer removed his cap, and he stepped inside the house.

"Oh!" Elizabeth was just coming from the kitchen carrying a tureen filled with soup.

"It's all right, Elizabeth. This young man says he needs to speak to me in private. Step into my study, Captain—"

"Jones."

"Captain Jones. Would you like some soup?"

"No, thank you. I've just eaten."

"Suit yourself." Zimri then escorted the captain into his study, casting an admonishing glance towards Georgia in the process. Elizabeth returned to the kitchen.

Zimri closed the door behind them. "Have a seat by the window, Captain. You'll have a view of what's left of my rose garden."

"I apologize for my men, Mr. Rhodes. Sometimes they think that civilian property is theirs for the taking. I have strict rules—"

"I suppose we should be grateful we have anything left at all." Zimri made a gesture towards his crowded bookshelves. "This is my inner sanctum, Captain. My retreat from the world. Now what is it you wished to speak to me about?"

The captain went to the window and looked out at the rose garden. "How do you get them to bloom in November?"

"They're perpetual hybrids. I've cross-bred them to withstand colder temperatures so that we have them nearly every month of the year except for January and February. Are you a student of horticulture?"

"Horticulture? No, I'm afraid not. But it's remarkable what you've done with them. They're beautiful to behold—especially in the midst of these...these troubled times."

"Yes, they are troubling, aren't they? Have a seat, Captain."

The captain turned around and looked for a chair. Finding one, an armchair, he sat down.

"Now what can I do for you, Captain?"

Captain Jones reached into his breast pocket and extracted an envelope. "I have a letter for you."

"My, my—this seems to be the day for letters." Zimri sat at his desk. "May I ask from whom?"

"From a lady."

"A lady? Anyone I know?"

"See for yourself." Captain Jones handed him the letter.

Zimri examined the envelope. It had his name on the front and nothing more. No postmark, no return address. On the back, however, was a wax seal. "Before I open this letter, Captain Jones, may I ask how you came by it?"

"It was given to me by my mother."

"Your mother? Do I know her?"

"It seems that you did. She's deceased."

"Oh, I'm sorry to hear that. What was her name?"

"Cora Rinaldi."

Zimri sat motionless for a moment, then looked again at his name on the envelope. Of course it was Cora's handwriting. Why didn't he recognize it? "Your mother was a great friend of mine. I admired her very much. How long has it been since—"

"Two years ago. Of malaria."

"Malaria?"

"Some call it swamp sickness. She contracted it years ago while leading an escape of slaves in South Carolina. It recurred from time to time. Finally, it was too much for her, combined with other ailments."

Zimri continued to stare at the fine script on the envelope. He pulled a letter opener out of his desk drawer and slit the top edge open so as to avoid breaking the seal, which contained the imprint of a ring. He would examine the seal more closely later.

9 August, 1862

Dearest Zimri,

Alas, it has been too many years since we last embraced at the coach station in tiny Louisville, Georgia. I always meant to write you—God, how many letters I began only to destroy them!—but I feared that you would misinterpret them, or that Elizabeth would become upset upon seeing a woman's handwriting on the envelope.

Thanks to you, my love, I was able to continue my work with what is now known—famously, or infamously, depending upon one's point of view—as the Underground Railroad. I have made numerous forays into the South since then and have freed perhaps as many as two thousand slaves. And but for my uncharacteristic carelessness at Lynwood, each and every mission was a success, with no casualties on either side. I believe my only failure was due, at least in part, to my emotional involvement with the denizens of Lynwood, both black and white. I wanted to free all of the slaves, and to punish Randolph for what he had done to me. The former was not practicable, and the latter was nothing more than the desire for personal revenge. Both caused fatal delays in my plans.

Randolph's fate, of course, you are quite aware of. I only regret that I was unable to free poor Pliny before he was driven, as a grieving father, to raise his hand against his master. Hanging is a sad end for such a kindly old man.

I can imagine you at this very moment, my darling, sitting at your desk reading these words. You are no doubt older and wiser, as I am. Have you grown fat? I daresay, it would not matter to me if you have. Even with graying hair and a pot belly, you would be the most attractive man I ever encountered. Could it be that inner beauty, that goodness of your soul, which you never acknowledged, that shines through your manly features so brilliantly?

We never completely know ourselves, do we?

But I hope you will come to know the young man who is sitting before you at this very moment. His name is Antonio. He is your son.

Zimri, astonished, looked up from the letter at 'Captain Jones.' The young officer simply stared back at him uncomprehendingly. Yes, there was a resemblance. He returned his eyes to the letter.

Forgive me, darling, for not informing you of this matter before, but I was too afraid that it would upset your life. I know that you love Elizabeth, and she you. And I know that though you love me, you could never leave Elizabeth to live with a gypsy adventuress. Nor would I have expected you to. I was no more cut out for marriage than you were for a life as a swashbuckling musketeer. It is enough for me to know that I have loved, been loved, and most of all, have given a child to this world that carries the best qualities of us both. I feel that I must be the happiest woman who ever lived.

Please give my fondest regards to Elizabeth, as well as to Charlotte and Fortunata. Where are they now? They must be grown with children of their own. How delightful! You are a grandpapa!

Au revoir, mon chéri,

Cora

Zimri folded the letter and returned it to its envelope. He looked up at the captain. "Did your mother show you this letter before she sealed it?"

"No, sir, she did not."

Zimri leaned back in his chair and stared at the young man for several moments. "What did she tell you about me?"

"Only that you were a newspaperman and that you risked your life to help her escape from the South Carolina plantation where she was born."

"Nothing more?"

Antonio looked puzzled. "No, nothing more. Oh—she said you had a way with roses."

Zimri smiled. The young man seemed completely ignorant of his origins. A son! He had a son! He stood up abruptly, startling the young captain, who seemed to interpret it as a signal that the interview was over.

"Well, I won't trouble you further, Mr. Rhodes. I'll just—"

"Why were you called Antonio?"

"My mother, as you probably know, loved all things Italian. She once told me I was named after Antonio Rinaldi, the architect. Another time she said it was after a character in one of Shakespeare's plays. I think she just liked the sound of the name, actually."

"And is your last name really Jones?"

The young man seemed surprised. "Why, yes. My father was an actor named Junius Brutus Jones. He and my mother formed an acting company that toured Europe and America before the war."

"She was a free spirit, your mother."

Antonio grinned. "She was that. No doubt about it."

Zimri started to say something but checked himself. Instead, he came around from behind the desk and extended his hand. "Thank you, Captain Jones. It has been a pleasure to have met Cora's son."

"The pleasure's mine, Mr. Rhodes."

"Are you sure you won't stay for some soup? Or perhaps we can—"

There was a knock on the door.

"Zimri?" Elizabeth appeared. "I thought you might want to know; Solomon's at the back door. Betty's with him. They look as if they haven't eaten for days."

"Solomon? We hardly have enough for—"

"I'll have one of my men bring you some fresh meat and produce, Mr. Rhodes," Captain Jones said. "And some eggs, too. After all, they—"

"Then you'll stay and dine with us?"

"That's very kind of you, Mr. Rhodes, but I've got to keep the men moving."

"I understand. We'll be very much obliged for the food, Captain."

"It's my pleasure, Mr. Rhodes. I know times are hard. Good day to you, sir. Good day, Mrs. Rhodes."

Captain Jones started for the hearth room, where he was met with an admiring gaze from Georgia. "Good day, Miss."

Zimri escorted him to the front door. The captain stepped out onto the veranda and placed his cap on his head.

"Captain?" Zimri said.

"Yes, sir?"

"You will write, won't you?"

"Write? Well, yes, of course. If you like."

"Perhaps we can meet again—after the war."

The captain looked first at Zimri, then at Elizabeth. "Why not? Perhaps we'll have some stories to tell. Well... I have to be going now."

After the captain had left, Elizabeth, whose arm now encircled Zimri's waist, studied the expression on his face. "You look pale, Zimri—like you'd just seen a ghost. What did that young man want with you?"

"He's the son of an old friend of mine in New York. His mother died recently."

"Oh, I'm sorry to hear that. What did he say his name was?"

"Jones. Antonio Jones."

"Well, for a Yankee soldier, he seemed like a very well-mannered young man."

"He should be. His mother was quite a lady."

She kissed him on the cheek. "And he's sending us some eggs. Eggs! We haven't had eggs for a month! I'll ask Betty to help me in the kitchen. There's a thousand things she can do with eggs!"